The Crumbling Fortress

Books by Willi Heinrich

CROSS OF IRON

CRACK OF DOOM

MARK OF SHAME

RAPE OF HONOR

THE LONELY CONQUEROR

THE CRUMBLING FORTRESS

THE
CRUMBLING
FORTRESS

BY

WILLI HEINRICH

Translated from the German by

MICHAEL GLENNY

THE DIAL PRESS
New York · 1964

The Crumbling Fortress

Chapter I

"What's his surname?" asked Marcel. He sat leaning against the mountainside on a narrow path which merged at that point into a rockslide. Far below he could see the bright ribbon of the road up which they had come, snaking its way along the valley, still in the shadow of the mountains. On the far side of the valley the mountains were even higher. Their peaks and ridges gave off a reddish glow in the strong sunlight and farther to the north they reared up into a great massif in the empty sky.

"All I know is that he is called Boris," replied Georges. His face was damp with sweat and he gazed down the mountainside to the spot where three hours before they had left the road and begun the climb. A foaming river ran alongside the road, a greenish tinge in the surface of its crystal-clear water.

Georges could feel the cool of the rock through the sweat-soaked material of his tunic. From beside him came the heavy breathing of Marcel, who sat with eyes closed and face towards the sun and talked on: "I can't help it, but this is a terrible place. There are no birds here. Have you noticed?"

"Yes," said Georges. He got up, walked over to the foot of the slide and looked towards its upper end where a steep cliff rose upwards. The sun was behind him so that he had a clear view of the cliff which was about six hundred feet long and a hundred and fifty feet high. Hardly distinguishable among the crags at the top were the flat ramparts and pillboxes of a fort, semi-circular blocks of concrete with weapon-slits and massive gun platforms along its flanks.

1

"It's not manned," said Georges, "you can see that."

"No you can't," said Marcel, "you'll only be able to tell when you're up there and then it'll be too late."

Georges, twenty-five years old and very tall and thin, sat down again on the path beside him and let his legs dangle over the precipice. He wore a red check shirt under the thin linen tunic, black velveteen trousers and lace-up hobnailed boots. Marcel, dressed more poorly, was half a head shorter, with sturdy legs and a round face covered with long stubble.

"Stop moaning," said Georges. "Who do you suppose is manning it?"

"I don't know," answered Marcel, "but if Vieale feels like it, he'll finish us. Nowadays you can't trust anybody in France any more. They're all with the Resistance. Where's the Italian frontier, anyway?"

Georges pointed with outstretched arm to the other side of the valley. "In that direction, probably along the ridge after next. The fort must be part of the second or third line of fortifications."

"I'd rather be in Italy," muttered Marcel. "There's all hell loose in France now."

"It'll be just as bad in Italy."

They sat for another five minutes, then Georges got to his feet. "Come on. We'll bypass the fort to the left."

Marcel spat on the ground as he stood up and started to clamber up the rockslide behind Georges. It was flanked on both sides by steep rock walls which drew closer and closer the nearer they came to the top. The slide was so loose that the stones rolled away beneath their feet, carrying small avalanches over the precipice. Halfway up was a dried-up watercourse which made the going easier; here they rested for a few minutes and then went on.

As they approached the cliff wall the fort disappeared from their angle of vision and it was a good hour before they reached a spot from which they could traverse round the wall and climb past its left flank to the ridge. Now they could see the fort again. It lay about fifty yards above them and was only recognizable from that point by a tower, sitting on the cliff-top like a huge bell; the sight of the great toothless mouth of its gun embrasure gave Marcel a spasm of disgust and fear. He breathed in quick gasps, as if at any moment expecting the sharp challenge of a sentry to ring out.

Georges had by now reached the top of the ridge. He climbed

2

on to a flat rock and let out a whistle. "Seen something?" said Marcel, panting. As Georges did not answer he hastily climbed up behind him and he could not have looked more surprised if the elegant boulevards of Nice or Cannes had appeared instead of the brightly colored tiled roofs which they now saw. There must have been about fifty houses, huddled together on a terrace-like outcrop beneath the fort. Behind them a narrow valley opened out, and to the west rose a limitless sea of mountain peaks whose bare rock shimmered in the harsh, vertical midday sunlight.

Marcel felt the sweat running down his body. He turned and looked at the houses and noticed the empty casements, the crooked walls, the parched grass growing between the paving stones of the single street, and he felt horror at the thought of having to spend an indefinite time here—weeks maybe, or even months.

"Do you know what it makes me think of?" he asked in dismay.

"Don't bother to tell me," replied Georges, and he looked round for a way to climb down to the village. He discovered a narrow path which came down the mountainside above them and disappeared between the boulders. It snaked and twisted down to the village and Georges strode off down it, walking away with the impatience of a man who wanted to put an end to a burning uncertainty.

They had not gone far before the boulders thinned out and the path widened, dropped steeply and led towards the houses. Georges stopped so suddenly that Marcel ran into him from behind. He was opening his mouth to speak, when he looked past Georges and saw a thin old man coming towards them with a bucket in his hand. He wore a suit and spectacles; his head bowed so that they could see his gray hair.

"Who's that?" whispered Marcel. "Boris?"

Georges shook his head. Vieale had described Boris as tall and broad-shouldered. The unknown man was now about ten paces away from them. He could not have noticed them yet because he still kept his head lowered, but like a horse which catches wind of something he stopped dead and looked up. Behind the thick lenses his pupils dilated with fright. Then he turned round and ran back down the path clutching the empty bucket to his chest like a shield. The two men watched in amazement as he stumbled wildly off, tripped on a stone and dropped the bucket which clattered to the ground and rolled down the slope until it stopped, caught in a bush.

3

"What's the matter with him?" asked Marcel with surprise.

Georges did not reply. His whole attention was on the gray-haired man, who had fallen on his hands for a second but at once got to his feet again and dashed into one of the houses on the right-hand side of the street, from whence he emerged a short while later with another man whom Georges at once recognized as Boris. He heard Marcel say something and shook his head impatiently as he continued to watch Boris, who now stood, head cocked to one side, beside the old man; he looked quickly upwards and then calmed him with a gesture.

Georges decided to stop playing hide and seek. "Stay here," he ordered Marcel. Erect, he strode toward the two men. When he reached the place where the old man had dropped the bucket he veered from the path and climbed cautiously down the steep drop. The handle of the bucket had caught in the thorny branches of a bush and Georges had some trouble in disentangling it. As he turned round he saw Boris standing on the path above him. His right hand was in his pocket, his bearded face expressionless.

They looked at each other for a second, then Georges stuck his arm through the bucket's handle to leave both arms free and clambered up to Boris on all fours. There he put down the bucket beside him on the stony ground and said as calmly as he could: "Vieale has sent us."

"To me?"

Georges nodded. "We are Germans and we're on our own."

"Deserters," said Boris. He had gray eyes, widely spaced. His sunburned face was framed in a thick, light brown beard and it struck Georges that everything about him gave an impression of size and forcefulness.

He looked past him towards the old man, who had not moved from where he stood in the street. "Who is that?"

"He came a fortnight ago," answered Boris, taking his hand out of his pocket. "Some Resistance people brought him and his daughter up here. They're political refugees from Germany."

"That's all we need," muttered Georges.

Boris watched him expectantly. Then he gave a slight smile. "How is Monsieur Vieale?"

"He can tell you that himself. Are there any more people living here?"

"No. If by that you mean the Resistance, you needn't worry. There's no danger until the day after tomorrow."

"Have you spoken to them?"

4

"They know I'm here."

"What else do they know about you?" asked Georges.

Boris turned and looked down at the old man. "I've told him that I'm an escaped Russian prisoner-of-war. The Resistance come up here once a week by car and bring food for them both."

"Otherwise you've told them nothing?"

"No," said Boris curtly.

"I must know, so that I don't give you away," said Georges, satisfied. "Where does the car come from?"

"From Escarène. Have you heard anything of the Americans?"

"I suppose you know that they've landed near Toulon?"

Boris's head jerked up. "Toulon? When?"

"Seven days ago. Didn't you know?"

"No. Then the war will soon be over."

"Looks like it," said Georges. "My name's Georg—my friend's Marcel."

"Marcel isn't a German name."

"It could have been if we'd won the war. We must warn Vieale. He wants to come up here tomorrow with his wife and son."

"Up here?" queried Boris, sounding surprised for the first time.

Georges turned round and beckoned to Marcel. "We have twenty-four hours. Within that time we've got to think of something."

He waited until Marcel had joined him and then said, "This is Boris. Pretend you know nothing about him."

"Why?" asked Marcel with surprise.

Georges nodded towards the old man. "German emigrés."

Marcel went pale. "Damn!"

"I'll tell him who you are," said Boris. "Wait here."

As he walked towards the old man Georges told what he had learned. "This is going to be bad for Vieale," he added. "I don't know what we're going to do."

"I had a feeling that something would go wrong," muttered Marcel.

"You've been having that feeling for the past three years. Quiet; here they come."

They watched as Boris and the old man rapidly approached them. "Herr Knopf would like to know from what part of Germany you come," said Boris.

"From Konstanz," answered Georges, and watched the old man approaching them, an embarrassed smile on his hollow-

5

cheeked features. He looked first at Marcel and then turned to Georges with a gesture of apology: "I lost my head. I had no idea that you were fellow-countrymen of mine. Are you going to stay here?"

"Perhaps," said Georges and turned to Boris: "Have you anything to drink?"

"Herr Knopf was just going to fetch a bucket of water."

"From the river?"

Boris laughed. "It's four hours' walk to the river. We have a spring. Did you come over the mountain?"

"We lost our way. If you don't mind we'll go with you to fetch the water. We are very thirsty."

Boris exchanged a few whispered words with Knopf, then bent down to the bucket and said in a tone of indifference: "It's a steep path."

"We like climbing," said Georges with a grin, and turned to Knopf: "Do you want to go back to Germany?"

"I don't know yet," said Knopf. "I lived there for sixty-four years."

"When did you leave?"

"Two years ago."

"Lucky for you," said Georges.

He let Boris lead the way and walked beside Marcel towards the mountainside. The path narrowed between boulders and began to climb steeply. Looking back Georges saw the old man still standing on the path and watching them. The farther they went the sheerer grew the mountainside on their left. Finally the path dropped sharply to traverse a vertical cliff and follow the line of the valley, first southwards then eastwards. After walking along it for about ten minutes, a narrow gorge was revealed which made an opening twenty yards wide in the cliff-face to their left. Its bottom, covered with loose stones, was reached by a row of rain-smoothed steps which had been hacked out of the rock. After climbing down them and up the far side they were on the path again and found themselves looking down half-right into a deep valley. It lay surrounded by sheer mountains, its floor covered by a thick wood.

After another hundred yards the path took a sharp turn to the left, then widened slightly and came to an abrupt end at a wall

6

of dark slate which jutted at an acute angle from the mountain-side.

"Here we are," said Boris and stopped.

"Where are we?" asked Marcel, who had halted behind Georges and now stood looking around. Georges too stared about amazed. In front of him was the slate outcrop, to the left the mountainside and to his right a sheer drop towards the wooded valley.

"I came here three times before I saw it myself," said Boris and laid his hand flat on the outcrop of slate.

Georges, standing close to him, now saw clear water running over his fingers. At first glance it seemed like magic but then, as he looked upwards, he realized that the whole surface of the rock was covered by a thin coating of water. He took a step, craned his head back and tried to discover where the water came from. Slightly to the left of the outcrop the cliff-face broke up into a maze of enormous boulders, stones and rockslides stretching away out of sight.

As he looked up Georges felt his stomach heave, and shut his eyes for a moment to repress the sudden feeling of dizziness. "It's miraculous," he said. "I just don't understand where the water comes from."

"Must be a broken pipe," said Marcel, who was incapable of being impressed when he was hungry. He tried to catch some of the water in the hollow of his hand, but Boris showed him a better way. Sticking out his lower lip he pressed his chin against the rock and let the water run into his open mouth.

When they had quenched their thirst, Boris laid the bucket at an angle against the rock and put a stone under it. "It takes half an hour to fill up," he said. "If the ground weren't so stony I would have dug a hole to collect the water in."

"Where does it run away?" asked Georges. "Into a cleft?"

"If you lie down on the ground you'll see it. The rock underneath is hollow. The water must come from an underground lake. It used to be piped to a fountain in the village, and the fort also was supplied from the same source. Let's sit down, we have time enough."

"One can hardly tell that you aren't a German," said Georges as they sat down. He looked down into the valley.

"I had plenty of time to learn it," said Boris. His voice was deep, and when he laughed he showed two rows of strong teeth, some dark but the rest very white. He wore a tattered shirt unbuttoned to the waist, which exposed his muscular, hairy chest, and tight, dark-gray trousers. His shoes were in holes and from the right one the sole hung loose. With his great round face, his wild beard and his skin tanned by the wind and the sun, he looked like a Russian peasant. But Georges knew that he had been no peasant.

He felt automatically in his pocket, then realized that he had no more cigarettes. He looked at Marcel, whose eyes had closed with fatigue. Georges still had no idea how he was going to carry on; the appearance of the emigrés had upset all his plans. Normally he would not have worried about them, but he had eaten nothing for twelve hours, the way up had been heavy going and from what he had heard the mountains were swarming with Resistance men.

He looked again at Boris. There was something about him that he didn't like. He sat rather hunched up and Georges wondered about him. "While we're here," he said, "we might as well find something that will make the bucket fill quicker. A piece of tin would do."

Boris gave a thin smile. "Why bother? The day won't be any shorter if the bucket takes one hour or two hours to fill. Here you have time on your hands. Besides, you can't stay here. Knopf may not give you away to the Resistance, but his daughter will for sure. She hates everything German."

"How old is she?"

"Maybe seventeen; still half a child."

"If she's seventeen she's not a child any more," said Georges. "I have the feeling that you don't like us being here."

"I won't deny it," said Boris calmly. "I'm glad to have found a spot which is more or less safe. If you stay you spoil the only chance I have."

"Or so you imagine. As soon as you appear anywhere they'll arrest you and hand you over. You can't stay hidden in La Peine forever."

"Not forever, no. Perhaps times will change."

"You don't really believe that."

Boris was silent and Georges decided to try another angle. "We've taken three days to get here," he said. "We must have something to eat and we must rest. Then we'll see."

"You can rest and you can eat. I have no objection to your staying here until tomorrow."

8

"That suits me fine," said Marcel, who had been listening sleep-ily. He was glad to be lying down and were it not for his hunger he would have been quite happy. "I don't think much of this hole anyway. We should be able to find somewhere better."

"Such as a nice apartment in Nice," remarked Georges sar-castically. He turned to Boris again. "I still don't see what it mat-ters to you. After all, you ought to be glad of our company. Knopf and his daughter won't stay here much longer and then what are you going to say to him when he invites you to go with him?"

"I'll tell him that I'd rather stay here until the war is all over. I'm sure he'll understand."

"All right, then. I'll make another suggestion. We'll stay here until tomorrow and then we'll go and find Vieale. Somewhere we'll find a place where we can wait until Knopf and his daughter have gone and then we'll all come back here and join you. Agreed?"

"What does Vieale want here?"

"Didn't he tell you?"

"No."

"He was a prisoner-of-war in Germany for two years," said Georges. "A relative who was in some Ministry used his influence for him with Laval. He was released, sent back home and made mayor by the Prefect of the Alpes Maritimes. Now the people in Eys are angry with him because he was released early while his pals were still in a prison camp and because he got the job of mayor. For that there are quite a few who are just waiting to get a rope round his neck."

"I thought it was something of the kind," said Boris, and stood up. He walked over to the bucket, looked inside and stood for a moment gazing absentmindedly. Then he turned round. "Sup-posing we do as you suggest and supposing we are found here. What then?"

Georges looked at Marcel who was now listening intently. "That depends on who finds us. Vieale is bringing our things with him."

"Your things?" asked Boris sharply.

"We left our weapons and uniforms with Vieale."

"Weapons?"

"Two brand-new machine carbines," said Georges grinning. "We only got them four weeks ago. Vieale advised us to leave

9

them with him in case we were seen on the way. They would have looked a bit funny with this." He pointed, still grinning, at the thin linen tunic.

Boris looked hard at him. "So you mean to shoot?"

"If I have to."

"It's up to you."

"It was never up to me when I had to shoot."

"They all say that. Now I'll tell you something. You're not going to do any shooting and you're not going to stay here. I'm sorry about Vieale, but I can't have any trigger-happy fools up here."

"He's mad," said Marcel. Then he said angrily, "You can't talk to us like that."

Georges stood up. "Don't get worked up, boy. The bucket's full, we can go now."

"We'll go when we've finished our conversation," said Boris coldly. "I shall tell Knopf that you are only spending one night here. Tell Vieale that he can't come up; it's too dangerous for him."

"For him or for you?"

"The Resistance have nothing against me. Escarène is fifteen kilometers from Eys, where Vieale is mayor."

"That means nothing."

"Perhaps not for you, but it means plenty for Vieale. Ask him whether there are people living in Escarène who know him. Apart from that, La Peine is not a pleasant place to live, otherwise the original inhabitants wouldn't have left it."

"They left it," said Georges, "because the road is blocked with rubble."

"It's not blocked. There was a landslide below La Peine which carried away two hundred yards of the road. But that's not the point: the people were not evacuated because of the road. You've seen the fort, haven't you? When the French built it they had to blast into the mountainside. They went as deep into the rock as they could and when they had finished they discovered that the mountain was hollow. Cracks appeared in the concrete ramparts, they shifted and now it's only a question of time before the whole westside collapses and buries La Peine beneath it."

"Good God!" said Marcel. "Are you serious?"

"I learned about it from Vieale. I've been up in the fort, too. The

10

barracks are half ruined, and in the pillboxes you can easily put your head through the cracks in the concrete."

"You're trying to frighten us, of course," said Georges rather uncertainly. To Marcel he said, "Have you ever seen a hollow mountain?"

"Anything can happen in a place where there aren't any birds," growled Marcel. "Perhaps it's something to do with the underground lake."

Georges paused for a moment, then he said: "I'm surprised that Vieale told all this to you and not to us. Does Knopf know about it?"

"He heard about it in Escarène," answered Boris. He picked up the full bucket and pointed in the direction from which they had come. "You know the way now. I'll take longer than you with this bucket to carry."

"We can help you," said Georges.

"There's no need for that."

Georges went ahead of Marcel. When they were some distance from Boris, Marcel said, "I don't understand why you took all that from him. Is it because Vieale told you he had a pistol?"

"We need him," said Georges.

The return route took them sharply downhill and Georges gave one backward look. The Russian was about fifty paces behind them. "You know I'm not scared of a pistol."

"That's why I'm so surprised. Why do we need him? Or do you really want to stay here in spite of everything?"

"In spite of what? La Peine is the one safe place in the whole area."

"You call that safe!" Marcel gave an angry shout of laughter. "I have never seen such a mass of disadvantages heaped together in one spot. We should have crossed over to Italy after all. Why don't we try to go farther north? Then at least we'd be nearer home."

"You're going to have to realize that you're just as far from home at Annecy or Annemasse as you are at La Peine, and the sooner you get used to the idea the better it'll be for both of us. Which do you prefer—a few weeks at La Peine or the other thing?"

"You're talking to me as if I were an idiot," answered Marcel, who was beginning to lose his temper. "The only thing you seem to forget is that in a few weeks the problem will be no more solved than it is today. So far I've done everything you've told me; I don't mean to start a discussion now as to whether it was right or wrong, but you're up against it now and later on you'll remember what I'm saying: you're doing the wrong thing."

"All right, you can turn round and go," said Georges. "You came of your own free will."

Marcel was just starting to reply, but they had reached the gorge and had to give their full attention to negotiating the slippery steps without falling.

Marcel could see that Georges was furious from the way he climbed up the far side. He had always looked up to him and tried to be like him. He was so dependent upon him that he had even tried to adopt some of Georges' personal mannerisms, such as his drawling speech, the way he knocked the ash off a cigarette or stood with his hands on his hips. However, from the very moment when they had met Vieale his blind confidence in Georges had been shaken. As he clambered up the gorge and then, tired and hungry, followed Georges along the mountain path he recalled the conversation that evening three days before, when their troop train had stopped in Eys, no one knowing why until the order came to halt and await fresh orders. Vieale had received them in the house that Georges had picked for their billet. He had put glasses on the table and fetched a bottle of wine from the cellar, heavy red Beaujolais, and had said, "When you have drunk that it won't matter to you that you are losing the war."

"Who says we're losing the war?" Georges had countered. Then they had talked for a long time. Vieale's wife had joined them and then his son, whom Vieale had sent to the cellar to fetch another bottle of Beaujolais. There was only one thing for them to do, Viele had explained—after Georges, made talkative by the wine, had told him their whole story—they must hide in the mountains until the war was over and people had come to their senses again. Then they should go to Germany and wait to see how things developed. He knew a safe place in the mountains.

A safe place! thought Marcel grimly. The fellow knew very well why he was sending us up here and he had said nothing about the hollow mountain. He may have been afraid we'd change our minds, but if so he didn't know Georges. Georges was glad to clutch at a straw like this after all the years of acting as if he had a patent solution up his sleeve for every problem.

He sighed a little, then quickened his pace to catch up with Georges and said, "What's the hurry? We've plenty of time."

Georges stopped and looked back up the path. Nothing was to be seen of Boris, and Georges decided to wait for him. "If only I knew what was going on in that fellow's head," he said.

"Why bother? You credit him with too much sense. He's like all Russians."

Georges shook his head. "He knows now that Vieale is bringing our weapons with him. He's sharp enough to have realized that he won't be able to stop us from staying in La Peine with his pistol."

"He can't with his pistol alone, but he can with the help of the Resistance men."

"I've thought of that too. Here he comes." Boris had now come into sight round the last bend in the path and as he saw them signaled to them to go on.

"Doesn't seem very eager to talk to us," muttered Marcel. "He treats us like my father treats his workmen. Shows how much our stock has fallen. Funny how quickly it happens as soon as you haven't got a gun in your hands."

"One day when you get home," said Georges, "you can sit down and write a thesis on it."

They set off again and soon reached the place where the houses of La Peine could be seen between the boulders.

It was early afternoon and very hot. To the south a bank of weirdly-shaped cloud was forming over the mountain-tops, which seemed to be trembling in the heat. The air was very still, and Marcel, wearily keeping pace with Georges, felt his fear returning. He looked mistrustfully at the houses with their crooked walls and peeling plaster. Only the narrow church tower seemed to be in good condition, even though the hands were missing from the faded clock-face. The empty belfry windows yawned beneath the flat, rust-brown tiled roof, whose color reminded Marcel of the garish Riviera posters in travel agencies. In the past he had always wanted to go to Nice. It had often been talked about at home, but it was one of his father's immutable habits to choose a place for the holidays from which he could easily and cheaply keep in constant touch with his business by telephone.

Georges stopped and waited for Boris at the spot where the rocks gave way to the smooth steep slope leading down to the village. Below the houses the mountainside was a sheer, almost vertical cliff. From where they stood Georges now had an even

13

clearer view of the jutting outcrop on which La Peine stood. The double row of houses ran parallel to the rocky mass, about a hundred and fifty feet high, which towered behind it and was topped by the fort.

Georges was so absorbed by the view that he was not aware of Boris's arrival. Only when Boris spoke to him did he turn and notice that the Russian was smiling.

"Thought of something funny?" asked Georges drily.

Boris shook his head. "I was laughing at you. In those clothes you look like *maquisards*."

"Oh, really?" said Georges, setting off again down the path, followed by Marcel and Boris. "I don't know what you think is so funny about them. No one around here seems to be wearing a double-breasted suit."

"What's that?" asked Boris.

Marcel snickered. "He doesn't even know what a double-breasted suit is, Georges! Don't be too hard on him, he's a Russian. I've never understood. . . ." He broke off. They had reached the first houses and Marcel had happened to look up at the cliff-face. It was his first sight of it so close above him. It did not rise vertically up to the fort but leaned right out over the roofs of the houses on the right-hand side of the street. He was almost sick and for a second felt an urge to run away. He glanced at Georges, who was also looking up at the cliff. "Useful when it rains," said Georges after a pause, and turned to Boris, standing beside him with a strange expression on his face. "You didn't tell us that the cliff was overhanging. Has it always been like that?"

"Yes, always," replied Boris. "You see it when you climb up."

"Then there's nothing to worry about—or is there?"

"Not if there were no crack in it. There's nothing holding it since the crack developed; it's hanging free."

Carrying the bucket he walked past them towards a house about thirty yards along the right-hand side of the street. At first sight it looked like all the others, but then Georges noticed that it had shutters and a door. The red-painted shutters were open; on one of them two slats were missing and the hinges were rusted so that the house stood out from the rest like a vain, painted old woman. It had two stories and five asymmetrically placed windows of different sizes.

Georges was still standing lost in thought when Boris came out of the house with the gray-haired old man. They paused in front of the doorstep and Georges and Marcel walked over to them.

14

"Boris tells me that you only want to stay here for one night," said Knopf.

"Then I suppose we shall," replied Georges. "Have you anything for us to eat?"

Knopf nodded. "We'll bring you something." He and Boris went back into the house, closing the door behind them.

"That was plain enough," growled Marcel. "Time for us to find a place for ourselves. I'm beginning to get fed up with them. Do they think we're lepers or something?"

"Perhaps."

Georges sat down on the middle step of the three leading up to the door and looked down the street. It lay in the shadow of the houses and was no more than half a dozen paces wide. To the north it sloped sharply downwards. The cobbled surface was stepped at regular intervals and both rows of houses stood in two straight lines directly beneath the overhanging cliff.

Marcel had remained standing, irresolute. "If you ask me . . ." he began.

Georges interrupted him. "Shut up! Sit down, you're keeping the sun off me."

Marcel looked round. "What do you mean? It's not shining here."

"You're in my light all the same. You're too fat."

"Want some of it?" asked Marcel. He sat down beside Georges on the step and groaned with pleasure. "Ah, that's better. I'm not moving from here for at least an hour. All we need now is a bottle of beer."

"I'd say Ovaltine was more your speed. Didn't your mother always give it to you?"

Marcel grew red in the face.

"And a nice glass of milk every morning," said Georges.

Marcel looked at him threateningly. "You know I can't stand it when you talk like that."

"Sweet little Marcel," said Georges unmoved. "I really think she could stick a knife into me now and twist it round and round. She could scratch out my eyes with her long red fingernails and tear off my skin in strips. If she lives to be a hundred she'll never forgive me for what I've done to her sweet little Marcel. And yet she used to think a lot of me once. Didn't she always change her dress when I came to see you?"

"Be quiet!" shouted Marcel, furious.

"The latest Paris fashion," said Georges. "She can't have been

15

more than eighteen when she married your father. A girl only does that if the man's got a lot of money or if she's slipped up. Judging from your face it was a slip-up."

"Georges!" said Marcel.

Georges gave him a friendly slap on the back. "All right, boy. But you must admit she was a knock-out. With her figure she looked like a film star. I was crazy about her."

"You!" Marcel stared at him in astonishment, then shook his head and grinned. "If somebody else had told me that I might have fallen for it. But women were always running after you."

"Silly bitches," said Georges. Marcel laughed. He slid down to the bottom step and leaned back. "They used to chase me too," he said, "but for a different reason. You didn't need a father with money. One day I'll get caught; that's what'll happen."

"Your father didn't get caught."

"Depends how you look at it. A woman like my mother isn't the ideal wife either. She's too . . ." He was silent. Having laid his head back he could see the house-front and for a moment a girl's face appeared at one of the windows. Marcel sat up in a flash and twisted round to get a better look at the window. Like the others it had neither frame nor pane and from below the ceiling of the room could be seen, but now the girl had disappeared and Marcel wondered how long she had been standing there listening to them. Puzzled, he turned to Georges, who immediately stood up and looked at him questioningly, disconcerted by his strange behavior. Before Marcel could explain, the door opened behind them.

"It took a long time," said Boris. "Our stove is burning badly."

He held in his hands a plate with two large lumps of meat on it and under his arm there was a piece of bread. "The bread is Herr Knopf's. There's one plate. It's the only one, so don't break it." He gave the plate to Georges and the bread to Marcel, nodded to them and went indoors again.

Georges looked up from the plate into Marcel's bewildered face. "Your mouth's hanging open."

"God almighty!" said Marcel furiously. "I can't stand this much longer. I've never met a Russian with good manners before."

Georges smiled. "He's playing Santa Claus to the naughty boys, but he doesn't know yet just how naughty we can be. Eat up or the meat will get cold."

"What with? My fingers?"

"Go on, Mummy can't see you now." He was about to sit down

16

again on the step when he noticed that Marcel was staring suspiciously at the house.

"What's the matter?" he asked.

"Come here," replied Marcel. He crossed the street to the house opposite and sat down on the step. Georges followed.

"It's better over here," explained Marcel. "We can at least see the people who are listening to us."

"Who's listening?"

"The old man's daughter. She was standing up there at the window."

"What, just now?" Georges at once stood up and turned round, plate in hand.

"Not just now, but earlier, before the Russian came out. I happened to look up."

"Why didn't you tell me then?"

"I didn't have time."

Georges bent over him angrily. "And did she hear what you were saying?"

"I don't know, and even if she did it needn't stop us from eating." He took the plate from Georges and sniffed the meat. "Not bad! Let's see what it tastes like."

When they had finished eating Marcel wiped his greasy fingers on his trousers. "Now for a cigarette. I'd smoke sawdust if only I had some."

Georges said nothing. After a while he asked: "What did she look like?"

"It happened too quickly," said Marcel reflectively. "I really can't remember much about her looks—except for her eyes. They were very dark."

"She's almost too young for my liking," mused Georges. He leaned his elbow on his knee and gazed up at the window.

"Why?" asked Marcel. "The younger the better. They all get old soon enough."

"That's not what I mean. Her father said he had lived in Germany for sixty-four years, remember?"

"Didn't he say sixty?"

"He said sixty-four. Once I hear something I don't forget it. I figure that he left Germany, say, two years ago; add that on and he must have been forty-nine when the girl was born."

"My mother was eighteen. The other extreme."

It can happen, of course, thought Georges. Why not? His thoughts wandered for a moment and he tried to imagine what

17

Marcel's mother must have looked like at eighteen. Then he heard Marcel's voice, preoccupied with much duller matters.

"I wouldn't have told him anything," he was grumbling. "What business is it of his where we live? Now he'll want to know which street. What made you choose Konstanz of all places?"

"Because I couldn't think of anything better on the spur of the moment," replied Georges, his thoughts returning to reality. "Besides, it explains our accent."

"All the same, I wouldn't have said Konstanz. Almost every German goes to Konstanz at least once in his lifetime. Perhaps Knopf even knows people there. No, I would have said nothing at all, and if he comes back and tries to pump us I'll send him back to his daughter."

He carried the plate over the street, put it on the step and returned to Georges. "They can wash it up themselves. I'm not walking all the way to the spring because of a plate. What do we do now?"

Georges stood up. "Look for a roof over our heads."

"Agreed," said Marcel and yawned. "God, am I tired. What beats me is why people should be so crazy as to build a village here."

"They were afraid of the Saracens," said Georges, as they walked down the street side by side. "Up in the mountains they were more or less safe from them."

"When would that have been?"

"No idea, but before the first world war, anyway."

Marcel laughed. "Not good enough, Georges. Think of your doctor's degree."

"No chance of that now."

"Bad luck for us."

"It won't worry me—but your mother! She had to have a university man in the family. Her husband's bank account doesn't count for much now that every grocer has taken to driving round in a Buick. She wanted to hand you round at parties on a silver salver."

"Why must you always go on about that?"

"Why indeed?" said Georges, and looked up at the houses on both sides. Their uniform method of construction gave them something of a military look: there they stood, two companies of veterans drawn up in single file along the street, itself made with equal uniformity with fourteen rows of cobbles after every three steps. Each house stood a little lower than its neighbor and at

18

every third house the drop was a little less than between the other two. A cool dampness blew out of the empty doors and window frames, and the walls, bare of plaster, gave off the smell of rotting wood.

They walked about fifty yards down the street and the row of houses on the left-hand side opened out into a semi-circular square in which stood the church. Its porch gaped open to the street as if still awaiting the faithful congregation of La Peine, but behind it was nothing but a pile of rubble, the remains of what had once been the nave, reaching as far as the tower which stood above the ruins like a tombstone. On the valley side the square was enclosed by a low wall and as Marcel, who reached the wall before Georges, looked over it he jumped back.

"God!" he said, pale, and looked at Georges, who was now also leaning over the wall. The church was built on a pulpit-like outcrop projecting from the main cliff-face and rising a sheer three hundred-odd feet from the valley like a gigantic rostrum. The western row of houses formed an unbroken wall along the line of the cliff, seemingly built into the mountainside. For the first time Georges was able to see the valley floor. It was narrow, overgrown with thick scrub, with broken boulders of all sizes scattered among the bushes. On the far side, too, the mountain rose steeply. On its lower reaches grew a scattering of olive trees, after which the slope became a bare, unassailable barricade of gray rock. Northward the valley tapered, but a terrace jutted from the west side and obscured the view after a short distance while the southern arm of the valley was visible until it changed direction.

A little later Georges also discovered the pass. He followed the line of the road, clearly traceable through the olive wood on the other side of the valley. Where the valley turned eastwards the olive trees came to an end, and the road vanished into a hollow and reappeared, six hundred feet higher on the north flank of the mountain at the point where it blocked the southward-running valley. But there the distance was so great that Georges could no longer follow it with the naked eye—presumably it wound up the mountainside. In the center of the mountain's ridge there was a deep wedge-shaped cleft which Georges took to be the pass. Behind this mountain was another and behind that a few dozen more, their peaks probing the soft blue of the sky. An immense stillness of an almost physical intensity lay over everything as if a volcano of silence had erupted and buried the landscape.

Marcel turned to Georges. "Shall we go on?"

19

"What did you say?" Georges had been far away. He was disappointed that even from here he could not see the point where the road crossed the valley. He did not wait for an answer and continued: "We must go on a bit farther. I want to see where the road crosses over."

"Why are you so interested?"

"Because we can't afford not to be interested in anything here."

Looking north, they turned to the street, which ended farther down in a gateway of one of the houses which stood at right angles to the other houses. It was bigger than the rest and had a small square tower with a pointed roof on which was a long rusty iron pole.

"I like that," said Marcel and stopped. "There's something carved in the stone work up there."

"It used to be the town hall," said Georges. Marcel spat on the ground. "Of course, there must be somewhere for the bureaucrats, even up here. That's the place where I'll sack out."

"Please yourself," said Georges absentmindedly. Something else had caught his attention. Just in front of the town hall the cliff wall which hung over the entire length of the village like a crooked claw came to an abrupt end, and he could now see how its massive north shoulder straddled the main ridge.

He walked quickly over to the gateway with its three-foot-thick arch and dark steps on either side leading into the house, and emerged on to a round open space at the end of the village. Like the square in front of the church it was enclosed by a low wall which started from the right-hand corner of the town hall, described a semi-circular arc and bounded the space on the western and northern sides. On the eastern side, where the mountainside sloped up towards the ridge, there was no wall. In the exact center a slim cypress grew out of the dry soil. On the open side a steep path skirted the cliff, climbed towards the ridge and joined a road which, at the point where it rounded the flank of the mountain, disappeared into a tunnel, bored in the northern face of the cliff. Georges followed its path northwards through numerous tunnels, until it suddenly stopped and the western face of the mountain broke off as if some supernatural force had wrenched it away. With its torn skin of shattered rocks the mountain here looked like a mortally wounded giant, dying in agony.

Farther on, about five hundred yards up the valley, Georges made another discovery. The bold arch of a viaduct spanned the valley, stretched between the lowering mountainsides and looking absurdly small and fragile in the distance. Georges gazed back at the cliff-face above, then looked round for Marcel whom he had completely forgotten for the last few minutes. He was nowhere to be found, but then he heard his voice; it sounded as if he were sitting in a cellar. As Georges followed the sound he realized that Marcel must be hidden between the eastern line of houses and the overhanging cliff. To get there he had to skirt the long front of the town hall and take a path which led up to the road. He climbed a few hundred yards and could then see along the narrow gap between the cliffs and the backs of the houses. As they were built close to the mountainside the light there was very dim. Large rocks lay scattered on the ground and on one of them stood Marcel. When he saw Georges he came quickly towards him, jumping from rock to rock.

"They've got windows at the back," he said, "so they could look straight out at the rock."

"Why not, if it amused them," said Georges.

They went back to the village square, where Georges stopped and shook his head. "Not far to go to Heaven when somebody died here."

"Nor to hell either," said Marcel with a grin.

They glanced over at the mountains opposite, whose outlines were now traced more sharply than before in the melting blue of the sky. The sun stood low in the west, a cool breeze was blowing over the mountains and shadows were gathering in the valley like great beasts returning from pasture.

"It reminds me of something," said Marcel.

Georges had thrust his hands into his pockets, and walked once round the cypress tree, looking at it from all sides. Then he stopped and looked at Marcel.

"I'm definitely not one of them," Marcel continued, "but just imagine a church bell among all these mountains!"

"Why not a symphony orchestra, too," said Georges and turned his attention to the façade of the town hall. It consisted of thirty-foot-high walls with tiny windows like loopholes that were barred by iron lattice-work. Only the two windows in the tower were slightly bigger. Their dark, empty casements gazed over the mountains like the eyes of a blind man, and the rusty iron pole on top of the tower glowed red in the light of the setting sun. To the right of the gateway a pipe stuck out of the wall, and beneath it, built into the wall, was a large stone trough.

Georges walked over and stared at it. "It seems to have been the only fountain in the whole village. The water must have come from the underground lake. I suppose they must have built it here because this is the lowest spot in La Peine. How do you like the square?"

"Why?"

"I suggest we sleep here. Here we've got soft ground and fresh air. If we're lucky there may be some doors in the town hall still on their hinges. We'll fetch two or three of them and build ourselves a shelter."

"I'd prefer it to a house," said Marcel. "I saw a few doors farther up there."

"Let's have a look at the town hall all the same."

They walked in at the gate, up the left-hand stairway into a narrow, dark passage with half a dozen doorways on either side. The rooms were small, damp and completely bare. As there was nothing more to see in this part of the house they investigated the opposite wing. Here they found the same, so they returned to the street and walked along it until they came to three houses with closed doors. These they lifted off their hinges and dragged to the square.

"Where shall we put them?" asked Marcel.

Georges nodded towards a corner of the town hall. There they laid the doors in a row at a slant, which gave them a reasonably comfortable lean-to shelter.

"When Vieale brings our things," said Georges, satisfied, "we can even hang a groundsheet over the entrance. All we need now is some grass." They knelt down on the ground and pulled up enough of the withered grass to make a fairly large heap, then carried it into the shelter.

"That's enough," said Georges, and crawled back into the open. As he stood upright, he saw a man coming through the gateway.

"I hope I'm not disturbing you," he said.

Georges looked at his hollow-cheeked face. "People who bring us something to eat never disturb us."

"It's tomato soup," said Knopf, and placed a soot-blackened iron cooking pot on the ground. "I've added a little bread to it. It was too dry to eat any other way."

Georges looked round for Marcel who was still in the lean-to and had not noticed Knopf's arrival.

"Chow!" shouted Georges. To Knopf he said, "It was kind of you to have thought of us. Did you know that we were here?"

"I looked for you," replied Knopf. "I'm afraid the soup has got cold on the way."

"That doesn't matter," said Georges. He turned to Marcel who had now emerged. "Herr Knopf has brought us some tomato soup."

"Good for him!" said Marcel, delighted, and quickly bent down to pick up the pot. "Where shall we sit?"

"On the fountain trough," suggested Georges. He said to Knopf, "We've got nothing to eat it with."

"I've brought you two spoons," said Knopf.

While Georges and Marcel settled themselves on the edge of the trough, Knopf walked over to their shelter and glanced inside. "Why don't you sleep in one of the houses?" he asked.

"We're not very fond of old houses," answered Georges.

Knopf rejoined them. "I hope you like the taste. We have practically no more salt," he said.

"Tastes good even without salt," said Marcel, and Georges nodded agreement. The pot had been half full, and when they had emptied it their hunger was satisfied.

"All we need now is a cigarette," said Marcel.

Knopf felt in his pocket and produced a pack of cigarettes. He offered it to Marcel.

"It's too good to be true," said Marcel. He took two cigarettes, gave one to Georges, put the second one between his lips and lit it.

Knopf looked over the wall towards the mountains. "Look at that! I never knew what a sunset was like until I came to La Peine."

"Pretty good," said Marcel, also looking westward to where the mountains now rose blue and black above the milky vapor in the valleys, and the sky above looked like a pallet of colors. He noticed that Knopf had taken off his glasses and asked: "Are you far-sighted?"

"Yes," answered Knopf, amused. "Don't you care for sunsets?"

"Yes, only I don't show it. Whatever else you may think about me, I'm not a snob about that sort of thing."

"Why should I think badly of you?"

"People often do," said Marcel, who had not forgotten their cool reception that morning. "But I still don't see why I'm any worse than other people who happened to be on the right side."

23

"It's not necessarily pure chance which puts one on the right side," said Knopf thoughtfully.

Marcel gestured impatiently. "You can talk! Did you choose your own parents, might I ask?"

"Shut your mouth," broke in Georges sharply.

"Let your friend talk as he likes," said Knopf. "We might have been spared a great deal if only people hadn't grown tired of talking to one another at the critical moment."

"Anyway," said Marcel, "as soldiers we only did our duty."

Knopf smiled. "I don't doubt it, but just think what we might have avoided in this century without soldiers who only did their duty."

"You can put the question another way," said Georges. He had wanted to avoid this conversation, but now that the subject had arisen in spite of his reluctance, he dropped his reserve. "What would have happened without soldiers doing their duty? Do you think that the Communists would have sat back and rested on their laurels after the Russian revolution?"

"Perhaps you are right," said Knopf. "But you can't fight Beelzebub by making a pact with the Devil." He picked up the pot. "I would have liked to have stayed and chatted with you for a little about Konstanz, but it is getting dark and the road is bad. You said you didn't like old houses. Do you know Escarène?"

"No," replied Georges.

"I came across a remarkable proverb there," said Knopf. "Translated into German it means roughly 'Old houses never die.'"

"I've never heard it before," said Georges. "I can't see any sense in it either."

Knopf nodded. "I thought the same at first, but I think that it has a very profound meaning." He pressed the cigarette packet into Georges' hand. "Share them with your friend and I hope you get home safely. I used to have some friends in Konstanz who would have been very happy if you could have given them my regards."

"If you give me their address. . . ." said Georges hesitantly.

"It's no use," said Knopf. "I think they must be dead by now."

Boris came towards Knopf down the village street. He took the pot from him and said: "Did you talk to them?"

24

"Not much," replied Knopf. "Perhaps I am too old to understand them."

"I didn't get much out of them either," said Boris. "They're hiding something."

"What makes you think so?"

"It's just a feeling I have," said Boris, and fell silent. They were approaching their house and as they reached it they saw waiting for them a girl in blue three-quarter length trousers and a blue pullover, sandals on her bare brown feet. Her long black hair was combed over her left shoulder and fell to her waist; without it she would have looked like a boy, since her face was long and narrow, her nose straight beneath serious dark eyes. She had high, rather pronounced cheekbones and her cheeks arched inwards, emphasizing the strong and regular contours of her mouth.

"You've been away a long time," she said to Knopf. She had a deep, soft voice which had fascinated Boris the first time he had heard it. Although he had spent two weeks in the same house with her, she still seemed to him as enigmatic as on the day when she had first walked up the village street with her father. They had been followed by two determined-looking men with heavy rucksacks. He had told them who he was and since then they had treated him as a friend.

He stood for a while and listened to Knopf and his daughter talking, then turned and carried the cooking pot indoors. The house had five rooms, two of which were on the ground floor on either side of the narrow hall. Boris bunked in one of them, the other being the kitchen. Here there was a cooking-stove made of stone, from which the iron rings were missing, and a makeshift table which Boris had nailed together out of old planks. On it lay crockery for two people, a few glasses and two saucepans. In one corner, near a heap of firewood, stood the bucket. Otherwise the room was empty.

Boris filled the pot with water from the bucket, carried it to the stove and put it over one of the holes. Although it was almost dark in the kitchen, his movements were rapid and sure. There were still some embers among the ashes in the stove, on which he laid some wood and blew until it caught fire. Then he went into his own room. It contained nothing but his bed. He had put it up in the farthest corner, because of the open window, and it consisted of a heap of straw piled up against the wall to a height of two feet. To keep the straw in place Boris had boarded it in with

25

planks and big stones, and now, with a blanket given to him by the men from Escarène, he slept in reasonable warmth and comfort. Before that he had slept on a heap of dried leaves which he had dragged up from the valley in a sack. Knopf and his daughter slept on mattresses that they had brought with them from Escarène. A week ago they had been given a paraffin lamp. Boris lit it and carried it into the kitchen. He put it on the table and made sure that the water in the pot was hot. He washed it out with a cloth, threw the dirty water down a sluice in the floor, then went back to Knopf who was sitting in the dark on the steps and talking to his daughter.

As Boris approached them, Knopf moved over to one side and said cordially: "Come and sit with us. I'm not so tired tonight. Perhaps it's because of the good news we have had."

"You mean about the Americans landing at Toulon?" asked Boris.

"Yes. As soon as the Germans have withdrawn we can go back to Escarène. You will be coming with us, won't you?"

For a whole fortnight Boris had been waiting for this question to be put to him and he answered it as unconcernedly as he could: "The war isn't over yet, even if the Germans do withdraw from these parts. I think I'll stay here for a few weeks more."

"You may find it rather lonely when we've gone."

"Perhaps," said Boris and looked over the roofs at the starlit sky. Then he laughed quietly. "Or rather, I don't think I will. I grew up in a village half the size of La Peine. It was three days journey by cart to the nearest town."

"What did you do for a living?"

"My parents had a small farm," said Boris. He had never told Knopf anything about himself, but the thought of his imminent return to Escarène, which would also mean Anna leaving his life forever, saddened him and made him forget his reserve.

Knopf lit a cigarette. He had grown to like the Russian for his laconic manner, and the occasional monosyllabic conversations with him had aroused the wish to learn more about him. He also felt grateful to him. Since they had been in La Peine Boris had quietly and unquestioningly done most of the work. He did the cooking, fetched wood and water and had seen to it that their living conditions in the damp, empty rooms were steadily improved.

"So you always lived in a village?" he inquired, picking up the conversation again.

Boris shook his head. "No. The last twenty years in Gorky. I studied there."

Before Knopf had time to express his astonishment, Anna broke in. "What did you study?"

This pleased Boris, since she rarely asked him questions. "My last job was teaching languages at the high school."

"Why did you never tell us that?"

"It didn't seem important."

"You are not a stranger any longer," said Knopf with warmth. "You have helped us a great deal and whether you taught in a school or worked in a factory before the war does not make us any less grateful. It has always surprised me how well you speak French. Your German would be explained by your having been a prisoner."

"You speak French better than I do, although you weren't a language teacher."

"He has studied languages a great deal," put in Anna. Her voice suddenly had a lively ring and she looked at Knopf. "Can I tell him?"

Knopf shook his head. "Another time. It's getting late. I would still like to know," he said to Boris, "how you managed to reach the high school."

"I owe it to the Communists," said Boris. "At that time I didn't understand much about politics. I went to school in Gerovka; it is five kilometers from our village. One day a commission came to the school. We were given a test and after four weeks my father was sent for to go to Gerovka. They told him that I had won a scholarship to Gorky. Of course my father agreed to my going. He still had my brother at home, who was five years older than I was, to help him with the work. Five years later the land was nationalized. Like all peasants my father tried to save what there was to be saved. Five times he went to the authorities in Gorky, but they wouldn't even see him. Then they did a new land survey and my brother knocked down one of the surveyors. He was sent to the mines for twenty years."

"Is he still alive?" asked Knopf quietly.

"I don't know. I've never heard from him since. My father, who was standing by when it happened, was sent to prison for a year. When he returned home he was ill. I saw him twice again. A few months later my mother died too; it was too much for her."

He stood up and looked through the open door into the house.

"I've left the lamp burning. We've nearly finished the paraffin."
To Anna he said: "Shall I bring you a blanket?"

"Don't bother, Boris," she said.

It was the first time she had called him by his name and Boris
could feel his heart beating harder. He went into the kitchen
and put out the lamp. When he rejoined them his voice was as
calm as before. "Perhaps you could go down to Escarène a bit
sooner, then we shan't need any more paraffin brought up."

"Why don't you ever think of yourself?" said Knopf. He was
so astonished at Boris's unselfishness that there was silence for a
while until Anna turned to Boris: "You must hate the Communists very much. How could you bring yourself to fight for
them?"

"I was captured very early in the war."

"And before that? I'd like to know what goes on in a man's mind
when he has to fight for a government he hates."

Boris hesitated. He could hardly resist the temptation that
the question offered him. Perhaps it was the last chance to tell her
everything, but the mere thought that she could despise him for
it was unbearable and he said: "War doesn't give you much time
to think about such things."

Knopf sighed and stood up. "I think we'll go to bed. If I start
thinking about it all I just get a headache."

"So do I," said Boris.

He went indoors with Knopf, while Anna remained sitting on
the steps. They had done the same thing every evening since they
had been in La Peine. The first evening Boris had tried, after
Knopf had gone to bed, to start a conversation with Anna, but she
had made it clear to him that she wanted to be alone. Usually
she stayed outside for an hour, until the men had gone to sleep,
and when Boris had once remarked that she would catch cold,
Knopf told him that she had been just the same in Escarène. There
she had often sat out of doors half the night watching the mountain tops and gazing up at the stars.

This evening, too, Anna stayed out on the steps. Later she
walked to the end of the street, where the houses ended, and took
the narrow path to the spring as far as the great rocky boulders.
One of them looked like a giant beetle; it had a trough-shaped
indentation in its broad back, very comfortable for sitting in.
It was her favorite spot and difficult to reach. First she had to
climb on to another slightly lower rock and from there pull herself
across, but she had done it so often that she knew every handhold

28

by heart. Then she sat up there, the stored-up daytime warmth of the rock on her back and the soft breath of the stars in her face.

She dreamed of whatever came into her head, letting the disjointed images pass one after another before her mind's eye. There were people and things, a red dress with short sleeves, a house beneath old trees, a woman in a dark coat, then a uniform, a truck, and again a face in front of a blue lake with white clouds in the sky. The same pictures returned again and again and she would contemplate them a little longer to see if they were really the same, but without interest and only out of a weary, aimless sense of duty. These shoes, she would think, were too clumsy for her feet and those bracelets too costly for her. She was talking to a man who had suddenly appeared at her side and asked her the time, but she remembered that a nebulous figure had warned her against talking to strange men and she broke off the conversation and glided on. Somewhat later she was lingering in front of a shop window, full of expensive furs without price-labels, until a fat woman came up to her and tearfully told her that her husband had not written to her for four months. She tried to comfort the woman, but more women were standing behind her and they were all weeping. Then another truck came and the women climbed into it, pushed by men with red faces who shouted and laughed coarsely. She wanted to stay and watch the truck, but someone seized her by the hand and she walked beside her father down a broad street with smart shops and then a man came towards them who had often sat in their house and taken her on his knee. She looked at him, but the man turned aside and looked hard into a shop window as if he didn't know her, and her father hurried on.

And she remembered the many humiliations in school, how the girls used to giggle when her name was called out and the pitiless eyes which stared at her wherever she went. She had stood in front of a mirror and examined her face and her body, and compared herself with the other girls without understanding why she should be different and uglier than the ugliest of them, who were never stared at or laughed at—until she was old enough to understand why she was different, why her eyes were the wrong eyes, her lips not pure lips, and from that moment she felt the injustice like a physical pain.

This evening, as he always did, Boris heard her return. He never went to sleep until he heard her light tread on the steps and as always his heart stopped for the fraction of a moment in

29

which Anna passed his door. Like all the other rooms it had no door and Boris could see the hallway from his corner. Although he put out the lamp it was never completely dark in the house; enough starlight gleamed through the slats of the shutters for him to recognize Anna's outline as she quickly passed by.

He heard her climb the stairs to her room, which was over his, while her father slept in a small room over the kitchen.

He had known a girl in Gorky who had been fond of him, and perhaps they would have married if there had been no war. She was not beautiful and not even as clever as was expected of the wife of a high school teacher in Gorky, but she had a way of listening to him and comforting him which had always drawn him to her. When things were difficult she would come to him and he would lay his head upon her breast, until the harsh odor of her body aroused his senses. Then she gave herself to him with the calmness of a woman for whom the thought of a man no longer held any illusions.

Anna, on the other hand, was an utterly different type of girl, and when he saw her in the evenings sitting hunched up on the steps, he felt tempted to stroke her head. But he was never quite sure how he felt about her. With the girl in Gorky he had known quite well: with her broad hips, her strong, stocky legs and her big, soft breasts she looked like most of the other women in the town. There was already something maternal about them long before they experienced the pain of childbirth, which was perhaps what the men in Gorky looked for in their women.

Now when he thought back to that time it often seemed to him that it was hardly worth the trouble to exert himself for the little that life still held for him. He had finished his studies, had a responsible job and a girl who loved him. Even if he had stayed in Gorky he would not have attained much more than that. Perhaps a few salary increases, perhaps even another girl, but it would not have been like the first, and the raises in salary could never have reproduced the feeling that he had experienced at the sight of the first money he had earned for himself. Nothing would have been more than a mere repetition, and he found that he could now think about it quite calmly and without sadness.

Chapter 2

After about four hours on the march they reached a deep gorge with overhanging sides which leaned inwards and formed a roof over the road and riverbed. Water dripped down from the high, smooth rock walls and an icy cold blew in their faces. Beyond a railing along the left-hand side of the road the river surged with unimaginable violence like an unleashed, spume-tossing monster between great boulders obstinately stemming its flow with their massive weight. Dotted with pebbles, the road hugged the cliff as if terrified of the fury of the river, or crawled into one of the many tunnels which yawned with a kind of enticing languor at every bend in the noisy, spray-laden green twilight of the gorge.

The roar of the river made talking impossible and Marcel had long since ceased to try to make Georges understand what he was saying. He sauntered along behind Georges, his hands in his pockets, stopping occasionally to glance over the railing into the water or to look up at the towering walls of rock.

With the greater part of their journey behind them they could now afford to slacken their pace. They had set off from La Peine while it was still dark, and were soon due to reach the spot where three days before they had taken the wrong turning and reached La Peine from the rear. But then it had been the middle of the night and they had not even been able to see the cliffs on either side of the road. Vieale had advised them to march by night and to spend the days in some safe place. In case they lost their way and got into the wrong valley, he had likewise given them instructions as to what to do, and Georges had meanwhile had occasion to admire his foresight and his excellent knowledge of the country.

They now had to traverse a long tunnel, and as they emerged into the open the valley broadened. The road crossed over a steel bridge to the other side, at the same time drawing away slightly from the river. In between road and river ran a narrow meadow, and a hundred yards farther the road re-crossed the river by a larger bridge built of wood. Georges was puzzled by this and unconsciously quickened his stride. He then realized that it was not the same road but another which branched off at this point and wound its way up a desolate valley which up till now they had been unable to see. There was a signpost at the bridge and as Georges saw it he gave a low whistle. He stuck his hands on his hips and waited for Marcel who joined him at a leisurely pace, put his arms akimbo in the same way and stared at the signpost. It had two arms, one pointing westwards towards the desolate valley, the other in the direction from which they had come. The writing was hardly legible and Marcel peered at it dubiously. Then he glanced at Georges, whose face wore a knowing grin. "So this is the way to Escarène," he said and looked up the wild valley. "Looks as if there's another pass before you get there. Do you remember which way Vieale said we should go when we came to the fork?"

"Keep right," said Marcel.

"That would've been correct if only we hadn't turned right too soon. We never got as far as here."

"All I know is that we followed the river."

"We did, but not far enough. I see now where we went wrong. In the darkness we mistook the crossroads for the fork and turned eastwards a few kilometers too early."

"But we did reach the river again!"

"That was wrong. Vieale said expressly that we should keep away from the river. If you'd use your head a bit you'd remember that before the road rises up to the pass, the river flows northeastwards. It's the same one we drank from yesterday morning before we climbed up to the fort."

"I suppose so," said Marcel without interest. He looked expectantly down at the meadow, across which the river-bank was easily reached. Here the current was not so strong as in the gorge and the sight of the clear water made Marcel feel violently thirsty.

"How about a bit of a cool-off?" he said with a businesslike jerk of the thumb.

32

"We're stopping here anyway," replied Georges, and climbed towards the meadow down the steep scrubby slope by the bridge. The grass was thin and short, liberally sprinkled with small stones. Some small bushes with red, poisonous-looking berries grew by the river bank. Here they found some shallows where they were able to wash and quench their thirst. The meadow was still in the shade and Marcel shivered.

"I'll catch rheumatism if I stay here much longer," he said morosely, and looked at Georges who was standing with his legs widely planted on two stones and washing his naked torso. "Isn't it too cold for you?"

"Gets the blood circulating," answered Georges, wiping the water from his chest with his arms. "We should have brought a bit of soap and a towel with us."

"Not to mention a toothbrush," grunted Marcel. "Vieale seems to think we live like pigs."

"I don't know how pigs live, but he meant well."

"It wouldn't have killed us to have brought a few things like that. Look at my beard! Another couple of days and I'll look like William Tell."

"What, with your bandy legs?" asked Georges with a grin. "Gessler would have died laughing."

"You don't look much better," Marcel muttered.

He walked a little way from the bank and looked for a place where he could lie down. Below the embankment of the road, about five yards from the bridge, was a spot which was less stony and covered with a slightly thicker growth of grass. There he sat down and waited for Georges who was lingering by the river and making a careful examination of the surroundings.

Downstream the valley broadened out, the mountains grew less savage and their sides were overgrown with thick scrub. From where he stood Georges could see southwards down the valley for about three hundred yards, then it disappeared from view where it swung to the south-east. In that direction the road did not cross the valley again, and the river too kept to the right-hand side of the valley on which the sun now shone. It would not be long before the meadow also was in sunlight.

As Georges looked up the valley he saw the steel bridge. Beyond it the valley narrowed into the gorge. Opposite him the road to Escarène led up the wild valley in serpentine curves, looking like a broad, gently rising watercourse, its surface lightly strewn with stones. This valley too was only visible for a short distance

33

as its sharp bends closely followed the contours of the mountain.

Finally Georges took another look at the bridge. It was planted on eight strong piles rammed into the riverbed, across which were laid two long tree trunks, their ends resting on masonry built up on each bank. Across them lay clumsy half-rotten planks and the wooden railings on either side looked as if a puff of wind would have blown them down.

Georges sat down beside Marcel, who lay on his back in the cold grass with his eyes closed and his hands clasped behind his neck; he had spread out his tunic underneath him as the ground was still wet with dew. Having had only a few hours' sleep the night before, Georges could feel his eyelids growing heavier. Originally he had not meant to leave La Peine so early, but towards dawn it had grown so cold in their lean-to that they had both awakened and decided to set off while it was still dark. Fortunately their early start had meant that they had the pass behind them before the sun had risen over the mountains, which would otherwise have added the heat to their problems. Now they could gladly have done with a little warmth: they were frozen, and the long, tiring march on empty stomachs had taken toll of their strength.

As he gazed at the sunny mountain slopes on the far side of the valley, Georges debated whether it wouldn't be more sensible to have faced the journey in the heat of the day and to have let Knopf give them something for breakfast before they set out. If Vieale didn't turn up until evening it was going to be a long day. He knew that Marcel was thinking the same thing. It was not difficult to pursue this line of thought a little further, and for the first time since they had left Eys he found himself wondering what would happen if Vieale did not come to La Peine.

Georges had never doubted his honesty for a second, and had relied almost blindly on his promise to bring their belongings up to La Peine. He had given them the civilian clothes, a little food and a small map, which Georges had kept in his pocket along with the compass which had helped them to find their way over the mountains. They had not, in any case, had much time to think of another solution. After his talk with Vieale he had gone back to company headquarters, where Ritter had pointed to a chair, sat down and stared at him with his cold eyes. . . .

"So you want to clear off," he had said. "Have you thought it over carefully?"

"Yes. If you agree."

34

Ritter crossed his legs. In the mottled camouflage uniform he looked like some wild animal; there was even something feline about his movements. "When you joined us in Heilbronn," he said, "I looked at your papers. I called for you and asked you whether you still wanted to carry on with us. I expect you were surprised that I did so."

"I still am," replied Georges.

Ritter grinned, his upper lip curling. "I wanted to satisfy my conscience. Did you think I hadn't got one?"

"I don't know you well enough to answer that one."

"You are intelligent, but not quite as intelligent as you are honest. After I had read through your papers I knew that you would desert at the first opportunity. You needn't be shocked by that—I would do the same in your place."

"I'm not shocked," said Georges, smiling.

Ritter gave him an icy stare. "If I had wanted to have your answer I would have asked for it. I never could stand your people. You are narrow-minded and complacent—a nauseating hodge-podge of European prejudices without ever having done anything for Europe. And that's why you hate us, too."

"You forget one thing," said Georges. "You forget that it was Switzerland which refused to break off diplomatic relations with Germany in 1917 when the United States asked us to. As for the help we gave Germany through the Red Cross . . ."

"Rubbish!" Ritter cut him off with a violent gesture. "You told me all that in Heilbronn when I asked you why you had come over to us. A policy of re-insurance, that's all it was. Probably you were still too young to think like the rest of your heroic countrymen. I have nothing against you personally, but as an officer I've no time for you—at least not in my outfit."

He stood up, walked round the desk with a creak of boots and then sat on it beside Georges, looking down into his face. "In Heilbronn I left the decision to you as to whether you stayed with us or not. If you had deserted in Germany you would have been caught sooner or later. To save your skin you would have pleaded that I had left you a free agent and—let me finish what I'm saying, I don't really care whether you would have done so or not. I would simply have denied having said anything of the kind and that would have been that. But that's not the point. Since I've been in command I've not had a single deserter."

"If I understand you rightly . . ." said Georges. Ritter interrupted him a second time. "So far you have understood nothing."

35

He took a sheet of paper from the desk and studied it carefully. Then he looked at Georges. "The Americans have landed at Toulon. According to the latest reports they are not only advancing on Marseilles and Grenoble, but they are coming this way too. We have had orders to withdraw over the Italian frontier at the first contact with the enemy. Reconnaissance patrols are to observe and report all enemy movement." He replaced the paper on the table and stared at the corner of the room for a few seconds, then looked at Georges again. "I have already sent out a patrol. It was supposed to contact another unit in Nice and should originally have pushed on towards Cannes. Now a new order has just been received which forbids us to move beyond Nice. The telephone line to Nice is cut, probably sabotage. I have sent runners to try to catch the reconnaissance patrol, but in the circumstances I think it advisable to send a liaison officer as well. It is quite a dangerous job; attacks on German soldiers by the so-called Resistance fighters have been increasing lately. A liaison officer could easily fall into their hands."

Georges was listening attentively. "Yes, that could happen."

"Glad to see you still remember some of our training," said Ritter drily. "Are you prepared to take on the job?"

"Of course," said Georges, getting up to go. Ritter pushed him back into the chair. "Just stay sitting on your backside. I'll let you know when I want you to disappear. Have a brandy."

"I could even manage a double."

"You're going to need it," said Ritter, fetching a bottle and glasses. "Guaranteed genuine French," he said, as he filled the glasses to the brim. "And after three years of German occupation too. You must admit that we've been very sparing with it."

He swallowed the whole glassful, sat down on his chair and looked at Georges. "What do you think of the whole business?"

"I've got out of the habit of thinking."

"That's a soldier's duty. However I feel sure you know exactly what you want, although I don't quite see what there is left for you to want. Do you intend to wait for the Americans?"

"I could've waited for them in Germany."

"With fifty per cent less chance than here. Why don't you do as your father told you in his letter?"

Georges stared at him in horror. "What do you know about my father?"

"When we were in Heilbronn I had to censor two letters. One was addressed to you, the other had been written by you. You don't really think it's pure philanthropy, do you, that makes me risk my own neck by assisting one of my own officers to desert? How stupid do you think I am?"

"I should have thought of that," said Georges, very pale.

Ritter grinned. "That's what comes of losing the habit of thinking. If I have to make my living one day selling lavatory brushes or toothpaste, it'll simply be because I once let other people do the thinking for me. Your father is an officer in your cardboard army. I read it in your documents. He seems to me to be a reasonable man and if I were you I'd put up with a few years behind bars instead of starting out on an odyssey in the hope of evading capture indefinitely. You wrote to him that at a certain time and place you would go underground until the whole mess was over. If somebody else had got hold of that letter you wouldn't need to be worrying about your future now: you'd have none. You took the oath of allegiance like every other soldier and your officer's uniform is no protection against censorship, in spite of which I saved your skin by not reporting the contents of your letters. Do you need anything else?"

Georges emptied his glass. "Only some ammunition, but I can get some before I go."

"So you don't intend to let them lock you up?"

"I'm a restless person," replied Georges. "I need elbow room and space to move."

"Watch out that you don't have to get along with rather less space than your own people are prepared to give you. Must be a nice feeling for you to have. I suppose you imagine that one day they'll have a red carpet and brass band out to welcome you as they used to for the Crusaders when they returned from the wars. Or didn't they have brass bands in those days?" he asked in a mocking voice.

With tightly pressed lips Georges looked into his empty glass and said nothing.

"Why so silent?" asked Ritter.

"I'm thinking about the censorship. It was the first time I'd ever mentioned it in a letter. Up till then I'd hoped that the war would end differently."

"People are usually disappointed by the way wars end. It was just your bad luck that this particular letter was censored. But you haven't answered my question."

"I've a lot to thank you for," said Georges.

"And so you think you can put up with being lectured?

37

Don't get any wrong ideas, though. I told you I just want to satisfy my conscience. If you're married to a parson's daughter you can't help having occasional scruples—and besides, damn it, I can't stand your people. How often do I have to tell you?"

"I haven't forgotten," said Georges and stood up. "I'd like to take someone with me."

"Take anyone you like. The chief thing is for you to clear off as fast as you can."

Georges smiled. "In an hour at the latest. My men know that I'm a Swiss. I don't think they'll believe the story of an ambush by the Maquis."

"Do your men write the casualty reports?"

"No."

"All right, then," said Ritter and refilled their glasses. "Drink that up. I suppose at your age one might still believe all that propaganda about the crusade against Communism, but today it's irrelevant. Crusaders are a bit out of date since they invented jet planes."

"I realize all that now. After all, anybody can make a mistake."

"Well, they say experience is cheap at any price. . . ."

"It's priceless," declared Georges, and replaced his empty glass on the table. He waited to be dismissed, but Ritter simply sat motionless in his chair and stared gloomily into a corner. After a while he said: "I was in Zürich once before the war, though only on the way through. Did you ever live in Zürich?"

"I was born in Lausanne."

"Ah, Lausanne. I only know it by name. Must be a nice place. I've fathomed what it is that you Swiss have against us. Don't start telling me again that there were others who thought differently; one only needs to read your newspapers. Even before 1933 you disliked us. In those days it was the Prussians, now it's the Nazis and tomorrow it will be somebody else. I can only suppose you have some secret homemade recipe against it, that's all."

"Against what?" said Georges.

Ritter turned and stared at him, his features suddenly flat and expressionless, and said angrily, "Against your own stupidity, man. Can't you see you're getting on my nerves?"

"I didn't mean to," said Georges, and went out. . . .

He had waited a moment outside the door in case Ritter called him back, but nothing had happened. Georges had walked over to his quarters where Marcel, waiting for him, was already getting

38

uneasy; they had discussed final details with Vieale, exchanged their uniforms for civilian clothes and Vieale had led them along a narrow, dark street until the houses stopped at a crossroads and they had taken the road leading due north into the mountains.

And now they lay on their backs in the short grass by the river, waiting for the sun to emerge any minute over the long mountain ridge behind them, whose shadow still covered the eastern half of the valley like a damp cloth.

Georges looked down at Marcel, who lay beside him with eyes closed, chewing a stalk of grass. He looked worn out and depressed. When Georges recalled how he had looked three years before, his face seemed to be the face of a stranger and he wondered whether his own face had undergone a similar transformation. Perhaps it was simply because they had not shaved for days, or perhaps it was due to their exertions of the past few hours. It would hardly be surprising, though, if the last three years had aged them both: they had been through the crucible which tempered men and changed them forever.

But what have I done wrong? thought Georges. I only did what millions more did in equally good faith and I don't see why I should pay for it with a further five or six years in prison. All right, so it would have been better to have stayed at home, but how was I to know that three years ago? And then that deadly boring school, as if there was nothing in the world more important than economics and commerce. Always the same old trash, the same old phrases flogged to death, cards in the café in the evening, the family outing to Lucerne or up the Utliberg on Sunday and every morning the nice cup of coffee and the nice bacon and eggs while the world outside goes berserk. Nothing to do with us, of course; Herr Richle's chances of getting into the Federal Council at the next cantonal elections are just as important as any little world war that the Prussians have hatched up to amuse themselves.

Doesn't it make you laugh, Georges? Yes, because the same people who have done nothing for the past five years except drink their nice little cups of coffee and pile up their nice little francs will interrupt their nice little lives for half an hour, put on their deadly serious face and condemn you in the name of their nice little democracy to a nice little spell in prison for treason by foreign

39

enlistment in time of war. Then they'll go back to their nice little jobs with the warm feeling of having done their bit in defense of the constitution.

He spat in a spasm of disgust and said to Marcel: "If you've finished chewing your bit of grass, perhaps you can answer one question."

Marcel lazily opened his eyes and pushed the stalk into the corner of his mouth with his tongue. "All right, if you've nothing better to offer. . . ." he murmured indistinctly.

"You'll last out all right until Vieale comes. Have you ever once thought about anything except food?"

"Yes. During the exam," replied Marcel, grinning. "Hope you don't have any more bright ideas. I've had enough for the moment."

"This one's harmless," Georges assured him. "You were going to tell me yesterday why your mother isn't the ideal woman to marry. From what I remember there was always an awful lot of kissing and 'darling' this, 'darling' that, and so on. Aren't they happily married?"

"The answer to that depends on how you define it."

"Define what? Marriage?"

"No. Being happy. Perhaps they're happy by most middle-class standards. But otherwise. . . ."

"Well?"

"You know I don't like talking about my family. Nothing matters now, anyway."

"Why not now?"

"Oh, hell," Marcel took the grass out of his mouth. "Let's not start that all over again. I hope they'll send us some money when they know where we are. I'll write to them as soon as I can. Perhaps they can send it poste restante."

"What, to La Peine?" asked Georges. "To be collected from the town hall, first floor, second room on the right. You can forget about that for the time being. If you're lucky they can even get you out of it by paying: twenty thousand francs, say, for each year of imprisonment. Shouldn't be difficult for your father."

"Do you really think so?" asked Marcel quickly.

"Not impossible. There are only two things money won't buy you, happiness and immortality."

"I've never even thought about it," said Marcel, fascinated by the idea. "If he really——" He broke off and looked uneasily at

Georges. They were both thinking the same thing, although neither was willing to say it aloud. They sat silently for a while until Georges gave a brief laugh.

"He'll pay that much alone to get you away from me. 'Whatever I do is done only for my family,' he once said to me. Do you remember?"

"He said it almost every day."

"Only for his family," mocked Georges. "Day and night in the shop. First it was two stories, then four and finally the whole building. And all for his family! No time to go on holiday, no time to go to the theater, no time for . . . I suppose one has to be married twenty-five years to understand it. I don't like marriages where the husband is nearly twice as old as the wife. It makes me think of two people who sit down to a meal: one starts eating half an hour before the other but they must both finish at the same time. Your father would have been better off if he'd stayed single, then he would have had nothing but his shop to live for and nothing would have been any different. What is it, do you suppose, ambition or what?"

"They didn't have the same interests," answered Marcel, indifferently.

"They did have one thing in common," said Georges. "Their love for their dear little Marcel."

"They liked you too, you know."

"Your mother rather more than your father." Georges said it without a trace of conceit, and as he looked at Marcel he saw that the other was grinning. He looked at him suspiciously. "Or didn't she?"

"Oh, yes, she did." Marcel raised himself on one elbow and pulled out of the ground a handful of grass. "But perhaps not in the way you imagine."

"Oh, really? How, then?"

"I never told you before. She once asked me to tell you not to come and see us so often. She used to get rather annoyed with you sometimes."

Georges went first red, then white in the face. "When did she say that?"

"About six months before we crossed the frontier. We were sitting at table, she, my father and I. Somehow the conversation got around to you. She said she liked you better when you were younger, you were too full of yourself nowadays and . . ." He trailed off, looking at Georges sitting beside him with clenched

41

teeth. As Marcel did not continue, Georges slowly turned round towards him and said, "Well . . . and what?"

Marcel became suddenly serious. He realized that it was as if he had begun this conversation meaning to fire blank ammunition and had mistakenly loaded with live rounds. He gestured nervously. "That's all. She didn't say any more."

"Listen," said Georges, and he knelt to stare Marcel full in the face. "You don't have to tell me. You can keep it to yourself if you like, but if you do, things will never be the same again between us, do you see?"

Astonished, Marcel stared at him, then dropped his gaze and mumbled: "You take everything much too seriously. You were four years younger then."

"What did she say?"

"That you needed longer than most other boys."

"To do what?"

"To grow up."

"No," whispered Georges. "No, she didn't say that."

"Why should I lie to you about it?"

"She can't have done," said Georges, his face the color of chalk. "Then why did she change her dress every time I came to see you?"

"Because she was always changing," said Marcel, who was also growing irritated. "She even used to change when a workman came to the house. She had nothing else to do but change. What else could she do with those great piles of clothes, for God's sake? I tell you it was like being in the theater—nothing but into the wardrobe, out of the wardrobe all day long. It was just a kind of mania, that's all."

Georges said nothing. Of all the disappointments in his life this was the greatest. He felt himself humiliated and deceived in a particularly shameful way. For a few seconds he felt as if he had been suddenly disemboweled and the last trace of his past life had been finally smashed. He could scarcely prevent tears of fury coming to his eyes.

He stood up and walked with leaden steps down to the river, where he sat down on a stone by the bank and stared into the fast-flowing stream. This spot was already in sunlight. A small green lizard darted along the sand among the dead leaves and branches washed up between the stones. Motionless, Georges watched it dive through a puddle and make for his shoe; it stopped, gave an exploratory flick of the tongue and then clambered on to the sun-warmed leather of his toe-cap, where it contentedly closed its eyes.

As the day lengthened even the violence of the river's torrent seemed to abate. It now sounded like the noise of a gigantic turbine whose rhythmical hum made the warm air reverberate back and forth across the valley. But Georges was unaware of this. He sat on the bank of the river, his body hunched as if from internal pain, staring at the little lizard on the cracked leather of his shoe. Its armored back was marked with brown zigzag lines, its horny eyelids flickered occasionally in the sun. Georges gazed at the middle of the river, then back at the lizard. He tried to decide whether or not he would kill it but his mind kept returning to the many times he had sat next to the woman and talked with her.

Of course she had never let anything slip, had always treated him with the polite reserve of her class, with the superiority of the great lady, yet he would have been prepared to bet heavily on having often enough caught a flash of something else in her eyes which belied her self-confident manner.

You fool, he said to himself. You never got beyond the calf-love stage and now you're having to face up to it. With this thought he heaved the lizard into the river with a violent kick. He watched as it struck the surface of water, sank, then surfaced seconds later about two yards downstream. It climbed on to a rock whose razor-sharp edge cleft the waters in two. Then the lizard turned completely round at the rock's highest point and remained staring rigidly at the far bank.

Georges watched it, disappointed. Something else they didn't teach you at commercial high school, he thought. Or did anyone ever tell you that lizards can swim? Perhaps it was just cast up on the rock by the current—could have been I suppose, but still—to be able to grasp and hold on at that speed . . . !

Not bad, he thought approvingly, you're not so easily done for, you little beast, are you? How about this, though! He bent down for a stone the size of a clenched fist, weighed it appraisingly in his hand and hurled it at the lizard with great force. It flew so close to the creature that it looked as if it had hit it, but the lizard moved not a fraction of an inch from where it sat and continued to stare unblinkingly at the opposite bank.

I'm a little out of practice, thought Georges. Besides, I'd throw better if I stood up. Not bad, though, from a sitting position and considering how long it is since I used to do that sort of thing. He got up and looked around for a suitable stone. On the bank he found one, bigger than the first, rounded on one side and with a sharp edge on the other. It fitted smoothly and firmly into his palm and he looked at it with satisfaction. Then he returned to where he had been sitting, measured with a glance the distance to the lizard and drew back his arm for the throw. At that moment the lizard moved. It slowly turned round and stared at Georges, its flat head shimmering in the sunlight.

Georges dropped his arm. Something in the creature's behavior disturbed him. He stood irresolutely for a few moments, then threw away the stone in disgust and sat down lost in thought. It seemed to him that a cloud had obscured the sun, although the sky over the mountains was as blue as ever.

Marcel had been watching him. From where he lay he could even see the lizard, and as Georges dropped the stone he involuntarily sighed with relief. Since Georges had stood up and walked into the bank Marcel had been ceaselessly occupied with the question as to whether it had been wise, at this moment, to revive old memories. He would have liked to spare Georges the lesson if he himself had not been touched on the raw by Georges' arrogant insistence. He could more easily have borne the crowd of spoiled idlers with which his mother had chosen to surround herself had it not been for the infuriating complacency with which each of them thought himself secure in her special favor. And the fact that Georges, his friend, had turned out to be just like the rest of them was sufficient to shock him. Even so, he had by no means told him everything and he remembered very well how it had all begun. His mother had been late for dinner, as she was every evening. He and his father were already at the table. At last she came in and his father had put his newspaper to one side and looked at the clock. "It's nearly time for me to go," he had said, and she had pouted and replied: "I know, Ralph, but it's Tuesday today and the dressmaker's been to see me. . . ."

He tucked a corner of his napkin between his neck and his collar and said nervously: "I'm sorry, I was preoccupied with other things. Didn't you once tell me that she came on Thursdays?"

"That was five years ago. I suppose you won't have any time to spare tomorrow evening either?"

"Tomorrow?" He recollected, frowning, then shook his head firmly. "No, in fact, I've a very important——"

"As you have every evening, Ralph," she interrupted. "Some more toast?"

"Yes, please."

"You too, Marcel?"

"Two slices, please."

She looked at her husband. "I have some tickets for the circus. It's three years since I went to the circus."

"I'm sorry. Take Marcel if you like."

"I'd like to go with Georges," said Marcel. "I'm doing something else tomorrow evening."

"You're always doing something else."

"Oh, don't exaggerate, Mama."

"Yesterday evening you were out with Georges and the evening before, too. Don't you think it's about time you spent an evening here?"

"Three days ago I stayed at home all evening."

"And you remember it because it was so exceptional. I'd like a word with your father now. And please tell Georges not to come here so often."

Marcel left the room without a word. He pulled the door behind him enough to leave it slightly ajar and stood there listening. He could clearly hear his father's voice saying: "My dear, I simply don't understand you. If you want to talk to me about the boy I beg you to do so in private. And now of all times, when I've more than enough to worry about with other things. To my mind you over-dramatize everything. I don't doubt that no one in your family ever went to cowboy films. As for me I rather enjoyed seeing one now and again when I was younger and you must admit that it hasn't had a noticeably bad effect on my character. Why don't you let the boy go if it amuses him? Oh, God, it's past eight o'clock already. What did you want to say to me?"

"I hope you consider your son worth five minutes of your time. Your indulgence with him borders on irresponsibility. If the shop seems more important to you than your family . . ."

"But of course not, my dear. I am simply overworked, that's all, and I don't see what all these trivialities . . ."

"We are discussing Marcel. Do you call that trivial?"

"I didn't mean it like that. I can't force the boy not to see Georges any more. After all, this is not the Middle Ages."

"Thank you for the innuendo about my family, but I——"

"I made no innuendo about your precious family. You're so touchy that it's impossible to carry on a rational conversation with you. I am well aware that certain of your relations raised their eyebrows when I——"

"Couldn't we consider this subject as closed once and for all?"

"With pleasure, as far as I'm concerned. It was you who

45

brought it up. As if I had nothing better to think about. Georges'
father is an officer, an honorable, respected man. Why should his
son be any different?"

"He has inherited his father's adventurous streak. If he had had
his way Switzerland would have abandoned her neutrality in 1914."

"His wife was German, of course."

"All the more reason not to let Georges forget that he was born
in Lausanne and not in Berlin."

Marcel heard his father clear his throat impatiently. "Forgive
me, my dear, but I really must——"

"I've almost finished. We have different views on Georges——"

"But we haven't at all. If you think that Marcel would be better
off if he saw less of him. . . . I feel sorry for the young man somehow. I imagine it must be dreadful to grow up without a mother.
Didn't he once say that she died giving birth to him . . . ? Well,
I know, these things happen, but then having a father who is always traveling half round the world. That's not any sort of family
life. Did you want to say something?"

"No, not about that. I don't know what it is, Ralph, but whenever
Marcel goes off with Georges, I have an unpleasant feeling. I can't
sleep at night until he comes back. He's growing away from us."

"But what nonsense! Marcel growing away from us! It simply
isn't true. The boy couldn't wish for better parents and I'll swear
he knows it. When he has his summer holidays why don't you go
away with him to St. Moritz for a few weeks and give your nerves a
rest? As soon as Georges' father retires from the army, which can't
be far off now, he'll have more time to devote to his son. Then all
this fuss will peter out by itself. Now I really must go. I have someone coming to see me from Geneva."

As he was about to leave the dining-room Marcel quickly ran to
the other side of the hall and opened the door of the lavatory. Then
he slammed it and turned round to meet his father who was coming
into the hall at the same moment. He stopped, glanced around
quickly to make sure that nobody could overhear them and said:
"Your mother has been rather upset lately. You should think of
her a bit more than you do." Marcel nodded indifferently. "If only
I had more time," his father went on. "As soon as you leave high
school it will be better. Let's see—you'll soon be in your fifth term,
won't you?"

"Third," said Marcel.

His father gazed at him in vague surprise. "Oh, only the third?
I somehow thought you were farther than that. What a time it

46

takes." He looked at his watch. "Well, now . . . will you come some of the way with me?"

"I still have to change."

"I should have changed too, but now I haven't much time. What a nuisance all this . . . That jacket suits you very well, by the way. Where did you get it?"

"You gave me the material as a Christmas present."

"Oh, of course, so I did. It still looks so new. Do you need some money?"

"Not today."

"Well, if ever you run short . . . O.K., my boy?" He patted Marcel on the cheek and quickly left.

Marcel watched him go without concern. As he climbed the stairs to his room he grinned slightly. Don't think you can separate us as easily as that, he thought. You have no idea!

That evening he went with Georges to a small café that had a dubious reputation, where they had a considerable amount to drink. "Have you seen the paper today?" asked Georges.

"My father hasn't let it out of his hands for a second."

"The Germans have landed in Tripoli. You watch, the British will be kicked out of Africa now."

"Marvelous!" exclaimed Marcel admiringly. Georges nodded thoughtfully. "My father is full of it. One day . . ."

"What?"

"I've just about had enough. Look at us—watching the war in the newsreels, drinking, cramming stupid economics, sitting around. Just look at the women! They turn up their noses at us. They're all uniform-mad and when the war's over they'll marry a German with the Iron Cross. Now I'm just waiting for them to attack the Russians and that'll be the green light. My father has heard rumors; something's going on near the eastern frontier of Germany. You know what he thinks about the Communists."

Marcel laughed. "Just like mine. He hardly gives a thought to politics, but when somebody mentions the Communists he gets furious. He was more annoyed about the Nazi-Soviet Pact than their little blitzkrieg against France."

"He doesn't know a thing about politics. Look, it was obvious, they had to make that pact to protect their rear. They learned that much from the First World War." Georges tapped his forehead with his index finger. "You've got to use your head in politics. Just you wait, in a few weeks . . ."

But the few weeks became a few months, and in the meanwhile

47

they discussed it frequently. Then when the attack on Russia came, Georges showed his hand and asked him whether he wanted to join him. After three sleepless nights and three feverish days he joined Georges, with all the spirit of a great adventure. The night that they crossed the frontier near Waldshut in pitch darkness they had the feeling that they were approaching the center of an event which had set the universe turning like a great wheel. The encounter with the German frontier guards, their removal to Waldshut, the many interrogations and waiting for weeks under close guard until they were released and simultaneously posted to an infantry division—they experienced it all in a kind of fever of heightened perception.

Now, as Marcel looked back, it seemed to him that he had spent those days in a state of intoxication; it had taken a long time to sober up. From Waldshut to within sight of the suburbs of Moscow and then in the opposite direction, farther and farther back and more and more sober until the end of the line in a deserted meadow somewhere in the mountains, there were no illusions left and nothing but a hollow feeling inside. The universe had not been set in motion, not one river had changed its course, not a single ant had left its heap, and the sun shone as it had always shone before. Nothing had changed yet everything was depressingly different and Marcel realized that it would stay like that forever.

By late afternoon the lizard was still squatting on the rock in midstream. It had grown very hot and Georges had taken off his shirt and jacket. Even though his eyelids were drooping with tiredness he could not let himself go as Marcel had done, who now lay snoring with his mouth wide open. The fear that Vieale might drive past without seeing them had lodged itself in his brain like a thorn and would not let him rest. He sat facing south and gazing at the far side of the valley where the road wound away in bend after bend. It lay in glaring sunlight, and whenever he closed his weary eyes they seemed to turn into two glowing balls which burned slowly into his skull. But the most painful sensation was his hunger. He doubled up his body, filled his mouth with gastric acid and imagined that his head was an empty vessel rocking weightlessly back and forth with every movement. It no longer helped to drink the cold river water or chew the leaves from the bushes that grew on the bank. They tasted bitter and brought on an attack of nausea. He did not trust the red berries. He had crushed one of them between his fingers and found the sweetish, insipid smell repellent. He even found that the cigarettes which Knopf had given him had become tasteless.

However all this would have been bearable had not his doubts about Vieale's honesty grown with every hour of waiting. They seemed to spread through his body like a cancerous growth, cramping his breathing and persistently eroding the hard core of hope which until now had resisted all setbacks.

For the last quarter of an hour he had forgotten to watch the lizard, and as he now glanced at it again he saw that it had dropped its head on to the stone and closed its eyes. It had an exhausted look, and as Georges watched it he felt a pang of conscience.

Perhaps you should have killed it, he thought. It was quite illogical to throw it into the river and then to have scruples after it had saved itself by climbing on to the rock. This wouldn't have happened to you a few weeks ago. It's not like you, Georges, you could never stand contradictions and this is a violent contradiction. A text-book example of the primitive way we can react without realizing it. If Vieale gets here before the sun sets over the mountains you will wade in, fetch the lizard and let it go in safety: if he doesn't come at all or comes later you will throw stones at it until it's dead.

He had grown stiff from sitting for so long and stood up with a grimace, shaking each leg in turn and massaging his cramped muscles. He felt a soreness on the skin of his naked chest and as he looked down at himself he noticed that he was quite sunburned. Better watch out, he thought and quickly put on his red-checked shirt. A glance upwards showed him that there was only an hour or so until the sun set. In half an hour at the latest its lower edge would touch the line of the mountains on the far side of the valley and then it would be time for Vieale to keep his word; if he doesn't, thought Georges, as he watched the lizard, he will have you on his conscience and I swear I'll make him pay for it.

He thrust his hands into his pockets and sauntered over to Marcel, who still lay on his back but with his mouth now shut. In the clothes that Vieale had given him he looked like a tramp. His thin, pale, gray linen tunic was worn out at the sleeves, the pockets torn and the middle button missing. The blue-gray velveteen trousers were covered with stains, the knees bagged and the trousers were too big for him. He had pulled them in at his waist with an old leather belt, and a length of white, hairy leg showed below the turn-ups. His socks had slipped right down and partly covered the

49

tops of his mud-encrusted hobnailed boots, a remnant of his army uniform. He wore a pink shirt unbuttoned at the navel revealing a white, fleshy chest. His round face with its protruding ears, bushy eyebrows and heavy stubble was tanned a healthy reddish brown, while his long, light-brown hair hung in disorder over his forehead.

As Georges approached him he opened his eyes and said lazily: "Hello."

"Hello, boy," Georges grinned, "lucky there aren't any trees round here; you would have sawed through them with that snore of yours."

Marcel slowly straightened up and with a groan gripped his head with both hands. "My head feels as if someone had been hitting it with a stone."

"Serves you right. I must have told you a hundred times not to sleep in the sun."

"And a filthy taste in my mouth!" said Marcel, and spat with disgust. Then he looked at Georges. "What if you have said it a hundred times? Where is there any shade in this bloody place? God, I wish we'd stayed in La Peine. What's the time?"

"You only have to look at your watch."

"My watch has stopped. But I can always ask Vieale," he added bitingly.

Georges sat down beside him on the grass and pulled his cigarettes out of his pocket. He handed one to Marcel and lit it for him before taking one himself. "Vieale will come all right," he said. "If not today then in three days' time at the latest. We'll borrow his Citroën, tie one end of a rope round his neck and the other end to the back bumper and make him run all the way to La Peine. That'll teach him to keep his word."

"I really believe you would," said Marcel, and carefully put his burning cigarette on a stone. He stood up, walked down to the river, washed the foul taste from his mouth, watched the lizard for a few seconds and then went back to Georges, who had drawn his knees up to his chest and was staring at the sky with a deep frown.

"But you don't really mean it," said Marcel. Georges drew at his cigarette and blew out the smoke through his nostrils before replying: "I don't know yet."

"All right, then," said Marcel and flopped to the ground.

"But I do know one thing," Georges continued. "He won't get away with it. We'll fix him in the same way they've fixed us these last three years."

Marcel regarded him anxiously. He could not agree with Georges' way of looking at things. "I mistrusted him from the start. Yesterday when I——"

"Shut up," said Georges harshly. "If it turns out to have been a mistake to have trusted him, I will personally make up for it."

They sat for a while without speaking. Georges watched the mountain ridge on the far side of the valley, whose two peaks resembled a huge magnet drawing the sun towards it. A cool breeze blew down on them from the gorge, a blue-gray butterfly fluttered across the meadow and the red berries of the bushes along the river bank shone evilly among the soft green of their leaves.

Marcel sighed. "Know what I'm thinking about?"

"I'm not a mind-reader," replied Georges.

"I'm thinking of what Knopf said. About it not always being a matter of chance that you were on the right side in the war."

"Oh, leave it alone," said Georges. "The more you think about it the stupider you get."

"Still, you can't go on blaming yourself forever."

"Do you blame yourself? I know exactly where I stand. Perhaps you remember how our newspapers suddenly shut up when the Germans entered Paris after their four-week campaign in France. Not another word was said about the Jews, they started off about the Russians instead. I bet you anything you like that on the day the Germans declared war on Russia there were lots of Swiss who slept soundly for the first time since the end of the Russo-Finnish war. We did too, the only difference being in our case that we did more than make pious funeral orations over the Finns. And if it now turns out that we were on the wrong side all the time, it's not our fault but simply the fact that a thing always looks worse in the long run than it did at first sight."

"All the same," said Marcel obstinately.

"Go and shut yourself in a monastery," said Georges, and stood up. He walked a short way down the bank to a point where the river widened slightly. He sat down and stared at the flashing green water.

They're all the same, he thought contemptuously. I've never met one who sticks to his convictions when he's up against it. It's so much easier to swim with the current; you only have to float and if you always follow the fashion you won't be ashamed of being seen in old rags. Sound policy, my boy; make a note of it for the future.

He moved his head slightly and saw that the sun's lower rim

51

would soon touch the ridge. He bent to pick up a big stone and walked along the bank with it to the place where he had kicked the lizard into the water. It had not changed its position and did not even twitch when Georges threw the stone over it into the stream. He still had a few more minutes and sat down on the gently sloping edge of the river. Without once looking round at Marcel he knew that he was being watched, but this did not worry him.

I shall prefer it if I don't hit it to begin with, he thought. I'm sure to get it with the first throw, anyway. I'll finish him off quickly, as quickly as Marcel's mother finished me. The little beast, he thought, the little beast.

For a while he stared at the water without realizing what he was doing. The conversation with Marcel had stirred up memories, and in his mind's eye he saw his father's face with its long narrow nose, its broad, deeply-lined forehead and white hair cut *en brosse*. For as long as Georges could remember he had never looked different, except that the lines on his forehead had grown a little deeper with the years; otherwise he had not changed, and whenever he walked through the streets in his uniform women still glanced after him. Although he seldom talked about his profession, Georges knew that he had a key post in the defense planning staff and for that reason he did a great deal of traveling, but Georges had never even been able to find out the precise name of the staff on which he worked. When Georges first mentioned that he too would like to become a regular officer, his father had reacted strongly against the idea. At the time Georges had just left boarding-school, where he had made friends with Marcel, who had witnessed the conversation. His father had told him that he could choose any other career he liked except that one. He had advised him to study something, and since Marcel, on his father's insistence, was due to start a course at the commercial high school for a Bachelor of Commerce degree, Georges had decided to do likewise.

In the mood he was in at the time he might as well have decided to become a taxi-driver, and he had long borne a grudge against his father for having prevented him from becoming a soldier. Until they had had that talk, three years and a month ago on a sultry Sunday afternoon. Georges remembered quite clearly how his father had been sitting at his desk when he entered his study. He was adding up a long column of figures and Georges stood beside him until he had finished his work and turned to face him. What is it, old boy? his father had said. He had always addressed him with these words, and now they echoed so clearly in Georges' memory that it seemed as if his father was sitting beside him on the bank watching the river. Georges imagined himself saying: "We looked at it from every angle, but we never really thought seriously about it."

And his father said: "You didn't but I did. I would never have put on a uniform without thinking about it beforehand."

"You didn't say anything at the time."

"No, I didn't."

"Why not?"

"When a soldier goes to war he mustn't think of any alternative. Otherwise he'd be like a man who has to cross a wide river and hangs a stone around his neck before setting out."

"Ah, the morale factor!"

"Precisely. Just as no soldier ever seriously believes that he himself will be killed. He may often think about it; but he won't talk about it."

"That was the way I always felt."

"As I would have expected of you, old boy!"

"It seems as if it happened only yesterday," said Georges. "You weren't even surprised."

"No."

"You looked at me, then you got up and sat down again on the edge of your desk."

"It was the first time that I had ever done such a thing."

"That's why I'll never forget it. It was so unlike you. I admired you so much. You only once disappointed me."

"Making you go to the high school, I suppose."

"Yes. Still, I ought to be grateful to you for it."

"Really?"

"One must keep the two aspects separate: how it seemed then and how it has turned out to be since. So you sat down on the edge of your desk and gave me one of your cigarettes. You were very serious. . . ."

"No wonder. After all, we weren't simply talking about the weather."

"For once, no. You asked me whether I had thought it over and I replied that for the past year I had been doing nothing else. Then you said you would have gone with me if you hadn't been an officer."

"Naturally."

"So you sympathized with me all the time?"

"As a soldier—yes. As a Swiss officer—no."

53

"And it was the soldier in you which did nothing to prevent my going?"

"Yes and no. There was more to it than that."

"What, for instance?"

"Because if I had been you I wouldn't have let anybody hold *me* back."

"We assumed," said Georges, "that the Germans would win the war. I could then have returned to Switzerland with German citizenship and no one would have dared to prosecute me. Everything depended on who were the winners."

"As in every war."

"And still you let me . . . I mean, if only you had made some attempt to stop me. Your motive seems unconvincing, at least for the sacrifice involved. I suppose it was a sacrifice, letting me go?"

"Was it a sacrifice!"

"Then you must tell me everything."

"I'll try. Why do you think I became an officer?"

"Because your father was an officer."

"And his father too. There was tradition but no achievement."

"Aren't they the same thing?" asked Georges.

"Well, let us say no achievement of which we as soldiers could have been proud. Look at me. For forty years I have been working on plans which have never been used."

"And probably never will be used, either."

"Hardly, because if it ever came to war there would be new plans, new ideas and new people. It was the same with your grandfather. He planned as hard as I do; today his plans are a joke. One day people will laugh at my plans too."

"They're out of date?"

"Out of date before they can even be put to the test. Every day a new problem arises before I have solved the old one. Anything that I start on turns to dust in my hands. I am like a cook, but nobody comes to eat my cooking, so the food is spoiled. A life wasted."

"What is the reason?"

"In the first place, technical progress. We can no longer keep up with it. We aren't prepared to make the same sacrifices as others. Nowadays an army equipped like ours is as bad as no army at all."

"That's why we have a policy of unreserved neutrality?"

"Even that is no substitute. The world is on the move and we are a part of that world. Today the alternatives are no longer war or unreserved neutrality, but freedom or tyranny."

54

"We are a freedom-loving people," said Georges.

"In a selfish way, yes. We love our freedom, but we have never been prepared to risk anything for the freedom of others."

"And that's why——"

"One should never choose to be a regular army officer in a country which for more than a century hasn't had the need to take that profession seriously."

"You're a laughing stock."

"That is by no means the worst of it. We can't even take ourselves seriously any more. We are like a theater company that has been rehearsing the same play for years without knowing whether the show will ever open. Even that would be bearable if the actors weren't forbidden to accept engagements in other theaters. Since we prohibited Swiss enlistment in foreign armies in 1859 we have been prisoners of a policy which is as out of date as our army. If people are no longer free to fight for a supra-national idea and if need be to die for it, they are forced into purely egotistical nationalism."

"The Communists have realized this."

"Unfortunately, yes. You cannot subordinate an international threat to national interests without doing violence to yourself."

"I thought that perhaps we might be involved this time."

"It's too late for that now."

"So it seems. I understand it all now, but I still want to know what I should do."

His father shrugged, and turned aside.

"You don't know either?" Georges asked him.

No reply.

"That's the trouble," said Georges to himself. "When it comes to the pinch one is completely alone."

He pulled a thick bundle of his father's letters from the inner pocket of his jacket. "You still owe me an answer," he thought, looking down at the letters. "I tore up your last letter in which you told me to report to the nearest Swiss consulate, because it wasn't the right answer. We can't agree on that. Perhaps you even realize it and think the same as I do. I am almost certain that you do, but you felt it your duty to write this letter and are now secretly glad that I have torn it up. I will tear up the other letters too, and bring this dialogue between us to a close, so that we can start another which will perhaps last longer than three years—although it must be one based on different premises. You might find it unpleasant if we started off again with this pile of letters hanging over us; I think we'd both prefer to forget the mistakes we've made."

He pulled the rubber band off the bundle, put it down beside him in the grass and began to tear the letters one by one into tiny pieces which he slowly scattered in the river. At the last letter he hesitated. He looked at the envelope with its Swiss stamp, read the address with its field post office number then pulled the letter out and hesitated for a second before he quickly crumpled it in his fist as if to suppress the sudden impulse to preserve it. The feeling soon passed; he held the crushed letter and envelope for a few more seconds, then dropped them both into the river and watched them float downstream and disappear.

As he looked up he noticed that the sun had already half disappeared behind the line of the mountain ridge. In ten minutes or so the whole valley would be in shadow. Georges knew that now he would not kill the lizard. The moment was gone by and he was glad of it.

Chapter 3

Pierre Fournier lived in one of the last houses on the road leading northwards out of Escarène, where the road with its double line of shady chestnut trees followed the narrow mountain stream up the twists and turns of the valley until it branched off to cross the pass. There the valley narrowed to a thin strip between the steep mountains, their sides overgrown with chestnuts, fig trees and pines; beyond, flanked by savage peaks, lay the head of the pass. On the foothills sloping towards the rugged crags on either side of Escarène the inhabitants had built vineyards. To prevent the vines from being swept away by rain they had hacked terraces out of the hard soil and shored them up with walls. From below they seemed like monumental stairways. Southwards the valley widened until it met a rocky spur, covered with a fine growth of chestnut trees, which split it in the middle into two valleys, one of which led off to the south-east, the other to the south-west.

The village itself consisted of about a hundred and fifty houses hidden away among vineyards; within small gardens, behind gnarled olive trees and low red granite walls, between innumerable alleyways and steps, the haunt of cats and dogs; with brightly painted shutters, the wood cracked by sun and wind, soot-blackened chimney pots and shady corners where the men of Escarène would sit at noon to read their newspapers. A narrow burn flowed through the middle of the village. Its banks were built up with masonry to a depth of about six feet, and it divided the village street into two halves linked by little wooden bridges. In spring-time when the alpine snows melted the stream turned into a torrential river; then the men would fetch out their fishing tackle and tell for the hundredth time the story of Gérard Boulanger who, at the turn of the century, had caught a trout the size of a pike. And towards evening they would go to the village square behind the church to play boule while their wives, big straw hats on their heads and carrying great baskets of wet linen, would walk home from the wash place or exchange a last piece of gossip before putting the soup on the stove.

By day, when the sun scorched the flat, tiled roofs, hardly a soul was to be seen on the street. The men were in Nice, where they worked in the factories, others were in their vineyards weeding, binding the heavy vines and reckoning up how much money the vintage would earn. The women had work to do indoors, if they were not helping their menfolk or looking after the goats which grazed on the steep hillsides.

Outwardly the war had not changed Escarène. People seemed to go on living as they had always lived even though the food situation had deteriorated and many even went hungry. This outward appearance, though, was deceptive and no one knew it better than Pierre Fournier who assumed the leadership of the men of Escarène when darkness fell and they collected their automatic weapons from a cave hidden among the vineyards. These had been dropped on the mountainside by parachute after British agents had started to help organize resistance against the occupation troops. By then Pierre Fournier had already had his first experience of guerrilla warfare. He had been a sergeant in a brigade of chasseurs manning the forts on the Italian frontier between Menton and Barcelonette. When the line had broken under the attack of the Italian divisions he had made his own way to Escarène, burned his uniform and gone back to his former occupation. He had owned a small joinery business, with five men working for him, but trade had never picked up after the occupation, and as time went on Pierre had lost interest in the work. A bachelor and without ties, he had packed a suitcase and gone to his sister in Lyons with the idea of taking a few weeks off. But the few weeks became half a year. His brother-in-law, a Socialist deputy before the war, had become the leader of a Resistance group and in six months Pierre had learned enough from him to go back to Escarène and start up his own underground unit. It was another three months before his brother-in-law sent the British agents to Escarène and airplanes dropped arms to them. The agents stayed only a few days in Escarène on their way through to Nice, told about a big invasion being planned, distributed English cigarettes and, what was more important, gave Pierre a small portable radio transmitter.

Trained into an effective team the men of Escarène had done more for France than they were ever able to do before or after the outbreak of war. They were proud of their successes, and when in the early evening of that day Pierre Fournier drove his truck back from Sospel he had no inkling that his most difficult operation was just about to begin.

He had had an exhausting day and was glad to drive the truck down the last straight stretch of the chestnut avenue, past the first gardens and up to his house. Beside him in the cab sat three other men. As the truck stopped they climbed out and touched their caps to Pierre; one of them asked him: "Nothing tomorrow?"

"I don't know when we'll be back from La Peine," replied Pierre. He turned to the shortest of the three: "We'll leave in time to be up there at about midday. I'll put the stuff away myself tonight."

"Good," said the man who was called Gaston. He had a pale face and black eyes.

Pierre turned towards the house. Single storeyed, with whitewashed walls and green shutters, it stood in a pleasant garden shut in by a low wall whose entire length was overgrown with bougainvillaea hanging down to the ground. From a broad wicket gate in its left-hand corner a gravel drive led past the house to a smaller building, also whitewashed, which housed the joinery workshop. Beside it stretched a long, dark storage shed.

The garden had a well-tended look. Pierre spent a lot of time on it and grew all his own flowers from seed. As well as flowers he had some large cacti, and in front of the house stood three decorative olive trees, whose silvery leaves glinted in the evening sunlight. About fifty yards behind the house the vineyard terraces began to rise and above them, like the enormously magnified ruins of an old castle, the savage mountain landscape with its weather-worn crags, blue-black cliffs and jagged ridges reared itself skywards.

Before going indoors Pierre put the truck away in the shed. It was a blue, covered two-and-a-half tonner, with rusty mudguards and tires worn down to the canvas.

The front door was on the far side of the house and as Pierre turned the corner he saw a man sitting on the steps. He was of medium height, inconspicuously dressed, had a smooth, young face, slightly protruding ears and wore a beret. Pierre stopped, surprised. He did not know the man and felt automatically for the

59

pocket in which he kept his British army revolver. "What are you doing here?" he asked the man. The stranger stood up and looked at him appraisingly. "Monsieur Fournier?"

"That's me," answered Pierre.

"I've been waiting for you for three hours," said the man. He had a harsh voice which did not fit his young face. "I suggest we talk indoors."

Pierre hesitated. He half turned and looked across the garden to the street. On the far side two men stood talking. Now they looked over and Pierre turned to the stranger again: "Come in."

He unlocked the front door, showed the unknown man in and led him into a room which was in semi-darkness. He pushed back the shutters to let in the light and turned towards the stranger, who had stayed near the doorway and was looking round the room. It was small, with pale blue wallpaper and brightly colored curtains. White goatskins covered the waxed floorboards. In the middle stood a table with four chairs, by the wall a heavy sofa and in the right-hand corner by the window was another table.

"You're very comfortable here," said the stranger. "May I sit down?"

Pierre pointed to the table with the four chairs. He himself stayed by the window.

"You've come a long way," he said.

The stranger looked surprised. "What makes you say that?"

"Your shoes. You only find that red dust farther to the west, where the big quarries are!"

"They didn't tell me too much about you," said the stranger and smiled. Then he took a piece of paper out of his breast pocket, put it on the table and went on: "When you have read that the introductions will be complete."

Pierre walked over to the table and studied the paper carefully. "I had an idea that was what you were," he finally said, and sat down opposite his visitor, "although I had put you down as English."

"How did you notice that I'm not French?"

"From the way you speak. You have a slight accent."

"That's bad," said the stranger, whose name was James Bordon, an American citizen. "You are the first Frenchman who has noticed it."

"They're not all as clever as I am," said Pierre. "What do you want me for?"

60

"I want to get to know you. I've heard a lot about you in Nice."

"And that's what brought you all the way here?" Pierre grinned. "Go and tell that to the marines. Those people in Nice need someone to pull their chestnuts out of the fire again."

"Not the people in Nice," said James Bordon. "I represent Headquarters, American Seventh Army, which landed at Fréjus on the 15th August. I simply got your address in Nice. I have an important job for you."

"Go to Sospel. Louis has more men than I have."

"I have to see him too."

"Then good luck to you." Pierre lit a cigarette. "There's a mountain pass in between. You'll be sweating."

"With your truck we can be there in an hour."

"You're out of luck," said Pierre. "I've just come from Sospel. They can do their own dirty work. I'm not going to lift a finger for them."

"Had some trouble?" asked James Bordon. Pierre stood up and went to the sideboard. He was about five feet seven inches tall, wiry, had long black hair which stuck out in a fringe under his beret. A long diagonal scar crossed his right cheek. He had got it five years ago when he had tripped over a plank and fallen on his face on a circular saw. His skin had the dark coloring of all mountain villagers. He was dressed in blue workman's trousers and a sleeveless striped shirt which he wore outside his trousers.

He took a bottle and two glasses from the sideboard and put them on the table. "Do you like red wine?" he asked.

James Bordon nodded. "Is it your own?"

"Yes and no. I leased out my vineyard ten years ago. It was too much work for me. One can have either a vineyard or a joinery; both together are more than one man can run. *A votre santé!*"

"*A la vôtre!*" replied Bordon and drank. The wine had a sourish flavor and left a smoky aftertaste in the mouth, but after the third mouthful James Bordon no longer noticed the sourness. He licked his lips with his tongue and said: "This has got something!"

"When you've drunk two glasses of that," said Pierre, "you won't be able to stop—and after the fifth glass you'll start singing."

"Then I had better stop with the first," said Bordon and looked at his watch.

61

Pierre gave him a somewhat mocking look. He leaned both arms on the table and inquired softly: "What do you want from Louis?"

"What do you think of him?" countered Bordon.

"We used to work well together. He is a reliable man, but he's lost his touch. He's got too many there telling him what to do. When he began there were a dozen men in Sospel working with him; now there are so many that even he has lost count. It's none of my business. I have fifty men in Escarène, although I could have twice that number, but with that fifty I know where I am. If I had anything to do with organizing it, the Resistance would have been built up on very different lines."

Bordon grinned. "We Americans are pleased with you, anyway. You've saved us a lot of work."

"And for that you'll leave us behind even more when you go," said Pierre bitterly. "You Americans! What do you know about France? You come over to Europe in boats, play at war for a bit and then clear off again."

"Now listen," said Bordon, "we didn't come to France for the fun of it. As a Frenchman you should have a slightly better opinion of us."

"Do you think so? Are you banking on our gratitude? What for, exactly? For leaving us in the lurch in 1940? That was when you could have earned the gratitude of the French, but now! You didn't come over to liberate France! You just want to finish off the Germans, now that the Russians have done most of the dirty work for you."

James Bordon gave a slight shrug. "You are a difficult man, Fournier. While we are, as you put it, just finishing off the Germans, we happen to be freeing France too."

"You couldn't knock the Germans out without liberating France. There's a big difference, Monsieur. You're not setting us free because France means anything to you, you're doing it because you need us, especially after you took such a knocking in Italy. Don't think I object to your good intentions; you've come four years too late for my liking, that's all. Something has happened in France in those four years which can't be put right by your invasion and that's what I've got against you. If you had come into the war when the Germans marched into Poland, this wouldn't have happened to us. Until the collapse in '40 there were just Frenchmen; after it France was split into two camps. One was for

62

Pétain, the other against him. It goes right down through families, turning fathers and sons into deadly enemies."

"I haven't been in France long," said James Bordon, "but it seems to me, from what I've seen, that the people are united, body and soul."

Pierre finished his glass and wiped his mouth. "For the moment, yes. But you wait a few weeks and then things will look different. Three months ago the cowards behind Pétain saw that their time was up. They came over to the Resistance in droves to get themselves a quick alibi. Nowadays they make out that *they* were the ones who started up the Resistance, whereas in fact they are worse than useless. Not long ago I said to Louis, you can shoot away as much as you like, but do it so that the Germans don't catch us. A few weeks later his fools clobbered a few Boches three kilometers beyond Sospel. Twenty-four hours later the Germans were on to them. Louis pulled his crew up to the Col de Braus and they had a pitched battle which cost them twenty men. Afterwards he was furious because I made no attempt to bail him out with my fifty. If you want to play at generals, I said to him this afternoon, go and join the Liberation Army; they'll give you a lovely uniform, a few stars on your shoulder-tabs and maybe even a pension for your old age. The man's an idiot and besides . . . but that wouldn't interest you."

"It interests me very much," said James Bordon patiently. "I have more ties with Europe than you think. My grandparents were born and died in Germany."

"Is that why you came over?"

"That would hardly be enough. We Americans know what we're fighting for."

"You don't make it very obvious," said Pierre grinning. "If we'd had a decent government in 1940 we wouldn't have needed you. But that will all change now, provided the Communists don't stick a spoke in the wheel. That's what I was going to tell you just now. Louis is a Communist. I've got nothing against Communists so long as they haven't got a gun in their hands. They're already making sure that their men get elected mayor wherever there's a vacancy."

"Why do you let them get away with it?"

"What are we supposed to do? Shoot them? They were among the first to join the Resistance. Probably not because they were better Frenchmen than the rest, but because they were organized. The only person they're afraid of is de Gaulle."

James Bordon smiled. "He's a queer one."

"He is the only general," said Pierre, his voice rising, "who is any good at all. Apart from him I've got no time for soldiers. My grandfather was a Republican and my father was killed in 1907 during the rising of the southern wine farmers. That revolt was smashed by Clémenceau. Since then soldiers haven't been welcome in my family, but I won't hear a word said against de Gaulle. Would you like another glass?"

"If we have finished chatting."

"Right you are," said Pierre with a grin. "After all, you wanted me to do something for you, didn't you?"

While they had been talking dusk had fallen. Pierre switched on the light and went over to the window. "I don't think, though, that you're going to have any luck," he said, and closed the shutters. "Why do people always come to me?" He went back to his seat, filled the glasses, drank with relish, smacked his lips and continued: "You go to Louis, he's got the men, they'll do anything provided they are rewarded by a good job afterwards."

"I have a mission for Louis, too."

"Then go and see him. He's got enough people to do my part in it as well. I don't like being told what to do."

"Good," said James Bordon and stood up. "I'll go to Louis. They told me in Nice that Louis would do it if you wouldn't take it on."

"They told you that, did they!" Pierre laughed, furious. "That's nice to know. That means the Communists are behind it. They prefer Louis because he's one of them. As long as they needed me no one worked better than I did."

James Bordon wiped the sweat from his forehead. He was near to giving up, but his father had worked his way up from a clerk to being the owner of a big firm of wine merchants, and along with some of his other qualities Bordon had inherited his toughness. He said: "You could prove to them that you can still do a better job than anyone else."

"Could!" sneered Pierre. "Could? I already have. They just won't admit it any more."

"They do admit it," said Bordon. "They did not say that Louis worked better than you. I explained what the job was and they said that in their opinion you were the only one who could bring it off. However, they thought it most unlikely that I could persuade you to take it on and that was why they advised me to try Louis as well."

64

"Then why didn't you go to him straight away? And what gives them in Nice the idea that I wouldn't take it on? Do they think they can just write me off like that? He'll do that, he won't do that! I'll show them what I can do!" He shook his head, grinning. Then he realized that James Bordon was still standing up and he said: "If you want to go, go; otherwise squat down again and tell me what it's all about. Then I'll tell you what I think of it and whether I'm prepared to do it. How old are you, by the way?"

"Twenty-five," said Bordon and sat down again.

"Still pretty green," said Pierre. "Where are your troops?"

James Bordon pulled a map out of his pocket and laid it on the table. "In the Lyons area. They're making good progress. The army's objective is to push up the lower Rhône Valley and at the same time to make a flanking movement through Grenoble to block the route north to the German troops in the Rhône Valley."

"Have they succeeded?"

"Partly. Since the eighteenth the Germans have been in general retreat. They are trying to reach the upper Marne, the Saône and the Italian frontier. Up to yesterday morning we had taken twenty thousand prisoners. I hope there will be more."

"There could have been more," said Pierre, "if you had dropped parachute troops in the Rhône Valley. The Germans had at least ten divisions stationed on the coast. It could have been a French Stalingrad, but your generals won't take any risks. I don't think much of your generals. They could have learned something from the Germans."

"Such as how to lose a war?" asked Bordon, anger creeping into his voice for the first time.

Pierre laughed. "Ah, now you're talking like a regular army man! You're all touchy on that point. I just wanted to see how thick a skin you've got. I must say you can stand a lot for your age. Where did you learn it?"

James Bordon fell back exhausted against his chair. "In France, if you want to know. You French have a remarkable aptitude for getting off the point."

"It's in our blood. How are things round Marseilles and Toulon? You've been stuck there for a week now."

"Not since yesterday. The Germans have surrendered."

"Good," said Pierre with satisfaction. "And Nice?"

"Nice is due today. Can we go on now, or do you want to know more?"

"What's happening at Briançon?"

65

James Bordon glanced at the map. "It may have been taken by now. It was to be a joint assault with the Resistance."

"Thanks, that's all I wanted to know. Nice will fall today and you are already in Lyons and Grenable. Apart from the coast road there are three points between Menton and Modane where they can cross the frontier into Italy. Three crossing points in two hundred kilometers and the one at Briançon is probably already barred to the Germans. That leaves the Col de Larche near Barcelonette and the Col de Tende. Good, that is quite clear now. What is their strength and where are they coming from?"

"We don't know exactly," replied Bordon in a tone of admiration. "It could be a regiment, but it could be as much as a division. When our tanks were on their way up from Marseilles to Grenoble they bumped into some retreating German troops at Château-Arnoux. They fought a delaying action, but they were not motorized and we overran them. Some of them disengaged and got away to the east and followed the N202 through Digne."

"Why didn't you pursue them?"

"They blew up a bridge behind them. We can't move until it's repaired."

"How long will that take?"

"Our engineers reckon it will be ready in forty-eight hours."

"By then they will have such a start that you'll never be able to catch them."

"That's why I'm here," said James Bordon. Pierre nodded. For a few seconds he sat thinking, then raised his head. "The N202 leads to Nice. Since, as you say, Nice will be taken today, the Germans are denied the coast road. They must turn off the N202, either over the Col d'Allos to Barcelonette or . . ."

"Or?"

"Or push on farther up it as far as Plan-du-Var. There they can take a minor road, the D206, over the Col de Brouis. After crossing the Col de Brouis the D206 follows a long valley and joins up farther north with the N204 which comes from Nice and leads to the Col de Tende."

"And over the Italian frontier," said Bordon. He followed the route on the map with a pencil and looked at Pierre. "What's the area like?"

"Quite good for our purposes," answered Pierre reflectively. "But it's too unsafe for me until I know how strong the Germans are. I'm not so crazy as to take on a whole division."

"All you have to do is to hold them up."

"Doesn't make any difference," said Pierre scornfully. "If they got self-propelled guns or tanks with them they'll make mincemeat of us. I'm thinking of something else." For a while he stared into space, frowning, shook his head a few times, then said: "If only I knew that they wouldn't take the road to Barcelonette. . . ."

"Can't we prevent them?"

"They've got to cross the Col d'Allos. If Louis co-operates, then they'll never get over."

"That's roughly what I had in mind," said James Bordon with satisfaction. He looked at the map again. "I'll ask Louis to position his men on the Col d'Allos. Do you trust him to make a good job of it?"

"The Col d'Allos," replied Pierre, "is not like the Col de Braus. Tell him to blow up the bridge past Colmars. It crosses a deep gorge. If the bridge is blown the Germans will be forced to leave their guns and tanks behind and Louis can easily pick off any of their infantry who get over. He only has to post his 'army' on the cliffs on either side of the road and not even a mouse could slip through."

"I'll tell him that. Do you think he'll do it?"

"As long as you don't tell him that it was my idea. You must use tact and make him believe that he thought it up himself."

"Thanks for the tip," James Bordon smiled. "He seems to be as complicated as you are. Then that only leaves the Col de Tende and you will have to occupy that."

Pierre drank a mouthful and banged the glass back on the table. "I don't *have* to do anything, get that into your head once and for all. When I do something I do it of my own free will. And we can leave the Col de Tende out of the reckoning from the start. If Louis occupies the Col d'Allos he's taking no risk, because from there it's a good twenty-five kilometers to the Italian frontier. The Col de Tende, on the other hand, is right on the frontier. At the first rifle-shot we would have the frontier guards firing at us from the rear. When were the Germans in Digne?"

"At five o'clock this morning."

"That's all right," said Pierre. "From Digne to Colmars it's roughly seventy-three kilometers. Even if they move fast they can't be in Colmars before tomorow morning. I estimate they'll need another day to reach Plan-du-Var. So we have enough time. . . . You don't happen to know whether they have tanks with them?"

67

"When I left Nice," answered James Bordon, "we still had no definite information."

"Then we'd better assume that they have."

Bordon looked at the map. "That would mean that they could get there tonight."

"Not a chance," Pierre contradicted. "There are three passes on the way, and besides, I don't believe the tanks would push on and leave the infantry behind. In mountainous country tanks are helpless without infantry. The earliest we ought to expect them is tomorrow afternoon or evening. It's only annoying that . . ."

He stopped, took off his beret and scratched his head. "Damned annoying," he said.

Bordon waited expectantly.

"You'd never imagine," said Pierre after a while, "that I could hold up a whole division with my fifty men, would you?"

"If Louis sent you reinforcements——" began James Bordon.

Pierre cut him off sharply: "Louis is not going to send me any reinforcements; you can forget that idea altogether. I'll do this thing on my own or not at all."

"But you say yourself——"

"Wait until I've finished. You don't yet know what I've got in mind. I don't want a great mob, all telling me what to do next. Afterwards they'll say I couldn't have managed it without them. Why don't you send us some troops from Nice? On the N204 they could be here with their tanks inside three hours."

"First," said James Bordon, "Nice is not yet completely in our hands and second we need the troops there to push on through Menton to the frontier. We cannot split up our forces any further. It will be a few days yet before we've landed enough divisions to start an advance northwards from Nice."

"And by then the Boches will be over the hills and far away. Your American generals are no good. They play for safety too much. War is not a slow foxtrot, Monsieur, and anybody who didn't realize it by 1939 should have learned from the Germans how fast war can move when the generals are any good. Who knows what the result would have been if Hitler had given his generals a free hand? It doesn't bear thinking about. Now I'm going to tell you how I see this business. We will send the Germans up a road which comes to a dead end in the mountains. This will make them lose so much time that they'll pull their tanks back and we can pick off the infantry. That is as much as I can risk with my fifty men."

"The idea's brilliant," said Bordon, fascinated, "how do you propose to do it?"

"If the Germans want to reach the Col de Tende from the N202, they can only do it by way of the Col de Brouis. They will be forced to go up the long valley which I mentioned just now. That is the D206, a bad road, but it joins the N204, which leads to the Col de Tende and there's no other way."

"Yes, I see it," said James Bordon, who was studying the map again.

Pierre stood up and started to walk up and down the room with rapid strides. "Then you'll notice that a little farther on the valley forks. The right-hand fork leads to the junction with the N204, while if you go straight on the road runs through a gorge with vertical cliff sides and a fast-flowing river, which it crosses by a steel bridge. About two hundred yards in front of that is another bridge, a wooden one, which carries a small road leading to Escarène. Perhaps you saw it on your way here."

"I didn't notice it," said James Bordon. Looking expectantly at Pierre he said, "I still don't see what you're driving at."

"You'll soon see," replied Pierre, satisfied with the impression he was creating. "My aim is to make the Germans, when they reach the fork, march straight on instead of turning right."

"Good idea, but you could never make them do it," said Bordon sceptically.

"Oh yes, we can." Pierre sat down again at the table. "Why do you think the Germans have never caught us yet? Just because we're quick and clever? That is not enough. In this game you must be able to use your head as well as your gun. We've led the Germans on, drawn them away from the big Routes Nationales down lonely side roads and then finished them off at our leisure. It was easier than you might think. One only had to fix the signposts a bit and we've made that our speciality. It pays to have learned an honest trade."

He laughed and emptied his glass. Then he went on: "You might object and say that if you had been in the Germans' place you wouldn't have been so stupid as to fall for it, but believe me you would have fallen for it too. If you've been marching for thirty kilometers and you come to a fork with a signpost which shows fifteen kilometers to Nice by one road and twenty-five by the other, which would you take?"

"The one with fifteen kilometers, certainly," answered Bordon.

Pierre nodded cheerfully. "You see? We thought the same.

Even if you have a good map you'll fall for it. You'll say to your-self that it must be a short cut that isn't shown on your map. That can happen in the French Alps. A signpost can't be wrong, you'll say to yourself. A signpost must be right because they always are right, all over the world. It's bound up with human laziness, Monsieur, and if the Germans find a suitably fixed signpost at the fork of the D206, then those same Germans who have just got away from your tanks by the skin of their teeth and whose only thought is to get over the French frontier as quickly as possible will take the shorter route without a moment's hesitation. And this apparently shorter route is a road which is not shown on their map because it has been blocked by a landslide. It stops just before La Peine. The village is uninhabited and lies beneath a disused fort. If we succeed in steering the Germans up this road, they only have two chances. They can either pull back and find that they can't cross the river any more, because in the meantime we will have blown up the steel bridge, or they can abandon their vehicles and heavy weapons and climb over the landslide debris until they come to the point where the road is passable again. There they have to go through a long tunnel and in the tunnel there will be a few of my men."

"A few?" James Borden sounded uncertain.

"That will be enough. There's a bend in the middle of the tun-nel, where I shall set up a machine gun. As soon as a German ap-pears in the tunnel mouth, he's a dead man. One machine gun at this spot can hold up an entire army, provided there are no heavy weapons. Farther up the road towards La Peine there are still more tunnels. Even if the Germans succeed in driving us out of the first one they won't gain much. Of course they will go all out to reach La Peine, because once there they can cross the ridge, down the other side of the mountain and rejoin the D206. If the worst comes to the worst, we've always got the fort. From there with even a few weapons you can dominate the entire length of the ridge. I will divide up my men between the tunnels and the fort."

"I don't know the district," said James Bordon. "If it's of any interest to you, I think your plan's a good one, but———"

"It's of no interest to me," interrupted Pierre. "I'm not so mad as to take on an impossible task."

Bordon nodded. "Of that I have no doubt. Apart from the road, is there no other means of reaching La Peine?"

"Not on this side. Anybody who tried to would break his neck."

"Now I begin to see. I'm just trying to imagine what the Germans will do as soon as they realize that they can neither go back nor forwards. There must be other ways of getting out of the valley."

"Perhaps, if they drop everything they've got. Look at the map. You can get a rough idea of the terrain if I tell you that the road runs first through the gorge, then over a small pass and from there down into the valley. The Germans can't get out of the gorge, the pass runs between unclimbable peaks and the valley is flanked by vertical cliffs. Of course there is one way of getting out of the valley—on the north side, where the road runs along a viaduct. From there you can climb up the side of the valley until you reach a ridge; but for anybody who doesn't know his way about our alps, it's a risky business because by then you are over nine thousand feet up. Even if the Germans tried to reach the frontier by this way they would lose so much time that your troops could catch them. When are you expecting them to be there?"

"By tomorrow morning at the latest," replied Bordon. "Where is your radio?"

"In a good place up in the vineyards. I have put three men on it who take it in turns to keep in permanent contact. Do you want to send a message?"

"Yes, to our headquarters in Toulon. Your corresponding station in Nice has had a direct link with H.Q. for a week. We'll tell them our plan so that they'll send some troops here as quickly as possible. Where do you want them?"

"On the D206, where else? If they came in time before the Germans spotted the trap, we shouldn't have to blow up the bridge; if we blow it up your engineers will have to build a new one to let your tanks across to chase after the Germans."

"All right," said Bordon. "But don't forget to allow for the rear guard once the main body of the Germans has passed."

"I shall not allow for it," retorted Pierre with dignity. "As soon as the German main body is over the bridge, the signpost at the fork will point in the right direction again. I shall need one of Louis' men to blow up the bridge, though. I've never dealt with such things. Louis has two or three who learned it up north. Tell him that it's to be the steel bridge by the gorge and then he'll know how much dynamite we need. When the Germans have crossed the bridge I'll send two men after them to give us good warning when they turn back."

"You're a remarkably gifted man," said James Bordon, "in the

71

American army you would have been on the General Staff long ago."

"In the American army," said Pierre, "that wouldn't have been surprising. Now I'm going to collect my men. . . ."

"You needn't do that yet," said Bordon quickly. "Louis has to get moving tonight. He has farther to go and if I am too late in getting to him . . . You will drive me to Sospel, won't you?"

"What would you have done if I refused to drive you?"

"Guess."

Pierre looked into his cold eyes. Then he stood up, walked to the window and pushed back the shutters. "Come here for a moment," he said. James Bordon went over to him and Pierre pointed across the dark street to the house opposite. Although it was unlighted, Bordon saw several men sitting on the doorstep and the glowing ends of their cigarettes. "How did you manage that?" he asked in surprise.

Pierre closed the shutters before answering: "We were seen going into the house together. As soon as a stranger appears in Escarène he is shadowed. Simply a safety precaution."

"I noticed nothing," said James Bordon. He returned to the table with Pierre, grasped his half-full glass and emptied it with one gulp. "One lives and learns."

Pierre shrugged his shoulders. "We can't afford to be careless."

"Nor can we. Above all we can't afford to let a whole German division slip through our fingers because of the obstinacy of one Frenchman. War is a serious business."

"Very true," said Pierre. "Now for calling me obstinate I won't drive you to Sospel."

Both were standing in the middle of the room and James Bordon still had the empty glass in his hand. He slowly replaced it on the table and looked at Pierre. "I warn you, Fournier," he said quietly. "I am here as a soldier and am acting under orders."

"I know that," said Pierre. "It would be a pity if anything happened to a fine man like you."

"So you don't want to drive me to Sospel?"

"I have things to do here. We must be off good and early tomorrow and in the meantime there are still a few things to be done."

"If I don't reach Sospel in time you may just as well stay in bed tomorrow morning. Then the Germans will march straight over the frontier."

72

"I did not say," explained Pierre, "that you wouldn't get to Sospel in time. I merely said that I would not drive you there."

"There's no difference."

"Oh yes, there is. We have another car here, and I shall arrange for you to go to Sospel in that. Or were you counting on my company?"

"Hardly," answered Bordon, and once more wiped his forehead. Pierre sat down again and refilled the empty glasses with wine. "Let us drink another glass to Free France, Monsieur. Or won't your American self-consciousness let you?"

"Not that so much as the fact that your country is as responsible as the Germans are for the mess in Europe."

"Did you learn that in some college?"

"I make up my own mind on politics. At the University in St. Louis we had a history professor who used to say that France was like a woman getting on toward fifty: she can't do it any more, but she goes around acting as if she could."

"What can't she do any more?" asked Pierre, his head cocked to one side.

"You know," replied Bordon.

"Now you're starting to get red in the face," said Pierre grinning. "Do go on. I want to hear what comes next."

James Bordon leaned over the table toward him. He was livid. "I want to tell you something, Fournier. They described you to me in Nice as strong and self-willed, but you're not self-willed, you're nothing but a querulous old woman and disgustingly conceited as well. I don't deny you're intelligent, but intelligence with both these other characteristics makes up a combination which I cannot abide. I've come across it everywhere in France and you oughtn't to be surprised if we Americans, after what we've seen here, never lift a finger for France again. And believe me, I'm not the only one who thinks like that. If there's ever a third world war, you'll be on your own."

"You think so, do you?"

"Yes. No country in the world is going to be crazy enough to drag you out of the mire for a third time. We didn't come over here to be laughed at by you people. Because of you I stopped studying, postponed getting married for three years and gave up a hell of a lot of other things. This has nothing to do with politics. I don't give a damn what our government thinks about France and whether it thinks we should be in the war. As far as I'm concerned

73

you can think what you like about America, that's your business, but we're not in Europe because we have to be. Economically it's finished anyway. We came into the war in spite of that as the result of a free vote of the American people; that could change tomorrow and when this war's over there *will* be some changes in America, that you can rely on."

"I doubt it," said Pierre as he savored a mouthful of wine. "You Americans will come over to Europe ten times again whenever your interests here are threatened."

"Fournier, you're wrong about America. Once we realize that what we have to lose in Europe is not worth the risk of a war, public opinion will turn and no government in Washington can do a damn thing about it."

"Then it's no good," said Pierre. "It's the government that should take the responsibilities and not the people. The people are stupid and lazy and will do anything for a quiet life. If our government had let itself be influenced by public opinion in 1940, the Germans would be absolute masters of Europe today. There are times when a government must act against the will of the people when it is convinced that war is the ultimate means of saving the country."

"That will always be a matter of opinion."

"That has nothing whatever to do with it. What's the good of letting yourself be bitten by a snake in order to find out whether it's poisonous? Much better kill it at once. What our country lacked in 1940 was a man with a myth, that is why the Germans beat us. Even the Russians would have been lost without their Stalin. That's why we French have had no luck since Napoleon. He was our last great man."

James Bordon made a slight grimace. "It surprises me to hear you of all people say that. Just now, it seems, you had no time for soldiers."

"Napoleon," said Pierre sharply, "was a statesman; remember that when you talk to a Frenchman. He did more for Europe than you ever learn in your schools in America. If he had been born a hundred years later we wouldn't have needed a single American to help us finish off the Germans."

"So you may like to think."

"I do, if you don't mind. I also like to think that you Americans are incapable of sitting by and looking on when Europe is under a dictatorship. The days are gone when it didn't matter to an outsider what happened in Europe. And now kindly write down

74

what I have to radio to Nice. I've better things to do tonight than to sit here and listen to you putting the world in order." He rose and left the room.

James Bordon stood frowning for half a minute, then took paper and fountain pen from his pocket and set to work. He had just finished when Pierre came in with four other men. They grinned awkwardly when they saw Bordon and touched their caps. Gaston went up to him and shook his hand while the other three hesitated in the doorway and looked at Pierre, who turned to the American: "Done it?"

Bordon gave him the paper. "I hope you can read it."

"Do I look illiterate?" asked Pierre, and read it carefully through. Then he passed the sheet to one of the other men and said: "Make sure you get an acknowledgment and don't forget to ask who took down the message. If anything goes wrong later no one will admit having received it."

"You'll send it in code, of course?" put in Bordon quickly.

Pierre looked at him with scorn. "We encode everything. Only a fool would transmit something like this in clear." He turned to the man who had the message. "Hurry up. Better transmit it twice. They always need their ears washed in Nice."

The man nodded, grinned at James Bordon and went. Gaston had sat down on Pierre's chair and was talking to Bordon. The other two approached the table. One wore a black leather jacket with a red scarf round his neck.

"This is Jules," said Pierre to James Bordon. "He has a car and will drive you to Sospel." He turned to Jules. "On the return journey I want you to bring back the man who is to blow up the bridge for us. Drive him straight up to the bridge, to give him plenty of time to lay the charge before tomorrow noon." To Bordon again he said: "Give my regards to Louis. Tell him that we're on our way. If he gets difficult shoot one of the curls off his head; that always works with Louis. He was in the army for four years, but give him a pistol or a rifle and he can't even hit a corpse."

The men laughed and Gaston said: "They say he's pretty good in bed. The woman he's got at the moment used to be in a brothel in Nice. She turns pale when he so much as looks at her."

"I think it's time I was going," said James Bordon. He walked up to Pierre, "I hope you won't mind, Fournier, if I don't shake your hand. Perhaps we will meet again, when we've finished with the Germans, and then I can make up for it. At the moment I find it rather hard to do."

"The Englishmen felt the same, too," said Pierre. "I can't think why."

"Probably because of your charm," said Bordon, and opened the door. Out in the garden he stopped, took several deep breaths of the cool night air and looked up at the starry sky. A little later he heard Jules's step on the gravel path and his voice: "I had to ask him something. Sorry to keep you waiting." Together they walked through the garden to the street, where a red Citroën stood under a lamp. "She still goes well for her age," said Jules. "I need her for my business."

"What sort of a business have you?" asked Bordon politely.

"A bakery. You know, the people in Escarène won't buy anything but white bread, and no baker in France can live on that alone. Before the war I specialized in pastry, you earned more that way, and the sweet stuff sold very well in Nice. My wife looked after the shop up here by herself. Since the war, of course, it's been hopeless. For the first two years we could manage, then at least we got a regular ration and if you knew what you were up to you could always get some stuff on the side. But now . . ."

He had stopped beside the car and spat on the ground. "This is a useless bit of the country, Monsieur. We have neither wheat nor rye and whatever we need we have to bring in from miles away. Just look at the soil! It produces nothing, I tell you. Do you know . . ." He lowered his voice. "If we weren't able to scrounge a bit of corn from over in Italy now and again we would have starved to death long ago. They call it smuggling, but if they won't give us anything to eat what else can we do? It's a dirty, dangerous business. The frontier guards watch for us like hawks."

"Things will get better soon," said James Bordon. Jules nodded. "Let's hope so. What I wanted to say was . . ." He looked over the garden wall. "You mustn't get angry. It's just his way and he doesn't really mean it. He's our best man for miles around. The people here would die for him. Ten years ago he had some bad luck with a woman. You know how these things happen?"

"He told me nothing about that."

"Christ, man! If you ever see him again, for God's sake don't say that I told you. He's a good fellow, but where that's concerned . . . better keep off the subject. Come on, let's go. We've enough to do tonight."

He opened the car door for Bordon and waited until he had seated himself, then walked round to the driver's side, climbed in behind the steering wheel and lit a cigarette. "By the way, what do you do in America?" he asked. "I mean when there's not a war on."

"I was a student," answered Bordon. "My father has a business. It was his idea that I should take it over one day."

"And you don't want to?"

"It doesn't interest me."

"What were you studying?"

"Physics."

"Don't understand a thing about it," said Jules as he started up the engine. "Nobody can tell me anything about my trade, but physics! I don't even know how to spell it. Do you live in New York?"

"No, in St. Louis."

"Nice town?"

"A very nice town."

"Home's always best," said Jules. Bordon was silent. Before the car moved off he looked past Jules and saw that Pierre was standing at the open window and looking out at them. His narrow head showed up clearly against the bright light from the room, and Bordon had the impression that he was waving to them. He could see no more as the car drove off and Pierre, who was not sure whether James Bordon had noticed him waving, watched the car for as long as he could see its red rear lights. Then he shut the window and joined Gaston and Roger at the table. They each had a glass and Gaston asked: "Were you rude to him?"

"No harm in it," replied Pierre. "He's intelligent and I like him, but in Cannes and Marseilles they must have had a reception like a winning football team. It does them good to find out that there are other Frenchmen who won't creep up their backsides, otherwise they get delusions of grandeur. Right, now listen."

He described his talk with James Bordon and concluded: "We'll split up into three groups. The first group takes up a position near the blown-up bridge and waits for the Americans. The second occupies the tunnels near La Peine and the third goes to the fort. It will probably be the last job we shall do. . . ."

"*And* the most dangerous," broke in Roger. He was a tall, hefty man in his fifties, sunburned with black hair falling over his forehead. Beside him Gaston, with his lanky figure and pale, hollow-cheeked face, looked like a dwarf. Roger had a deep, booming voice, Gaston spoke like a boy whose voice was just breaking. He lisped slightly, as two of his front teeth were missing. His age was hard to judge. He could as well have been thirty as forty. He now looked at Roger and said: "If you're afraid, we'll take someone else in your place."

"Don't talk like a fool," Roger replied. "If I say it's our most dangerous job so far that doesn't mean I'm afraid."

"It's no more dangerous than the others," interrupted Pierre. "I'd even say that we've done more dangerous ones in the past. At any rate it's a worthwhile one and a good finale. They'll be talking about it all over France."

"They'll give you the Legion of Honor," said Gaston. "When it's all over I'll go and spend a few months in a sanatorium and get my lungs put right."

"Where will you get the money from?" asked Roger. "A sanatorium's for rich people."

"Pierre will help me," answered Gaston. "If they give him the Legion of Honor they'll have to do something for his comrades too."

"You'll go to a sanatorium," Pierre assured him, "even if I have to pay for it out of my own pocket. Your wife will be glad to get rid of you for a while. Now we'll go and give out the orders. We've two passes to cross tomorrow, so I can't take more than a dozen at a time in my old crate, or she'll stall on the way. We'll have to make three journeys."

"Tonight?" asked Roger.

Pierre shook his head. "Daybreak will be early enough for the first truck load. By the time we've got the weapons out and fixed the signposts it will be nearly daylight. My idea is to take the first twelve straight to La Peine. Jules will first of all drop his at the bridge and then drive straight back here. Then I will follow him a bit later and bring Monsieur Knopf, Boris and the girl with me. They must hide in the vineyards until it's over. Have you got room for them in the cellar up in your vineyard?" he asked Roger.

"There's room all right, but no one can sleep in that foul air."

"They can come down to sleep," said Gaston.

"Too dangerous," Pierre objected. "We'll have to reckon with German stragglers straying towards Escarène."

"What about putting them in the cellar where we have our radio set?" asked Gaston.

Pierre reflected. "If there weren't the girl," he then said. "I couldn't let her."

"Of course not!" said Gaston and grinned.

"Don't be offensive," said Pierre, his voice rising. "You know I won't stand for it."

78

"I didn't mean it like that," said Gaston in an appeasing tone. "You should have married, Pierre, you're a natural father."

"He still could, at his age," put in Roger. "Once he's got the Legion of Honor all the women will be running after him." Pierre reached for his glass. "To hell with the Legion of Honor, you hear me? I haven't been fighting for medals. The girl has lost her parents and I have promised my sister and her husband that she'd be in good hands with me. I should like best to keep her here for good. I've always wanted a daughter."

"He wants a daughter but he won't marry," said Gaston.

"I do believe," said Roger, "that even if he did he would have nothing but sons."

"All of them heroes, like him," said Gaston and giggled.

Pierre looked at him with contempt. "When you laugh you look even stupider than usual. Besides, you can't talk; any son of yours would be an idiot like his father."

"Now you're being insulting," said Gaston in an affected voice.

"True, isn't it?" said Pierre grinning. "Look at you, married ten years and not a squeak to show for it. You haven't got the imagination to think what it must be like to have a daughter. A girl's much better than a boy. She stays closer to her parents and when she's grown up you can marry her off nicely. If I had a daughter I'd bring her along when we go and teach the Boches a lesson tomorrow, just to show her what sort of a fellow her father is. God, I've never regretted not marrying for a moment, but I tell you a daughter like that wouldn't be at all bad. I had never realized it until those two came here. No, I don't want a boy, believe me. What about you, Roger? You slaved away for yours for twenty-three years and then he goes and marries a slut in Marseilles and you never see him again. That wouldn't have happened if you'd had a daughter. A daughter never forgets her parents."

"You can't pick and choose," said Roger gloomily. "You have to take what comes your way. Yes, if I had a second son or even a daughter for that matter. . . . Why are we sitting here talking?" he interrupted himself brusquely. "Where else will you put her if you won't let her into the radio cellar? Mind you, she can stay in my cellar for as long as she likes, but it's no pleasure, I can assure you. There's water leaking into it from somewhere."

"We'll have to find a cellar higher up," said Pierre. "I'm just trying to think which one would do."

They discussed it for a while until Gaston struck the table impatiently. "We're just wasting time," he said. "Wait till the men

79

are here. Perhaps one of them will have a sensible idea. After all it's only a question of two or three nights; it won't kill them. If we take them up some bedding they won't sleep much worse than they do in La Peine. In the daytime they can sit outside. You must just tell them not to run around outside at night."

"Good," said Pierre and stood up. "Roger, you take the bridge, Gaston the tunnel and I'll keep an eye on things from the fort. Gaston will probably have the most to do. As soon as I see that you can't hold out any longer I will occupy the next tunnel and cover your withdrawal."

"He's being funny!" said Gaston to Roger. "He's going to cover my withdrawal! Did you hear? He must have heard the word in the army." He gave a sarcastic laugh and looked at Pierre. "Have you ever had to cover me yet?"

"No, I haven't, but nor have we ever taken on a whole division before."

"A division that has to pass through a tunnel is as strong as the number of soldiers who can fit across its mouth. What perhaps could be dangerous are hand-grenades and mortar bombs, and for that we'll throw up a barricade. You can go to sleep in the fort if you like. I'll wake you up when it's all over."

"All right, I'll take over the tunnel and you can bed down in the fort."

"Christ Almighty!" said Gaston in fury. "The man's as touchy as an old maid. How are you going to run the show if you're stuck in the tunnel? Am I the boss or are you?"

"I am, and you can shut up."

"How many men are you giving me?"

"Fifteen."

"Fifteen. That's a whole damned regiment. What will I do with a crowd like that in a narrow tunnel? All I need is three to man the machine-gun."

"If one of them is wounded," said Pierre, "then you only have two left and if two are wounded, all you have is one."

"Yes, you're right," Gaston said, slightly abashed. "You always were good at mental arithmetic. But I won't have any wounded."

Pierre stepped close to him. "Listen to me, Gaston, if you won't take this business seriously I'll put somebody else in your place. It's not a question of your having any men wounded or not, it's something that we must allow for in any case and then you'll need people to carry them up to La Peine. Don't you see that if something goes wrong I don't want wounded men lying about in my field of fire?"

"All the same why do you always have to look on the black side?" said Gaston.

Chapter 4

That morning Boris was again up before sunrise. With his shoes in his hand he went barefoot into the kitchen. He had thrown away his only pair of socks the day that Knopf and his daughter had come to La Peine. They had had big holes at the toes and heels and he had been afraid of Anna seeing them. So he now washed his feet every morning, which he had not done as long as he possessed a pair of socks. He collected the bucket from the kitchen and set off on his morning walk to the spring.

He loved the hour before sunrise when the air smelled of fresh dew, the mountains stood out in crystal clarity and pink clouds floated across the clear sky. Then the flapping of the loose sole of his shoe no longer worried him, and he even fitted the noise to the rhythm of a song which he hummed to himself as he walked.

As he was alone he could move quickly and reached the spring in a quarter of an hour. As the bucket filled he took off his shirt and washed his face and body with the ice-cold water. To clean his teeth he used some of the fine sand from the ground; lacking a toothbrush he had to make do with his fingers, but he was well practiced by now and the fine damp sand was effective enough. Then with a comb which only had a few teeth left he combed the hair back from his forehead, put on his shirt again and looked at the bucket. It was three-quarters full and Boris decided to waste no more time in waiting for it, since he would have to fetch water again during the day.

For the last few minutes he had become aware of a definite yet inexplicable feeling of unease, and he returned to the village as fast as the bucket would let him. His inner tension only relaxed when the houses came into veiw between the boulders and the sight of the deserted street partially relieved his disquiet. He put the bucket on the steps and looked down the street. It was still in the shadow of the overhanging cliff. Only to the south and west were the mountain peaks bathed in pinkish light as if from invisible floodlights and the sky was slowly gaining color.

Boris stood for half a minute more in front of the house, then he carried the bucket indoors and set about removing the cold ashes from the stove. Having laid paper and wood he lit it with a match and blew on it until the wood caught fire. As he was doing so he suddenly felt that he was being watched. He looked over his shoulder and saw Anna standing in the doorway. After a second's confusion he quickly stood up and smiled. "I didn't hear you coming," he said. "You're up early."

She came into the kitchen and held her narrow hands over the fire. "I was frozen last night. If we stay here any longer Pierre will have to bring me a second blanket."

"You could have had mine," said Boris. He looked at her hands, almost transparent over the glow from the stove.

"I used some of my clothes as well. Have those two already gone?"

He understood immediately who she meant. "I don't know. I don't think they would have left so early. If you like, I'll go and look."

She crossed to the window, opened the shutters and looked out. "Perhaps we ought to take them something to eat. It wouldn't matter to us: we are getting more supplies tomorrow. You might see to it while I go and wash."

Boris gazed at her in astonishment, unable to understand her change of attitude. His own dislike of the two Germans had various grounds; their presence not only increased the danger of discovery, but could lead to trouble with Pierre. Boris felt absolutely convinced that both of them would shoot at the first opportunity once they had a gun in their hands. As they were deserters there was the added danger that the German troops might be searching for them. Besides these, though, there was another reason why he did not want them to stay in La Peine and although he told himself that it was irrelevant, he knew that he was jealous. He wanted the remaining days that he would spend with the girl to be undisturbed and had no wish to share her company with the two Germans.

83

He was upset by the sudden interest which Anna was showing in them, and he tried to make her change her mind. "I don't
know whether those two are worth so much trouble," he said.
"Anyway, they were expecting to contact someone today who
was supposed to bring them food."

Anna turned quickly round. "Did they tell you that?"

"Not in so many words." He hated lying, but could see no other
way to avoid mentioning Vieale. "I happened to hear it as they
were talking together. They know some Frenchman who is willing to help them."

"Where are they going to meet him?"

"I don't know that either. Somewhere in the mountains."

"Perhaps they have a long way to go," said Anna. She looked
out of the window again. "I wonder whether it was right to send
them away."

Shaking his head, Boris walked over to her and stood behind her.
"Why do you bother about them? After all you've been through!"

She turned round and looked him in the eyes. "Please don't
keep reminding me of it. I haven't forgotten it and I will think of
it when I have to."

A note in her voice made Boris cautious. He shrugged his shoulders. "It was you who wanted to send them away."

"So did you."

"Because I didn't trust them; I said so to your father."

"Why didn't you trust them?"

Again Boris hesitated. He wanted to avoid worrying her by
telling her too much. That could wait until it was unavoidable and
he said evasively: "Men in their situation will stop at nothing. Shall
I ask them if they want to stay here?"

"Only if they raise the matter themselves. Otherwise it would
look bad."

"I agree," replied Boris with relief. "If you give them some
more to eat you will have done more than anyone else would have
done in your place. Do you want to wash here?"

"I'm going to the spring. You must hurry with the food, or they
will have gone." She went towards the door and turned before
leaving. "Don't hold back on bread. We get fresh tomorrow."
She said it with such seriousness that Boris gazed at her in amazement. A little later he heard her leave the house.

Carrying a towel she stopped for a moment in the street and
looked up at the sky, then took the path to the spring. She
walked very quickly, and although she did not once glance back,

84

she knew that Boris was watching her from the window. He did so whenever she left the house and she had grown used to it. To-day, though, it annoyed her and she was glad when the path disappeared among the boulders and Boris could no longer see her. On some days she was particularly fond of him and had to take care not to show it. She thought of him as a brother, a great affectionate bear who now and then earned a friendly stroke of his fur, but he might have misunderstood her and the thought of that frightened her. She had never really been fond of anybody except her parents. Often she froze with loneliness and then she liked having Boris at hand to warm herself from his unexpressed tenderness and kindness.

She was not surprised that he had been a teacher, for she had realized from the first that he was highly intelligent, although he had seldom spoken about himself and indeed had never uttered a superfluous word. In this he resembled Anna herself, and she felt that this was probably why she felt herself drawn to him. Their conversation of the evening before had not only confirmed some of her suppositions about him, but had also had a further significance for her as she had for the first time extended her sympathy to another person, whereas until then she had reserved it entirely for her own fate. Even her more conciliatory attitude towards the two deserters was a natural consequence of this new-found generosity of feeling. It was a new quality that she had discovered in herself and she was still uncertain what to think of it.

Now as she strode along the narrow path and felt the cool of the morning on her face, saw the sun rise over the mountains and inhaled the distant odor of the sea, she suddenly felt a violent longing to be in some other surroundings. She had almost forgotten what it was like to walk the well-kept street of a great city, to watch fountains playing or stare at passers-by from a café table. All that was so far away that she could only recall it with an effort and often it seemed as improbable as if it had only existed in her imagination like visions from another world.

She reached the spring and took her soap from a rubber bag which she had put in her trousers pocket. She took off her blue pullover to wash herself. To keep her long hair from getting wet she wound the towel round her head into a turban. Although Boris had unearthed an old tin bowl which served them as a wash-basin, she often went to the spring. She was always afraid that someone might appear and see her standing half naked. Often when the heat in the village became intense she used to douse herself all over with cold water from their bucket. At home she had had a big bath surrounded with black and yellow tiles and although she could hardly remember it, she had never forgotten those tiles.

Having dressed again she looked at herself in a small mirror. It was cracked in the middle and distorted her face a little. However she seemed satisfied with what she saw and carefully replaced the mirror in the little bag. A woman in Escarène had given her a lipstick, but she felt embarrassed to go around wearing make-up and she had only used it in secret until it was used up. It had tasted of raspberries, and she had determined to buy another lipstick like it one day when it would no longer embarrass her.

She looked carefully around to make sure that she had left nothing lying about, then started on the return journey. It was already getting warmer and the cloudless sky promised yet another fine day. It was almost nine weeks since the last rainfall, and she often wished the weather would change. She loved sitting by the window and looking out at the rain as it pattered on the roofs or slid in drops along the telegraph wires like little boats. There were no telegraph wires in La Peine, but from her window she could watch how the rain was whipped across the valley by the wind and the mountain-tops vanished in cloud.

Now as she walked along the rocky path, cheerful and refreshed, she started thinking again about the two men who had sat under her window the previous afternoon. Knopf was waiting for her at the door. He was greatly relieved to catch sight of Anna, and taking a few paces towards her he said reproachfully: "You were away for over an hour."

"I was thinking," she replied, and looked back along the path. "The wind has shifted today; you can smell the sea."

"You are being careless," said Knopf. "Only yesterday you saw how suddenly strangers can turn up here."

She linked arms with him. "I'm not a child any more. Is Boris back?"

"He's in the kitchen. The two Germans had already gone."

"Gone!" She stopped and withdrew her arm from his. "But they can't have gone! Did he look properly?"

"Their lean-to was empty and not a trace of them was to be found anywhere."

"That is amazing." The news dismayed her more than she cared to admit and she bit her lip with disappointment.

Knopf looked at her inquiringly. "I thought you'd be glad to hear it."

"Yes, I am." She had collected herself again. "Of course I'm glad." She looked over at the house, where Boris had just appeared in the doorway.

"Let's have breakfast," he said. "The coffee's ready." He was wearing a shirt that was too tight for him. Knopf had given it to Boris as he had only possessed one, but he could not quite button it over his chest and it bothered him whenever Anna looked at him.

He turned to her and nodded towards the other end of the village. "They had already gone. They must have started out in the night, because I couldn't see anything of them on the road. At first I thought that they might still be held up where the road has been cut by the landslide, so I watched it for a good quarter of an hour. I'm surprised they left so early and I only hope it means nothing sinister."

"Why should you think that?" asked Knopf, astonished.

Boris continued to look at Anna, who had pricked up her ears as he said his last words. "They might think of coming back."

"To La Peine?" Knopf could not understand him. "Then why should they go away?"

"They didn't want to go."

"But no one forced them to leave!"

"It depends on how you look at it. We made it quite clear that we preferred to see them gone."

"I suppose we did. But I had the feeling that they weren't particularly keen to stay."

"They are meeting someone in the mountains," said Anna. "Boris told me. He's bringing them food."

"I know nothing about this," said Knopf to Boris.

"It only occurred to me this morning. I pieced it together from one or two things they said."

"Most mysterious!" Knopf looked anxiously down the village street. "But I can still see no connection with your notion that they intend to come back here."

Boris realized that he had said too much. I shall either have to come clean with him or keep a tighter rein on my tongue, he thought. He had in fact already told Knopf that there was a man in Eys who had given him the pistol and advised him to hide out in La Peine, but had refrained from giving his name.

87

As he went indoors with Knopf and Anna, he resolved to straighten things out to the extent of telling Knopf the truth about himself. He had already delayed it too long and it was better to make a clean breast of it now than for Knopf to discover the facts by chance or at a more awkward moment.

They had breakfast in Anna's room. Boris had slept there up till a fortnight before. In choosing this house he had not only selected one at the southern end of the village and therefore nearest to the spring, but had also looked for one which was still more or less habitable, and this was one of the few without a tile missing from the roof. It also had a deep cellar which was cool enough to keep meat and other perishables fresh for a few days. Some of the shutters he had fetched from other houses and carefully fastened to the windows where they had been missing.

To reach Anna's room they had to go upstairs. Of the five rooms in the house three were placed one above the other in two stories on the right-hand side, while on the left-hand side there were only two rooms and one story. The original owner had solved the problem by making the rooms on the right-hand side lower than those on the left. Only the kitchen on the ground floor was slightly higher, whereas the rooms above it were little more than cupboards which were so low that Boris hit his head on the ceiling when he stood up. Yet Knopf had insisted on sleeping in the room over the kitchen and had firmly rejected Boris's suggestion that they should change places. The entrance to his room was about halfway up the steep stairs; there was then a narrow landing which led to Anna's room, and a few steps farther up was the door to the second room, but it was never used. The toilet was behind the kitchen and consisted of a tiny windowless room with a round hole in the floor. Even here Boris had achieved some more civilized arrangements with the simplest of means. The only table in the house really worthy of the name stood in Anna's room. Pierre had dragged it up the mountain on his back. He had even brought her a chair, but Anna made Knopf use it when they sat down to eat at the table. She herself sat next to Boris on a plank made into a makeshift bench by being supported at each end by large stones. They had placed the table near the window. From there they could look out over the roofs of the westerly line of houses to the mountains beyond, and when the sun shone through the window at midday, the bare, peeling walls lost their usual ugliness.

Anna had arranged her bed in the same corner that Boris had chosen in his room. Boris had pushed a few bundles of straw un-

88

derneath the mattress to raise it off the bare floor. Two dresses and a thin raincoat hung on a nail. The rest of her belongings Anna kept in an old leather suitcase near the foot of her bed, another gift from Pierre.

On the table were three plates and a pot of coffee. Today Boris had broken more bread into it than usual and sweetened it more strongly. They had no more milk and Boris was relying on Pierre bringing them a few bottles the next day. A week previously he had written him out a long list of the most urgent necessities.

Scarcely a word was spoken during the meal. When one of the men had an empty plate Anna looked at him inquiringly. If he nodded, she took his plate and refilled it. Knopf was usually satisfied with one while Boris, who had a good appetite, often emptied four platefuls at breakfast.

Today, however, Boris seemed to have lost his appetite. The thought of what he had to say weighed on him like a stone and when he firmly said he could eat no more after the first plateful, Knopf looked at him in amazement and said that he was surely not serious.

"Yes, I am," replied Boris and looked at Anna's face, who had glanced up from her plate and given him a speculative look.

"I hope you're not ill, Boris."

This was the second time that she had used his first name and he blushed with pleasure. At the same time he felt that in doing so she was making matters harder for him and he was already half resolved to put off saying his piece until later, although his conscience at once rebelled against the idea and he felt disgusted with himself. He forced himself to smile as he replied that he was certainly not ill and there were always some days when he felt less hungry than usual.

"I don't know what it is to be ill," he went on. "I once had a cold, but that was at least ten years ago."

"How I envy you," said Knopf. "For me it is the exact opposite. I have forgotten what it is to be healthy."

"You will be one day," said Anna and got up. "I'm going for a walk. I want to see where those two slept last night."

"You will not!" said Knopf with a sharpness which Boris had never yet heard in him. As if frightened by the tone of his own voice he immediately sank back and said imploringly: "Stay here, Anna. It is too dangerous."

Here Boris broke in. He suddenly saw a means of easing his own difficulty and said quickly: "It is no more dangerous than

89

usual, you know. Even if they were to return, they couldn't be back here before the evening."

Knopf thought for a few moments then said to Anna: "Don't be away for long."

"I'll be back in ten minutes," she answered and went out.

Boris watched her go downstairs. He felt a constriction in his throat which he tried to remove by swallowing a few times and looked at Knopf, who was smiling apologetically.

"I know you must think me absurdly frightened," said Knopf. "It is deeply ingrained in me by now, I'm afraid." He looked out of the window, where Anna's footsteps could be heard as she left the house. Then he put his hands down on the table. "You want to tell me something," he said levelly.

Boris stood up and walked over to the window to collect himself. Without leaning out he could see Anna about fifty yards away, and as he looked after her walking so lightly and gracefully down the street he was reminded of a timid fawn.

"I should have spoken to you long ago," he said without turning round. "I hope you won't hold it against me for not mentioning it until now."

"You should know me better than that," said Knopf. He had taken off his glasses and was polishing the lenses with a white rag.

Boris turned round. He remained by the window and crossed his arms on his chest. "I think I know you better than you know me."

"That was true until yesterday," said Knopf, busy with his glasses. He now put them on and looked at Boris. "You told us a lot about yourself."

"But not everything. I was not taken prisoner, I gave myself up. I am what is called a deserter, and whatever the motives are for doing it, it is an ugly word. In every language."

"It depends on how you say it," said Knopf. "You know our language well enough to know that. It can be a word of abuse as well as a term of admiration. So you wanted to tell me that you're a deserter."

Boris nodded.

"I guessed it; since yesterday I knew for certain. You had no alternative but to desert. I would have been disappointed had you not done so."

"You can't mean that," said Boris harshly.

Knopf smiled. It was a habit of his, and when Boris thought

about him later he remembered that Knopf had almost always been smiling.

"You know I mean it," he said.

"Then I fail to understand you."

"Why?"

Boris hesitated. He had not yet got over his astonishment and sat down at the table before replying: "I gave myself up to the Germans."

"Well? Am I not a German? Do you want to see my papers to prove my nationality? I was born the son of German parents in a German town with a German name. To be precise you have in me a representative of that very Germany to which you wanted to give yourself up. You just happened to come to the wrong address, that's all. It was the same house that you were looking for, but there were different people living in it, or rather they were not different. They were still the same people, but they had changed rooms within the house. The people who used to live in the cellars and attics had taken over the rooms on the ground floor and the real owners had to make do with the cellars. But you couldn't have known that."

"Tell me, Knopf, do you want to go back to Germany?"

"I still don't know whether I will. But I told you that I am a sentimental man. I suppose you are capable of weakness, but I don't see you as being sentimental—or am I wrong?"

Boris sat down on the bench. "We Russians have two peculiar characteristics: we like drinking and we like suffering. However, let's forget that. What will your daughter's reaction be?"

"To what? To the fact that three years ago you had the courage of your convictions and acted accordingly? Her reaction will be exactly the same as mine. Incidentally Anna is not my daughter."

"She's not your . . ." Boris broke off and sat motionless for a second. Then he nodded and his voice was quite calm as he said: "That explains everything."

"And you mystify me," said Knopf looking at him attentively.

Boris drew his hand over his forehead. "I need a little time," he said. It still seemed to him so extraordinary that he was unable to find the right words to give Knopf an answer. "They were only little things," he said after a pause. "I explained them away by saying that I am a Russian and don't quite understand your mentality."

"I think I can grasp what you're referring to," said Knopf. "Anna and I didn't seem close enough for me to be her father."

91

"No one could reproach you," said Boris.

Knopf smiled. "Apparently one could, or you wouldn't have mentioned it. It's true, people notice that I have had no children of my own. A bachelor never strikes the right note however hard he tries. I have never lived for anybody except myself."

For a few seconds he looked thoughtfully at the floor, then shrugged his shoulders as if to shake something off and went on: "I expect you want to know why I said Anna was my daughter."

"You are under no obligation to tell me."

"Morally I am. Confidence can only be rewarded with confidence. It's not even a very long story. Her father was my brother. He was a big banker in Düsseldorf, where I also lived. When the time came to leave Germany his wife was in a hospital. Kidney trouble, a sad business; he couldn't leave her. He was afraid that she wouldn't stand the strain of a journey. By then he had already been forced to give up his house. The medical superintendent of the hospital let him know that he could no longer be responsible for keeping my sister-in-law there. He was a good man and he did everything within his power. We moved in with some friends who even before we arrived had six people living in three rooms. They gave over their kitchen to us, helped us as far as they could, but it was no sort of life. And one day they came and took my brother. He was never heard of again.

"They left me alone—then. I was a journalist, an author, and a few books of mine had been translated into other languages, but I knew that it couldn't be long before it was my turn. When a temporary improvement occurred in my sister-in-law's health, I put her and Anna on a train and went with them as far as Trier. Originally I meant to take them to Switzerland, but I had been advised not to. The German-Swiss frontier was too strongly guarded, and many of us had been caught. Friends in Luxembourg helped us over the frontier at night and took us by car to Lyons in unoccupied France, where we managed to find lodgings with a French family. The man's name was Laurat and he was a member of the Resistance. He meant to help us get to Spain via Marseilles, but it was too much for my sister-in-law. She should have had an operation. At night she often shrieked in pain so loudly that she could be heard in the street.

"Then the Badoglio government was set up in Italy and the Germans had marched into what had been the unoccupied zone. Lyons became more and more dangerous for us. Laurat advised us to go to his brother-in-law in Escarène. You know him: he is

Pierre. I realized that we had to leave Lyons, but by now my sister-in-law couldn't be moved. She knew it. One evening she called me to her and told me that she had only a few more days to live. She made me promise her to look after Anna; the rest I have told you already. She poisoned herself with sleeping pills the same night. A sound heart would have survived the dose; even two years earlier it wouldn't have done her much harm. She was only forty and she clung to life; I wouldn't have thought her capable of suicide, in spite of all she had been through. She only decided on it when she began to fear that her illness might indirectly endanger her daughter's life. It must have been a very hard and lonely decision to make."

He stopped and slowly stood up. Boris watched him as he walked to the window and looked out for a few seconds before continuing: "We came to Escarène. Pierre helped us greatly. He treated me like a brother, Anna as if she were his own daughter. When the Germans started combing out the Maquis in the villages about a fortnight ago he brought us here. He has a great heart, little Pierre, and that's why I think that he will find a way for you too. It was he who advised me to say that Anna was my daughter in case we should meet strangers. As protective coloring, as he put it. You know what Frenchmen are. But in your case it no longer seems to be necessary."

"I am very grateful to you," said Boris.

Knopf turned round to him. "What for? I've told you why I want to be honest with you. You were with me."

"Not quite."

"Tell me, then. We are allies now."

Boris looked into his brown eyes. He had quite suddenly resolved to tell him everything. After this talk he could not have brought himself to conceal anything more from Knopf without having a bad conscience.

"Mine is not a very long story, either," he said. "I can tell it to you in a few words. You never asked me who sent *me* to La Peine."

"You will have had your reasons for not telling me."

"To be sure." Boris lit a cigarette while he considered how to begin. Having found the thread he said: "We had been recently moved to Bordeaux. A new road was to be built, a strategically important road, I think, though I don't know the exact details of it. Before we could start work the invasion began. We were confined to our camp and simply sat around waiting. Then we heard that we were to be moved back to Germany, but it was too late for that. The British and the Americans had made a breakthrough, all roads north and west were blocked. The only way open was southwards and I suppose that is why we were sent to Marseilles. There we spent a few days in an empty factory. Then we were put into freight trains again and passed through Cannes and Nice to Menton. Do you know the place?"

"I've never been there. Isn't it part of Italy?"

"The Italians annexed it during the war, but before that the frontier was a few kilometers eastward of it. However, at the very point where it crossed the frontier something was wrong with the railway line. Perhaps it had been blown up by the Maquis or something; nobody knew what it was. We sat day and night in our freight trains. There was nothing to eat and the soldiers guarding us could tell us nothing. They were mostly older men, good-natured and rather careless. For the first two days they were strict about guarding us, then less and less so. On the fourth night I was able to escape. It was the first chance I'd had since we came to France, otherwise I'd have done it sooner. Above all I wanted to get out of Italy and back to France. I didn't trust the Italians, the situation in Italy was extremely confused, whereas the French usually helped an escaped Russian prisoner-of-war.

"By nightfall I got on to a road which led into the mountains. Although I hadn't eaten for days, I kept going until morning. The road was steep. With many bends it went farther and farther into the mountains, or so I imagined. In actual fact it described a great semi-circle and finished up farther west by the sea again. I only realized this when it got light. I sat down and considered the situation. A kilometer away I saw the sea, the same railway which had brought us from Marseilles to Menton and beyond the railway a small village. It was Eys, but I only discovered that later.

"I didn't feel like turning back and I needed food. As long as it was daylight I didn't dare go into the village. I found a place to sleep and then I went down to Eys when it got dark. The people there were afraid. Nobody would take me in, until a woman sent me to the mayor. Yes, he took me in. He's called Vieale, and although he had been pro-German he kept me hidden in his house for a week. Then he gave me the pistol, these clothes and some food and sent me to La Peine. I was to come to him if I ever needed anything. I didn't need anything more from him and I never even thought I should see him again. However, I was wrong."

"Why?" asked Knopf.

94

Boris stared hard at him. "Those two Germans came from him too. He sent them up here and said that he would come here himself the following day—which is today. He was afraid of being condemned as a collaborator when the Germans leave."

"So they lied to us," said Knopf.

He sounded disappointed and Boris bit his lip. "Put yourself in my position," he then said, "I didn't know how you would react. I didn't want to worry you."

"You have worried me much more by not telling me this until now," replied Knopf and sat down on his chair again, his features tense with anxiety.

Boris watched him. When he could no longer stand the silence he cleared his throat. "I know how contradictory it all sounds, but . . ."

"You don't have to explain," Knopf interrupted him. "You were thinking of Pierre; I quite understand your motives. Nevertheless I can't help feeling that you did the wrong thing. If this man, this . . ."

He stopped and looked towards the window, through which they now heard footsteps. "That's Anna," he said quickly. "For the time being we'd better not tell her anything about this. I must think it over first. Do you think Vieale is dangerous?"

"How could I? He helped me. He's strange but I think he's a good man."

"Then we'd better let him come. I expect I can get Pierre to agree with me. Go down or Anna will catch us here like a couple of conspirators." He looked disturbed, and Boris, who now regretted having told him about Vieale, went out in silence.

He met Anna in the kitchen, filling the pot with water before putting it on the stove. As she heard him coming she turned round and nodded to him. Boris walked on out of the front door, sat down on the steps and looked down the street. If it had been a mistake to tell Knopf about Vieale, there was nothing to be done about it now. He regretted a mistake once made, but that was all. Further anxiety was useless and he thought no more of the matter.

As it was still early in the day he decided to see to the firewood. There was not much more in the kitchen and if Pierre came tomorrow he would not have much time to concern himself about wood. There was always so much to discuss and Pierre was bound

95

to bring a bottle of wine with him. It was the only variety in their monotonous existence in La Peine and Boris looked forward to these visits.

First he went into the cellar. The entrance was at the end of the hall and it meant climbing down some extremely narrow, steep stairs. At the bottom two doors led off a pitch-dark little lobby into the cellar rooms. Both were very low with tiny windows giving on to the street, through which filtered enough light to make a lamp unnecessary.

Boris turned to the right-hand of the two doors, bending down to avoid knocking his head. Near the window a flat rectangular flagstone lay on the ground; Boris had found it behind the house, dragged it into the cellar and washed it. It now served as a clean shelf for their provisions, which had become greatly reduced in the past week. Nevertheless they would still last a little longer. Boris himself supplied the meat; he had found out from Vieale that there were wild pigs in the thick woods below the spring. Otherwise they were only to be found on the Italian side of the Col de Tende, where the local people had started to hunt them since food had begun to run short. Probably a few animals had fled into the next valley and had multiplied. Three days ago Boris had shot a fifty-pound wild pig with his pistol.

He pulled a torn sack from one corner of the cellar. He put it over his shoulder and went out again to the street. Through the open window he could plainly hear Knopf's voice talking to Anna. He guessed they were talking about him and stopped for a moment, listening. Then with long strides he set off down the street, through the town hall archway and up the steep path to the road. About fifty yards to his right the road vanished into the fort: he turned in the opposite direction. It was downhill and he made good progress. The road surface was a good as new. It had hardly been used by the time the troops had been forced to evacuate the fort, but now it was spattered here and there with stones which had rolled down the mountainside. Boris counted fifteen tunnels, often very narrow but all of them with at least ten feet of headroom, along the short stretch to the place where the landslide had occurred.

It was hot on the road. Boris could feel the heat of the asphalt through the worn-out soles of his shoes. All around was quiet and he walked through the stillness as if through deep water which opened before him and closed soundlessly in his wake. The only sound in the vast space between road and steely blue sky was the

clatter of his loose shoe-sole. Not a sound besides this, not a murmur between all the mountains, on all their peaks and in all their
valleys but this one sound and he felt that the whole world was
listening with bated breath. For a moment he felt tempted to take
off the shoe.

But he now had to watch his step more carefully. While until
now only single pebbles had lain around, he gradually found more
and more, and in many places he was forced to clamber over quite
formidable heaps of stones. Then he reached the last tunnel. It
was longer and wider than the others, but where the road
emerged again into the open there was nothing but a chasm where
the landslip had torn away the mountainside and road.

There were two ways of getting past the ruined stretch. It
could be circumvented by climbing up a very steep slope behind
the tunnel and traversing about two hundred yards along the foot
of a cliff-face as far as a rockslide, which led down to the road
again. This route was nearly twice as long as the other, which led
through the middle of the rubble. To go this way meant climbing
down about one hundred and fifty feet on emerging from the
tunnel. Here there was a flat outcrop, sticking out like a giant's rib
from the torn flesh of his chest. From there after only a short
climb the far side of the road could be reached. Boris had used
this way ever since he had been at La Peine. But it was not only
shorter; it was also more dangerous as the outcrop, covered with
loose stones, frequently narrowed to a sloping path on the edge
of a sheer precipice. It consisted of reddish porphyritic granite, and
when the sun shone on it the contrast with the dull gray of the surrounding mountains gave it the aspect of a livid, mortal flesh
wound. Pierre too had taken the lower route when he had brought
Knopf and Anna up to the village, and Boris used it now, even
though he was not aiming to reach the other side. After only a few
yards he reached his goal.

Jammed between the fallen boulders and torn into pieces were
the remains of an olive grove which the landslide had carried
down with it. Boris dropped the empty sack and gathered as many
of the scattered branches as would fill it. They were easily snapped
and he broke them up into convenient lengths, then heaved the
loaded sack on to his shoulder.

The climb back to the tunnel was laborious, but after stopping
several times to regain his breath he finished the climb. For the
return journey he needed nearly twice the time, although he never
stopped to rest. Only when he reached the small square in front

97

of the town hall did he drop his load on the fountain trough and massage his aching arms with both hands. After wiping the sweat from his face and taking a few deep breaths he went on his way.

Walking with his head down, he could just see a few feet in front of him and only looked up when he heard his name called. It was Knopf. He was standing in front of the ruined church and watching him. Boris walked over to him and let the sack slide off his back to the ground. His knees were trembling slightly and he could feel his cramped leg-muscles twitching.

Knopf shook his head. "How often must I tell you, Boris, not to climb down there in the full heat of the day? The wood could have waited until this evening."

"What you can do in the morning . . ." said Boris and wiped the sweat from his forehead again.

Knopf smiled. "You've got it a bit wrong. It goes: 'Don't put off till tomorrow what you can do *today*.' "

His cheerful tone told Boris that their talk had left no ill-will. He too gave a smile. "I never could manage German proverbs. I prefer to have this job over with for the day."

"I have been making myself useful, too," said Knopf. "I have been to fetch water."

"You shouldn't have done that. It's too much of a strain for you."

"Not at all. I need to do it now and again to keep up my self-confidence. Believe me, Boris, there's nothing worse for a man than to feel superfluous, and whenever I can do something to counteract that feeling I'm quite willing to exert myself a bit."

Boris lifted the sack on to his back and they slowly walked up the street. "I have talked to her," said Knopf after a pause. "She agreed that it would have been better if we had been able to see this man Vieale. I'm not holding it against you. It's only a pity that our conversation of this morning didn't take place a few days ago."

"I'm sorry," said Boris. "Maybe we would never have had it at all if those two Germans hadn't turned up."

"That occurred to me too and you're certainly right in thinking so. Here we are. Turn round, I'll take the sack for you."

"No, I'll carry it straight into the kitchen," said Boris. Knopf stood awhile outside until Anna called him in to eat.

There was stew of meat, potatoes and tomatoes, and Boris had three helpings. This prompted Knopf to remark with a knowing wink that his loss of appetite seemed to have been only temporary. Boris, realizing how well Knopf understood him, looked over to Anna slightly abashed, but she had not noticed this little incident and merely asked whether Boris had remembered to include matches on the list of things for Pierre to bring.

"I don't remember," answered Boris. "Do we need any?"

"I still have a full box in my pocket," said Knopf. He had finished his plate of stew and suppressed a yawn. "The air in La Peine makes me tired," he declared. "I never asked Pierre how high it is. Have you any idea, Boris?"

"If you walk all the way up here it can seem like 10,000 feet, but I am sure that it's not more than 4,500."

Knopf stood up. "I must go and lie down for half an hour or so." When he had gone Anna turned to Boris. "However did you stand being completely alone in La Peine for a week?"

"I'm used to it. I've often had to be alone."

"When you were a prisoner?"

"You can be alone even when you're surrounded by people," replied Boris.

He shrugged resignedly. "It doesn't matter anyway, you're leaving soon. Are you glad?"

"My uncle is delighted. The air here doesn't suit him at all."

"What about you?"

"I often long to be in a big town. I love big towns. I liked Lyons very much, though perhaps I'd miss the mountains after such a long time spent in Escarène. My uncle thinks you ought to come to Escarène with us."

"So he has told me, too."

"Don't you want to stay with us?"

"It's not a question of wanting to or not; people like me cannot choose—we have to take what comes."

She said nothing for a few seconds, then asked quietly: "Does the fact that you can never go back to Russia make you very sad?"

"No." Boris rose quickly. He piled the empty plates on top of the pot and looked out of the window for a moment. "I will wash up. Why not go and lie down for a bit, like your uncle?"

"I'm not tired. If I had a book I would read it. Have you read much?"

"Yes, I had to."

"Didn't you enjoy reading?"

"I had more than three hundred books at home," Boris replied, picking up the pot and crockery.

At the door he heard her voice calling after him: "Boris!"

Turning round, he saw that she had got up. "I'm sorry that it makes you so sad," she said.

Boris stared at her for a long time. Then he nodded and went downstairs. Her words rang in his ears all day long and that night he dreamed of her.

He had other dreams that night, but only this one remained clearly in his memory when he awoke the next morning.

After breakfast he walked a little way down the street with Knopf. They discussed Pierre, and Knopf said that this time he was proposing to bring Gaston with him. Gaston lived near Pierre in Escarène and had often come over in the evening for a game of cards. "If you can perhaps leave me alone with them for a few minutes," Knopf went on, "I'll tell them all about you and I am convinced that they will understand. Your only danger is from the Communists. Pierre and Gaston are not Communists. I trust them implicitly."

"What would be the object?" asked Boris. "I can't spend the rest of my life in Escarène."

"It will be enough if you can stay there until the war is over. Perhaps I can still persuade Anna to come back to Düsseldorf with me. Then you could come with us."

"Do you think I'd be safer there than here?"

"That will be my concern. Anna's parents had some good friends in America and I know a few people who won't let me down. Whatever happens I must go to Germany for a few weeks."

Boris watched his hollow-cheeked profile. He had not shaved that day and the black stubble accentuated the sallowness of his skin. "Paying off old scores?" asked Boris, when Knopf did not go on.

Knopf smiled bitterly. "With whom? I shall need all my time to straighten out what is left of my life. If you have lived over half a century in Germany there is no place at the moment for any feeling except pain and sorrow. Shall we walk on a bit?"

"Did Pierre tell you when he would come?"

"No, but I expect it will be towards midday, as before."

"Then I'll stay here," said Boris and pointed to the low wall behind the church. "From here you can see the car coming."

"Providing one has eyes like yours."

"Can't you see the road?"

100

"Without eyeglasses it's too far and with glasses I can only see the olive grove as a green blob of color. If you don't mind I think I'll go and keep Anna company. I don't like her sitting around in the house by herself, she thinks too much."

"She gets it from you."

Knopf gave him a questioning look. "What do you mean by that?"

"Just a feeling of mine. Has anyone ever told you that you are a good man?"

"Oh!" Embarrassed, Knopf took off his glasses, turned them round in his hand and put them on again. "I think the postman once did in Düsseldorf, when I gave him a particularly big tip."

They both laughed and Boris said: "Well, he knew."

"No, no," Knopf shook his head. "It was a lucky chance, that's all. I recall it very well because it was a memorable day for me. I gave him fifty marks when he brought me a telegram: it was from a foreign publisher, accepting my first book."

He gave Boris a friendly nod and walked a few paces up the street, then stopped, turned half round and said: "No one is ever as good as they would like to be, Boris. See you later."

Boris waved. As Knopf walked up the remainder of the steep street he was smiling. He was still doing so when he reached their house and met Anna in the hall.

She looked at him questioningly. "I was just coming to look for you both. Where is Boris?"

"He wants to wait for Pierre. He thinks he can see the car coming as far away as the olive grove. How are you getting on?"

"I'm in the kitchen. I've put some water on to boil. If you put on another shirt I'll wash that dirty one. What are you so pleased about?"

"Pleased? What makes you think that?"

"You look so cheerful."

"Do I really?" Knopf wiped the smile off his face with his hand. "Perhaps it's because Pierre is coming today. All right, I'll go and change now—and I must shave at the same time. Can I have some hot water?"

"It'll be hot by the time you've changed."

She returned to the kitchen while Knopf went upstairs to his room. When a little while later he came down again dressed in his clean shirt, Anna was sitting on the steps in front of the house. He brought down his shaving gear and propped up a little mirror on a window ledge beside the front door.

"My razor blades are coming to an end," he said to Anna. She watched him soap his face, but her thoughts were elsewhere. After a while she asked, "Will he go with us?"

"Boris?" Knopf stopped shaving for a moment and looked towards her. "I think he will. At least, he hasn't refused to."

"Yesterday he didn't know whether he would," said Anna. "It seems to me he doesn't know what he wants."

"He knows very well. If he didn't know it wouldn't be so hard for him."

"I don't understand him," said Anna pensively.

She stared at the tiny ants which were climbing up the sunny wall of the house. They were one of the numerous minor nuisances which the abandoned village seemed to employ as weapons against its new inhabitants. There were ants in the rooms, ants in the cellars, ants marched in almost endless columns up and down the street, crawling over all obstacles, and if a person sat down on the ground they immediately had ants in their clothes. But it was a harmless variety, and Anna was used to them. She looked at Knopf again, who had now finished lathering and was wielding his razor.

"It's not really so hard to understand," he said after a pause. "I used to know two Russian emigrés in Düsseldorf, who had even managed to do quite well. One of them had his own car and he had a radio shop right opposite the station. You wouldn't remember now, but your father used to buy quite a lot from him. Whenever you talked to him you could guarantee that after two minutes he would bring the conversation round to the subject of Russia, and then there was no stopping him. After five minutes you knew what his house looked like, after ten minutes you knew his whole family and in half an hour you could have given him a lecture on Russia yourself."

"Why didn't he stay in Russia?"

"He was very wealthy, what they call a capitalist exploiter. Fortunately he had been able to transfer part of his fortune to Germany in good time, but whenever he talked about Russia, tears came to his eyes. The Russians are very fond of their country. I'd like to help Boris; I'm sure I could do something for him in Germany."

"You mean in Düsseldorf."

"I know you never want to go there again. Even if I could I wouldn't force you to go back there, although you can't spend the

102

rest of your life running away from memories. But I'm not saying that to try to make you change your mind."

He had finished shaving and went into the kitchen to rinse his face. Then he came back to Anna who had not moved from her seat on the steps and was tracing imaginary figures in the street cobbles with the toe of her sandal.

Knopf unscrewed his razor, cleaned it meticulously and wiped it on his towel. Anna did not fail to notice his frequent impatient glances down the street and she said: "It's too early yet. We had finished lunch before they arrived last time."

"Pierre keeps to no timetable," answered Knopf, looking at his watch. "It is eleven o'clock, if my watch is right. I haven't been able to check it for a fortnight. Remind me to ask Pierre."

"I still don't understand Boris," said Anna. "How can one long to go back to a country which is bound up with so many unhappy memories?"

"He must have other, happy, memories too. Just as I have."

"You are not Boris."

"I'm glad I'm not. If I never go back to Germany it will be as a result of my own decision."

"Or for my sake."

"Or for your sake, Anna. I promised your parents to stay with you."

"Is that the only reason why you do?"

"Have I ever given you cause to ask that question?"

She did not reply and Knopf sat down on the steps beside her. He took her hand in his. "When we left Düsseldorf," he said, "you were fifteen. Before that you had to spend three years hidden in an attic; your parents dared not let you out into the street. Do you remember the tiny kitchen in which we lived, all four of us—your parents, you and I?"

"I'll never forget it," she said slowly. "The window looked out on to a narrow courtyard. Then there was another house and behind that house a tree. From our window all you could see were its topmost branches. Without that tree I would often have forgotten whether it was spring or autumn. Why do you mention it?"

He dropped her hands. "Because you must come to terms with the past by yourself. I will go with you wherever you wish and not only because I promised your parents I would. I've watched you grow up. When my brother married your mother I spent three or more very lonely years. He was the younger, but my father wanted

103

him to take over the bank—which was quite right: he was wide awake, businesslike and energetic whereas I was cast in a rather different mold. I was happier buried in my books, studied law for form's sake, just managed to get as far as my doctor's degree and that was the summit of my worldly ambition. I went back to my books, started to write myself and . . . well, that was how it was. But your father was not only the most businesslike of us two, he was also what is called a good-looking man."

He stopped talking and gazed down the street again. To the north a bank of black cloud was spreading over the mountain-tops. Knopf looked at it for a few seconds then continued: "We had known your mother since childhood. Our parents were friends of her parents; it had begun as a business connection. We were both fond of her, your father and I, and we often quarreled over her, even later when we were grown up. Once I had to go away on a two-month trip. When I came back they were engaged."

He paused again, as if it were an effort for him to go on; then he looked at Anna, who sat motionless listening to him. "It took me a long time to get over it. I hated my brother then. It may seem strange to you, but forty years ago I could be extremely selfish and malicious. I only became reconciled with them when I saw how happy your mother was with him. You were the immediate cause of this. From the moment you were born I returned to their house after not having entered it for years. I still have something left from those days."

From his coat pocket he pulled out a worn leather wallet from which he extracted a post-card sized photograph. The paper was yellowed, the corners bent and Knopf smoothed it out before pressing it into Anna's hand. "Your mother gave it to me on her twentieth birthday. It might be a snapshot of you. Would you like to keep it?"

Anna stared at the photograph, then raised her head. "It must be hard for you to part with it."

"Not so much now," said Knopf with a smile. "After all, I have you. It's the only picture we have of her. And since we're talking about your mother, there is another thing you ought to know. She wished her body to be brought back to Germany after the war."

"When did she say that?"

"Her last night in Lyons when she called me to her."

Anna looked again at the photograph. Then she laid it carefully beside her on the step and asked: "Why haven't you told me any of this before?"

"Because I knew it would surprise you."

"Do you imagine it surprises me any the less now?"

"You're older now," said Knopf. He leaned over towards her. "The war is nearly over, Anna. It has set half the world on the move, but now even the dead are longing to return home. Is that so hard to understand?"

"You weren't going to try and influence me," she said, and looked past him at the black cloud bank in the sky.

"No," said Knopf. "I didn't want to influence you, Anna."

He got awkwardly to his feet, climbed the steps and went into the dark hallway. Hearing a noise behind him he turned round to see Anna come running towards him. She seized his hand and for a moment pressed it to her face. It was wet with tears and she at once released him and ran out of doors. There she bent down, picked up the photograph of her mother and ran up the street.

Knopf quickly turned back to the door. He saw her at the end of the street running towards the boulders and watched her for as long as she remained in sight. Then he heard steps coming up from the lower end of the village and turning round he noticed Boris. He was walking quickly and his face had a strange expression which Knopf had never seen on it before. When he stopped he looked in the direction in which Anna had disappeared. "What's the matter with her?" he asked.

"We were talking about her mother," said Knopf.

Boris turned half round and said: "There's a car coming."

"Pierre?"

"It's not Pierre. Is there another car in Escarène?"

"One. A red Citroën."

"This car's not red. It's dark colored, black or blue. I couldn't see it properly."

"Please fetch Anna back," said Knopf after a long pause.

Chapter 5

Now, with the approach of evening, the cool breeze had dropped. The daytime heat still radiated from the soft grassy soil and it was pleasant to lie on it and to feel the gentle warmth on one's back like an electric blanket. Georges watched the night striding along the valley, hanging black veils over the mountains as the pale gray sky darkened and lit its stars. The low bushes along the bank seemed to have been transformed into a group of gnome-like beings who stared into the water with bent backs. Up the valley at the mouth of the gorge the roar of the river now rang like the distant sound of a train rumbling over a great bridge.

Georges thought back to those evenings in Zürich when the city crept indoors and the chill breath of the mountains swept through the streets. He thought of the many hours which he had spent on the terrace of a café, the garden of a restaurant or by the side of the lake. He had always kept these memories and had never been as fond of any other city; yet at the same time he had felt hemmed in by it. Often he had the feeling of being stifled and had walked restlessly through the streets, driven by a vague longing akin to intoxication. He had often stood on a street corner and watched the clockwork play of the traffic lights which with a single blink of their colored eyes made men freeze in dumb obedience or pelt across the street in a jostling mass as if driven over by some whip-cracking tyrant. Every time he had imagined himself as one of those crowds, and had felt a violent disgust. He was simultaneously repelled and bored by this regimented activity; he could no longer appreciate its mindless perfection, having himself been involved in it *ad nauseam,* and he felt it as a form of compulsion against which his personality rose in rebellion.

Long before he had had time to think out its meaning for the individual he was sick of this perfect civilization. There was nothing left but to let oneself be carried along, ride the well-laid tracks and idolize the achievements which made this possible. Having been unable to participate in creating the world as it was, he despised all those who lived by perfecting the ideas of their forerunners, because they had no more of their own to offer. He often wished that the world would one day revert to its primitive state, and he sought this in reading adventure stories, in the romantic landscapes of American cowboy films, with whose heroes he identified himself and in so doing buttressed his sagging self-respect. But in the long run even this had been no substitute for constructive activity.

Added to a marked sense of justice and a natural distaste for all forms of coercion, his time at boarding school had been passed in the care of a teacher who bore an almost personal hatred of the system in Russia and of Communism as an ideology. It had been the most powerful impression which Georges had retained from this period and since his father—although on more generalized grounds—held similar views, this attitude had grown stronger with the years and had become for Georges the core of his dissatisfaction with his environment. The Spanish Civil War, the attempted Communist *coups d'état* in other countries, their growing strength in the parliaments of Europe and the guileless naïvete (as it seemed to Georges) with which the world reacted to Communist provocation had all provided almost boundless stimulation to the strong but undirected idealism of his nature. Suddenly he had felt himself no longer superfluous. He considered that he had formulated a viewpoint which, it seemed to him, was more important than any of those great discoveries which had changed the world; for however great these changes may have seemed they had little significance when compared to the ideology which threatened to enslave the world.

Whenever he thought back over the past three years, he often had the impression that since that dark night when he had crossed the frontier with Marcel it had never properly been daylight again. Now and again a little glimmer of light, a short flash like distant lightning, a strange glare over the tired faces. Now this glare was visible again, even through closed eyes; then when he opened them it was still there, quite distinctly cleaving the black horizon and

107

coming nearer and nearer, more and more hopeful, until it suddenly vanished. He had experienced it too often now to be deceived. A trick of the over-stimulated senses, visions of wish fulfilment from the subconscious. But there it was again, no longer on the horizon and shining clearly on the mountainside . . . the river . . . the road . . . and . . . and . . .

It's not true, thought Georges, it's not true. It can't be true, but if I'm not dreaming it must be true. I must get up, get up quickly and . . . "Marcel!" he said aloud. "Marcel, Marcel!"

They were both on their feet at the same moment, as the meadow was bathed in a bright light, the bridge, their faces and everything around them. Then they stormed up the steep embankment to the road; about fifty yards distant a car was approaching them, headlights blazing, its outline invisible to their dazzled eyes. But who could be driving to La Peine at this hour except Vieale, thought Georges, and he ran towards the car which now slowed down, steered towards the right-hand verge and stopped.

"Vieale!" shouted Georges breathlessly. "Hello there, Monsieur Vieale!" He stood laughing by the car door, which now swung open as a short, broad-shouldered man in a beret got out, walked up to Georges in bewildered astonishment, seized both his hands and stared at him, speechless. Then he looked into the car and said: "It really is them, Madame Vieale! It's our friends!"

He embraced Georges and beat a tattoo on his back. "*Mon Dieu,* believe me, I thought my eyes were playing me tricks when I suddenly saw you standing on the road. I know that face, I said to Madame Vieale, if you just picture it without the beard it must be our friend," he said at the top of his voice and turned to Marcel, who came up to him with a grin.

While they shook hands Georges walked round the car and helped Madame Vieale to get out. She was about forty, neatly built and the same height as her husband with an oval face, pretty blue eyes, a tiny red-painted mouth and dimples in her cheeks. Her reddish hair, except for a few strands on her forehead, was quite covered by a checked headscarf. She wore a plain woolen dress and low-heeled shoes which made her seem smaller to Georges than his memory of her. They exchangd a few words in French while Georges stared through the open car door into the dark interior, until he finally asked her what she had done with her son.

She hesitated and looked over at her husband, who had joined them when he heard what they were talking about. "I changed my mind," he replied for his wife. "He is with friends in Nice. But

108

please tell me how it was that you needed nearly five whole days to get from Eys to here. Did you stop somewhere? I suppose," he said to his wife, "they met a pretty girl on the way! We could fit one of you into the car since we didn't bring Philippe with us. Look at that!"

These words were directed at Georges, who had made no attempt to interrupt his flow of words and looked at him as he switched on the interior light of the car. It was stuffed to the roof with luggage, clothes and bedding. Only the front seats were clear.

"We have brought everything we could get in," said Vieale as he switched off the light. "If Madame Vieale had had her way we could have filled a truck. She wanted to pack all the furniture."

"Just you wait and see how they'll loot the house," said the woman.

"No they won't," Vieale contradicted her. "I locked it and Armand has promised me to keep an eye on the place. He's in the gendarmerie," he said to Georges. "I suggest we take one of them with us now, unload the baggage and then fetch the other one. We can be back here in two hours. Are you hungry?"

"He wants to know whether we're hungry, Georges," said Marcel. "He must be crazy."

Vieale looked uncertainly from one to the other and asked Georges: "Well, are you hungry?"

"We've eaten nothing since yesterday evening," answered Georges.

"Since yesterday evening! Wait a moment." Vieale wrenched open the car door and fetched out a large yellow bag. "Our nose-bag," he said cheerfully. "We were unfortunately a bit late because we had to go to Nice and leave Philippe. You see, it's better for the boy to be in proper surroundings. Above all he has to go to school." He looked round. "Where can we sit down?"

"On the embankment," suggested Georges.

Vieale turned to his wife: "Fetch yourself a blanket, *mon chou,* otherwise you'll find it cold."

He crossed the road with Georges and Marcel, where they sat down on the embankment in the light of the headlamps. Vieale opened the bag and took out some rolls wrapped in paper, which he distributed to the two men. "There's cheese and sausage in them," he said. "*Bon appétit, Messieurs. Mon Dieu*, I almost forgot the most important thing of all!"

He ran back to the car and spoke a few words to his wife who had found a blanket and returned with him to the embankment.

109

Vieale was swinging a bottle in his hand. "Beaujolais!" he cried. "I expect you'll remember it. Have a drink before you start eating."

He gave Georges the bottle, helped his wife to spread the blanket on the grass and sat down on it beside her. He looked on with satisfaction as Georges pulled the cork out with his teeth, put the bottle to his mouth and took a great gulp. The heavy red wine flowed smoothly down his throat, and at once produced a pleasant feeling of warmth. Then he unwrapped the rolls, bit heartily into one and slowly and pleasurably chewed the white bread thickly spread with cheese.

Vieale waited until they had finished eating and then asked: "How long have you been here?"

"Since this morning," replied Georges. He washed the crumbs from his teeth with a mouthful of wine and pulled the cigarette pack out of his pocket. He first offered it to the woman, then to Vieale and Marcel and lit their cigarettes in the same order. "We lost our way," he then went on. "We turned right too soon, at the first fork."

"I warned you specially against that," said Vieale. "But then in that case you ought not to be here at all!"

Georges nodded. "We have come from La Peine," he said, and told how they had climbed up from the other side and met Boris.

Vieale listened without once interrupting. By the light of the headlamps Georges saw that his face had changed color, but his voice sounded calm when he asked: "Did you hear any names mentioned?"

"No. But Boris thought it probable that there are some men you know among the Maquisards."

"Quite likely. I have been in Escarène a few times."

Georges watched him expectantly. It seemed as if Vieale had forgotten their presence. He stared absentmindedly into the night while the skin on his cheeks alternately stretched and slackened. From the side his face seemed carved out of wood. He had a strong chin, a straight powerful nose and big ears, one of which was half-covered by the beret pulled down on that side. His thick hair, combed straight back, was black and slightly graying at the temples, his broad forehead deeply lined. Under his coat he wore a dark brown suit.

He now turned to his wife, who sat silently beside him with her head down. "If I had had any notion of this, *mon chou,* I would have left you with Philippe." He took a wallet from his coat and extracted from it a sheet of paper. "Take a look at that," he said

110

to Georges. "We found it yesterday morning stuck to our front door with a drawing pin."

Georges looked at the paper and passed it to Marcel who grinned slightly.

"Do you see what it's supposed to represent?" asked Vieale.

"Doesn't need much imagination to see that," answered Marcel. "A gallows with a noose, drawn in red ink. Somebody must be playing a joke."

"I wish they were," said Vieale. He took the paper from him and put it back in his wallet. "What is significant is the time at which it happened. A few hours after your German comrades pulled out."

"Pulled out?" asked Georges quickly.

"It happened quite suddenly," said Vieale. "It was already dark when we heard running in the streets. We looked out and saw them tumbling out of their billets. Five minutes later they marched away."

"Do you know where to?"

"In the direction of the Italian frontier; we could find out no more than that. The Americans must be nearly in Nice. When we were with our friends we could hear their guns. People say they have taken Cannes; it was obvious along the road to Nice. There were German soldiers everywhere. Then we drove over the Grande Corniche, otherwise they would probably have requisitioned our car. They all seemed very depressed."

"I'm not surprised," said Georges slowly. He looked at Marcel. "We didn't get away a day too soon. Ritter must have known even more than he told me."

He gazed reflectively over the dark meadow towards the far side of the valley, where the outline of the mountains stood dimly out against the starry sky. Although he told himself that it meant nothing to him whether his regiment was still in Eys or not, the news moved him deeply. For the first time since he had left Ritter he realized the full significance of his action in all its finality. As long as it had still been possible he had not for a moment thought of turning back, but now that it was too late to go back he felt like a man who sees a bridge collapse behind him and is uncertain whether he would not have wanted to cross it again.

Marcel seemed to be thinking the same thing. He sat on the embankment with bowed head, his features inscrutable. He seized the bottle of wine, took a swallow and handed it to Georges. "Have a drink," he said. "It helps."

Vieale, who guessed what they were thinking, agreed with him.

111

"It's always the best thing for a man in the end. Since Pétain has been in charge the government has been running an anti-alcohol campaign. Personally I'd rather see a man holding a bottle than a rifle." He looked at his wife. "What do we do now? It would be best to drive farther north, but we haven't enough money to live anywhere where we're not known. And Nice is too dangerous for me."

"Why is it?" asked Georges. "After all, it's a big enough town for a couple of people to go underground."

"If you have money," Vieale countered. "Life is going to get costlier. We've never had to go hungry, Madame Vieale and I, but we had to think of the boy, and any money we could save went into the business. I trained as a motor mechanic. When the first war ended I was twenty. I got my master's certificate when I was twenty-eight, a year later I met Madame Vieale. By the way, she comes from Menton. Did I tell you that?"

Georges shook his head. "I was working in Menton then," Vieale went on. "Madame Vieale had a job at the hairdresser's where I went to be smartened up every fortnight. It was about the time when I was thinking I should set up on my own account. No, not a repair shop as you may be thinking; I had bigger plans. In those days hire-cars were just coming into fashion. The motor industry was developing so fast that the business had a sound future. We had to wait another three years, though, until we had the money for our first car. It was a Citroën, a rotten old crate compared with today's models, but were we proud of her! Weren't we, *mon chou?*" he said to his wife.

She nodded. "We called her by my name," she said, looking at Georges.

"And we got married the same day," said Vieale. "My brother was still alive then. These clothes," he pinched Georges' sleeve, "are his. He was almost as tall as you and five years younger than me. He stopped one near Dunkirk in May 1940. Anyhow, the Citroën, our 'Denise,' was a good start. Eighteen months later we bought the second and when war broke out there were seven. We had put every franc we had into them; buying them was expensive and so was the maintenance, even though I did all the repairs myself. Then came the war and they requisitioned six of my seven cars for the army. Today they must be running around somewhere in Paris or Germany; I never saw one of them again, not a centime's compensation did I get and finally they took me too. The last straw came when I was taken prisoner."

112

He was silent for a moment and then went on: "I'm only telling you this to explain why we have no money. If we were to go to Nice I would have to find a job, and that's too dangerous for me as long as the mob has control. I only have to be seen by someone from Eys and then I should never have another peaceful moment."

"Then we must go to La Peine after all," said Georges. "Why didn't you tell us that the cliff wall will cave in one day? Were you afraid that we wouldn't go with you if we knew?"

Vieale did not answer at once. He looked over his shoulder up the dark valley, to where the river boomed through the gorge. "Madame Vieale knows about it too and she's coming with me," he then said.

Georges grinned. He was amused by the way they both spoke of each other in the third person. He nudged Marcel: "Get it?"

"He knows what he's doing," said Marcel.

Vieale laughed and clapped him on the shoulder. "No one has ever spoken so honestly, Monsieur. No, I was really not afraid that you wouldn't come too if I told you, but why should I make a long speech about it when you could find out much better for yourself on the spot. The cliff will hold up for another hundred years yet."

"Let's hope so," said Georges. "Then I suppose you have no better suggestion?"

"Perhaps by tomorrow morning something may occur to me. I must confess to you quite frankly that I am slightly unhappy, though. More than anything I am disappointed in Boris."

"I couldn't stand him from the very start," said Marcel, and spat on to the meadow below.

Vieale scratched his neck. "Usually I can trust my judgment of people. Of course he must have been surprised when he heard that we wanted to come to La Peine too. I told him nothing about it at the time because I wasn't entirely sure whether it would be necessary. Added to which I never like putting all my cards on the table until the right moment. I really don't know what we can do."

"Then I'll make a suggestion," said Georges. "But first you'd better switch off the headlamps. There may be others moving around in the mountains at this hour. You need only leave the sidelights on."

"I was just thinking the same," said Vieale in agreement. While he walked over to the car, Georges spoke to Marcel. They spoke German to prevent the woman from understanding what they said. "You haven't got much to say for yourself," said Georges. "How about putting the great brain to work?"

113

"You can't expect any normal person to have brilliant ideas around midnight," replied Marcel.

"You don't have any in the daytime either," Georges assured him.

He waited for Vieale to rejoin them. In the last half-hour it had grown cold. The woman draped a corner of the blanket over her shoulders, and for a few seconds they leaned against the embankment without a word, listening to the monotonous drone of the river. The mountains stood up black against the sky and below them the crickets whirred.

Georges turned firmly to Vieale: "Let's suppose, Monsieur, that the Resistance men don't come to La Peine any more and we would have to live there for a few weeks with Boris, Knopf and his daughter. Would we have enough food?"

Vieale pointed his thumb over his shoulder. "Look at the car. Half of that load is food. We have a sack of flour, pies, jam and sugar. I've been preparing for this move for more than four months and you can be certain I've forgotten nothing."

"Have you gone short to save all that?"

Vieale laughed. "Not entirely. It would have been hard, though, without the five hundred liters of gasoline that I kept hidden in the cellar. I bartered it for food. Gasoline is as scarce as butter nowadays."

"So you think we'll manage?"

"Yes. Whenever we need anything I can get our friends in Nice to bring it up. I can guess what you're thinking. You're wondering how you're going to prevent the Maquis from looking after their protégés, Knopf and the girl."

"I was just going to tell you how we should do it," said Georges. "Have you brought our uniforms with you?"

"They're in the trunk, although I don't see why you want them."

"When we left you I didn't know that we would need them again. They're not the sort of things you part with too easily. Besides, it would have been too risky for you to dispose of them. Now listen, Monsieur. Tomorrow morning the car from Escarène will come up to La Peine with more food supplies. Put yourself in the place of the man driving the car and imagine that on the way, let's say in the olive grove near La Peine, you suddenly saw two German soldiers with machine carbines standing in the roadway. What would your reaction be?"

Vieale pursed his lips as if to whistle, then nodded thoughtfully.

"I would think that the fort had been occupied by the Germans. Is that what you meant?"

He's intelligent, thought Georges appreciatively, and went on: "Exactly. You would then think that the people to whom you were carrying food had either been caught by the Germans or had managed to get away in time. In either case it would be pointless for you to risk your own skin any further. You would turn round and drive back to Escarène as fast as you could. I should like you to tell me now whether you think that you would have another alternative which I haven't thought of."

Vieale stared at him for a while, then turned to his wife and said: "He is a genius, *mon chou!* What do you say?"

"Why ask me?" she replied. "I'm not a man."

"I sometimes think you act like one," said Vieale and laughed. But he quickly became serious again and said to Georges: "I think you're right. Only you must reckon with two possibilities; you must count on a stronger troop of Maquisards coming back sooner or later to make sure whether the fort really is occupied. And you must allow for Boris and Knopf not playing our game."

"I've thought of that," said Georges, with satisfaction. "Have you no more objections?"

"No," said Vieale firmly.

Georges nodded. "Of course we must frighten Knopf and Boris into acquiescence. I suggest we tell them that the Germans have brought up reinforcements and have halted the Americans. Besides which, we will say, the mountains are crawling with German troops. This would explain why the car from Escarène failed to reach them, from which Knopf and Boris only have to draw their own conclusions. Like that we shall make them into our allies, as they are as keen as we are not to fall into the Germans' hands. It's all a question of gaining time."

"Rather complicated," said Vieale thoughtfully.

"Only at first sight. What seems to you to be complicated?"

"We would have to keep Monsieur Knopf and his daughter with us longer than is actually necessary. Besides, we shall have to reckon with them getting to Escarène sooner or later and telling the whole story."

"Before it gets to that stage," declared Georges calmly, "we shall know where we stand with them. Boris will come to terms with the situation and we can probably talk Knopf round. He seems to be a reasonable man. The only element of uncertainty is the daughter. I'll take care of her. From the moment we arrive in La Peine it will be *we* who decide what's to happen. Do you agree?"

He directed his last words at Marcel, who shrugged his shoulders. He didn't like the whole business. They had discussed it the previous night, although not in such detail, but it had been enough to make him uneasy. He noticed that his own attitude to Georges had changed lately. He regarded him more critically than before and had begun to have his doubts, whereas previously he had been content to follow Georges' lead blindly. He was unwilling to admit to himself that this change in his thinking had a very human cause, but in the last few days the times had grown more and more frequent when he remembered his pale blue Chrysler coupé, sitting uselessly in the garage for the last three years. At such moments his view of Georges was at its most critical, like a woman after her wedding who wonders whether the man she has married is worth the sacrifice of her former life. These thoughts often went so far as to arouse in him almost a feeling of hatred for Georges.

"You do what you like," he now said.

Georges looked at his face from the side. "I can't do everything by myself," he said in a tone of irritation, and turned again to Vieale who was talking softly to his wife. "We haven't many chances," Georges said to him. "I can't believe that the Resistance will go on sending men up to La Peine once they know, or think, that the fort is occupied by troops. We shall just have to keep our eyes open. I'd like to see anybody getting to La Peine if I don't want them to. Of course you are twenty years older than I am. . . ."

"That has nothing to do with it," Vieale interrupted him. "It's obvious to me that you have thought everything out very carefully, and that is the main thing." He looked at the luminous face of his watch. "It is half-past twelve. Have you already decided where you want to carry out your plan?"

"You know the pass," said Georges. "When you start coming down on the far side of it the road passes through a hollow. About there. We mustn't be visible from La Peine. The question is, though, would it be better for us to spend the night here or in the olive grove?"

"Yes. . . ." Vieale looked hesitantly at his wife, then at Georges again. "One is as uncomfortable as the other. At least we should have water here."

"How long does it take to drive from Escarène to here?"

116

"There are two passes on the way. I would say about an hour and a half."

"Yes, then we can stay here," said Georges. "I am certain they won't leave Escarène so very early."

Vieale agreed and said to his wife, "Are you tired?"

She shook her head. "Not a bit. I do think it's getting chilly, though."

"I'll fetch you another blanket," said Vieale.

Georges stood up quickly. "I have a better idea. Have you a knife?"

"What do you want it for?"

"Farther down there are plenty of bushes. I think they are pretty dry. We can make a fire."

"I should have thought of that myself," said Vieale. "I have a small axe in the car. Shall I come with you?"

Georges looked at Marcel, who was squatting sleepily on the ground. "Stay with your wife. We two can go."

"I'll fetch you the axe," said Vieale.

Georges nodded and leaned over to Marcel. "What's the matter with you?" he asked in German.

"I don't know," replied Marcel. "I suddenly feel so funny."

"Feel bad?"

"No, something else. I don't like it. If only we hadn't let ourselves in for this."

"You can turn that record back three years and start playing it again. Pull yourself together. What will this woman think of us?"

"I don't care what she thinks. Why should we stick our necks out for these people?"

"Sometimes you make me sick," said Georges, and turned towards Vieale, who came across the road and gave him the axe. It was small and sharp. Georges put it over his shoulder. "Come on!" he said to Marcel.

After what seemed to Vieale an extremely long wait, he looked impatiently at his watch. "They've been gone a very long time. It will be light in three hours. I must remember to ask what their surnames are."

"I don't think they want to tell us, otherwise they would have done so already."

"If that's so I'd better not ask them. Do you think we ought to do what Georges is proposing?"

"What else would we do?"

117

"It's playing with fire, but Georges was an officer, after all. He must know what he's doing. Look, I think they're coming."

He looked down the road and saw the two men emerging from the darkness laden like mules. Each was carrying under his arm two large bundles of faggots, from which they had chopped off all the leaves and whose ends dragged along the ground behind them.

"God, what a job," said Georges. "This stuff is as prickly as a hedgehog."

"Have you hurt yourselves?" asked Vieale.

"Only a few scratches."

They walked down the embankment and dropped the branches on the meadow grass. Georges wiped his hands on his trousers. "I'll fetch a few planks from the bridge. They'll burn longer. Have you some paper?"

"I'll get you some," said Vieale. As he walked over to the car, Georges looked round for Marcel. He stood slightly to one side, hands in pockets, staring into the night.

"Dreaming?" asked Georges. As Marcel did not answer, Georges walked up to him. "If you go on like this," he said coldly, "you'd better go on your own. I don't need you."

"You've never needed me," said Marcel between clenched teeth.

Georges stared at him in silence. Then he took the axe and climbed on to the bridge. He knocked away two thick railing posts, struggling to master his ill temper. While he and Marcel had been gathering the firewood they had had a quarrel, because Marcel had said he was damned if he was going to run around like a servant for Vieale. His sudden obstinacy had infuriated Georges. They had often quarreled, but never with such venom as in the last twenty-four hours. When he thought about it he had the feeling that something alien had come between them. It annoyed him because he did not know what it was, because however he imagined the future it was unthinkable without Marcel and his blind dependence. His feeling of responsibility for him had become a kind of motive force which perpetually drove him on, and every time he challenged Marcel to leave him and go his own way, he almost shook with fear that he might one day do so.

When he tried to fix the moment of the change in Marcel's character, he always came back to the day when they had arrived in Eys and had deserted the same night. It seemed that from the very moment when they had taken off their uniforms, Marcel had altered in an indefinable way, which was as mysterious as it was annoying to Georges and it made him unhappier than he cared to admit to himself.

When he had chopped down the third post he heaved them on to his shoulders and returned to the camping place. Vieale had meanwhile pushed a small screw of paper under the pile of sticks and lit it. His wife stood near by and watched Marcel loafing idly about on the meadow, which had grown wet with dew. Even the air was now damp and cold and Georges froze in his thin tunic. He laid the posts crosswise on the sticks and watched how the fire worked its way crackling upwards and began to lick the posts with red tongues.

The fire lit up the meadow. Georges held his hands over it and eyed Vieale. In his thick coat he seemed by firelight to be even broader-shouldered, and his slanting beret gave his face a slightly piratical look. When he noticed that Georges was staring at him he returned his look and said: "I think we could all do with a brandy."

"I think so too," said Georges, and looked round for Marcel who was still standing slightly apart. "How about a brandy, boy?"

Marcel came over reluctantly. He looked frozen to the bone and had his hands deep in his pockets. "Brandy?" he asked.

"I'll fetch it," said the woman quickly and went to the car. Vieale climbed up the embankment behind her and fetched the blankets down. He spread them out on the ground and gestured hospitably. "Sit down, Messieurs!"

They squatted down on the blankets and Vieale dispensed cigarettes. The wood in the fire popped like champagne corks, sparks flew up and burned out as they fell. Vieale's wife returned with the brandy bottle and sat down beside them. She gave the bottle to her husband, who passed it round, took a hearty pull himself and sent it round again.

It was the hour before dawn; surrounded by cold, damp darkness they sat as if on a warm little island, the distant drone of the river in their ears and the mountain breeze blowing cool over the damp grass and fanning the flames.

She's still pretty, thought Georges to himself, and looked at the woman's face reddened by the fire. She sat unconcernedly with her legs apart and he saw the piece of white flesh where her long stockings ended.

Beside her Vieale was chatting to Marcel about Zürich, and Marcel was telling him that at home he had his own car and a sailing boat. Vieale asked about the make of the car and they talked shop for a while, the wife listening and showing a tactful interest.

119

As Georges looked at her legs again she noticed his glance and smilingly changed her position so that he could only see her legs as far as the knees. He listened with half an ear to the conversation between Vieale and Marcel, while watching the stars grow paler. Only when Vieale spoke to him did he turn and ask: "What did you say?"

"I said you seemed unusually quiet. What are you thinking about?"

"Nothing in particular," replied Georges and looked at Vieale's wife again. He now noticed that she had taken off her headscarf. She wore her hair combed straight back, divided by a narrow parting in the middle. In the firelight it looked more copper-colored than red; even her face, enlivened by the heat, had a coppery sheen, and Georges was completely absorbed in the sight of her.

"I was just asking your friend," said Vieale, "why you joined up with the Germans."

"That's a long story," said Georges. "Most people don't lift a finger for their convictions; we at least tried."

Vieale laughed. "That's the shortest version of a long story I've ever heard."

"We didn't go over until they attacked the Communists."

"You mean Russia."

"It's the same thing."

"Not for me," said Vieale. "You know, I like the Russians as people. They had bad luck with their history; it can happen to any nation. Look at the Germans. I don't suppose they ever dreamed that they would be dragged into such a shambles. It's something that comes like a natural disaster: suddenly it's there."

"To hear you talk," said Georges, "one would think you were a Communist."

Vieale grinned. "Now that they've labeled me a collaborator I can hardly qualify as a Communist, can I?"

"But you defend the Communists?"

"Because I'm tolerant."

Georges shot another quick glance at the wife, who was listening to the conversation with a smile. "As I see it," said Georges, "there are only two alternatives: one is either for or against the Communists. Tolerance will get you nowhere. Perhaps you might discuss it with Boris sometime."

"We got along excellently together," said Vieale.

"You can keep Boris as far as I'm concerned," said Marcel.

120

"That man is neither fish nor flesh. If he had really been anti-Communist he would have fought against them."

"Not everybody cares to shoot his own fellow-countrymen."

"The Communists had no objections to it."

"Boris is no Communist."

"We're just talking round in circles," broke in Georges. "Boris isn't a Communist, you aren't a Communist, most people don't want the Communists, but what do they do? His father," he nodded towards Marcel, "is a rabid anti-Communist too. When the Germans went for Russia he was wild with enthusiasm. And as for his mother, she's so fine that the word Communism never passes her lips. For her it's the equivalent of a mob of filthy guttersnipes. But when her son lit off to help the Germans clear away that mob, you should have seen the letters she wrote. And they're all the same. They all scream when they hear what the Communists are doing but no one will lift a finger to do anything about it. They'd rather just wait until one day they come knocking on their front door."

"It needn't come to that," said Vieale. He picked up the bottle and held it up to the firelight. "We've nearly drunk it all. There's no point in taking the rest with us." He gave the bottle to Marcel. "Have a drink, Monsieur!" He turned to Georges. "We've not much more time. It will be light in an hour."

At last he tore his eyes away and looked at the sky, where the stars were fading in the day's first light. It was starting to turn gray. The wind had dropped. The outlines of the landscape began to emerge like great ink-blots in the hazy morning light. The black woodwork of the bridge assumed a shadowy reality, and up the valley, where the river widened, a milky haze hung over the water. The air bore the scent of distant woods into the valley and the meadow grass lay flattened by heavy dew.

Slowly the fire burned out. Georges poked around with a half-charred stick in the embers, which lay like a blob of red paint in the circle of white ash. Although he had not slept in the last forty-eight hours, he felt fresh and ready for action. Since drinking the brandy he no longer even felt the cold. He felt its vitalizing warmth in his blood and his head was clear. Near by he heard Vieale talking to his wife. They spoke so softly that he could not understand them and he turned to Marcel, who sat with crossed legs looking depressed.

"The fire's going out," Georges said to him. "We might fetch a few more posts to burn."

121

"Is it worth it?" asked Marcel dully.

Vieale broke in: "Madame Vieale thinks we could make some coffee. And we have some cakes too."

"I could do with some of those," said Georges.

As he and Marcel went over to the bridge Vieale busied himself with water for the coffee. His wife fetched some cups, and when ten minutes later she dropped coffee into the boiling water and the brown, bubbling drink gave off its sharp, appetizing smell the men sat down expectantly round the fire. Georges said: "It's almost like being at home."

He turned to Vieale. "It's not much fun in Germany nowadays. Not for a soldier who knows no one. You can't forget the war for a second—even when you go to the toilet. Let's not talk about it any more."

He put his empty coffee cup on the ground between his legs and said to the woman: "You don't seem to mind sitting out all night on the cold grass."

"I hope there won't be another night," she said drily.

Georges smiled. "Even if I can promise you nothing else, you will sleep tonight in La Peine and you will sleep as well as if you were at home. Perhaps, Monsieur," he turned to her husband, "you wouldn't mind fetching our belongings from the car. We are civilized creatures and like to wash before we go to war."

They went to the car while Madame Vieale collected the crockery.

It had now grown so light that the car's sidelights were unnecessary. Vieale switched them off and opened the trunk. "We'll have to pull everything out," he said. "I put your things right at the bottom in case we were searched on the way."

"What luck that you got through safely," said Georges. "You took a great risk."

"We waited too long, that's all. It's always the way. Let's start. I put most of it into sacks because we had to carry it a little way to the car."

"You certainly took some stuff with you," said Georges, as they emptied the car. "What are you going to do with the car?"

"I'll show you when we get there. I've got a good place."

"Thought of everything," said Marcel.

"One must use one's head, Monsieur."

With three working they were soon finished. There were five sacks and three leather suitcases, plus a few odds and ends and a

122

box of crockery. "It's amazing what goes in there," said Georges with surprise.

"It's only a matter of knowing how to fit it in," said Vieale. "Here are your packs, here are your uniforms."

"The guns?" asked Georges.

Vieale pulled out two longish objects wrapped in canvas. "Are those machine carbines?"

"The latest model," replied Georges. "With locked breech-block. The only thing wrong with them is that we got them three years too late. Look at that."

He dropped the canvas cover and held the gun in his out-stretched hand. It had a short barrel and bulky breech-housing from which jutted the pistol-grip and cranked bolt. The metal parts were oiled and shining black.

"This is where the magazine goes," said Georges, showing Vieale the place. "This is the safety catch and the backsight is adjustable. I'm not mad on firing it but it's good to hold. It seems to fit so snugly into your hand. Can you understand that?"

"I'm probably too old for it," said Vieale. "I always feel sick when I look at those contraptions. I may have felt the same myself once, but in the meantime I have discovered that there are other things which fit even more snugly into your hand."

"There's a Frenchman for you," said Georges to Marcel.

They helped Vieale to put the sacks and cases back into the trunk and then carried their own things over to the campfire, where they piled the uniforms into a heap and opened their rucksacks.

"Here is the ammunition," said Marcel and laid a big, heavy bag of brown canvas on the ground. "You packed the magazines in your kit."

"We'll do that later," said Georges. "First I want to wash."

He took out what he needed for washing and walked down the gentle slope of the meadow to the river. There he took off his shirt and enjoyed himself by thoroughly cleaning his teeth. This done, he returned to the campfire, sniffing the morning air as he went, that indefinable smell of damp turf and dew-laden grass which he had smelled every day before sunrise for three years, without knowing how many more times he would be there to smell it; perhaps it was this that made it so pleasant.

As he reached the fire he saw that Vieale was holding a uniform tunic in his hand and examining it.

"Good quality stuff, this," said Vieale. "Our army was never equipped like this."

Georges turned to Marcel, who had opened his rucksack on the ground between his legs and was fumbling about inside it. "Looking for something?"

"I'm taking stock," explained Marcel. "I can throw away half of it. I've at least ten pairs of socks with holes in them."

"Throw them in the fire," said Georges. He sat down beside him and picked up the gun. "We'll burn the uniforms too. We need only keep the camouflage overalls."

"Do you mean these?" said Vieale. He pulled a mottled overblouse from the pile of uniforms, made of multi-colored canvas with big pockets and a hood. "Waterproof?" he asked.

"Absolutely," replied Georges. He turned to Marcel. "If you want to wash do it right away. Time's getting on." To Vieale he said: "There's not room for all four of us in the car. I'll sit on the fender."

Vieale looked sceptical. "You'll fall off at the first pothole."

"Not if you drive slowly. The road's strewn with stones. You won't get out of second gear all the way. Let's load up now and get going."

"As soon as I've had a wash," said Marcel and set off.

Georges helped Madame Vieale to fold the blankets. When that was done he set to work on the uniforms. Vieale watched him pull all the badges and medal ribbons from the jacket and lay them in a pile.

Georges threw the uniforms into the fire, then pulled the wide camouflage trousers of checkered canvas over his clothes. They hung down over his shoes and he tightened them round his ankles with draw-strings, which were sewn into the material for the purpose. Then he slipped the suspenders over his shoulders, pulled the blouse over his head and buckled on the broad leather belt. He pulled a crumpled peak cap from his pack and jammed it on to his head.

"At last you look normal again," said Marcel, still occupied with his camouflage trousers. He laughed furiously. "Never thought I'd have to put these old sacks on again."

"Last time, boy," said Georges.

The sky in the east was beginning to lighten. Morning came in rainbow colors over the mountains and gilded the clear peaks. The slopes on the western side gleamed like sandstone with a reddish sheen which softened their hard outlines and gave warmth to the landscape. Even the river changed color. The dull gray of its stream was broken up by reflected light which illumined its emer-

124

ald-green depths, danced over the twinkling surface and made the dewdrops glisten on the grass. Soon the whole meadow was flashing with light and the river was transformed into the silver streak of a comet which sped through the valley like an arrow and dissolved in the pale mist of the horizon. It was day.

Georges stood by the open trunk of the car and looked southward to where the silver arrow vanished. Then he took the heavy rucksack from Marcel and gave it to Vieale who stowed it in the trunk. "You can take your guns with you in the front seat," he said to Marcel.

Vieale's wife was already seated in the car and Marcel squeezed in beside her. "It will be rather a tight fit," she said and laughed.

"Oh, that doesn't matter," Marcel assured her.

Georges came to the window and spoke to him. "Comfortable?"

"We're all comfortable," said Vieale, who had climbed in behind the steering wheel.

Through the open window Marcel gripped Georges by the arm and said in German: "For the last time, Georges, couldn't we drop the whole plan?"

"It's too late now," said Georges and sat on the near-side fender. He waved to Vieale. "Off you go! What are you waiting for?"

"Look at that!" said Vieale and pointed down towards the meadow where a thick yellowish-black cloud of smoke was billowing out. "What have you been burning?" he said to Marcel.

"Ten pairs of old socks," said Marcel, in equal astonishment.

Georges burst into laughter. He was still laughing as the car drove over the steel bridge to the far side of the valley and slowly made for the spot where the valley narrowed into the gorge. Behind the dusty windshield Marcel's face, round and bearded, grinned beside the woman's shoulder, and whenever Georges turned and looked at him he started laughing again.

He's priceless, Georges thought happily.

Chapter 6

The D206 is a minor road and the only cross-country link between the N204 and the N202 in the Département of Alpes Maritimes. While the N204 leads north-eastward from Nice over the Col de Tende towards Italy, the N202 starts about three miles west of Nice where it branches off from the coast road, runs first northward to Plan-du-Var and then makes a sharp turn to the west to join the N85 just short of Digne. Near the point where it changes direction lies Plan-du-Var and a few miles farther to the north the D206 starts. It goes first eastward, climbs two small passes and eventually drops into a north-south valley. A bridge carries it over to the eastern side of the valley, from whence it follows the river northward up the valley and into the mountains. After about six miles the road forks. Straight on it leads to La Peine, while the D206 parts company from the river, makes a wide bend through a narrow valley towards the north-east only to return in a north-westerly direction to the river, from which point it climbs another pass and shortly beyond that links up with the D204.

The road to La Peine, on the other hand, continues in a straight northerly direction, past the wooden bridge carrying the road to Escarène, crosses the river by a massive steel bridge built by French army engineers and snakes its way along the left side of the gorge to a point where the gorge forks. Straight on the gorge opens out into a valley, closed on three sides, while to the right the river disappears into a deep ravine; at first the road maintains its original direction along the floor of the valley then leaps at the western flank of the surrounding mountains in an audacious hairpin bend and makes for a pass which opens out between sheer cliffs on the northern side of the valley.

Beyond the pass there is another valley forming a V-shaped cleft in the surrounding mountains. Its head points south, while at the lower end it splits into two arms, one eastward and one northward. The eastern arm is about a mile long and overgrown with a thick wood which climbs some of the way up the sides of the valley. The northern arm looks bare and harsh; it is only relieved by a thin growth of olive trees along the left-hand side. Facing the pass, on a conical mountain which forms the apex of the triangle at which the two mountain chains meet, lies La Peine. It is built on an outcrop, which projects like a jutting underlip from the side of the northward-running valley. Above it, like a giant's head, rears the great massif crowned by the fort.

In a hollow of the valley between the pass and La Peine, overshadowed by two boulders which lay like gigantic dice beside the road, sat Georges and Marcel. They had arrived there four hours before, and Vieale had driven the car up to the olive grove where he and his wife were waiting for them. The place where they sat was well-chosen. From here they commanded the road as far as the pass.

Georges sat leaning against a boulder, his legs crossed, the gun lying across them. Marcel was even more comfortable. He lay on his side with his head in the crook of his arm and chewed a grass-stalk while he stared fixedly down the road. Both were silent, and whenever they did exchange a few words it was only to break the spell of the sleepy stillness which lay over the valley like an invisible blanket. Now and again Georges glanced over his shoulder uphill to the edge of the olive grove. After a four-hour wait he was beginning to grow impatient. It was eleven o'clock and his fatigue increased in equal ratio to the growing heat of the air in the valley. Only with an effort could he keep his eyes open, and whenever he looked down into the peaceful valley with its sun-warmed stones, the dark green wood in its eastern arm and the thick undergrowth, he was overcome by a strong though completely illogical feeling of calm and security.

"What are you thinking about?" asked Marcel, but immediately forgot the question when he looked towards the mountains and saw that a blue beetle was creeping down from the head of the pass, moving slowly down the serpentine curves and drawing behind it a white plume of dust like a transparent veil. Georges had seen it too and they both stared at the blue beetle, which grew bigger at

127

every bend. Then it was no longer a beetle and they could clearly make out the outlines of a truck, its windshield flashing in the sun.

Georges stood up and looked at Marcel, who had gone white in the face and was watching the truck with half-open mouth.

"It's them!" said Georges stepping on the road. It ran steeply out of the hollow up the right-hand flank of the mountainside, traversed along the sheer cliff eastward for about three hundred yards and then began its series of hairpin bends leading to the pass. Following a sudden impulse Georges glanced behind him, where he saw Vieale and his wife coming down the road. They could not yet have noticed the truck, because the stretch of the road where they were walking was screened by a bend.

Their unexpected appearance bewildered Georges so much that for a few seconds he paid no attention to the truck, which had meanwhile reached the last bend and begun to move down the long straight stretch towards the hollow. Now Vieale must have seen it. He suddenly stopped, seized his wife by the hand and ran with her to the boulders beside the road. As they disappeared from sight, Georges turned back to look at the truck and saw immediately that it had halted. It was now about four hundred paces away and stood poised on the steep road like a horse shying away from a chasm.

Right, they've seen us, thought Georges and looked round for Marcel. He saw him standing three yards back on the roadside, his face still white. As Georges stared at him he came hesitantly up and said in a voice hoarse with excitement: "If they've got guns they can knock us out on the spot. We're standing here like a couple of targets."

"We needn't stand here any longer," said Georges. "They know now that we're here."

He walked to a low rock on the left side of the road and positioned himself behind it so that he could keep the truck under observation. Marcel quickly followed him. "What are they waiting for?" he asked nervously.

Georges gave no reply. His hands were damp. He wiped them on his trousers and laid the gun on the rock in front of him. A glance behind showed him that Vieale and his wife were still hidden between the boulders. Now that he was no longer sitting in the shade he realized how hot it was. Farther up the road, where the hollow narrowed to a mere cutting, a breeze was blowing. The branches of broom waved gently to and fro, and over the mountains a falcon sailed through the blue sky.

128

"If they don't do something soon in that crate up there," said Georges, "I'm going up to say good morning to them."

"For God's sake don't go and do anything stupid, man," said Marcel, terrified. "Look, someone's looking out from the back."

"That's not just someone. There are three or four of them in there," said Georges, shielding his eyes against the sun with his hand. At the same moment the truck started to move backwards. The noise of its powerful engine could be heard down in the hollow. Georges watched the driver stick his head out of the window as he reversed, while the head looking out of the back disappeared.

"They're clearing off," said Marcel. He grinned with relief and nudged Georges with his elbow. "They're really clearing off."

"I'd like to know why they're pulling out," said Georges.

He had an unpleasant feeling, and when the truck stopped as it reached the first bend, he felt the sweat running down his face. Something's wrong, he said to himself. Boris made out that they would come with two men, but it looks as if the whole truck's full of them.

"They're stopping again," said Marcel uneasily. "Why are they doing that now?"

Georges wiped the sweat from his face. "We'll soon see."

"You said yourself that they would turn back as soon as they spotted us. Why aren't they going?"

"When I said that," replied Georges, "I was counting on there being only two men. But there are——"

He broke off and stared intently at the truck as the door on the driver's side was flung open. In spite of the great distance they could see a man jump out and vanish behind the truck. When he reappeared two other men were with him. They stood beside the truck for a while, then one got in again while the others moved to the roadside. The truck started up and maneuvered back and forth until it had turned round.

Georges could now see its rear. The bow-shaped superstructure of its load platform was open at the back, the inside dark, and although Georges strained his eyes he was unable to make out how many men were sitting in it. Then the truck drove away rapidly uphill towards the pass. The two men who had stayed behind stood for a time on the road and seemed to be watching the truck go. Finally they sat down on the embankment beside the road, their faces turned towards the hollow, and moved no more.

Georges slung his carbine over his shoulder, glanced at Marcel's perplexed face and walked back into the road, where he kept a lookout for Vieale. He knew that the two men were watching his every move, and for a few seconds fury and disappointment made him incapable of making a decision. As Vieale did not show himself he turned to Marcel, who was still standing behind the boulder and staring up at the two men. "Find Vieale and go back to the car. Wait there for me."

"What are you going to do?" asked Marcel anxiously.

Georges looked up at the two men. "I'm going to take a closer look at them. Do as I tell you." He started out, walking rapidly up the road, unslinging his gun to carry it in his right hand.

It was about five hundred yards to the bend where the two strangers had taken up station. Even after the first fifty yards Georges could feel the sweat running down his whole body. The heat was doubly strong under the thick weatherproof camouflage suit. The sweatband of his cap stuck clammily to his forehead. He took it off and stuck it in his belt. Another fifty paces and he was out of the hollow; the road drew nearer to the steep mountainside, and with every step that he took the valley dropped a little lower to his left. He did not take his eyes off the two men for a second. They sat motionless by the roadside watching him. When he did look back he saw three black dots on the far side of the hollow moving slowly along the road. This made him feel slightly easier, and as he strode on he pushed back the safety catch of the gun with his thumb.

He was now about three hundred paces from the men. High above him he saw the second hairpin bend on the road. Then Georges noticed that the two men had stood up. They were of equal height, poorly dressed, one bareheaded, the other wearing a beret. In their hands they held short-barreled sub-machine guns. They must have had them lying beside them and as he saw them Georges felt his heart stop for a moment. He stopped and looked back.

The three black dots had now disappeared beyond the hollow. If it came to a fight he would be quite alone and he knew his chances were small. The two men had the hairpin bend behind them with its corner of dead ground against his fire, while he was without cover on the open road and completely exposed to the fire of their automatic weapons. But his thought disturbed him much less than the question of what had become of the others who were still in the truck. From where he stood he could see no farther up the road and he would have given a lot at that moment to know where the truck had disappeared to.

130

He looked at the men again. Although he could not see them properly it seemed to him that they were considerably older than himself. The bareheaded one wore a red kerchief round his neck, and to judge by their movements they were talking to one another. Now they turned round, walked round the bend a short distance up the road and stopped again. Their strange behavior increased his tension and he suddenly had the feeling that they were trying to delay him. He looked across the valley to the wedge-shaped peak at the junction of the two mountain ranges; he remembered how two days before he and Marcel had climbed up the other side to La Peine, and then a terrible thought came to him.

He turned round and walked down the road, slowly at first and then faster, stopping occasionally to look back at the two men who had again taken up their previous position and were staring after him, but they made no attempt to follow him; he soon regained the hollow and took the steep road leading to the olive grove.

On this side of the mountains the heat was even more unbearable, and the dusty road threw off the heat like a kiln. Despite this he did not stop once and by the time the worst of the slope was behind him and the road had leveled off slightly towards the olive grove he could hardly keep on his feet. For the last two hundred yards he could only drag himself along with bowed head. He looked up when he was nearing the olive trees and heard Marcel's voice calling his name. He saw him standing in the middle of the road. Neither Vieale, his wife, nor the car were to be seen. He walked weak-kneed up to Marcel, who looked horrified at the sight of his face.

"Where's Vieale?" asked Georges. He found talking difficult and he was panting with the strain of the climb.

Marcel jerked his thumb over his shoulder. "Behind the bend; the car can't be seen from there. What's the matter? Did you talk to them?"

"I changed my mind," Georges replied. He mopped his face with his handkerchief, then hurriedly replaced it in his pocket. "We must get to La Peine as fast as possible, otherwise the Maquisards will be there before us."

Marcel stared at him in astonishment. "Do you think they're going on to La Peine after all?"

"I don't know. It was just an idea."

"But if they want to get there they must come past here!"

"Did we come past here the first time we went up to La Peine?"

131

"Damn! Of course!" said Marcel and the hand holding his gun trembled.

Georges changed his machine carbine from his right to his left shoulder. "Perhaps they won't. Did you ask Vieale why he didn't stay with the car?"

"The wait was too long for him," said Marcel and looked nervously down the road. "He started to get worried."

"That's a habit he will have to lose. It was unbelievably stupid of him. Those fellows most certainly saw him and his wife."

"It frightened him badly," said Marcel.

"Much good that is to us. Come on, now; we must move. I won't feel safe until we're in La Peine."

Five minutes' hard marching brought them past the turning where Vieale had concealed his car. He and his wife were sitting beside it on the embankment. Georges immediately noticed that the woman had taken off her coat. In her blue, short-sleeved dress she looked like a young girl. Vieale too had removed his coat and jacket and rolled up his shirt sleeves to show his hairy, muscular arms. When he heard them coming he jumped to his feet and ran towards them.

"At last!" he shouted with relief. "We felt we were sitting on hot coals, waiting for you for so long." He stopped in front of Georges and looked at him expectantly. "Did everything go all right?"

"We wouldn't be here if it hadn't," answered Georges. "We must drive on at once."

"What about the two men?"

"Nothing to worry about. Once we reach La Peine they can do what they like."

Vieale hesitated. "Your friend told me you wanted to talk to me."

"I did want to, but I've changed my mind. You must put our camouflage suits back into the car for a while. You shouldn't have let yourself be seen, Monsieur."

"I'm sorry," said Vieale in embarrassment. "We just couldn't bear sitting about and waiting any longer."

"You'll have to get used to bearing it for a few weeks now. I do what I can, but if you don't listen to me I can't vouch for what happens."

"That doesn't sound as if everything did go as well as you say," said Vieale sharply. "You're hiding something from us."

Georges looked over to Vieale's wife. She had stood up and

132

was slowly walking towards them. "I'm not hiding anything from you," he answered. "We'll have to be careful, but I already warned you of that this morning. As soon as we're in La Peine I'll have a careful look at the surroundings. I like to feel sure." He smiled at the woman. "I'm sorry you had to wait so long."

"We were careless," she said.

Georges shook his head. "It was all right. Nothing happened, don't worry."

He laid his gun on the ground and pulled off the trousers of his camouflage suit. Marcel did likewise, then they packed them in the trunk of the car. As he shut the cover Georges shot an appraising glance overhead. The pile of cloud to the north had grown a great deal bigger and was eating up the blue from the sky with its sulphur-yellow jaws. The mountains too were changing their color, as if a dark veil was dropping over them.

"How do you like the look of that?" said Georges to Vieale, who had stopped close beside him and was also staring at the sky.

"It looks like a nasty thunderstorm," replied Vieale in a worried voice. "Once it starts here in the mountains it's like hell let loose."

"Then let's hurry up, so that we get a roof over our heads," said Georges as he picked up his gun. He slung it across his back and waited until the others were seated in the car. Then he climbed on to the fender and Vieale started the engine.

Through the wood the road surface was good. The trees had held up the stones rolling down from the mountainside, but as soon as the road ran into the open for the last five hundred yards before the viaduct it was covered with stones. Vieale had to throttle back and steer carefully between rocks and stones.

The viaduct rested on two tall piers, firmly anchored in the rock-strewn floor of the valley. At this point the valley narrowed almost to a ravine, widened out again after the viaduct, and after taking a crooked course between the encroaching mountains it came to an end at the cliffs which shut it off to the north. There was still a good two thousand yards of the valley in front of them, and as the car rolled over the viaduct Georges noticed a wide path which led up the right-hand side of the valley and disappeared behind a jutting outcrop. When they had walked down the same road two days previously he had been unable to see it, and he was wondering where it might lead to when Vieale brought the car to a halt.

"It leads to my garage," he said, pointing to the path. "There's a quarry behind the fort. It was working when they built the fort. You can easily drive up there; I'd show you if we had more time.

133

The workmen blasted a cave in the rock-side as a protection against falling stones. It's just big enough to get the car into. As soon as we've unloaded I'll drive it down there."

"We won't make it before this thunderstorm breaks," said Georges.

Vieale looked up at the sky. "Perhaps we will. First we'll put all the baggage in the tunnel on the other side. We can wait there until it's over."

He drove on and steered the car round a sharp right-hand bend. It was now so steep that he had to drive in second gear. Soon they reached the first tunnel, after which the road surface became extremely bad. Georges was forced to dismount several times and remove big stones before they could continue. It took them half an hour to travel from the first tunnel to the spot where the road ceased, and at the same moment that Vieale stopped the car in front of the gap the sun darkened and a violent gust of wind whirled a cloud of dust across the road.

Georges quickly jumped down from the car and looked upwards. The sky was now the color of basalt, the ragged-edged clouds chased sulphurous wisps of vapor before them and the thunder was rumbling in the distance as if an enormous iron barrel was rolling downhill. Georges waited until Vieale emerged from the car.

"We won't make it," he said to him. "The weather may break at any minute. Let's take what we can carry and go and sit over there in that tunnel. Open the trunk, I want to get out my groundsheet."

While Marcel and the woman got out of the car Vieale opened the trunk. Georges put the groundsheet in his pack, which he now dragged a few yards to one side. A glance at the car showed him that no one was watching him. He put down the groundsheet beside him, then took the ammunition bag out of the pack and hastily stuffed his pockets full of cartridges. He had just finished when Vieale approached him.

"We'll only take the three suitcases with us," he said. "They are easier to carry than the sacks. Madame Vieale will take the bag with provisions. We may get hungry if the thunderstorm lasts a long time."

"Let's hope it doesn't," said Georges. "That would just be the last straw." He looked round for Marcel, who was helping Vieale's wife unload the suitcases.

134

"You can take your rucksack," Georges said to him. "It won't hinder you if you're carrying a suitcase."

"What about the camouflage overalls?" asked Marcel. "Are we to leave them in the car?"

Georges shook his head. "We'll pack them into the rucksack."

Vieale and his wife were now also ready. They had to put on their coats again, and then Vieale carefully locked the car doors. Before they set off Georges took another look at the gap in the road; it was not a smooth break, but jagged and irregular, as if someone had broken a plank across his knee. They climbed with care down the steep slope until they reached the terrace-like outcrop. Here they were obliged to traverse the two-hundred-yard-long path which led round the landslip débris, and as Georges stopped to wait for Marcel to catch up with him he put down his suitcase and gave an appraising look over the long sheer drop below.

"I don't understand how this happened," he said to Vieale. "The mountainside must have slid down like a toboggan."

Vieale laughed. "It was more than a toboggan, Monsieur! There was once a three-hundred-foot cliff on this spot. It crashed into the valley and took a fair chunk out of the mountain with it. That's why that great hole is still there. The granite didn't shift, but the layers of other sorts of stone above it were torn away with the falling cliff. Let's hurry and get across. If the storm gets up it will blow us off this ledge like scraps of paper."

They had covered about three-quarters of the way and were just negotiating a tangled mass of jagged branches and tree-trunks when it quite suddenly grew dark. Involuntarily they stopped and stared at the sky, to see a jet-black stream of cloud racing over the valley above them. Almost simultaneously a lurid serpent of flame lashed across the sky, a violent gust blew down from the mountains and then there was a clap like an exploding gas tank.

Georges felt the woman's hand clutch his coat sleeve, and in the second of quiet that followed the thunder he heard Vieale's voice utter a curse. The next squall announced its coming with a thin whimper which rose to a shrill howl, and as they went on their way in violent haste the first big raindrops splashed down on them. But the worst part was now behind them and the full violence of the storm only struck them as they panted up the last steep stretch to the road. This time Georges felt the woman's hand on his leg and he waited until the storm slackened off for a moment, then climbed the last few yards dragging her behind him; he threw the

135

suitcase on to the roadway and pulled her up with his free hand. For a second their faces touched and Georges kissed her on the mouth. It happened without his willing it and afterwards he never knew how it could have occurred. The woman at once pulled herself free and he watched confusedly as she ran into the tunnel. Then he heard Vieale's voice beside him: "Take this suitcase for me, Monsieur, I'm completely out of breath."

Georges helped him up on to the road and watched Marcel who was now struggling up the last stretch. In a moment they were all running through the mountain rainstorm into the tunnel. Here it was so dark that at first they could see nothing. They put down their suitcases and Vieale looked round inquiringly. "Are you there, *mon chou?*"

"Here I am," his wife replied. She was standing on the right-hand side of the tunnel, and Vieale was only able to recognize her when his eyes had accustomed themselves to the gloom. He walked over to her and they spoke quietly to one another.

Georges had stopped beside Marcel at the mouth of the tunnel. After the incident with the woman he was nervous, and the whispering between husband and wife increased his uneasiness. Although he thought it unlikely that she would tell her husband about it, he still cursed his impulsiveness.

You must have gone mad, he said to himself, people just don't do those things, my boy. It was unforgivable, and if she does tell him that you kissed her you're going to spend an uncomfortable few weeks. Vieale is not the man to laugh it off if he catches you at that game.

The longer he thought about it the more worried he became. He had already decided to find out what they were talking about when the thunderstorm broke in full force. The entire landscape was brilliantly lit up, and for a fraction of a second the outlines of the mountains were etched against the black sky, then the flash of light vanished with a shattering crash and their place of refuge turned into a wind tunnel. Georges felt the force of the storm seize his body, spin him round and take away his breath, while the pattering rain outside the tunnel rose to a steady roar. He heard Marcel shout something incomprehensible, and almost simultaneously they bent down to pick up the cases and ran, half propelled by the wind, deeper into the tunnel. They joined Vieale and his wife, who had pressed themselves flat against the wall, and they all ran through the darkness illumined by ceaseless flashes of lightning as far as a sharp left turn of the tunnel; as they turned the

136

corner they saw the farther mouth of the tunnel forty yards on, gleaming like a gray patch in the darkness.

Here the storm blew less violently. Georges noticed that it was most bearable on the inner side of the tunnel and said: "We can sit on the rucksacks. If we're lucky it'll be over in an hour."

"We've been very lucky already," said Vieale. "If the storm had caught us out on that ledge we'd be down at the bottom by now." He was breathless from running and he leaned exhaustedly against the rock.

"We'd be better off sitting in the car," said Marcel between chattering teeth. "This place is as drafty as a sieve."

Georges looked at the woman. She had so far said nothing and her persistent silence was making him gradually more uncomfortable. He unbuckled his pack-straps, dropped the rucksack and said to Marcel: "Help me carry the suitcases over here. If we pile them up we can make a screen against the wind."

"We should have stayed in the car," Marcel repeated obstinately. "We only needed to squeeze up a bit. . . ." He broke off. The tunnel mouth was for a second flooded in dazzling light, then came a deafening clap of thunder. "For Christ's sake shut up!" he screamed in German.

Vieale burst into laughter. "We couldn't help hearing that, Monsieur. What did you say?"

"He was asking Christ to shut up," Georges translated with a grin. He now felt certain that Vieale's wife had said nothing and he grew bold. "Are you frightened too?" he asked her.

"Not so much as the time before," she replied.

"Then I'm sorry you were frightened then," said Georges. "It came so suddenly."

"Yes, quite suddenly," she said and he could hear from her tone of voice that she was smiling. Relieved, he clapped Marcel on the shoulder. "Come on, you idle old bastard! Give me a hand with those cases."

With Vieale's help it was not long before they were sitting huddled together on the rucksacks and screened from the wind by the pile of suitcases. Madame Vieale asked: "Would anybody like something to eat?" She sat between her husband and Georges, who could feel her legs alongside his own and he thought he could sit there forever.

"I'm not hungry," said Vieale. "But if the Messieurs will have something I will eat too."

"Then let's all eat," Georges proposed. It was still pitch dark in the tunnel and they could hear the storm lashing the mountain outside. Only the flashes of lightning had grown less frequent and the thunder, too, sounded more distant. Madame Vieale handed round sandwiches; when they had finished eating they lit cigarettes.

Georges heard Madame Vieale sigh beside him and as he was about to put his hand into his pocket he touched her hand. He waited for her to pull her hand away, but she left it there and he cautiously took it in his and stroked it. She had long smooth fingers, cool to the touch; he pushed his fingers between hers and squeezed them, and she returned the pressure. Then she slowly withdrew her hand and said: "I was just thinking about Philippe."

Georges came abruptly to his senses. The lust which had blazed up in him at this contact sank down as if the woman's words were a bucket of water which she had thrown over him. He felt the blood rush to his face and sat motionless for a few seconds. Then he quickly stood up and said in a hoarse voice: "Do you often think of Philippe?"

"Does it surprise you?" asked Madame Vieale.

"No," replied Georges. "No, it doesn't surprise me."

Vieale laughed. "Madame Vieale is a model mother, Monsieur. She lives only for her family."

"However hard it may be at times," she said.

"Don't you believe it," said Vieale. "That's just her way of talking. I know Madame Vieale."

"Do you know me?" asked his wife.

"Do I know you, *mon chou!*" In the dark Vieale put his hand in her lap for a moment. "Don't we know each other?"

"If you say so," she answered, "then I suppose you do." She looked up at Georges, whose face was dimly visible. "Why did you get up, Monsieur?"

"Because I'm going to La Peine," said Georges. "I want to be sure that everything's all right there before we all four arrive."

"Why shouldn't everything be all right?" asked Vieale in astonishment.

"You never know," said Georges. "A lot can happen in two days. I don't think anything has happened, mind you, but I just want to be certain."

Vieale also stood up. "But you can't possibly go outside in this weather, Monsieur. It's raining bucketfuls."

"I have my groundsheet."

138

"Let him," said Marcel. "We're used to marching in the rain. In Russia——"

He was interrupted by the woman. "Has this idea just come to you?" she said to Georges.

Georges shook his head. "I thought of it before we ever got here."

He slung his machine carbine muzzle downwards over his shoulder and slipped his head through the slit in the groundsheet so that it covered his whole body as far as his knees. "If I don't come back by the time the rain stops," he said to Vieale, "don't wait for me. I reckon we'll have to make four journeys to get all the baggage up there. I'll take a suitcase with me now."

"You'll kill yourself dragging it along in this storm," said Vieale.

Georges looked towards the tunnel mouth. "It's easing off a bit. There's no more lightning and rain never harmed anybody." He took the topmost suitcase from the pile and said to Marcel: "I need you for half a minute."

They walked down the tunnel together. Georges stopped at the mouth. "I didn't want Vieale to listen to us. He pretends he doesn't understand a word of German, but he was a prisoner-of-war long enough to have learned some. As soon as it gets light go and take a look at the road. I admit it's improbable that those two fellows would dare to follow us, but you must keep a lookout all the same."

"And if they do come after us?" asked Marcel.

"Shoot a round into the air. The sides of the valleys will carry the sound. I can rejoin you in ten minutes if I run. For the time being there's no need to keep Vieale informed. I'll climb down the slide a little and take a look at the road. Did I tell you that those two have got guns with them?"

"No!" Marcel looked terrified. "That you didn't tell me."

"Well, you know now. Don't let them come too near. They probably have automatic rifles or machine pistols, but they certainly haven't the same range as our carbines. You should be able to keep them out of range."

Marcel had not recovered from his fear. "But you told me only to shoot in the air. Suppose they fire at me."

"If they shoot at you, shoot back. I don't think they will, though, because they didn't fire at me even though I was a sitting target. If they really wanted to take a shot at you they'd have to climb past the landslide gap and they won't be so crazy as to do that. Look after the woman. If anything happens to her, you and I are finished."

139

"What's she to do with you?" grumbled Marcel. "Her husband can look after her. He's the one who sleeps with her."

Georges stared at him for a while. Then he turned round and strode out of the tunnel into the open.

Marcel gazed after him in amazement. "What's the matter with you?" he shouted. As Georges paid no attention he cupped his hands in front of his mouth and roared: "Go on, then! Go to the devil, damn you! I don't need you!" He shook with agitation and watched as Georges marched head down up the road, to be soon swallowed up by the swirling, low-lying shreds of cloud which covered the road.

All because of some bitch of a woman, thought Marcel bitterly, almost weeping with rage.

His last words had been inaudible to Georges. The storm was still so violent that it drowned any other sound, but it was at his back and he moved fast. The nearer he came to La Peine the worse the visibility grew, and in many places the clouds hung so low over the road that he was unable to see three yards ahead.

The rain beat with an even rhythm on the slippery asphalt, stretching out black and shiny beneath his feet. The lightning had almost stopped. In between the infrequent flashes, like the dull rumbling of a landslide, distant thunder rolled across the sky, growled along the valleys and died away in the monotonous roar of the rain.

To judge by the time taken he reckoned by now to have covered the greater part of the way. The distance seemed longer today, perhaps due to the suitcase which dragged painfully at his arm. He decided to take more of a rest in the next tunnel. If his calculations were right, the Maquisards' truck would need at least an hour to reach the point from which he and Marcel had climbed up to La Peine. Four hours could be added to that for the climb and it was out of the question for them to appear before late afternoon, if they appeared at all. He considered it doubtful, but he had come to terms with the idea and it no longer worried him. He did not believe that they would use force. Perhaps they just wanted to make sure whether La Peine really was occupied by German troops, and it would not be too difficult to convince them that it was, without getting seriously embroiled in a fight.

He looked impatiently ahead to where the dark mouth of the next tunnel was looming through the cloud. Georges quickened his pace and he had all but reached the tunnel mouth when he noticed two men.

They were standing in the entrance, and Georges at once felt a spasm of fear. Instinctively he reached for the gun under his groundsheet, but then he recognized them. He quickly approached them and asked: "What are you doing here?"

"We might ask you the same question," answered Boris.

"We were waiting for you," said Knopf.

Georges gave him a suspicious stare. "For me? You had no idea we were coming back."

"Boris saw the car. We thought it might be you and came to meet you. When the storm broke we turned round, but we managed to get as far as here. Where have you left your friends?"

"They're waiting until the rain stops," said Georges. He now felt safer and put down the suitcase. "I'm sorry we had to come back. Monsieur Vieale has bad news for you."

Knopf started. "For us?"

"He'll tell you," said Georges. "For the moment we must stay in La Peine." He looked at Boris. "I hope you don't mind."

"I've told you what I think about it," said Boris icily.

Knopf laid his hand on his arm. "We discussed the problem. La Peine is big enough for us all."

"I think so too," said Georges, and bent down to pick up his case. Boris quickly barred his way. "Why don't you stay here until the rain stops?"

"We've a car full of baggage. If we delay any more in unloading it'll be dark."

"The others are waiting, though."

"I don't mind the rain. Vieale has his wife with him."

"If you're going to La Peine," said Boris. "I'm going with you." His determined expression showed Georges that he meant what he said. He grinned mockingly. "Are you afraid that I'll clear you out of your villa?"

"Think what you like."

Georges put down the suitcase again. "Look here, I put up with your attitude for a whole day. Now I can't stand any more of it."

Boris looked at his shoulder, where the outline of the gun showed beneath the groundsheet. "Because you have your gun, I suppose?" he asked with a sneer. "You feel safer now than you did the day before yesterday."

"That's a pretty childish conclusion to come to. A man in your position has to be a bit smarter."

141

"In what position?" asked Boris. "In that of a deserter?"

Georges looked over at Knopf. As he betrayed no surprise, Georges nodded. "So it has occurred to you. Whether it's any use to you in the long run, time will tell."

Before Boris could counter him, Knopf broke in. He had listened uneasily to the altercation and now said: "I can't see what you two have to quarrel about. I'd rather you stayed with me, Boris. The rain may last for some time." To Georges he said: "I can't manage walking in this weather without a coat, otherwise I'd go with you both. But perhaps I may ask you to do me a favor —please tell my daughter where we are. In case the storm doesn't blow over soon, ask her to bring me my coat. Will you see that she does?"

"If I see her," said Georges. As he set off he felt Boris staring after him, and he wondered again what the Russian had against him.

He hates me, he said to himself. I shall have to watch out for him. And why didn't he want to let me go to La Peine alone? As if there was something there I ought not to see. Or is he really so naïve as to think that I would loot their house? I can't believe that, so he must have some other reason; but what? The girl? The girl, he thought, and stood still for a second. Of course—the girl! Why didn't I think of that right away? But still—that can't be it. He's at least twenty years older than she is and I simply can't imagine . . . impossible, he interrupted himself. Probably he's managed to arouse her sympathy. Now I'm just curious to see how she looks.

He had to take care now not to miss the way to La Peine in the thick cloud and mist. The drop on the valley side of the road was bottomless and nearly invisible. Its edge was formed by a narrow curbstone with a runnel-like depression, but which was inadequate to carry off the floodwaters of the storm. In many places the road was like a riverbed and little waterfalls cascaded down from the mountainside on the left. Now and again the crash of a falling rock could be heard. At every one of these Georges stopped and looked upwards, holding his breath. The mountain was invisible, shrouded in cloud, and Georges had the feeling that it was listening to every step he took. He walked faster, and when he finally reached the spot where the path branched downwards he felt warmer and quite relieved. He was not timorous, but this deserted, stone-spattered road, which wound like a narrow ridge between heaven and earth, stirred up a feeling of unease.

He stopped for a moment. His hope that the rain would stop had come to nothing. Below the road it looked even worse. There the clouds were massed into a thick fog. Strain his eyes as he might, Georges could not even make out the outline of the town hall, and the steep path vanished in the white vapor after a few yards. It was stony, much washed away by rain and cut diagonally across the flank of the mountain towards the foot of the great cliff which overhung the village.

Georges started cautiously down the path. The cliff rose over him like a gigantic shadow, and when he finally crossed the little semi-circular square with its cypress tree he felt like someone coming home after a long journey.

He saw the girl before he reached the gateway through the town hall. She wore a raincoat with a hood. Her hands were thrust deeply into the slanting pockets and she stood motionless in front of the gateway looking at him. He wondered that she made no attempt to run away, but she had probably noticed from his trousers that he was no soldier and had not been frightened by the sight of the German army groundsheet. He walked over to her, put down his suitcase and looked curiously into her face. It was not quite as he had imagined it, and when he looked into her eyes he understood why Marcel had said that her most striking feature was their color. They were amazingly big and deep brown, dominating her face. Her slightly hollow cheeks were emphasized by strong cheekbones, although her face as a whole gave an impression of being very narrow and her mouth, too, was narrow with a sharply drawn lip-line.

Rather nice, thought Georges, and said: "Good morning. Are you waiting for your father?"

"Did you meet him?" she asked, without returning his greeting.

Georges felt the same sensation as did Boris when he heard her voice for the first time. He looked at her in surprise and thought, from her voice she could be thirty. Aloud he said: "He's waiting in the first tunnel along the road from here. If the rain doesn't stop he wants you to take him his coat."

"I would have taken it already," she said, "but he made me promise to wait for him here."

"Perhaps it'll stop soon," said Georges, looking out of the gateway at the sky. Then it occurred to him that she was not talking to him as to a stranger and he asked: "How do you know me?"

"I saw you the day before yesterday," she said.

"When we were sitting in front of your house?"

"Yes."

"Did you listen to us?"

She was almost a head smaller than he and took a step back the better to see his face. "I did not listen to you," she said coolly. "When I came into my room I heard your voices and looked out of the window. What you were talking about was no business of mine."

"Then you are a well brought-up girl," said Georges. "In your place I would have made it my business."

"I know that some men are inquisitive."

Georges grinned. "You get like that in a war. If I weren't so inquisitive I should probably be dead by now. The only thing that arouses my curiosity is to know what it is you have against us; you didn't want us to stay in La Peine. Why not?"

"Who told you that?"

"Your friend."

"I have no friend," she said.

"Haven't you really?" asked Georges. As she gave no answer he sat down on the suitcase and wrung out his soaking wet trouser-legs. The gun got in his way, so he pulled off the groundsheet, unslung the carbine and propped it up against the wall.

"I was wondering," he said. "Are you really only seventeen?"

As she still did not reply he looked up at her and saw that she was staring at the gun. "Do you like it?" he asked.

She looked sharply away from the weapon and asked: "Why did you bring it with you?"

"Because I've grown attached to it," said Georges. "Later I want to hang it over my bed as a souvenir. Do you understand anything about guns?"

"No. Where are your friends?"

"They preferred to wait for better weather. Just like your father. Boris was a bit worried about you. He was determined to come with me."

"Then why didn't he?"

"Your father was against it. He was afraid he'd get bored without Boris's company. I thought Boris was your friend."

"You have a very vivid imagination, soldier."

Georges was taken aback by this remark, then he smiled. "My name's Georges. And the soldier business is finished. I'm a civilian now."

"All the same I shall call you soldier."

He stood up and said: "I'm afraid the rain will go on for some time. If I were you I'd fetch the coat and take it to your father."

She turned her face towards him. "I was just going to ask you to do it for me."

"I'm sorry," said Georges. "I hate refusing a girl anything."

"Won't you do it?" she asked.

Georges wiped the water from his wet, matted hair. "I'm here as a sort of billeting officer for the others. I hope you will understand when I say that I haven't time for anything else."

For a while she looked at him in silence. Then she turned slightly round so that her back instead of her shoulder was leaning against the wall and said: "You're not very polite, are you?"

"It's a question of self-control," said Georges. "That was never my strong point."

"What is your strong point?"

Georges smiled and stared for a moment at her beautiful slim legs. "That depends," he said and glanced at his watch. More than two hours had passed since the truck had driven up the pass. He had no more time to lose. "I must look round for a billet."

"Shall I help you?"

"Thank you, I can do it better by myself. You'd better go to your father, otherwise he'll think I've held you up."

"I'll tell him that you didn't hold me up."

"Listen to me, girl," said Georges nervously, "I don't want to cause any trouble here. If you'll just make your Boris drop this childish jealousy we can all get along together."

She looked at him, amused. "What makes you think that Boris is jealous?"

"I'm not blind. Do you want to marry him?"

"You're crazy, soldier," she said and smiled. It changed her face as sun changes a landscape after rain. Then she turned round, walked past him through the gateway and quickly up the village street.

Frowning, Georges watched her go. She walked slightly bent against the rain and the perspective made her bare legs seem even longer. She's got it all right, he thought. Watch yourself, boy.

He absentmindedly lit a cigarette, picked up his belongings and turned towards the staircase leading upwards from the right-hand side of the gateway. It was so dark that he had to feel his way up with his feet. On the topmost step he sat down, laid the gun beside him and thought about the girl.

"She dished it out to you all right, didn't she," he said to himself. "You're crazy, soldier. You have a very vivid imagination, soldier. Big guns! If she fires off a few more like that you'll be a mess, soldier!"

He chuckled to himself in the dark. Then he thought he heard steps and quickly stubbed out his cigarette. From where he sat he could only see a small area of the gateway. Now the footsteps became more distinct. They were coming from the right down the street, grew louder and then echoed away through the arch of the gateway and suddenly stopped; for a second there was quiet and Georges sat there grinning, waiting until the footsteps were heard again and died away. He remained sitting for another couple of minutes, then walked down the stairs and looked out. It had grown somewhat lighter, and here and there he could see the mountainside between banks of cloud.

Georges carried the suitcase up the empty village street. At the third house before the end on the left-hand side he put it down and took the path leading to the spring. He followed it for some way between the boulders, then climbed up to the ridge. The visibility was growing worse again, and when he reached the ridge he seemed to be standing in a boiler full of water vapor.

It took him a long time to climb down to the slide and he was twice forced to turn back and take a different route to avoid going over the edge. At the third attempt he was luckier and struck the slide. With every step downwards it grew brighter and this enabled him to move faster. Whereas two days before it had taken them over an hour to climb up the slide, he now needed a mere thirty minutes to clamber down it, after which he found himself on the narrow path near the spot where he and Marcel had stopped to rest; the valley, under its transparent veil of rain, was spread out at his feet.

For as far as Georges could see down the road there was no car or truck, although there were several places hidden from his view, and he decided to climb down a little farther.

Although it twisted and turned and frequently narrowed to no more than a foot in width, the steepness of the descent allowed him to make rapid progress and in spite of the rain he was soon warm from running.

Once when he looked at his watch he was surprised to notice that he had already spent three quarters of an hour on his way down the path. Here it passed between two boulders, about six hundred feet above the valley floor, after which the view forward was cut off by a sharp turn to the right. The place might have been

146

made for an observation post. He could see the path in front, and the boulder to the right of the path had a slight hollow near its base. If he leaned his back against the hollow it gave him some protection from the rain, and he could conveniently keep the path and the road under observation.

To keep his feet from getting wet he drew his knees up to his chest and passed the time by smoking. The ground beneath him was damp and cool; he felt the dampness through his clothes as he watched the raindrops running races down the porous rock beside him. Suddenly there was a clink of metal against stone.

The movement with which Georges swung his head round occurred almost simultaneously with the noise. At the bend in the the road he saw a man with a rifle appear and behind him another.

Although he had reckoned with their coming, he was at that moment as little prepared for it as was a soldier who goes to war with a presentiment of death and is killed by the first shell. Had he been ready he would have fired into the air. What happened was like a chain reaction, and between the alarm bell ringing in his head to the reflex movement of his hands, the instinctive thumb pressure on the safety catch and the automatic grip on the trigger-guard, less time elapsed than his reason required to cancel out the short-circuit action of his limbs. He simply fired on the spur of the moment as he had done for three long years; in that time he had acquired the habit of firing a fraction of a second before his brain began to function.

The two men dropped full length to the ground and a third, who had emerged with them, disappeared like lightning behind the bend in the path. This was the last thing that Georges saw before he leaped to his feet and ran blindly up the path as far as its next turning. Then he panted for fifty yards straight up the mountainside, struck the path again and ran on without slackening his pace. Only when his wind failed completely and his chest hurt as if he had swallowed molten lead did he drop to his knees, lay his arms on the wet ground and his face on his arms. For half a minute he fought for breath, then turned round on his knees and looked down the pathway. The rain pattering on his ground-sheet interfered with his hearing. He held his head slightly to one side, closed his eyes for a moment and held his breath. Besides the rain there was nothing to be heard, and after waiting for a few seconds he heaved himself up from the ground and climbed on, leaving the path, directly up the mountainside.

By this means he cut off three loops of the path and felt then

147

that the danger of the men cutting him off by a similar move was past. It was his first clear thought since the incident. As he continued up the path and the rain cooled his flushed face his head also cleared. As it did so and he became soberly aware of what had happened he began to curse. You fired out of control, he said to himself, and that is far worse than when you do it deliberately; if you shoot deliberately you can stop when you have to. You've lost your grip, that's obvious. You're like an epileptic who gets his attacks now and again; as long as you have a gun you will shoot.

While talking to himself he had climbed a good stretch of the mountainside, and when he stopped again he noticed that the rain had stopped. The sky was still overcast, but the black thunderclouds had moved southward and in some places the cloud-cover was melting like snow in spring, thinning and changing color to a pale blue which rapidly spread; then it seemed as if a bunch of golden-yellow rods of light fell through a hole in the clouds on to the mountain-tops. They began to shine, the river, too, shone in the valley and made its rocky sides glow with reflected light.

Georges took off his groundsheet, folded it up and continued his way along the narrow path. He could feel a dull ache in the region of his heart and his thoughts turned ceaselessly round one point like a revolving disc on its axis. When he reached the slide an hour later and began the ascent towards the fort, the clouds had completely vanished from the sky as if they had been swept away by a storm and the afternoon sun burned hot on his face. His leg muscles hurt and he frequently had to stop until his heartbeat settled down, but he took no long rests and worked his way up the mountainside with the regularity of a machine. At the top of the slide he dropped on to the rock-strewn ground and rested for a few minutes.

The stones were drying quickly in the sun. After the rain the air was clear and pure and the sky was brilliant blue over the mountains. Georges wished that everything could again be as it had been yesterday and the day before, when he was free of the consequences of having shot the two men.

He took a handful of ammunition from his pocket, pushed six rounds into the magazine and clambered on upwards. At the ridge he stopped for a while and gazed over the mountains to the north until he heard a voice calling his name.

148

Chapter 7

"Let's hope the rain stops soon," said Vieale. "We must shift the baggage before it gets dark."

"It'll stop soon," said Marcel indifferently. The woman sat between them and said nothing.

Vieale shook his head with a sigh. "Something like this always happens. Are you very tired, *mon chou?*"

"Not too much," said his wife. "When we're in La Peine we can sleep as long as we like."

"We'll do nothing until the day after tomorrow," said Vieale. "We'll spend all tomorrow resting. Do you agree?" he said to Marcel.

Marcel nodded. He was still bad tempered from the quarrel with Georges and stared listlessly at the mouth of the tunnel to where the rain-soaked road disappeared round a bend.

Vieale gave him a cigarette and said: "You don't always agree with your friend."

"Not always."

"But you get along with him, don't you?"

Marcel waited before replying. For the past hour he had been unable to think of anything but the two Resistance men on the road. He liked the whole affair less and less the more he thought about it.

"He goes his own way," he finally said. "You never quite know where you are with him."

"You must know him very well. Otherwise why should you have gone over to the Germans with him?"

149

"It wasn't my idea," said Marcel gloomily. "Georges was always against the Communists. He said we should fight them because they cared nothing for the value of the human personality."

"He also seems to have something against his own country, Switzerland."

Marcel shrugged his shoulders impatiently. "I suppose it's too conservative and stuffy for him. I don't agree. I think we've done rather well with our neutrality. Why should we care about others? They don't bother themselves about us, do they?"

"If that's your view," said Vieale, surprised, "I wonder at your going with him."

"We'd known each other so long," said Marcel. "There are moments, you know, when everything goes sour. That was one of those times for me. I was fed up with sitting at home and letting myself be treated like a small boy."

"That's something you can learn for Philippe," said Vieale to his wife. "It's not as simple as you often seem to think."

"Philippe's still too young to worry about that," declared his wife. Her legs were crossed straight out in front of her and she was smoking a cigarette. "Once he's twenty he can do what he likes. Even now I give him a freer hand than you do."

"Too much freedom is not always the answer either," said Vieale, and scratched his chin. "One needs a great deal of sensitivity."

The woman turned to Marcel. "But your parents must have done a lot for you."

It sounded like a reproof, and Marcel felt that he had said too much. The quarrel with Georges had aroused the need to vent his feelings a little, but now he lost the desire to talk and said in a tone of finality: "That has nothing to do with it."

For a while nobody spoke, until Vieale started up again: "When did your friend become an officer?"

"A year ago, when I was shot in the lung. He could have been commissioned sooner and then he only did it so that he could visit me in the hospital during his officer cadet's course. When I came back he was company commander and fixed me a soft job in the company office."

"That was a bit of luck," said Vieale. "What is his surname?" The remark slipped out unconsciously and his wife dug him in the ribs. "Oh, pardon!" he said. "I didn't want to be inquisitive."

"We did agree to use only our first names," said Marcel, "but I don't see why you shouldn't know. Georges' name is Chabrier and mine is Egli. You'd better forget them, though, in case they slip out when Knopf or Boris are near by. We don't want them to know where we came from."

"Haven't you told them?" asked Vieale.

"One never knows how they might react. Anyway, it's no concern of theirs."

"Then we'll continue to call you Marcel and Georges. I'm glad though, that you——" He broke off and looked towards the tunnel mouth. "Wasn't that somebody's voice?"

"I thought it was too," said Marcel and stood up.

The road was still shrouded in cloud and the rain rattled on the macadam in great drops. But now the voices could be heard again, and seconds later the outlines of three figures emerged from the mist.

"We have visitors," said Marcel peevishly. "They seem to be in a hurry to welcome us."

Vieale also stood up and threw his cigarette away. "It's Boris," he said to his wife. "His beard has grown thicker. I suppose the man beside him is Knopf."

"Knopf and his daughter," confirmed Marcel. "Shall we go and meet them?"

Vieale nodded. "Yes, why not? Perhaps you ought to wait here, *mon chou*. I wonder why Monsieur Georges isn't with them?"

From habit Marcel slung his gun over his shoulder. "I expect he's still in La Peine."

They walked side by side down the tunnel and met Boris first, who wore no coat and was walking a few paces ahead of the others. The greetings between them were somewhat strained, and Boris did not fail to notice that Vieale hardly returned the pressure of his handshake. They exchanged a few perfunctory words, then Boris introduced him to Knopf and the girl; Marcel could only stare at Anna. He liked her at first sight and when she looked at him he gazed aside with embarrassment.

"This is an unexpected reunion," said Boris to Vieale. "When I left Eys I thought it was goodbye forever. Where is your wife?"

"She's waiting in the tunnel. Did you know that we were sitting here?"

"Your friend told us," replied Knopf. "We saw your car coming and wanted to come some of the way to meet you, but the thunderstorm held us up. Is it true that you have bad news for us?"

"We'll talk about that later," said Vieale evasively. "I suggest

151

we go back to Madame Vieale first of all. She's looking forward to meeting you."

"So are we," said Knopf and looked at Marcel. "So it was only *'au revoir'* for us, too. You left very early the day before yesterday."

"We went while it was still dark," said Marcel.

"We wanted to invite you for breakfast," said Knopf, "but you had already gone. Don't you two know each other?" he asked Anna.

The girl shook her head.

Marcel awkwardly gave her his hand. "If we'd known about breakfast," he said, "we wouldn't have gone so early."

Meanwhile Vieale was talking to Boris. He asked him how he was managing in La Peine.

"I like it here," said Boris. He was embarrassed because he had a bad conscience about Vieale. He brushed the rain from his jacket. "Did you have a good journey?" he asked, for something to say.

"Yes, we did." Vieale turned to the girl: "Isn't it too lonely for you in La Peine?"

"Sometimes."

"That I can imagine. For a young girl La Peine must be worse than a convent. You speak French quite as well as your father. Did you learn it at home or in France?"

"She learned it all in France," said Knopf. "We have been living in your country for two years."

"I had imagined your daughter as much younger," said Vieale. And to Marcel: "You never told me that Monsieur Knopf has such a pretty daughter."

"I didn't know it myself," said Marcel to the girl.

Vieale put his hand on Knopf's shoulder. "Come along, Monsieur, we don't want to keep Madame Vieale waiting any longer." He went ahead with Knopf and Marcel, while Boris and the girl stayed behind for a moment.

"Perhaps I'd better go back to La Peine," said Boris. "I don't like the thought of him being there on his own. You said you didn't see him again on your way back?"

"I purposely stopped and looked around for him."

"You must be careful of him," said Boris. "I don't like him."

"You've said that before. He didn't make a bad impression on me."

"He knows that you hate the Germans and so he's making a special effort with you."

152

"How does he know that?"

"I told him. Shouldn't I have done so?"

"Have I once said to you that I hate the Germans?"

There was a note in her voice which made Boris pay attention. "But you did tell me that you never wanted to go back to Germany again. Isn't that the same thing?"

"No," she said. "It is not the same thing."

Boris's mouth dropped open in astonishment, but she suddenly walked very quickly away from him and he saw that she no longer cared to talk to him. In any case he would have no more opportunity to talk to her, as she had meanwhile joined the others and Vieale was introducing them to his wife. "This is Monsieur Knopf," he said to her, "and this is his daughter. Isn't she pretty, *mon chou?*"

"She is very pretty," said Denise Vieale, smiling, and touched the girl's face with her hand as if she was going to caress it, then she looked at Boris.

Vieale cleared his throat. "Monsieur Boris has been telling me that he has settled in very well at La Peine."

"I'm glad," said Madame Vieale, giving Boris a fleeting handshake, and turned directly to the girl. "May I call you Anna? It's a nice name. I like it."

"If you like it," said the girl, "please call me Anna."

Vieale, relieved, gave a laugh. "I see we shall get on well together. But why are we standing up? We can sit down on the suitcases and have a bit of a chat until the rain stops. I think we have plenty to tell each other."

"I think so too," said Knopf. Although he had only exchanged a few words with Vieale, he liked him and his wife. Vieale laid the two suitcases flat on the ground and gestured to them to be seated. "Sit down, Messieurs! It's not so comfortable as home, but I don't expect you're fussy."

"No chance of that in La Peine," said Knopf, and lowered himself on to a suitcase beside Vieale, while Boris sat on the second suitcase.

"You can sit next to me," said Denise Vieale to the girl. "There's room for three on the rucksacks, isn't there?" she asked Marcel.

"Why not? There was room for four just now." He waited until Anna had sat down and said: "I can stand."

"Please don't," said Anna. "There's still room for you here. Or are you afraid of sitting next to a girl?"

153

"Do I look as if I am?" asked Marcel, who liked her more and more.

"Not while you've got your gun, at any rate. You drag it round with you as if you were still fighting."

"A soldier is married to his rifle," said Vieale, coming to Marcel's rescue.

"But he's not a soldier any more," said the girl. "Or do you intend to hang it over your bed when you get home?"

"Who wants to do that?" said Marcel in surprise.

"Your friend told me he wanted to hang it over his bed one day."

"Oh, him!" Marcel laughed. "He gets ideas like that. I'll be glad if I never see the thing again."

"Then why did you bring it with you?" asked Boris.

There he goes again, thought Marcel with annoyance, and said: "As long as there are people carrying pistols I prefer to keep it."

"Do you mean me?" asked Boris.

"I'm speaking generally," replied Marcel. "The war's not over yet and I don't want to be shot even by my best friend just because he had a gun and I hadn't. Ask Monsieur Vieale what he thinks about it."

"The times are unsafe," said Vieale. "I've been in two wars and I don't want any more to do with shooting, but nowadays it's as well to have a gun on you."

"Were you a soldier in 1914?" asked Knopf.

"I volunteered at eighteen. I persuaded myself then that I'd be missing something if I didn't volunteer. Since then I've learned otherwise."

"That happens to most people," said Knopf, "but then they forget it again. I was in the first world war myself."

"Were you?" asked Anna, in extreme surprise. "I never knew that."

"It's quite enough that I know it," said Knopf bitterly, and looked at Vieale. "We are all uneasy. I hope the bad news you have for us is not so bad as to affect our immediately safety."

"No, it's not," said Vieale. He had crossed his legs and lit another cigarette. "If La Peine were not absolutely safe I would have chosen another place."

"Well, that's a relief," said Knopf. "We were prepared for the worst. Now perhaps you'll tell us what you know."

Vieale hesitated. He suddenly felt inhibited and turned to Marcel. "You'd better tell him, Monsieur."

"I know no more than you," countered Marcel. It annoyed him that Vieale had thrust the unpleasant task on him. Georges would have told them at once, he thought. Or would he? He was usually clever enough to leave the dirty work to other people. "It looks as if the Germans are planning a counter-offensive," he said unwillingly.

"What makes you think that?" asked Knopf anxiously.

"They're bringing up new divisions. Our unit, for instance, only arrived in this area a few days ago from Heilbronn."

"I didn't know that. Then perhaps the war is going to drag on."

"Maybe. Anyhow, the mountains are crawling with German troops."

"Have you seen any?" asked Boris suspiciously.

"If we hadn't seen any," replied Marcel, "I wouldn't be able to tell you."

"Where did you see them?" asked Knopf. "In this area?"

"No, farther south."

Knopf turned nervously to Boris. "That would explain why Pierre hasn't come." To Vieale he said: "Do you know where the Americans are?"

"Not exactly. Apparently they are somewhere near Cannes."

"Then they've made good progress."

"They've made good progress," said Marcel, "because the Germans had no reserves in the area. What will happen now is hard to tell."

"Who is Pierre?" asked Vieale, looking at Knopf.

"A friend of ours from Escarène. He was to have come up to see us today."

"Oh, I see," said Vieale.

Knopf laid his hand on his knee. "You have no need to worry about him. If I have a word with him, he'll treat you as a friend. Boris and I have already discussed the matter. You needn't worry either," he said to Marcel. "I would just ask you, though, to hide your gun when he comes. If I tell him who you are and that you have had enough of this war, you will certainly have nothing to fear from him."

"Do you really mean that?" asked Marcel sceptically.

"I promise you. Pierre is only fighting the Germans who are keeping his country under occupation. He's rather a rough diamond, but fundamentally he's more humane than even he himself realizes. Anna and I lived with him for a long time."

"Well I'm . . ." Marcel was silent. He felt like a man who

155

has struggled up a laborious and dangerous path, only to learn that he has been going in the wrong direction. "Why didn't you tell us that the day before yesterday?"

"Everything happened so quickly," said Knopf. "If you hadn't left in such haste we could certainly have talked about it. You didn't tell us that the Germans were planning a counter-offensive, by the way."

"You didn't give us the chance. And we went away because we saw that we were not wanted."

"It was a misunderstanding," said Knopf.

Marcel stared perplexedly ahead for a while, then he looked at Vieale. "What do we do now?"

"That's easy," said Knopf. "You stay here." He noticed that Vieale has a distracted, worried look. "I thought that you would be pleased at my suggestion," he said with some resentment.

Vieale pulled himself together. "Of course we're pleased." He laughed with embarrassment and turned to his wife: "That's a weight off your mind, isn't it, *mon chou?* Or isn't it?"

"It most certainly is," she replied and said to Knopf: "Monsieur Vieale and I are very grateful to you. It wasn't an easy decision for us to come here, but we made up our minds weeks ago and there was no alternative."

"We must talk about that later," said Knopf. "I'll tell Pierre that it was you who helped Boris; that will carry more weight than anything else. Do you know Escarène?"

"We know it well."

"We've been there a few times," put in Vieale. "Does the name Michaud mean anything to you?"

"Monsieur Michaud? That's the mayor, isn't it, or do you mean someone else?"

"No, I mean the mayor. We have often met on official business. He's a bit old for the job now."

"Pierre says so too, but Michaud is very well liked."

"Because he stands everybody drinks," said Anna. "I've never seen a man who can drink as much as he can."

Vieale nodded. "So that's one way in which he hasn't changed much. I haven't seen him for more than a year, but he owns more vineyards than anyone else in Escarène. How much longer will he go on being mayor?"

"Until the war's over," said Knopf. "The people want Pierre to be his successor, but I don't think he will take office."

156

"What is Pierre's surname?"

"He can tell you that himself. It is more important that you tell me how you had to leave Eys. Boris had already hinted at a few things, but before I talk to Pierre I would prefer to make my own judgment. Do they accuse you of having collaborated with the Germans?"

"It's a lot of trumped-up nonsense," said Vieale. "A collaborator is a man who co-operates with the enemy and of these there are two kinds. Those who do it for personal gain and those who do it for better and less obvious reasons."

"Are you thinking of France when you say that?"

Vieale looked at him appraisingly. "That question is a trap, Monsieur, but I can put your mind at rest. I was actually thinking of other countries, although there were enough people in France too who shortly before and after the capitulation preferred working with the Germans to seeing their country go politically bankrupt—and without any thought of personal gain or loss. But the mob will never ask what their motives were and whether they really betrayed France or simply drank a glass of wine with a German soldier. They will kill them without discrimination."

"I can't believe that of the French," said Anna. "They are a civilized people."

Vieale laughed humorlessly. "My thanks for your good opinion of us, but the Germans are a civilized people too. In fact, the greatest crimes are committed in the name of civilization. It's not even the 'people' that commit them, it's the rabble. I'm glad I don't live in Paris or Marseilles; I've seen quite enough in Eys." He turned to his wife. "I'm thinking about Monsieur Duvet's little Yvonne. I would have liked to help her."

"That was her parents' concern," said the woman. "What could we have done for her?"

"Nothing, *mon chou,* but I can't get it out of mind." To Knopf he said: "She is eighteen and the daughter of a friend of ours. She worked as a salesgirl at a department store in Nice. Eighteen months ago she got to know a German soldier. You know how it is with young people. Love has nothing to do with nationality. One day he was posted away and . . . Well, they loved each other too much. Her parents soon found out, of course, and gave her no peace until they knew who the father was. A week later the story was all over Eys. Nobody would speak to the wretched creature and we have people in Eys, I happen to know very well,

157

who have much more on their consciences than she could ever have, but no, because she did it with a German they shaved her head and drove her into the streets naked."

Anna shook her head in disgust. "I would never have believed that the French could do such a thing." Turning to Marcel she said: "Would you let it happen if you were there?"

"No, I don't think so," drawled Marcel in reply.

"Well, what would you do, then?" asked Boris. Marcel's smug tone of voice infuriated him. He considered Marcel's answer to be a piece of bravado and he wanted Anna to realize this.

"That's my affair," answered Marcel. "At least as long as I had a gun I wouldn't allow it."

"You'd shoot, would you?"

"If there were no alternative, yes."

"Would your friend shoot, too?" said Anna to Marcel.

"Georges!" Marcel grinned. "I rather think he would."

"So do I," said Boris coldly. "You seem to be very fond of shooting. Haven't you had enough of it?"

Marcel flared up at him. "I don't have to justify my actions to you!"

"Not to me you don't," said Boris. He had not forgotten the frosty reception given him by Vieale. Also he was disappointed that Anna was siding with Marcel, and he determined to drive him into a corner. "I was just wondering about you, that's all. First you desert and then you want to start shooting again. Why did you desert at all? Because you saw that you were losing the war?"

Denise Vieale joined in. She had been listening with mounting excitement and now said to Marcel: "It's nothing to do with me, Monsieur, but I think you ought to tell him."

"*Mais, mon chou!*" said Vieale, trying to keep the peace.

"Oh, shut up!" His wife shook her head angrily. "This is all a lot of rubbish. Why did you go over to the Germans?" she said to Boris. "Because you had had enough of the Communists. Monsieur Egli and Monsieur Chabrier are from Zürich and voluntarily joined up with the Germans to fight the Communists. Why shouldn't everybody know it?"

For a few seconds it was so quiet that the sound of the rain could be heard in the tunnel. Knopf was the first to react. "So you are not Germans at all?" he asked quietly.

"You heard what she said," grunted Marcel.

"Why didn't you tell us in the first place?"

158

"Why should we?" asked Marcel, and looked at Boris, who was apparently unable to speak.

"You had to be careful," said Denise Vieale. She had been carried away by her temperament and now she regretted it. "Are you very angry with me, Monsieur?" she said to Marcel.

Marcel wavered. He felt that the situation was getting out of hand and was afraid of Georges blaming him. Above all, he was painfully uncertain to what would happen now. He cursed Georges for not being there. Once or twice he had been on the point of telling Knopf why Pierre had not come, but he dared not to do so until he had spoken to Georges. He decided to take the first available opportunity to mention it, to Vieale if to nobody else. But it would have to be done so unobtrusively as to prevent the others becoming suspicious. "I don't care," he said finally. "You must make it up with Georges."

"I don't understand all this," said Anna, who was most surprised of all. "How could you, a Swiss, join up with the Germans?"

"Russians joined up with them too," said Marcel.

"Not only Russians." Vieale was relieved at the turn which the conversation was taking. "There was even a Spanish Legion. Volunteer units from all over Europe fought for the Germans in Russia."

"Nobody ever told me that," declared Anna, and turned her gaze on Marcel. "Which of you is Monsieur Chabrier?"

"Georges," replied Marcel.

"Chabrier is a French name," said Knopf.

Marcel nodded. "Georges was born in Lausanne."

"It's a beautiful place," said Knopf to Anna. "When the war's over we may perhaps go there one day."

"Isn't Lausanne on a lake?" she asked.

"On the Lake of Geneva," answered Marcel. "But Zürich is on a lake too. If you ever come to Zürich you must come and see me."

Vieale laughed. "Monsieur Egli has his own sailing boat and a car. If I were you I should take him at his word."

"I could show you the whole of Switzerland," said Marcel to the girl. "You'd love Zürich. We could——"

He suddenly stopped. For a second he stared emptily towards the mouth of the tunnel. "What's the matter?" asked Knopf.

Marcel gestured wearily. "Nothing. I've just thought of something."

159

"I know what you're thinking," said Vieale, who had guessed his thoughts. "You've remembered that you can never go back to Switzerland."

"Why not?" asked Anna in astonishment.

"If they go back to Switzerland they'll be locked up for a few years. The Swiss are not allowed to serve in foreign armies."

Denise Vieale laughed angrily. "Holy Mother of God! What good do the Swiss think that will do? If a man wants to go and fight for something let him go and fight."

"Is that the reason why you didn't desert sooner?" said Boris to Marcel. This was his first contribution to the talk since its new turn.

"We wouldn't have got very far if we'd deserted in Russia, would we?"

"Then I owe you an apology," said Boris; it clearly cost him an effort. Before Marcel could say anything in answer, Knopf broke in: "What will you do now?"

"Wait until the war's over. Then perhaps we can go underground somewhere in Germany."

"That would mean, though, that you could never go back to Switzerland again."

Marcel was silent and there was a pause, until Vieale burst out: "This is what I have always said. We have turned Europe into a dozen separate cages and one day we will suffocate in them. Look at me: what did I do? I simply drew the logical conclusion from past history, that's all. I told people that there'll be no peace in Europe as long as France and Germany can't settle their differences. I did make one mistake, though. I should never have accepted the office of mayor. But put yourself in my position. When I came home from the prison camp, I had nothing. The mayor's job was a straw at which I clutched and perhaps some vanity was involved too. *Mon Dieu,* who isn't a little vain in some way? I wanted to show that stupid mob that a good Frenchman is not necessarily a blind fanatic. In the midst of the war we built a new school, started a kindergarten and improved our drainage. None of that would have been possible if I hadn't been on good terms with the Prefect; now that is held against me. Tell me, Monsieur, is that a logical attitude?"

"That is a question that can be argued ad infinitum," replied Knopf. "What was your job before the war?"

"We had a car-renting firm. Business was good."

He told how he had begun with one car. While the others listened, Vieale's wife leaned over to Marcel and said softly: "Are you still angry with me?"

"No," said Marcel, "not any more."

"And your friend?"

"I must talk to him."

"Has he a sailing boat at home too?" asked Anna, who was sitting between them.

"His father's not so well off as mine," replied Marcel. "He's an officer. A good sailing boat is expensive."

"You gave up a lot."

"You don't notice it until it's too late."

"Is it really too late?"

"What do you mean?"

The woman hesitated, then looked up and stared him straight in the face. "I am not a man, Monsieur. I can only tell you what I feel as a woman. If you had nothing to lose in Switzerland I would understand your not wanting to return. But your parents have no one besides you. What will happen to the business if you never go home again?"

"I don't care," said Marcel harshly. "I'm not going to let them put me behind bars for six years."

"Are you sure that it would be six years?"

"It may only be four. But it makes no difference."

"It's bad enough, I agree, but I can imagine it would be far worse if you were never to go home again for the rest of your life—or don't you really care?"

"That has nothing to do with it."

"On the contrary, it has everything to do with it," she contradicted him. "You're destroying your own and your parents' lives. You won't be the first person who's had to pay dearly for something they did in good faith, but you must stop and consider which is the greater price to pay. Boris would gladly have himself locked up if by that he could buy back the right to return home."

"I'm not interested in what Boris would do. I could never go back, even if I wanted to. Georges would never agree. Do you think I'd leave him here alone?"

The woman smiled. "No, monsieur, I don't think you would. But suppose he agreed: would you go back then?"

"Perhaps," said Marcel uncertainly. Then he said firmly: "But I would never do it alone."

"You don't have to do it alone. You must simply convince your friend that it would be the best thing for both of you."

161

"You try convincing him of something that he doesn't agree with!"

"Shall I try?" asked Madame Vieale.

"You can save yourself the trouble; he would only be furious with you."

"That doesn't matter. I simply think that your friend, too, should think of his parents for once."

"He only has a father. His mother is dead."

"Is he married?" asked Anna.

Marcel grinned. "That would be a joke!"

"Why?" asked Anna, astonished.

"He never had much time for girls."

"I'm surprised," said Madame Vieale. "Has his mother been dead for long?"

"Yes."

"Then his father is going to be a very lonely man without him. I will speak to him."

"I've warned you."

Anna gestured impatiently. "You behave as if you were afraid of him. What is so terrifying about him?"

"About whom?" asked Knopf. Having finished his discussion with Vieale he had become aware of the conversation between the other three.

"We were talking about Monsieur Chabrier," answered Anna grudgingly.

Madame Vieale noticed that the question had annoyed her and she turned to her husband: "Have you told Monsieur Knopf everything?"

"Yes. I hope he is now convinced that I am no collaborator."

"I was sure before he started," said Knopf. "But the conversation was valuable none the less. I now have a better idea of what I shall say to Pierre." To Marcel he said: "I would never have guessed that you were Swiss. When you speak German your accent is more Swabian."

"We spent three years in a Württemberg division."

"Yes, one picks up the accent very easily," said Knopf smiling. "Your friend is a long time away."

"Perhaps he's taking a rest," said Marcel and got up. "I'll just go and take a look at the weather. It seems to have stopped raining. Are you coming, Monsieur?"

His last words were spoken to Vieale, who immediately got to his feet. "Yes, I must look after the car."

"We will help you to carry up your luggage," said Knopf.

Anna interrupted: "You mustn't do that. It's too much of a strain for you."

"I can carry something small. Perhaps Monsieur Vieale has a suitcase which is not too heavy."

"Yes, we have," said Vieale cheerfully.

He walked beside Marcel round the bend in the tunnel to its northern end. They were both deep in thought. When they came into the open Vieale broke the silence. "It really has stopped raining. If I know anything about the weather in these parts the sun will be shining again in an hour."

Marcel said nothing. He was looking anxiously down the valley. Although low-lying cloud still hindered visibility he could now see a short stretch of the road and the olive grove on the other side of the valley. But neither here nor farther up the valley, near the viaduct, was there anything suspicious to be seen.

"See anything?" said Vieale.

"No. I was wondering, though, where those two men went during the thunderstorm."

"I've been wondering that, too," said Vieale. "We made a big mistake."

"It's easy enough to say that after the event. But I told Georges at the time that I didn't like the whole business."

"He was fairly laconic when he rejoined us in the wood. What did he tell you?"

"He only said that those two had rifles."

Vieale let out a cry of surprise. "Why should they want to come to La Peine with rifles?"

"That's what I'd like to know too," said Marcel and scratched his neck uneasily. "There's a catch in all this somewhere. If Georges doesn't come soon I'm going to fetch him. It's up to him to sort this thing out. I'm not going to burn my fingers."

"We must tell the others," said Vieale. "We can't simply keep it quiet. Perhaps the truck only drove back to fetch reinforcements. Have you thought of that?"

"Better ask Georges whether he's thought of it. He's afraid of something else."

"What?"

Marcel considered whether he should tell him. Georges had told him to tell nobody, but that was in different circumstances and he decided to make a clean breast of it: "He's afraid that

163

the Maquisards will try to reach La Peine by the same way that we got there two days ago."

"*Merde!*" said Vieale, appalled. He seized Marcel by the shoulder. "We must talk to your friend as quickly as possible. Did he tell you where he was going?"

"I imagine that he has climbed down some of the way on the other side."

"You must go after him. We'll say nothing to Monsieur Knopf until your friend is back."

They returned to the others, who were already getting impatient. "The rain has stopped," said Vieale. "Monsieur Egli is going ahead to fetch his friend. First I'll bring the baggage over."

"Can I help you?" asked Boris.

Vieale nodded vaguely. "If you like, Monsieur."

He watched Marcel pick up his own and Georges' rucksack and turned to his wife: "There is some light luggage in the car that Monsieur Knopf could carry, isn't there?"

"I'll give you a bag," said Vieale's wife to Knopf. "We can carry it together."

"I'll go with Monsieur Egli," said Anna. She had picked up one of the heavy suitcases and was waiting for Marcel, who was still struggling with the two rucksacks. At last he managed to sling them both on his back and said to her: "I walk very fast."

"Oh, I can walk fast too," said Anna.

Vieale had watched this scene with dismay. He would have preferred the girl to stay behind with the others so that Marcel could search unhindered for Georges. "This case is too heavy for you," he broke in. "Wait until we have the smaller ones here."

"No, I can easily manage it," said Anna. As she turned away she had a glimpse of Boris's disappointed face and said to Knopf: "I'll put on some coffee for you."

"Put it on for all of us," said Knopf. "I think we could all do with a cup when we get there." Anna nodded and walked into the open with Marcel. There she changed the case over to her other hand and tried to keep in step with Marcel's pace.

The clouds had cleared and the road surface was rapidly drying. A warm breeze from the south blew up the valley. The mountains reappeared, peak after peak stretching to the horizon, as if an invisible hand had suddenly jerked away a veil. Marcel and the girl trudged up the road without exchanging a word until they reached the next tunnel, where Anna stopped and said: "Can you smell it?"

164

Marcel sniffed. "No. What can you smell?"

"The sea. You can smell it whenever the wind is in the south."

"I don't know what the sea smells like," said Marcel. "How can you tell?"

"I can't describe it. It's as if there were suddenly more air."

She put down the suitcase and let her arm dangle. "Phew! It's heavy. What's inside it?"

"Clothes, I expect," said Marcel. "Would you rather take one of the rucksacks and I'll carry your case?"

"No, no. I let myself in for this, so I must put up with it."

As they walked through the tunnel and re-emerged on to the open road Marcel glanced furtively at her profile. She really is pretty, he said to himself, and when she makes the coffee I can scout around for Georges.

"Where did you meet my friend?" he asked aloud.

"At the gateway to the village. I was waiting for my father."

"So you were all alone during the thunderstorm?"

"Yes."

"Weren't you frightened?"

"No, I like thunderstorms. Do you?"

"When I've a roof over my head."

They had now covered nearly half the way and Anna kept changing the case from one hand to the other. Finally she stopped again and said: "I must have a rest. This case is full of stones, not clothes." She massaged her aching arms and make a face which made her look like a very young girl. Marcel watched her with a grin.

Pity she's got that coat on, he thought, I think she has a good figure. For a few seconds he gazed at her legs, which stretched out long and slim from beneath her coat.

Anna noticed him. She quickly pulled the coat down over her knees and said: "You mustn't look at my legs like that. I've been running through the rain and they're dirty."

"Oh," said Marcel with embarrassment, "I don't mind." He was annoyed at being caught by her and added: "I was thinking of something else."

"What?"

Marcel frowned, but this time his imagination fortunately came to his rescue and he said: "It's not easy to say. You know, we thought of you as someone quite different."

"Do tell me exactly what you thought," said Anna looking at him expectantly.

He avoided looking at the girl as he said: "Well, you see, according to what Boris told us about you we thought you were the unapproachable sort. I don't know how to express it better than that."

"Your friend said much the same," said Anna calmly. "Boris obviously misunderstands me, but perhaps that is my fault. He knows from my father that I never want to go back to Germany and has assumed from that that I hate all Germans. But that's not so."

"I'm glad," said Marcel, "but why didn't you want us to stay here?"

"That was my first reaction. My father must have told you that we had met no other Germans for two years. Don't forget the conditions under which we had to live. We trembled at the mere sight of a uniform."

"But you've no cause to be afraid of us."

"Not now. Besides, you're not Germans at all."

She watched him shoulder the heavy rucksacks, pick up the gun and pull up his trousers, which had slipped down below his hips. "They're too big for me," he said apologetically. "Vieale couldn't find a pair to fit me."

"How did you get to know him?"

Marcel told her the story as they continued on their way. "At first I didn't trust him," he said finally, "but he's all right."

"I like him too," said Anna, "and his wife is very nice."

"Yes," said Marcel, "she is nice."

They spoke less now, as the going got stiffer and they had to pick their way past piles of fallen stones strewn across the road. The sky cleared rapidly, and when they began the descent of the steep little path leading into La Peine the sun began to shine again.

As they walked up the shady village street, Anna scrutinized the houses on either side. Marcel noticed this and asked: "Are you looking for something?"

"I was wondering where your friend might be. Shouldn't we call out for him?"

"There's no hurry," said Marcel, who was beginning to be irritated by her interest in Georges.

They were silent until they reached the house. There they put down their luggage. As Anna straightened up she noticed a suitcase on the other side of the steps. "That was his," she said. "He must have been here."

Marcel nodded. "He's bound to be near by."

"Do you want to come in?" asked Anna.

"No. I must look for Georges first."

"I hope you find him," said Anna and went indoors.

Marcel chose roughly the same route that Georges had taken and climbed up through the boulders towards the ridge. Before he reached it he found Georges. He stood, his hands in his trouser pockets and his back towards Marcel, silhouetted against the skyline on the ridge. As Marcel shouted his name he turned round and looked down at him. Marcel waved with both hands. Then he dropped panting on to a rock and waited for Georges to clamber slowly down to him. Something in his behavior puzzled Marcel. He got wearily to his feet and looked anxiously at Georges.

"Where have you been, man?" he asked nervously. "Everybody's waiting for you. Have you seen anything?"

As Georges did not answer and merely threw down his gun, dropped the groundsheet and sat on the same rock from which Marcel had just got up, he felt a stab of fear. Sitting down beside Georges he asked: "What's happened?"

"Tell me first what's been going on with you," said Georges. "Did those two fellows show up again?"

"No. Even if they had it wouldn't have mattered. You don't know what's been happening in the meantime. We could have spared ourselves all that trouble."

"What could we have spared ourselves?"

"Everything," answered Marcel, and hastily described the conversation in the tunnel. "We've told nothing to Knopf yet," he went on. "Vieale agreed that we should speak to you first, but we must go back as quickly as possible because if the two Resistance men do appear and Knopf knows nothing about what happened, there'll be trouble. We must simply tell him exactly how it was. If he knows them as well as he seems to, he'll . . . He stopped and looked at Georges, who had paled several times during his story and was now as white as a sheet.

"Are you feeling all right?" asked Marcel.

Georges licked his lips, then began suddenly to laugh. He laughed violently and almost soundlessly, in a way that gave Marcel gooseflesh. Horrified, he punched him and screamed: "What's the matter with you? Have you gone crazy?"

Georges stopped, but remained for a few moments in his

hunched attitude, then lifted his head and looked down the mountainside to the village. In his normal voice he said: "So they know who we are?"

"It was none of my doing," said Marcel. "That woman told them. But it was a good thing, don't you see? If we had only told them at the start——"

"We must get out," Georges cut him off. "We must get out of here at once." He turned to face him. "At once, do you hear?"

"No," said Marcel. He felt as though someone had punched him in the stomach.

"They came up the path," said Georges. "The same path that we used. I don't know how many there were. When I saw them my nerves went. I didn't mean to do it; it all happened too quickly."

"So you——"

"Yes, I have, I have!" shouted Georges. "And I did it for you and for Vieale and for us all. Anyhow, while you were having your cozy little party in the tunnel I was out here on my own. Why didn't you come when I fired those shots? Didn't you hear them?"

Marcel shook his head dumbly. He still felt stunned and clutched Georges' jacket. "Did you shoot one of them?" he asked in a whisper.

"One or two, I had no time to find out. It doesn't matter anyway. We'll ask Vieale to let us have some food and then get out. If only I knew where to," he said between clenched teeth. "In these damned mountains it's a great deal easier to starve than to find any food. Perhaps Vieale can suggest where we might go, or we could throw everything away and try to . . . I could kick myself for being so stupid as to leave our papers with the company clerk. If we had them we could prove that we were Swiss. Perhaps I'll have an idea."

"Of course," said Marcel, and was suddenly completely calm. "Of course you'll have an idea. You always do have ideas."

His tone made Georges look up. "What do you mean?"

"I said you always have an idea," answered Marcel in the same tone of voice. "And your latest idea is to make out that this affair is really all my fault. You had been away for at least two hours before that woman told the truth about us. Even if I had got up at once and run after you it wouldn't have made any difference. This time I'm not falling for it, Georges. And there's another thing I'm going to tell you."

"What on earth's the matter with you?" asked Georges.

"Something that ought to have been the matter with me long ago. But let me get this clear: did they see you when you shot at them?"

"I don't think so. I was sitting down with the groundsheet over me. Besides, I was half hidden behind a rock. They were just as surprised as I was."

"In that case you can stay here and if you won't stay here, I'm not carrying on."

Georges thought that he had misunderstood Marcel's words. "What won't you carry on?"

"I won't carry on with you," Marcel repeated clearly. "I'm sorry to say this, but I've had enough. I warned you and you wouldn't listen to me. If you want to get away from here you will have to go by yourself."

He's pulling my leg, thought Georges, and grinned. "Is this supposed to be a joke?"

"No." Marcel stood up. For the first time in his life he knew exactly what he wanted and had never before made up his mind so firmly. "I'll show you that it's not a joke."

Before Georges could stop him he took the machine carbine from his shoulder and with all his force struck the muzzle several times against a rock. Then he threw it on to the ground and turned to Georges, who had jumped to his feet and was staring at the gun. "No one can shoot with it now," said Marcel breathlessly. "Now perhaps you'll believe that I'm not joking."

Georges slowly raised his glance to Marcel's face, and nearly speechless with anger he muttered: "God rot your stupid guts, you fool."

"We'll see who's the bigger fool," said Marcel. "You with your ideas or me. Anyway, I've been thinking it over. I may go back to Switzerland after all."

"Oh, I see," said Georges. He walked right up to Marcel until they stood face to face. "When have you been thinking it over?"

"In the last few days. I don't intend to ruin my whole life just because of one of your ideas. I've never let you down; you know that. But I have more to lose than you have and if we pull out of here now we'll never have any peace. They'll catch us one day, so we've a better chance if we give ourselves up right away. What does it matter if they deport us and put us in prison? Even that will be over soon enough; but living on the run would be an endless agony. You could do as I'm going to do: stay here and play dumb. But I'm not running any more. I'm through with that."

Georges gave him a long and silent look, then bent down to pick up the gun. He held it up vertically and inspected the barrel. After examining the breech-block he detached the loaded magazine and shoved it into his coat pocket. "Where is my rucksack?" he asked.

Marcel made a stiff movement of his head towards the village. "In the street. I brought it up."

"Thanks," said Georges. With his own weapon over his shoulder and the other in his hand he began to climb up to the ridge.

"Where are you going?" Marcel shouted after him.

Georges did not reply. On reaching the ridge he turned right and climbed over half a dozen boulders until he reached a spot where the mountainside fell away to his left with a sheer drop of about a hundred and fifty feet. He threw the useless gun over the edge and watched it bounce off the mountainside, turn over once and disappear among the rocks. As he turned round he noticed Marcel, who had followed him. He stopped for a moment and looked at him as if he wanted to impress his face on his memory forever, but he did it without reflection and more from sheer absence of thought, much as one idly picks up something for no purpose and puts it down again. His feelings oscillated between painful surprise and a dull perplexity which was taking a growing hold on him and repressing the surprise. It gave him a feeling of emptiness, of having been drained; his heart was empty and his thoughts knotted in inextricable confusion.

As Marcel hesitantly approached him he turned round and clambered downhill in an instinctive urge to get away and be alone. He slowed his pace for a moment on the narrow path that led through the boulders to the village; behind him he heard the clink of a stone and assumed that Marcel was following him. Soon the path brought him to the end of the village street and there he saw the girl.

She was standing on the steps of the house and watching him as she had watched him from the town hall gateway, only this time she was wearing no coat. Her short-sleeved dress showed her knees; it had a round open neck and was belted at the waist. The rucksacks lay beside the steps; Georges walked up to them and picked up his pack.

Until this moment he had acted like a ball which once set in motion goes on rolling until its momentum is exhausted or until an obstacle blocks its path. In his case the obstacle was a girl and Georges was unaware of it until he had already slung his ruck-

170

sack, and his second's hesitation over which way to take made him look in Anna's direction.

She was leaning her shoulder against the doorpost and watching him with a look of tense expectation on her beautiful face. As Georges looked at her he felt his mouth go dry and looked away from her towards Marcel, who was slowly coming down the path. He carried the groundsheet in his hand, and as he reached them he threw it down and said: "You forgot this." He avoided looking at Georges and turned to the girl: "Are you still alone?"

She nodded, staring alternately at Marcel and Georges. "Where's your gun?" she asked Marcel.

"I don't need a gun any longer," he replied. "I've thrown it away."

Georges bent down to pick up his groundsheet, pushed it under the strap of his rucksack, then walked up the street and took the path between the boulders.

"What's the matter with him?" asked Anna anxiously.

Marcel sat down heavily on the steps. Since his conversation with Georges he felt miserable, and as exhausted as a man who has achieved something which he had believed to be beyond his strength, but has ruptured himself in doing so. As he watched Georges disappear he felt his eyes beginning to water and he might have got up and run after him if Anna had not sat down beside him and put her hand on his arm. "Have you quarreled with him?"

Her voice brought Marcel to his senses. He looked down at her and blinked a few times to drive off his tears, then nodded bitterly: "You can't talk to him. You never could. But I'm not running after him any more."

"Where is he going?"

"I don't know. Maybe right off."

"Altogether?"

Marcel nodded again. "I believe he would. When he loses his temper he doesn't know what he's doing."

"Then you should have stopped him from going," said Anna quietly. She took her hand from his arm. "What did you quarrel about? Because you had thrown away the gun?"

"Yes."

"I'm surprised at you," she said. "Why this sudden decision to throw it away? An hour ago I had the impression that he and you would never separate."

"I've changed my mind since then. It had to be done some

171

time. We couldn't take those carbines all the way back to Germany." He stood up uncertainly. "Perhaps I will run after him. He must be making for the ridge again."

"Where did you find him just now?"

"He was coming down the path towards me," said Marcel evasively. "Shall I go after him?"

"Why do you ask me? Couldn't you go and fetch your gun?"

"No good; it's smashed."

"Then run after him," said Anna. "Run fast."

From her seat by the steps, she watched him go. He walked faster and faster, until by the time he reached the boulders he was running.

She was just beginning to grow impatient at her uncle's long absence when she saw him coming up the street. Beside him walked Madame Vieale and both were laden with bags, blankets and bedclothes. Knopf had even put a pillow on his head and was carrying a small sack under his right arm. Anna dashed towards him and said reproachfully: "You shouldn't have carried so much. The doctor in Lyons told you not to strain yourself."

"The doctor in Lyons," said Knopf smiling, "obviously didn't know his job, otherwise he would have prescribed me much more exercise; it seems to do me a lot of good."

"We didn't want him to do it, Mademoiselle," said Denise Vieale. "We only wanted to give your father one bag. The rest he picked up himself."

"Sometimes men are more obstinate than children," said Anna, and took the sack and pillow from him. They had stopped in the middle of the street and Knopf wiped the sweat from his forehead. "Where is Monsieur Egli?"

"He ran after Monsieur Chabrier. They had a quarrel. Monsieur Egli threw away his gun," replied Anna. As they walked the rest of the way to the house she told him what had happened. "I can't imagine," she said finally, "where he intends to go all alone."

"He's a blockhead," said Denise Vieale, who had been listening. "He has nothing to eat with him."

Knopf waited until they had reached the house and put down their loads. Then he sat down on the steps and said to Denise Vieale: "Look at it my way. Today has produced so many surprises that one more or less makes no difference. With young people their hands and feet are always a fraction quicker than their reason."

"Even so I didn't think he would be so thoughtless," said Denise

172

Vieale. "And going off like that, without saying goodbye. . . ." she broke off and bit her lip with disappointment.

Anna was watching her closely. "You like him, don't you?" she said.

"Yes." The woman blushed slightly. "I like him in the same way that I like you, Anna. If I like somebody I make no secret of it. I tell people, too, if I don't like them."

"An admirable characteristic," said Knopf. "It only has the disadvantage that one ought not to exercise it all the time. Well, what do we do now?"

"I really must sit down," said Vieale's wife. "It's been a long day and an even longer night."

She put the pillow on the steps and sat down on it. Then she unbuttoned her coat, blew a strand of hair away from her face and looked round. "It hasn't changed a bit. So you live in this house?"

"It's no better looking than the others," said Knopf, "but it's the quietest street in which I have ever lived."

"It seems as if Pierre's not going to come after all," said Anna to Knopf. "Does it worry you?"

"No more and no less than usual. Still, while I was wondering why he hadn't come I thought of a good dozen harmless and natural explanations and that consoles me slightly. I'm sure he'll come tomorrow. Did you put the water on?"

"It should be boiling at any moment. But I shall have to go and fetch some more. And just look at my feet!"

"I noticed that they were dirty. I'm sure Madame Vieale will understand."

"When a girl has such beautiful legs," said the woman, "it doesn't matter if her feet are dirty."

Anna sat down beside her. "They've never been so dirty as they are today. It's because of the rain."

"Have you no stockings?"

"Some thick woolen ones. But I only wear them . . ." She broke off, for she suddenly saw Marcel appear at the end of the street. "He's alone," she whispered. "I thought he would bring him back."

Knopf stood up and they all stared at Marcel, who had by now seen them and slightly quickened his pace.

He looked deeply depressed and when he reached them he shrugged his shoulders helplessly. "I never saw him again," he said.

"Where did you look for him?" asked Anna.

173

"Everywhere. First I went up to the ridge and then I ran halfway to the spring. If he had been anywhere near he would have heard me. I called him."

"Then I don't see where he can have gone to," said Knopf. He looked at Anna who suddenly stood up and went indoors. "What are you going to do?" he called after her. As she did not reply, he fixed his gaze on Madame Vieale, who sat on the steps frowning and biting her lower lip. He noticed that the news had affected her strongly and said to Marcel, "Did you have such a violent quarrel, then?"

"I didn't quarrel with him at all," said Marcel, annoyed by his reproachful tone of voice. "I simply told him my opinion, that was all."

He turned to Madame Vieale: "You know how he is." But she refused to support him and stared away in silence. Annoyed, Marcel kept his eye on the door, wishing that the girl would reappear. He said to Knopf: "I never told him to go."

"Perhaps he'll change his mind," said Knopf consolingly. "When his temper has cooled down he'll have second thoughts. After all, you two have been through so much together that I can't seriously imagine how a little difference of opinion could separate you. But we must think about helping Monsieur Vieale; first I want to see how the coffee's getting on."

Presently, Knopf returned to the street. Madame Vieale was still sitting on the top step. Marcel was sitting on his rucksack with his back to the wall. He did not even look up when Knopf said that the coffee was ready and they could come indoors. "We have only one table," he added apologetically. "It's in Anna's room."

"Why bother with all that?" asked Madame Vieale. "We can drink the coffee out here."

Marcel got up. He did not know what he should tell Vieale, but he had already half decided to tell him no more than he had told the girl, because if Georges did come back—and Marcel clung to the notion like a drowning man to a piece of wood—he should not be met with more reproaches. He should be left to tell as much as he thought fit.

Now that he had cooled down sufficiently to feel an uncanny quiet from Georges's absence which grew more unsettling the longer it lasted, the first pangs of conscience made themselves felt and increased his unease. He could no longer bear to sit in idleness and said to Knopf, "I'll go and help Vieale. I don't want any coffee now."

174

"That's a pity," said Knopf. "By the time you come back it will be cold. Won't you have at least one cup?"

Marcel shook his head and walked quickly away.

"He has a bad conscience," said Denise Vieale. "I'd like to know what really occurred between those two."

Knopf sighed and sat down beside her. "These young people wear me out. I can never strike the right note with them and they always do the opposite of what I would in their place. Am I really so old or is it something else?"

"If it's any comfort to you I don't understand them either and I don't feel old enough yet to put it down to my age."

Anna appeared in the doorway. "Where is Monsieur Egli?" she at once inquired.

"Gone," said Knopf. "He didn't want any coffee and went off alone."

"To Monsieur Vieale?"

"Yes."

"Everyone here just runs off when he feels like it," said Anna. "I'm going to fetch some water. I've put the coffee on the table in my room. You and Madame Vieale can go up if you like."

"Won't you join us?" said Knopf, slightly hurt by her tone.

"No, otherwise it will be too late. Besides I don't feel like coffee." She disappeared indoors and Knopf stared after her with a worried look. "I don't know what's the matter with her. She's acting so strangely today."

"That sometimes happens with young girls," said Denise Vieale. She had her own ideas about Anna.

"Then I can at least invite you," said Knopf, rising.

They met Anna in the hall. She was carrying the empty bucket and had hung a towel over one shoulder.

"Don't stay away too long," said Knopf. "Pierre may come yet."

"I don't think he will," said Anna.

Deep in thought Anna walked rapidly along the path to the spring without once stopping, as she usually did, to gaze at the scenery or enjoy the hot sun of late afternoon. She reached the last few hundred yards before the spring more quickly than usual and was amazed to see a man lying on the path just short of the spring.

Anna recognized him before she could see his face. He had put the rucksack under his head, pulled up his legs and seemed to be asleep. His gun lay beside him.

She stopped, rigid with astonishment, undecided for a moment whether to run back or go on; as he did not move she took off her

175

sandals and walked towards him on bare feet. After a few moments looking at his face she was sure that he was asleep. She tiptoed past him, propped the bucket against the slate outcrop and turned round again. She could now have a good look at him. His long, narrow face with its narrow lips, the straight powerful nose and the thick beard had impressed her at first sight. She would have been unable to say exactly what had impressed her, for his features were neither attractive nor regular and his hair, which grew low on his forehead, looked as if it was rarely touched by a comb. Nevertheless she felt drawn to him, and as she watched him she realized how disappointed she had been when she heard that he had gone.

As if afraid that her stare might waken him she turned round to the rock and washed her feet. Then she dried them and when she was finished Georges said: "Wasn't the water too cold?"

She swung round and saw that he was sitting upright. Torn between the desire to run away and the urge to throw the wet towel in his face, she finished by doing neither and instead walked over to her sandals and put them on. Then she looked straight at him and said as coolly as she could: "Was it very funny?"

Georges stopped grinning. "Not exactly funny. You were so absorbed."

"So you weren't asleep?"

"No."

"You should be ashamed of yourself," said Anna calmly. She walked back to the bucket and turned her back on him.

Georges watched and waited. He took a cigarette, lit it and blew out the smoke. The girl had turned up at the moment when his deep perplexity had reached a critical stage. Running away had not solved his problem and had merely been a crude reaction caused by anger. Yet he had instinctively chosen a way by which he would avoid meeting Vieale and which eliminated any chance of stumbling across the Maquisards again. He had also had a raging thirst, so there was little choice open to him. His real problem only began to confront him when he had quenched his thirst and icy sobriety replaced his first wild urge to escape. The mounting conflict between his reason and his pride had reduced him to a state of paralyzing mental confusion; in the midst of this the girl appeared. He had seen her before she had noticed him and his relief was so great that he had shut his eyes the better to control his feelings.

He pushed the rucksack away from him and said apologetically: "I'm sorry, I didn't mean to annoy you. Or can't you take a joke?"

"You make rather curious jokes," she said.

Georges smiled. "Good, then I humbly beg your pardon. But don't keep your back turned to me and stop being a kipper."

She bit back a laugh and turned round. "What's a kipper?"

"Don't you know?"

"No."

"Your education has been neglected," said Georges. "A kipper is a smoked herring. You do know what a herring is, don't you?"

She nodded.

"Well then, imagine it dried and smoked and there you have a kipper. Wouldn't you like to sit on my rucksack?"

She hesitated slightly, then came and sat down alongside him on the rucksack.

"What are you doing here?" she inquired.

"I'm thinking."

"What about?"

"Oh, whatever comes into my head."

"Your friend told me you wanted to go."

"So he told you that, did he?"

"Yes."

"Did he also tell you why?"

"Because you and he had a quarrel."

Good, he hasn't given anything away, thought Georges. The news gave him satisfaction, although it did not immediately bear on his present problem. He said: "I didn't quarrel with him; he quarreled with me."

"You swore at him for throwing away his gun."

"Oh, did I? If he says so then I suppose I did."

"That sounds as if you disagreed."

"I'm an individualist; I always disagree."

"So I've noticed," she said in an ambiguous tone of voice. "Do you really want to go off alone?"

Georges frowned. He was sitting half a pace away from her on the ground and turned his body slightly in order to see her better. "Why does that concern you?"

"I'm just trying to imagine myself in your position, that's all. If you ask me, you're well and truly in the soup."

"That must give you great pleasure," said Georges flippantly. "I'm not the only one who's in the soup," he said. "It's a dilemma, but there is nothing much that you or I can do about it. Nor can the Germans, if it comes to that."

"What are you talking about?"

"I'm talking about the discrepancy," said Georges cheerfully. "About the discrepancy between good intentions and their result. Think what you like of me, but it was hardly my fault that the Germans were fated to commit national hara-kiri. The Germans I knew, with a few exceptions, were of the same opinion."

"I still don't understand what your opinion is."

"Then you haven't been listening properly."

"I was just thinking what you would look like without a beard," said Anna.

Georges laughed and leaned towards her so that his shoulder touched her. "You're not nearly as bad as I thought."

"Thanks." She nodded briefly. "I've learned a lot in the last few days. Or, more precisely, what my father used to tell me has been confirmed."

"I like him for that," said Georges. "What will you do when the war's over?"

"My father would like to go back to Germany. I may go with him."

"I plan to do the same. Only I don't know where to go."

"Your friend wants to go back to Switzerland."

"Did he tell you that?"

"Yes, but he will only go if you go with him."

"I'm surprised," said Georges. "Just now he said he would go back without me."

"Then he must have changed his mind."

"So it seems."

Anna smiled. "He invited me to come and see him there one day."

"To show you Switzerland."

"How do you know he said that?"

"I know our Marcel. He loves showing off with his car. You seem to have made a tremendous impression on him. I could almost believe that you were not unconnected with his sudden change of mind. Did you persuade him to return to Switzerland?"

"Not I; it was Madame Vieale."

"She interferes too much."

"She means to persuade you too."

"Me! She'd better not try."

"Wouldn't it be best for you?"

178

"Kindly let me decide what's best for me, girl."

"All right, soldier."

This annoyed Georges. "Will you stop this 'soldier' business. What are you trying to do, pull my leg?"

"I think it suits you."

She stood up and glanced at the bucket. She seemed disappointed, and Georges slowly pushed himself up from the ground and went over to her. "Why does it suit me?" he asked.

"Only a soldier could be as obstinate as you are. You should think of your father sometimes."

"Did Marcel give you that idea?"

"No. I'm saying it."

"And why do you say it?" He was standing near her in front of the dark wall of slate and noticed that the bucket was full to the brim.

"I would say it to anyone in your position," replied Anna.

"Really?" asked Georges, giving the bucket a gentle kick so that it upset and poured its contents over the girl's legs. She gave a terrified shriek and jumped aside. She stood and stared, first at the bucket, then at Georges, and finally at her own legs. As Georges made no move she said calmly: "You might at least apologize."

"Why should I?" said Georges. "I knocked it over on purpose."

"So I noticed. Why?"

"Because I wanted you to stay here," said Georges.

She went back to her place, sat down on the rucksack, pulled off her sandals and dried her legs with the towel.

"At least you can put the bucket back again," she said without looking up. "If I'm away for too long someone will come and fetch me."

"I wouldn't like that," said Georges. He threw his cigarette stub away and bent down to pick up the bucket.

"Why do you want me to stay here?" asked Anna.

"Guess," said Georges. His heart suddenly began to pound and he slowly walked towards her.

"I can't guess," she said. "You must tell me."

"Only if you want me to."

"Are you afraid to tell me?"

"No," said Georges. He bent over and kissed her on the mouth.

She let it happen, without doing anything, and when he took away his head she asked: "Was that why?"

179

Georges sat down on the ground in front of her and looked at her. "What are you really?" he asked. "A fish or what?"

"Perhaps a kipper," she said smiling. "Do I kiss properly?"

"You didn't kiss at all," said Georges. "You pressed your lips together."

"Shouldn't I?"

Georges felt a shudder run up his spine. He looked at her legs, which were so near to him that he was almost touching them with his mouth, and as he saw the soft curves behind her knees with their taut brown skin his body tensed with a dry, hot desire.

"Haven't you ever kissed anybody?" he asked.

She shook her head. "Not like that. Only on my cheek and once on my forehead, but that was a long time ago. How should I do it?"

"You mustn't press your lips together," said Georges dizzily. "You must make your mouth soft."

"Like that?" she asked and curled her lips outwards.

She had beautiful white teeth and Georges pulled her down to him so hard that she lost her balance and ended by lying with her back across his legs. He bent her head back and kissed her mouth, which was now quite soft, and her eyes, and then they were lying alongside one another on the hard ground and Georges felt her little breasts pressing against his chest, felt her firm, slim body and he forgot everything: his desertion, Marcel, the Maquisards and himself. Only when she began to plead and her eyes opened wide in sheer fright did he come to his senses, but he held her tight for a while longer and caressed her face until the fear went out of her eyes. Then he sat up and there was a feeling in his head as though he had drunk a whole bottle of Beaujolais.

Out of the corner of his eye he noticed the girl pull her dress over her brown thighs, sit up beside him and push her long hair out of her face.

"Phew!" she said breathlessly. "Are you savage."

"That's your fault," said Georges, in a voice which he didn't recognize.

She looked at him. "I didn't know it was like that," she said apologetically. "You frightened me." She pushed herself alongside him and gazed expectantly into his face. "Was it like that for you too?"

"Like what?" asked Georges thickly.

"It's not easy to say." She drew her legs up to her chest. "Like

180

a whirlwind," she then said. "I was sailing through the air and was afraid I would fall."

"You didn't fall," said Georges in the same clotted voice.

"No." She laid her head on his shoulder. "I held tight to you. Hey!"

"Yes?" said Georges.

She smiled up at him. "Hey, soldier!"

"I'll put you over my knee if you say soldier to me once more."

"Soldier," she said and went on smiling.

"What were you thinking?"

"When I said soldier?"

"No, just now."

"Nothing," she said. "Ought I to be thinking?"

"No," said Georges. "You shouldn't think at all. But would you do it with anybody?"

"Now you're crazy again," she said. "What do you take me for, anyway?"

"I'd like to know. But you did it with me."

"With you, yes."

"Why with me in particular?"

"I won't tell you," she answered, her head on his shoulder. "I'll never tell you."

"I know anyway," said Georges.

She put her hand on his lips. She had beautiful cool fingers with oval nails and she said: "Maybe. But you mustn't say it."

"Please," said Georges through her fingers. "Please, I promise not to tell."

"And not to ask any more questions?"

"And not to ask any more questions," said Georges. It struck him that he was talking to her as if they had known each other for twenty years.

"I think," said she, "that I'd prefer you without a beard."

"Then I'll shave."

"And then you'll kiss me again, will you?"

"Yes," he said, "then I'll kiss you again."

You're talking like a parrot, he thought. If Marcel could hear you he'd have a fit. Perhaps she has hypnotized you, so you're no longer normal. Have you gone stupid, or what's the matter with you.

"And you're not going to run away," said Anna. "You're going to come back to La Peine with me."

181

"I most certainly am not," Georges heard himself say, and he was relieved to recognize his own voice again.

She kept her fingers on his mouth for a moment, then took her hand away and asked: "Why not?"

Georges was silent. He had not wanted to tell her, but he did not know how he could avoid it. He lay on his back, shut his eyes and thought hard. "Will you help me?" he asked after a while.

"Yes," said the girl. Her face was so near to him that he could feel her breath.

"You must promise not to say a word to anyone about it."

"Yes," she said.

Georges opened his eyes and saw that she was leaning over him and looking at his mouth. He took hold of her long silky hair and wound it round his fingers. "If you tell anyone about it I shall have to go."

"I won't tell anybody."

"Not even your father?"

"No."

"I'll wait for you here," said Georges. "You must bring me something to eat."

"At once?"

"No, not until it's dark. And you won't tell them that I'm here. They mustn't find out. Do you understand?"

"No," she said and touched his mouth with her lips. "No, I don't understand."

"I'll explain everything this evening. You must go now, or they'll come looking for you. Will you find the way when it's dark?"

"I'll break my legs," she said and smiled.

Georges thought awhile, frowning. "Then we'll meet by the boulders. I'll wait for you on the path. Would that be better?"

She nodded and Georges let go her hair. "Then go now," he said. "And act as if nothing had happened."

"It may be very late before I come," she said. "I shall have to wait until they're all asleep."

"Then wait as long as you must. They must notice nothing."

"It's all so mysterious," she said. "Why do you make it so mysterious?"

Her face was close to his and her hair fell over her forehead and mouth; Georges pushed her hair aside and said: "If you don't trust me I can't stay here."

"Oh, you must stay here." Suddenly there were tears in her

182

eyes, and as she laid her face on his he could feel her whole body trembling. "You mustn't go away," she murmured. "Say that you'll stay here."

"We'll talk about that this evening," said Georges. "This evening, do you hear?"

She lay with her body half across him and he stroked her face and neck again. Through the neck of her dress he saw her little white breasts between the tawny brown of her shoulders, and his breath nearly stopped. Her mouth melted between his teeth like a lump of sugar and they held each other fast in an interlocking, interflowing embrace and were lost. When they drew breath again Anna pulled herself away and knelt beside him, both hands pressed to her face.

"Did I hurt you?" said Georges fearfully.

She shook her head and looked at him through her fingers. "I'm ashamed of myself," she said.

Georges laughed with relief. "You'll get over it. This evening you won't be ashamed any more."

He tried to pull her hands away from her face, but she only pressed them harder against it and said: "No, no, please."

"If you're going to be ashamed of yourself," said Georges, "I certainly can't stay here."

She quickly dropped her hands. "Then I'd better not. But what must you think of me?"

"That you're a sweet girl."

"You're just saying that."

"I think it too."

"I can't help it," she said helplessly. "I don't know what comes over me."

"Don't think about it."

"I'm frightened of it."

"I'll not do anything to you."

"No, I don't mean that," she said quickly. "I'm afraid because it hurts me so much. Here!" She put her hand on her breast. "Since seeing you this afternoon it has been hurting here. It's so violent, it frightens me."

"You needn't be frightened," said Georges. "Come here."

"I really must go now."

"Shall I carry the bucket for some of the way for you?"

"Better not. We might meet one of them. Promise me you'll still be here this evening."

"Yes."

"You must swear it," she said. "Put your hand where it hurts me and swear it to me."

Georges got slowly to his feet. The material of her dress was thin and smooth and Georges encircled her breast as if he were picking up a bird; he put his mouth against her neck and she said: "All right. Now I'm going."

He stood and watched her fetch the bucket and walk rapidly away without once looking back. Unthinkingly he pulled his cigarettes out of his pocket, lit one and sat down on his rucksack.

It had grown cooler. Georges sat with his head against the rock and tried to collect his thoughts, but his brain was drugged, and after sitting idle for half an hour he stood up and pressed his forehead against the slate. The ice-cold water ran down his face and dripped from his chin. Then he opened his rucksack, took out his shaving gear and soaped his face. He propped up a pocket mirror on the rucksack and knelt down in front of it. He had never before shaved in cold water, and when he was finished he had a deep gash on his chin and his skin burned like fire. He took a disgusted look at his face in the mirror and asked aloud: "Do you realize what you've started now? This is no harmless flirtation, as you'd like to think, and even if you did it simply because you could think of nothing better and because you want to make use of her to gain time for yourself, you're not worth a sou."

He stood up and washed off his face. Then he cleaned his razor, packed it back into his rucksack, and as he strapped it up his glance fell on the girl's towel. She had left it behind on the ground. He picked it up and held it uncertainly in his hand. It was still damp and smelt of perfumed soap. It was the same scent which he had noticed on the girl, and he said to himself that it was still not too late to shoulder his pack and march off.

But you don't want to march off, he thought, and you know it. You know quite well that you'd rather get yourself and the girl and the others into trouble than clear out; besides you promised her you wouldn't. You've even sworn it to her and it was a nice way of taking an oath, wasn't it! Very nice and very original and that stuff about getting them all into trouble is a bit of threadbare rhetoric out of a second-rate play. You're not going to get anyone into trouble if you stay hidden for a while and wait and see what happens in La Peine. At any rate it's safer than going back there, because if the Resistance men come they will automatically suspect you since you have a gun and no alibi for the time in question.

184

Not a bad idea at all, in fact, he said to himself, and the girl will take care of the food. You must just think very carefully what you're going to say to her this evening and whether it's wise to take her into your confidence. If she is so fond of those men from the Maquis she won't forgive you for having shot two of them.

Immersed in his thoughts he watched the night spread out along the valley and cover the wood with darkness. In a quarter of an hour it would be quite dark and Georges decided to move. The ammunition that he still had in his pockets he transferred to the rucksack. Then he slipped it over his shoulders and bent down for his gun. As he straightened up he heard from the distance the sharp crack of a tank gun and then again and a third time. For half a minute his limbs felt paralyzed and he stared incredulously in the direction from which the tanks had fired. No more shots were heard, so he set off as fast as he could along the path until he reached a spot beyond the narrow gorge from which he could see the pass. The growing darkness made it impossible to make out any details. Although the outlines of the mountain peaks still stood out sharply against the sky, the valleys were in total darkness and Georges stood, hesitating.

It must have come from the other side of the pass, he thought, perhaps farther. He knew that sound was very deceptive in the mountains and that the tank could as well have been immediately behind the pass as ten miles to the south of it, but he did not for a moment doubt that it was a tank. He had heard that nerve-shaking noise too often, and even at a greater distance he could have distinguished between that sound and the noise of a howitzer or a heavy mortar. As he feverishly wondered what the significance of the shots could be, a red glare flashed across the sky to the south and then followed the sound-waves of a heavy explosion many times greater in volume than the shots from the tank.

Georges felt his heart stop for a second. With a leaden feeling in his legs he leaned against the mountainside and stared breathlessly into the night.

Chapter 8

To make the falsified signposts seem as genuine as possible, Pierre drove after midnight with three men to a crossroads between Escarène and Sospel. There stood two rotten posts with weather-beaten, almost illegible signs. They dug them up, loaded them on to the car and Pierre took them to the workshop. He treated them first with paint and then with acid until the paint looked as if it were as old as the wood underneath it. Having done a few more minor repairs to the posts he called Gaston over and discussed a few details; shortly afterwards they were joined by Roger. "Jules is there," he said.

"Has he been to the bridge yet?" asked Pierre. Roger shook his head. "No."

"Why not?" asked Pierre sharply.

"Louis wouldn't give him any dynamite. He says he hasn't much left and what he has he needs for his own bridge."

"The damned swine," said Pierre, scarlet with fury. He stood up and walked several times rapidly up and down the room, then stopped in front of Roger. "Where is Jules?"

"He's eating."

"He's a damned coward," said Pierre contemptuously. "If I had gone there myself I would have got the dynamite. I can just imagine how he let Louis brush him off. He's no good. If he didn't have a car I would have kicked him out long ago. What did the American say about it?"

"Jules hasn't spoken to him."

"He wouldn't. So I suppose he has brought nobody with him who can handle the explosives?"

"No. Louis says——"

Pierre cut him off. "Save yourself the trouble. I can imagine what he says. He wants to pay us off for having refused to have ourselves massacred six weeks ago. He prefers to risk the chance of the Germans getting away."

"And if they do they will say it was our fault," said Gaston. "I bet he has lied to the American and told him that he has given us the dynamite."

"Of course he will have lied to him," said Pierre, dropping into a chair. "Jules was an ass not to make more of an effort to speak to the American. If I weren't quite sure that it's too late, I'd drive over there myself."

"It will be light in two hours," said Roger. "You'll never make it. The American will have left by now and so will Louis."

"Call it off then," said Gaston, and stuck a cigarette between his lips.

Pierre turned towards him. "What did you say?"

"Call it off," Gaston repeated. "We can't blow up the bridge without dynamite."

"Is dynamite the only way of blowing up a bridge?"

"No," said Gaston, his eyebrows rising.

"The mines!" said Roger, punching his forehead as he remembered.

Pierre grinned. "Louis never thought of that, although I told him only yesterday that we had captured forty German anti-tank mines. How many shall we need for the bridge?"

"Three," said Roger.

"Five," said Gaston.

Pierre looked at their smiling faces and said: "Ten. We'll take ten. With ten German mines I can blow up half a mountain."

"Detonator?" asked Gaston.

"Hand grenade and a hundred yards of wire."

"Two hundred would be better," said Roger. "Take stick grenades and attach two hundred yards of wire, then you can't go wrong. Better to be generous and run no risks."

Pierre stood up. "Fetch your men," he said to Gaston. "Besides you two I shall take ten with me. Six can get into Jules' car. He will drive behind us. When you get to the bridge, you, Roger, take my car and fetch the next contingent with Jules."

"I thought you wanted to go straight to La Peine," said Gaston.

"That can wait. First we must lay the charge on the bridge.

187

Get the mines down here and find the wire. And don't forget the hand grenades. If Louis' ears are any good he'll hear the bang as far as Col d'Allos."

"He thought he was being so clever," said Gaston. "He ambushes the Germans on the Col d'Allos while we are forced to let them escape over the Col de Tende because he wouldn't give us any dynamite. He will be the hero and we will be the fools."

"Or so he thinks," said Pierre.

Outside in the garden they divided; Roger and Gaston went up the street, while Pierre fetched his truck from the shed. He loaded the two signposts and pulled on overalls, then drove round to a small side-street off the main road. One of the houses belonged to Jules, who opened the door.

"Why haven't you reported to me?" asked Pierre.

"I met Roger and reported to him," answered Jules. "He was going to you."

"Did Roger send you on that job or did I?"

Jules said in an aggrieved voice: "Stop that, will you? What does it matter? I was hungry. I went off without having eaten anything. I was just coming to look for you."

"In future report to me and to no one else. Why didn't you talk to the American again?"

"Because he had already gone by the time Louis told me that he couldn't give me any dynamite. While he talked to the American he kept me waiting in another room for two hours and afterwards he came——"

"Typical," Pierre interrupted him. "If he had told you to go to Nice and count the benches on the promenade you would have done it. Take six men in your wagon and drive behind me."

He left him and returned to his truck. There he found Roger, Gaston and eight other men.

"How are you getting on?" he asked Gaston.

"We have four of the mines. Wire too."

"A few of you can go with Jules," said Pierre to the men. They had sub-machine guns and one carried a machine gun. "You stay with us," said Pierre to him.

Three others emerged from the darkness. Each one carried two mines, which they carefully deposited in the truck. In another five minutes the last men of the group appeared, carrying ammunition cases. When everything was loaded and the men seated in the truck, Pierre, Gaston and Roger climbed into the cab, switched

188

on the headlights and backed down the side-street to the main road.

"Has everybody brought enough food with him?" asked Pierre, as the truck accelerated up the chestnut-lined road.

"Enough for two days," replied Roger.

"If it lasts longer," said Pierre, "we'll get Jules to go and fetch hot food. Can you see him?" he asked Roger.

Roger craned out of the window. "He's there," he said. "Driving on his sidelights."

Gaston fell asleep with his head against Roger's shoulder and snored.

"High time the war finished," said Roger in a low voice. "Otherwise Gaston won't last much longer."

"We must send him away as soon as possible," Pierre murmured. "He even falls asleep standing up. It's the Germans being here that keeps him going. If they were to go he'd die the next day."

Roger drew at his cigarette and noticed that the sky was slowly turning gray. The mountains were beginning to close in on either side and the road had started to climb. "I still can't believe it," Roger began again. "No more war! That'll be the day."

"When it finally comes."

"It can't go on much longer."

"Let's hope not."

"I'm sure it can't," said Roger. "I'd prefer to be in Paris. It's a shame to be a Frenchman and never to have been in Paris. I want to go there once before I die. Wouldn't you?"

Pierre steered the truck round a tight bend before replying. "It's no place for poor people like us," he then said. "In Paris you need as much money in a day as you earn down here in a month."

"They might invite us. After we've been risking our necks at this business for a couple of years."

"No one will care a hoot about that when it's over. We'll go on the bottle for a few days and then back to the old grind just as we've always done. You in your vineyard and me in my joinery."

"I've always imagined it quite differently," said Roger. He threw his cigarette out of the window, crossed his arms and lapsed into silence.

Twenty minutes later, as the truck breasted the head of the second pass, a dazzling light flashed in their eyes and they saw the

189

sun rising over the mountains like a blob of violently luminous red paint.

The light wakened Gaston. He pressed his hands to his eyes and gave a dull groan.

Roger shook him by the shoulder. "What's the matter with you?"

"Leave him," said Pierre. "He always has a headache when he wakes up."

"Where are we?" asked Gaston, shielding his eyes.

"We're nearly there," answered Pierre. "In twenty minutes we'll be at the bridge."

Gaston dropped his hands. "Anybody got anything to drink?"

"Brandy," said Roger and gave him a small bottle. He watched him drink, then pull a face and shake himself slightly. "Do you want to poison me?" he asked with a gasp.

"If you don't like it," said Roger, "spit it out again."

"Let me sit by the window," said Gaston. "I need fresh air."

They changed places and Gaston stuck his head out of the window and coughed. "Damn!" he said, spitting on to the road. Then he looked over at Pierre. "Took you long enough to get here."

"Give me a new engine, then," said Pierre shrugging his shoulders. "With a new engine I'd make it in an hour."

"You ought to adjust the valves. They're making a noise like a telephone."

"It's not the valves, it's the gas. It's mud."

"Runs better on wine," said Roger and laughed.

The valley began to broaden out as the gradient of the road grew steeper. Pierre had to change down to first gear and put all his strength on the footbrake to slow the truck down sufficiently to take the sharp bends. The river was now in sight. They crossed it by a wooden bridge and Pierre brought the truck to such a violent halt that Gaston and Roger were almost catapulted through the windshield.

"Have you gone mad?" asked Gaston. Then he noticed a smoldering heap at the foot of the embankment of the road and he gave a shout of surprise. "What's that?"

"We shall soon find out," said Pierre and jumped out of the truck. The two men followed him and they ran down the embankment. Pierre poked about in the ashes with a piece of wood and fished out a half-charred scrap of cloth. He held it under Gaston's noise and asked: "What does it smell of?"

"My nose is blocked," replied Gaston and took the rag gingerly.

190

He showed it to Roger and dropped it from his outstretched fingers. Then he examined the grass and said: "There can't have been many of them. What do you think?"

"I don't think so either," said Roger. They stared at Pierre who was staring vacantly past the bridge and down the valley. "You don't seem to like the look of it, do you?"

Pierre slowly turned round to face him. "What did you say?"

"I said you didn't seem to like the look of it," Gaston repeated. "Do you?"

Gaston shrugged his narrow shoulders. "Don't know what to make of it. Suppose they were deserters. . . ."

"They were for sure," said Roger. "Otherwise why would they have burned their uniforms? They must have had civilian clothes."

"They can't have been gone long," said Gaston, and kicked the ashes. "It's still glowing. If we tried to catch up with them——"

"We've no time for that now," Pierre interrupted him sharply. "Besides we don't know which way they went. If they were making for La Peine we'll catch them anyhow."

He looked over to the truck; the men in the back had stuck out their heads inquiringly. At that moment Jules drove over the bridge. He leaned out of the window and shouted: "What's up?"

"Nothing," answered Pierre. "Unload and go back and fetch the next lot." He walked back to the truck with Roger and Gaston and Pierre pointed at the signpost. "That's one of them; the other is three miles farther, at the fork. You'd better do that one," he said to Gaston. "Take a few men with you. When you come back Roger will drive to Escarène. If there are any more left Jules must bring them. In three hours we'll have finished with the bridge and then I shall need the truck again."

"That's cutting it rather fine," said Roger reflectively.

Jules's men climbed out of the car. "Wait here," Pierre said to them. "Gaston will collect you in a minute." Then he drove his truck to the steel bridge at the mouth of the gorge, where his men dismounted and set about laying the mines on the bridge.

When the truck was empty Gaston asked: "What do we do with the real signposts? Throw them in the river?"

"That's too dangerous," replied Pierre. "Load them into the back. If they are too firmly planted drag them out with the truck."

Gaston touched the edge of his beret with his finger and took Pierre's place in the driving seat. Pierre and Roger walked on to the bridge. The men were standing around smoking and talking.

"We must first find a hiding place for the man who fires the

191

charge," said Roger and looked up the steep mountainside. "Where do you think?"

Pierre beckoned two men to him and gave one of them a roll of wire. Then he took another look at the opposite cliff-face. A little down the valley, in the direction of the wooden bridge, the side of the valley was strewn with boulders. Pierre pointed to one of them, as big as a house. "That's the place," he said to the two men. "You must get up there and throw down the roll of wire. But don't forget to keep hold of the end and don't throw it unto the river. You must throw it over the river."

The bridge consisted of two free-standing box trestles made up of riveted plates. They were about three feet deep, joined by a framework of transverse girders on which had been laid a reinforced concrete roadbed covered by a thin layer of macadam. The ends of the trestles rested on concrete abutments which jutted from the embankment into the river-bed. As Pierre leaned over the railing of the bridge, he noticed that from the downstream side of one of the concrete piers there projected two semicircular iron handles. He pointed these out to Roger and the other men and one said: "Looks like a drawer."

"More like a plug," said Roger. "That gives me an idea. Do you know what that is?"

"It's not difficult to guess," said Pierre with satisfaction. "I recognize it from my army days. All bridges leading to a fort have them. They are built-in mine chambers, closed by a concrete plug. You pull it out by those handles, pack in the charge and replace the plug."

"Somebody will have to go into the water to get at it," said Roger.

"Yes, but they won't have to go in very deep," said Pierre, pointing down into the clear water. About eighteen inches below the water level there was a projecting plinth wide enough to take a man.

Pierre pulled off his shoes and socks, rolled up his trouser-legs above his knees and climbed down the embankment. He cautiously picked his way through the shallows until he stood on the plinth within reach of the iron handles. He tried to pull them, but was unable to move the concrete plug, and returned to the bank.

"We must wait until the truck comes back," he said to the men. "I need hammer and chisel."

He took Roger aside. They sat down on the embankment and

192

rehearsed their plans step by step. "You must take charge of blowing up the bridge," said Pierre. "When Jules arrives with the last batch of men, send him ten or twelve miles down the road. There he must position himself and wait for the Boches. As soon as they appear he's to come back, tell you, and then drive his car a short distance up the side valley. You must do the same with my old truck."

"Clear so far," said Roger. He had rolled himself a cigarette and stuck it between his lips. "What I don't like about it," Roger went on, "is that you won't blow up the bridge yourself. If anything goes wrong it will be my fault. I've never done it before, you know."

"Nothing can go wrong," countered Pierre. "I've never blown up a bridge either, but it's a simple matter. You don't blow it up until you see the Germans coming back. You need do nothing but pull the wire; everything else works by itself. I don't care whether we catch the whole division; I'll be content with half. The main action will not be at the bridge but in La Peine, and there I certainly mustn't make a mistake or I shall be the one who gets blown up. With you I know it's in good hands."

Roger grumbled slightly but he felt flattered, and for a while they discussed details until Gaston came back with the truck. "All fixed," he said in his throaty voice. "How are things here?"

"Fetch me a hammer and chisel out of the tool chest," was Pierre's reply.

He explained the plan and finished by saying: "We'll tie the rope to the truck and pull the things out." Gaston fetched a stout tow-rope from the truck and Pierre once again waded into the water and knotted an end of the rope round the handles. Giving the free end to Gaston he said: "There's a hook over the back axle."

The tow-line fastened, Gaston sat down behind the steering-wheel and waited for Pierre's signal. He crawled forward a few inches. Pierre drove the cold chisel into the seam. Suddenly a concrete cube, weighing at least fifty pounds, jerked out of the abutment like a molar.

All the men gathered on the bridge to watch Pierre as he untied the rope, then peered into the mine chamber. It was about two feet high, of the same width and led deep into the abutment. Having made sure that the mines would fit into the chamber, he primed them and sent all the men away from the bridge with the exception of two who handed the mines down to him. Then

193

began the dangerous part of the job. He shoved five of the heavy dish-shaped mines one after another into the chamber like loaves of bread, took three stick grenades, lashed them together with a length of wire and screwed down their safety-caps. Then he removed the igniter-buttons, wrapped more wire round the igniter-cords and carefully jammed the grenades between the mines so that they could not move. He fastened the wire to the chamber wall with insulating tape, led the free end of the wire outside and looked around for Roger who had now opened the mine chamber on the other side and was climbing up the embankment.

"I'll do the rest," Pierre shouted to him. "You can go now."

Roger dried his feet, put on his socks and shoes and took Gaston's place in the truck. As he roared over the bridge and down the road the men looked after him and laughed. Gaston met Pierre on the bridge. "He drives like a madman," he said grinning. "There was a time when you wouldn't let him drive your truck."

"He's a safe driver," said Pierre. "He was driving a truck in the First World War. I don't care if the old crate does fall to pieces now. She's done her bit."

"Will you buy a new one?"

"If I can find someone who's fool enough to give me the money for it. For the business I need . . ."

He was interrupted by shouting and saw that the men on the bank were pointing upwards. Looking up at the mountainside he saw the head of a man appear over the skyline and then wave his arm. A second man came in sight a moment later.

"They've made it," said Pierre with satisfaction, and explained to Gaston what the two men were doing.

"Look out," he shouted to the others. "They're throwing down the wire."

Another minute passed, then the roll of wire fell in a wide arc, unrolling itself as it dropped, and crashed down in the middle of the road.

Pierre signaled to the two men. As they climbed over rocks and boulders to their position, Pierre walked back to the bridge, unrolling the wire as he went. He tied it to the railings and set about packing the charge into the second mine chamber. Gaston helped him to push the heavy concrete blocks back into their holes, and it was obvious that the joints were so wide that the wire would not jam. The two strands dangling from the mine chambers Pierre joined to a third wire, which he stretched across the river and made fast on the far side to form a bracing-line. Then he un-

194

tied the draw-line from the railings and leaned over the edge until he touched the bracing-line. He wrapped the free end of the draw-line exactly round its center, knotted it and made sure that it would not pull free.

"An expert would turn up his nose at it," he said to Gaston. "But I think it's good enough for our purpose."

"I think so too," said Gaston, and looked over the railing. "Let's hope those two up there don't take it into their heads to pull the wire now. It's pretty taut."

"That's due to the current," said Pierre, "but there's not enough tension to detonate the hand grenades. Now we must wait for Roger."

It was still early in the day. Pierre occasionally looked at his watch. He seemed nervous and Gaston, who did not fail to notice it, grinned. "If I were you I wouldn't worry. To get from here to La Peine on foot takes five hours. They'll be marching almost all the way uphill. We're bound to beat them to it."

"If I didn't know that perfectly well," said Pierre, "I would have driven after them at once. Even so it worries me. What are they doing in La Peine of all places?"

"I'll bet they've no idea that the road stops there. If they really are deserters they will have avoided the D206 as being too dangerous."

"Possibly," said Pierre.

Gaston picked his nose. "Of course they could equally well have been going in the other direction, towards Nice. Perhaps they haven't heard what's happening there."

"In that case they have already been in La Peine."

"Yes, they have," said Gaston, in a matter-of-fact voice.

Pierre lay down on his back and said between clenched teeth: "They can never go too far for me to find them."

"Nobody can," said Gaston, exposing his yellow teeth in a grin.

They waited more than an hour for Roger. Jules returned sooner. He brought with him another six men and set off again to Escarène to fetch the remainder. After going over the plans once more with Roger, Pierre put twelve men into his truck and seated himself behind the steering-wheel. Gaston was the last to climb aboard. He had fallen asleep again and Roger had been obliged to wake him roughly.

"You shouldn't have let me go to sleep," he murmured, as he sat beside Pierre. "Now I have pains in my head again."

195

"It's good for you to sleep a lot," said Pierre, as the truck drove off.

"One of these days I'll sleep long enough," said Gaston. "Till then I want to get what I can out of life. It's hot today. What's the time?"

"Ten o'clock. We're in good time. By four o'clock this afternoon I'll be back with you again."

"Do you think you can make it?"

"Provided nothing goes wrong. We'll be in La Peine at eleven; from there back to Escarène I shall need two and a half hours and another two and a half for the return journey. Only we mustn't lose any time. I'll pick up Monsieur Knopf at once and collect Roger and the rest of the men on the way back. Roger will then drive the truck up the valley behind the bridge, leave it there and go to his men. That reminds me—I never asked him whether he had filled up the tank."

"He surely remembered to do that," said Gaston. He took off his jacket and stuck his arm out of the window. "Damned hot in this crate of yours."

Pierre looked sideways at his face. They were still driving up the gorge, and the cool breath of the river was blowing through the open cab windows. "Are you really so hot?" asked Pierre.

"Aren't you?" said Gaston. Red spots were burning on his cheeks and he continually wiped the sweat from his forehead.

"I don't mind the heat," said Pierre.

"I'll be glad when it's winter again," said Gaston. "I can stand the winter better. I ought to live in Valberg."

"Perhaps you'll win the lottery one day, then you can build yourself a house in Valberg."

"When the war's over," said Gaston, "I'll buy some lottery tickets again. Do you think there'll be a chance?"

"Other people have been lucky before. But you'll have to stop knocking it back, or even the top prize won't do you any good."

"It won't do me any good at all if I don't win it," said Gaston. "Has anyone like us ever won it?"

"There are cases——"

"Oh, shut up," said Gaston. "I'm not a 'case'! I've been a poor wretch all my life and will always be one." He settled himself in his corner and went to sleep.

Pierre spat out of the window. He was always depressed after talking to Gaston.

They were now climbing up towards the pass. Whenever the

196

truck bumped over stones and potholes Pierre heard the men in the back cursing, but he could not afford to consider them now. As they crossed the head of the pass he saw a dark bank of cloud coming over the mountains. He cursed and gave Gaston a hefty punch. "Look at that," he said. "Not a drop of rain for nine weeks and now there's a thunderstorm brewing today of all days."

Gaston rubbed his eyes and blinked. Then he was suddenly wide awake. "Just our luck," he said. "And I didn't bring an umbrella."

Pierre grinned. "A drop of water won't do you any harm. You stink."

"You stink so much you can't even smell yourself any more," retorted Gaston. He watched as Pierre carefully steered the truck round the hairpin bends. Then halfway round the last bend before the hollow Pierre trod hard on the brake and they stared at two armed men in uniform standing in the road and looking up at them.

"What the hell. . . ." Gaston began and said no more. He looked at Pierre, who swallowed rapidly several times as if his mouth was full of water and his face was quite gray. "There are two more up there," he said, and as Gaston searched the road beyond the hollow he noticed two dark spots which suddenly disappeared between the boulders on the left-hand side of the road. The two soldiers in the hollow were now also on the move. They left the road and positioned themselves behind a rock which covered them up to the chest. Their multi-colored uniforms showed up clearly against the grey of the rock.

"This is a trap for sure," said Gaston and ground his yellow teeth. "But you're the boss."

Pierre was silent. His brow was covered with droplets of sweat. Never in his life had a decision cost him so much disappointment as when he changed into reverse and drove the truck backwards up the road.

Pierre brought the truck to a halt on the uphill side of the bend, leaned his face against the steering-wheel and sat silently for a while without moving.

"They may yet be all right," said Gaston. "Perhaps they were able to get away in time or have hidden themselves. If they have been caught it's too late now anyway." He paused, and as Pierre still said nothing, he said irritably: "Well, this isn't getting us anywhere either. Why don't you drive on and try and see whether we can get through? We can't do more than be killed."

Pierre lifted his head and stared at him vacantly. Then he

opened his door and jumped on to the roadway. He went round to the men in the back.

"We've seen them," said one. "What are you going to do?"

"We'll never get through alive," said another.

"Don't be so stupid," said Pierre, and beckoned two to get down. "You two stay here. I'll just drive a bit farther uphill until they can't see the truck any more. Wait for a quarter of an hour then come back to us. I want to know what they do when they see the truck drive away."

"Is that all?" asked one of the two.

Pierre nodded and mounted the truck again.

"What good will that do?" asked Gaston, who had been listening.

"There are two possibilities," replied Pierre as he drove the truck into the curve and turned it round. "Either they are sentries or they were going somewhere."

"Where to?"

"That's what I'd like to know," said Pierre. He had now turned the truck round and drove about a mile uphill towards the pass. Then he and Gaston got out and he said to the other men: "You can get out and stretch your legs now. But don't go far away."

He sat down in the sun on a rock and watched the black bank of cloud creep slowly over the sky. Gaston was standing near him and spat at an ant which was running across the road. He missed it, and filling his mouth with spit, he bent over the ant and dropped his mouthful onto the ant. Then he said to Pierre: "If they are going towards La Peine there might be an explanation: they are chasing the deserters."

"We'll find out," said Pierre.

The two men returned sooner than Pierre had expected. He listened to them with a frown and then conferred with Gaston. "We've only one chance," he said; "we must try to get up on to the ridge."

"Provided there are no more of them up there."

"We'll have to risk it. I must know what's going on in La Peine."

"I tell you we'll never get through. They'll shoot the truck to pieces."

"There's another way," said Pierre and jumped to his feet. He called to the men to board the truck. "Hang on tight," he said. "This is not going to be a picnic."

Roger saw the truck emerge from the gorge. He was standing in the road and directing the men to their positions by arm signals.

When he saw the truck coming he dropped his arms and walked a few paces to meet it. "Did you run away?" he asked in amazement.

"Something like it," replied Gaston. "I never knew till now just how fast an old wagon like this can drive when it's going downhill."

As Roger turned uncomprehendingly to Pierre, Gaston walked round the truck and looked into the back. The men were all lying on the floor and their faces were green and yellow.

"Let me get at him and I'll riddle his guts," said the man with the machine gun as he rose groaning to his feet. As if at a word of command the others began swearing in chorus. "Better to have no one driving than that madman!" shouted one of them.

Gaston gave a grin. "Stop bawling or we'll bring your wives too on the next run!" He rejoined Pierre and said: "They want to do you in."

"They can wait until tomorrow," said Pierre. He had told their story to Roger in a few words and Roger scratched uneasily behind his ear. "This could ruin the whole thing," he said.

"How are you getting on?" asked Pierre.

"My men are up in position. I've placed them so that they can't be seen from the road."

"Is Jules here yet?"

"Yes. I gave him one man and told him to drive a few miles past the fork and keep a lookout."

"Right. Now listen," said Pierre. "I shall take everyone from here who's superfluous. On the road I shall take there are no passes, and if we squeeze up a bit there's enough room. First we'll try to get up there from behind. If that is no good we'll block the road somewhere before it joins the N204 in the direction of the Col de Tende. As soon as the Germans are in La Peine they'll see the D206 and climb down to it. We'll wait for them in a suitable place which I will find. As it is I'm not too sure of the details of that area for the moment. Perhaps we'll be lucky and find a tunnel. Tell your men that there's a thunderstorm on the way."

"A storm?" Roger stared at the blue sky. "Where?"

"You can see it from the pass. You mustn't lose any time. There are enough rocks lying around to build yourselves shelter from the rain, but no one may leave his position. If the Germans haven't come by tomorrow evening send Jules back to Escaréne to fetch hot food."

"And for you?"

"Of course. I'll drive down when it's dark and fetch it." As

199

Pierre was talking to Roger, Gaston went over to a group of his men who were playing cards on the grass.

"Get ready," Gaston said to them. "We're all going together in the truck." He described what had happened and one of them collected up the cards. "We'll finish the game later," he said. "Is there room in the truck?"

"Yes, if you keep your stomachs tucked in," said Gaston. When his men and Pierre's group had somehow all squeezed themselves into the back of the truck he said: "We haven't far to go. We'll be there in an hour."

"We shan't need as much as an hour," said Pierre. "Are you comfortable?" he asked the crew in the back. The men laughed and shouted back a few jokes. "If you drive like that again," yelled the machine-gunner, "I'll shoot a hole in your gas tank."

"Remember to write a letter to your wife before you do that," said Pierre.

As he and Gaston climbed into the cab the sun vanished and it quickly grew darker. The storm broke upon them in earnest when they had passed the fork and were driving up the D206 along a narrow valley.

Pierre switched on his headlights and windshield-wiper. "If we're lucky," he said, "the worst of the storm will be over in an hour. I'm afraid Roger will get wet through."

"He's got a thick enough skin not to mind," said Gaston and curled up snugly in his corner.

Pierre now had to drive with great care. The rain was so violent that the windshield-wiper was almost completely ineffective. The dark sides of the valley were lit up by almost ceaseless flashes of lightning and the shattering claps of thunder drowned even the noise of the engine. The cloudburst lasted about half an hour, then visibility improved and Pierre was able to accelerate. The road followed the valley north-eastwards, then veered to the north-west and finally ran due west.

A look at his watch showed Pierre that they had been driving for over an hour. "We've lost time," he said to Gaston. "But for this storm we could have been there by now."

"What does it matter?" said Gaston, yawning. "It's always either too late or too early. We do what we can, that's all."

"If only I'd driven up yesterday evening," said Pierre bitterly. "I should have fetched Knopf then. But I swear one thing: if anything has happened to them I'll string a few of the Boches up."

200

Gaston shrugged. "Don't overdo it. You may have trouble with the Americans."

"In my private affairs," said Pierre, "no one tells me what to do; not even the Americans."

After another ten minutes' driving the valley widened out and they reached the point where the river joined the road again. They crossed it by a bridge and followed it until the valley took a swing northwards.

"Isn't this it?" asked Gaston.

"I'm looking for a better place," said Pierre. "There must be a wood somewhere. I've only been up this way once before, but . . ." He broke off. They had taken a sharp left-hand bend and there to the left of the road were some olive trees, which grew more numerous until they formed a small wood for about two hundred yards along the road.

"I wish I had your memory," said Gaston.

Pierre steered the truck off the road and halted a few yards inside the wood. "This will do," he said. "We'll leave one unarmed man behind; if anybody comes past he will say he's had a breakdown. The others must dismount and hide themselves until I get back."

"Until we get back," said Gaston.

"To be honest I'd prefer you to stay here."

"Perhaps you would," said Gaston. "But I'm just as keen to know what's going on in La Peine as you are. How many men will you take with you?"

"Five will be enough. If you come, too, that makes seven. As long as I don't know how strong the Germans are I'm not taking any risks. If they're in the fort none of us will get back alive. I shall in any case climb the last three hundred yards on my own."

"And if it's only those four Germans we saw earlier?"

"Then we'll deal with them and send a man back to fetch the others. Not a moment sooner."

They climbed down from the cab. The thunderstorm had moved southwards, but the rain was still falling. Great drops fell from the trees and Gaston turned up his coat collar. "If only I had an overcoat," he said peevishly.

"You can stay and sit in the cab," said Pierre.

"Put on a new record," said Gaston, and joined the men climbing out of the truck. He selected five men and brought them to Pierre who had meanwhile started talking to a hefty, bearded man.

"You're in charge as long as we're away," he said to him. "Split up in the woods so that you can't be seen from the road. If anything unusual happens send a man after us."

"Shall we take the machine gun?" asked Gaston.

Pierre shook his head. "It would only hinder us. It will be rough going."

He inspected the five men. None of them was older than twenty-five. Besides their weapons three of them carried a small sack fastened at the neck with string, and the other two each had an old French army ration bag hanging at his side.

"How much ammunition have you?" asked Pierre.

"Two hundred rounds apiece," replied Gaston. "That will do for a start."

Pierre slung his rifle over his back, gave his final instructions to the man with the beard, then set off up the road with Gaston and the five men. They followed it for about ten minutes, until they came to a path which wound its way up the right-hand side of the valley.

"This is it," said Pierre to Gaston. "I hope your lungs will stand it."

"They will if you don't rush on ahead of me," said Gaston, and led the way up the path. He set such a pace that the men had difficulty in keeping up with him. As the rain fell unabated they were wet to the skin after a quarter of an hour. Twice Pierre took over the lead from Gaston, and when they had been on the march for an hour he ordered a short halt.

Gaston sat down on a stone. He was breathing with wide open mouth, making a noise like a rusty engine.

"You can still change your mind," said Pierre.

"Why are you always bothering about me?" asked Gaston, annoyed. "I'll run you all off your feet."

"That's a good one," said one of them.

Gaston stared at him in fury. "Take care you don't swallow your false teeth," he said and stood up. He walked rapidly on, and when Pierre tried to hold him back he pulled himself free and said: "I know you've written me off already."

"Of course we haven't, you idiot," said Pierre.

The path into the mountains seemed endless. Although Pierre made several attempts to take over the lead from Gaston again, Gaston would not let him and each time he quickened his pace so much that Pierre was forced to drop behind. In time the rain slackened off and the sky brightened. Higher up, where the fort lay, the mountain was still hidden in cloud.

After two hours on the march Pierre began to think that he must have miscalculated the distance. Originally he had hoped to reach the fort in two and a half hours, but it now looked as if they would need twice the time. The path took another bend and Pierre, who was walking a yard behind Gaston, saw him fall even before he heard the shots; his face hit Gaston's leg as he fell, the whip-crack of the rifle in his ears, and when it was quiet he slowly raised his head and it seemed a miracle that he was still alive.

Dragging Gaston's inanimate body by the legs, Pierre crawled back a few yards and turned to look at the others' pale frightened faces. Then he took the rifle from his back, climbed over Gaston and hobbled on his knees to the bend in the path. From here the path ran for about two hundred yards up the valleyside and then disappeared at the next turning between two boulders.

After watching the way ahead for a few minutes he crawled back. They had laid Gaston on his back and unbuttoned his coat and shirt; Pierre bent over him and examined the three circular holes in the right side of his chest.

"His heart's still beating," said one of the men. "The bullets must be in him. They haven't come out at his back."

"Run!" said Pierre. "Send up five more men and bring a blanket. Run as fast as you can."

The man ran down the path in the rain. Pierre looked after him for a second, then gave his rifle and Gaston's to another man and pulled a pack of bandages from his pocket.

"Lift him up," he said to the men. Pierre bandaged him and they pulled off his bloodstained shirt. "Perhaps we'll get him through," he said. "We must take him to the hospital in Sospel. If we get him there alive you can all get drunk for a week on end at my expense. Put him on my back. One of you must hold up his feet."

He bent over until Gaston was safely on his back, then gripped his hands and carefully straightened up. One man put his arm under Gaston's legs and they slowly carried him downhill.

It was a laborious journey. The path was scattered with rocks made smooth by the rain and skirted many sheer precipices. They took turns at carrying Gaston but when the sun broke through the clouds an hour later they had covered a bare fifth of the way.

Even Pierre lost heart. But he was determined to bring Gaston to Sospel and he would not believe that Gaston was dead until he had heard the verdict from a doctor. Sometimes he thought that he felt a shudder go through the body on his back, and then he would

203

stop and turn his face round until he could see the lolling head with its yellow skin. He had always been fond of him; he was his only really close friend. Besides him there had only been two other people in his life who had meant much to him, but one had left him and the Germans had probably caught the other one, and if he had not schooled himself to keep his feelings to himself he would have sobbed as he went.

After three hours they were halfway down and they met the man coming to find them. They laid Gaston on the blanket, picked it up by the ends and carried him thus the rest of the way.

Pierre came last in the file and overheard the others talking.

"They must have been sentries," said one. "They occupied the whole mountain. If they'd been quicker off the mark they'd have got all of us."

"You've had the devil's luck," said another from the party which had just joined them. "How many were they, did you see?"

"No, but at least ten or more."

"If you ask me the whole plan was a stupid——" The speaker broke off; looking back over his shoulder he continued speaking so softly that Pierre could no longer hear him. But Pierre was not concerned. He agreed with what the man was saying, for since they had been fired upon he knew that he had made a mistake. The burned uniforms had caused him to underestimate the danger and he had agreed with Gaston that the soldiers they had seen were only part of a small patrol in search of the deserters. In fact it now seemed that the deserters had come from La Peine and were on their way to Nice. Now that Pierre was convinced that a much stronger German unit had occupied the fort and the village, this explanation seemed to him the most likely, even though he could not imagine why they should want to go to La Peine. At the same time the thought gave rise to a faint hope, as he felt it as good as impossible that Knopf and Boris should not have noticed the approach of so many troops. Perhaps they had been able to get away in time and had fled over the ridge.

Suddenly a noise from in front attracted his attention. The men carrying Gaston had stopped, and when Pierre caught up with them in a few rapid strides he saw that Gaston's eyes were open.

"He's alive!" said the man carrying his feet. "He just groaned."

Pierre bent over Gaston and said hoarsely: "It's all right, Gaston."

All the men had gathered round and stared at Gaston, who looked from one to the other. His nose stuck straight upwards and

204

there were drops of sweat on his forehead. Pierre wiped them off with his handkerchief and said: "We're taking you to Sospel. Do you understand?"

Again Gaston said nothing and Pierre thought he was too weak, but he was glad that he was still alive and took one end of the blanket himself. "If we hurry," he said, "we'll be down in an hour. Come on!"

They went on as fast as the way would allow. As the relays of carriers changed over on the move and the path grew gradually wider they made better progress. Gaston had closed his eyes again.

A bare hour more brought them to the road and they covered the last stretch to the wood almost at a run. There the others were waiting for them.

The sun had long since set behind the mountains and it was twilight in the valley when they laid Gaston in the truck. They had tried to give him a drink of wine, but he kept his mouth firmly shut and gave no sign of life.

Pierre discussed the situation with the man with the beard. He was called Raymond and was a butcher by profession. "If all goes well," said Pierre to him, "I'll be back by midnight."

"What do we do if the Germans come before then?" asked Raymond.

"No chance of it," said Pierre. "If they come it won't be before tomorrow morning. From the bridge to La Peine they will need four hours and another three to come down by this route."

"What do you mean, from the bridge?" asked Raymond. "They're sitting up in the village already."

"Those are not the ones that we are expecting. It is probably an isolated unit that has been cut off. The division that the Americans are expecting hasn't had time to get here yet."

"Let's hope they don't notice the trick with the signposts, otherwise they will take this road and come past here."

"In that case we can do nothing anyway," said Pierre impatiently. "You're not to get involved in anything before I get back. It may be that we shall only catch a fraction of the division in the valley. If the rest come past here you must leave them alone. They're certain to have heavy weapons. I'm only interested in the ones who are in La Peine already and any others who may join them. When they realize that the bridge has been blown up they will try to come down on this side and by then I shall be back in any case."

"Let's hope to God that you are," said Raymond. "You know

205

that I'm not afraid, but I should hate to be responsible for anything that went wrong. It has started badly enough already."

"The war started badly too," said Pierre, "and now we are winning it all the same."

He went to the truck and assured himself that Gaston was comfortable. Then he called two men and ordered them to sit beside him. "Hold him tight," he said to them, "so that he doesn't roll. If he comes to, give him something to drink."

He climbed into the truck and pushed another blanket under Gaston's head. Then he felt his pulse. His hands were so cold that Pierre felt a stab of terror. Feeling no pulse-beat he laid his ear to his chest and then he had the certain feeling that Gaston was dead.

He lifted his head and looked at the two men who had come into the truck with him; outside stood the others in a tight group, staring up at him, and although he knew that Gaston was dead, he said loudly: "He's alive. The doctor will operate on him and he'll be all right."

None of the men said a word and as he jumped from the tailboard they made way for him and avoided looking at him. He stopped and shouted: "He's alive, I said. Are you deaf?"

"All right," said Raymond. "If he's alive, that's fine."

"Don't you believe he's alive?" asked Pierre threateningly.

"If you say he is why shouldn't we believe you? You must know."

"I heard his heart beating," said Pierre. "And now I'm driving to Sospel and when this is over we'll all go and visit him. Or does anybody not want to visit him?"

There was an embarrassed silence and again Raymond spoke for them. "Of course we'll all go and visit him."

"Good," said Pierre, "but whether you believe it or not, I heard his heart beat."

He sat down behind the wheel, backed the truck onto the road and beckoned Raymond to him: "Listen; this will definitely be our last job and even if the whole division slips through our fingers I won't give a damn."

"If you think so. . . ." began Raymond, but Pierre interrupted him: "I've not finished yet. I was going on to say that I won't give a damn about the division as long as we catch the ones in La Peine instead, even it it's only ten men. But of those ten I will get every last man."

"Then stay here," said Raymond. "If you want to be sure of

getting them let somebody else drive to Sospel and you stay here."

"I have to talk to Roger," said Pierre. "Perhaps we will make a direct assault on them, but if so we will use both routes to make sure that no one escapes. I'll be back in two hours."

Raymond stared stupidly at him. "I thought you wanted to take Gaston to Sospel."

"He always wanted to be in at the kill," said Pierre through clenched teeth. "So he shan't miss this one."

He started up and drove down the road at full speed. He stared through the dirty windshield at the oncoming road, obsessed by only one thought.

This time it took him even less than an hour to reach the fork in the road. He wrenched the truck round a sharp right-hand bend, making the tires scream. For a few seconds he saw the river in front of him in the evening twilight, then he started to take the road up the valley. There was still three miles to go until the bridge, and when he approached the turning to Escarène, he suddenly saw men standing in the road and waving. Perhaps it was because he had not switched on his headlamps or perhaps it was because of his intense preoccupation, in any case he was so close to them when he recognized their German uniforms that he had not time to stop.

For a moment he felt that he was sitting up to his neck in boiling water, and then it seemed as if he had been struck by an ice-cold shower. Between these two sensations he first decided to make a breakthrough over the bridge, noticed at the last moment the monstrous colossus of a heavy tank blocking his path and reacted, seizing his last chance, by shifting down and driving at full throttle straight at the men. They jumped aside screaming, and now the empty road was in front of him and he drove at full speed up the valley; he had a hundred yards to go before the steel bridge when he heard a shattering crack and then another and with the third he felt the truck lift itself up as if it had driven over a mine. After that came a crash which completely deafened him. The entire surroundings lurched and swayed, while a terrible force bore down upon his shoulders. He saw the road dancing in front of his tilting radiator like a ribbon waving in the wind; he clutched the steering wheel and tried desperately to control the truck's wild movements. Several times it seemed as if it would crash over the steep embankment, but then it was in the middle of the road again with the radiator still tilted upwards.

When it stopped Pierre opened the door and jumped out. His

legs were trembling and he felt so ill that he almost vomited. A look at the truck showed that its back wheels were missing, and as Pierre looked back he saw three lifeless bodies lying on the road and behind them soldiers running towards him. At that he turned round and ran as fast as his legs could carry him over the bridge. A few soldiers fired after him without hitting him, then they ran across the dead men and stopped.

There were ten soldiers and a captain. He examined the dead men, searched their pockets and the bags hanging over their shoulders, and when he saw the ammunition he pursed his lips. Two soldiers had found a blood-stained blanket, a jacket, a bag of food and their automatic weapons.

The captain looked at them with an expert eye. "These are British Sten guns," he said. "We have made a good catch."

"One of them escaped," said a bemedaled sergeant. "Shall we chase him?"

The captain shook his head. He was an Intelligence staff officer of a division which forty-eight hours before had been in action against the Americans and had been forced eastwards off their planned withdrawal route. The latest order by radio from Corps Headquarters had ordered them to change their objective to a point on the Italian frontier near the Col de Tende, where the division was to take up a defensive position. Since then they had marched for a hundred miles without contact with the enemy. The captain had been ordered by the divisional commander to reconnoiter the line of march and find the shortest route; he had set off with three heavy "Hunting Panther" tanks and a company of infantrymen in trucks.

"We can't waste any time," he said to the sergeant. "Get the men mounted again. We're moving off." He noticed a soldier approaching him and dragging a large wooden post. The post had two direction signs at one end, and behind the soldier came another carrying a similar post on his shoulder.

"They were lying on the road by the truck," said the first soldier. "They are signposts."

"Signposts?" asked the captain in astonishment. It had now grown so dark on the road that he could not read the writing on the signposts. He switched on his pocket torch and gave a cry of surprise. Then he quickly opened his map-case, pulled out a map and shone the torch on it. The soldiers round him saw his face go pale, and after a pause he said hoarsely: "Schuler!"

The sergeant with the large number of medal ribbons stepped

up to him. "Do you remember what I said to you at the fork in the road?" asked the captain.

"You said that it wasn't marked on the map," replied the sergeant.

The captain turned round and ran to the truck. He shone his lamp into the back. The floor was riddled with shell splinters. There were three spades and a pickaxe in a holder on the right-hand side, otherwise the truck was empty. Only in the cab was there an automatic rifle.

The captain took it out and said to the sergeant: "Collect everything, including the signposts."

He ran down the road to the wooden bridge to where the tank had halted. The crew had got out and a young lieutenant in a black tank-suit came forward a few paces to meet the captain. His face held a worried expression and he said: "I only fired on your express order."

"Thank God you did fire," said the captain. "I congratulate you on your forthcoming promotion."

He left the puzzled officer standing and went to the signposts by the bridge, where he carefully examined the ground by the light of his torch. "As I thought," he said to the sergeant, who had joined him with the rest of the troops. "Do you notice anything?"

"It looks as if the soil had been freshly dug," answered the sergeant.

The captain took another look at the two signposts from the truck. Then he took one and stood it beside the signpost at the bridge so that their arms pointed in the same directions. "Notice anything?" he asked the tank lieutenant, who had still not grasped what was happening. As he shook his head the captain laughed angrily. "It's a trick, you fool! We were to be sent up the wrong road. Are you in contact with Division?"

"No, I'm out of range."

"Then call the rest of your troop. They must turn round and come back at once. Go on, man, what are you waiting for?"

The lieutenant had finally understood. He jumped onto his tank while the captain turned to the sergeant: "Get those dead bodies off the road and look sharp about it!"

He ran back to the tank, climbed up and looked through the commander's hatch as the lieutenant plugged in his throat microphone and retuned his transmitter. After calling up several times with no result he called the radio operator into the turret and they tried together. The captain watched with mounting nervousness.

"They can't be more than five minutes away, for God's sake," he said.

"What did you say?" asked the lieutenant, taking off his headset.

"Can't you contact them?" asked the captain.

The lieutenant shook his head. "They don't answer. It may be due to the terrain. But they must have heard the shots."

"We can't be sure. Drive after them until you regain radio contact." The other men of the crew had heard the conversation and climbed aboard.

"Drive as fast as you can," said the captain, then jumped down to the roadway and shone his lamp up the valley to where the soldiers were busy with the shot-up truck. They had thrown the dead bodies down on to the meadow and were trying similarly to dispose of the truck, but its rear axle lay so heavily on the roadway that they could not move it an inch. When the captain came running up to them the sergeant said: "We'll never shift it. The shell exploded under the rear axle and blew the wheels to bits. The tank could push it aside, though."

"Then it must, or it will never get past," said the captain, glancing impatiently towards the tank. As it had still made no move he cursed and said to the sergeant: "See what's the matter, Schuler."

The sergeant ran off. Three minutes later he came back and said breathlessly: "They have made contact forward. The tanks have turned round. They did hear the shots, but had to go forward a bit because they couldn't turn round in the gorge."

"Thank God," said the captain with relief. "Then we can leave the truck to them." As he walked beside the sergeant towards the tank he said: "We'll take the signposts with us. I want to show them to the general. They almost succeeded in fooling us."

"What on earth could they have been trying to do by switching the signposts?"

"If we had taken this turning we would probably have marched slap into the Americans. That's the last time I rely on a signpost."

The young lieutenant was standing up in the commander's cupola and said: "They'll be here any minute now."

"Warn them that there's a knocked-out truck lying across the road," said the captain. "They must push it aside. Have you made contact with Division, too?"

"Not yet."

"Then we'll wait at the fork until we have contact. But as a

210

precaution we must eliminate the wrong direction signs. Give me the paintpot."

The lieutenant handed him a small can of white paint and the men watched as the captain walked into the middle of the road where a great white arrow was painted on the macadam, its tip pointing up the valley. Below it was a number, and the captain painted a white cross above the arrow and painted out the number. Then he gave the paint-pot to one of the tank crew and climbed up himself. "Off you go!" he shouted to the lieutenant.

The driver started up the six-hundred-horsepower engine and forty-six tons of metal rumbled off and began maneuvering itself round.

The captain looked back up the valley from his place beside the commander's cupola. In the distance a speck of light emerged from the darkness, and as the tank roared up the road at 25 mph the bright spot at the mouth of the gorge grew larger.

The captain turned to the lieutenant who was standing with head and shoulders out of the commander's hatch and had put on his headset. "They're coming!"

The lieutenant looked back. At the same moment an ear-splitting noise broke loose. It sounded as if a dozen machine guns had started to fire at once, and then a column of flame shot up from the river near the mouth of the gorge and a shattering explosion swept down the valley. The men clung terrified to the steel sides of the tank, while the lieutenant disappeared into the turret and then a shower of small stones pattered down on them; the shockwave of the explosion was so violent that the two men were blown off the back of the tank. They at once jumped to their feet and ran shouting after it.

The captain had flattened himself against the commander's cupola. He did not straighten up until the rifle fire grew weaker and finally stopped. He ordered the lieutenant to halt. He now heard the shouting of the men who had fallen off and beside him someone began to groan.

"He's been hit," said the sergeant. "Can we bandage him quickly?"

The captain stared at him vaguely, then nodded and said to the lieutenant: "Are you still in contact?"

"They've driven back into the gorge," said the lieutenant in a husky voice. "The bridge blew up right in their faces. They're asking what they should do."

"Have they any casualties?"

"Ask them if they have any casualties," said the lieutenant into the turret. He listened to the transmission with his earphones, while the captain kept watch on the road as well as the darkness permitted.

The two men had now caught up with the tank and climbed on again. The sergeant laid the wounded man on the road and when the captain asked where he had been hit, he said: "In the back. Must have been a ricochet. If they had begun to shoot sooner we would have caught it properly."

The captain said nothing. The thought that they had literally been standing under the guns of the Maquis for a quarter of an hour sent a shiver up his spine. He looked up the valley again. The bright spot at the mouth of the gorge had vanished, but the distance was now so great that nothing more could be clearly distinguished.

"They have no casualties," said the tank lieutenant. "The trucks were still in the gorge. They say that the bridge is completely destroyed and that they can't move forward. They are firing at them from the mountainsides."

"If we hang around here much longer," said the sergeant, "they'll be coming after us."

He had bandaged the wounded man and gazed uneasily at the sides of the valley. The other men were also growing nervous, and looked at the captain, who was struggling to make up his mind. He knew that the division could not afford to lose a minute. The Americans were hard on their heels. They had been under air attack fifteen times in the past forty-eight hours and had suffered heavy casualties. The Americans were kept fully informed of all their movements and there were still thirty miles to the Italian frontier. If the division were to try to come to the rescue of the reconnaissance detachment it would mean a hold-up of at least twenty-four hours, which was the time the engineers would need to build an emergency bridge for the hundred and twenty men of the infantry element now stranded up the gorge. The two tanks would have to be left where they were and probably the trucks too, but now it would be no longer a matter of the fate of an infantry company and four trucks, but a question of whether the division reached the Italian frontier before the Americans caught up with them. He would have to justify his decision to the general, but he felt certain that he would approve.

He turned to the lieutenant. "Tell them that they . . . no, wait, I want to speak to First Lieutenant Cornelius personally."

212

He took the headset and microphone from the lieutenant. To the sergeant he said: "Lift the wounded man on to the back of the tank." Then he heard the first lieutenant's distorted voice in the earphones and he asked: "How are things with you, Cornelius?"

"We're behind the first tunnel," came the reply. "As soon as anyone goes near the bridge they start firing."

"Is there nothing you can do?"

"As far as I can see, no. The whole bridge has collapsed into the river."

"Listen, Cornelius," said the captain. "We came up the wrong road. We should have turned right at the fork. The signposts were purposely turned round. Try and break through forwards. You're bound to strike the D206 somewhere. We can't hold up the division."

He waited a moment, and as the other said nothing he asked: "Can you hear me?"

"I can hear you all right," answered Cornelius's voice. "I suppose you have no idea where the road leads to?"

"It's not shown on the map, but it must go somewhere. Can you turn?"

"We'll have to reverse up the gorge; no room to turn round here."

"All right, then don't lose any more time. We'll try and keep in contact with you. Perhaps it will work again when you're out of the gorge."

He took off the headset and returned it to the tank commander. "Get going!"

The lieutenant hesitated and looked up the dark valley. "Do you think we'll ever see them again?"

"How do I know! Why do you ask?"

"No particular reason," replied the tank lieutenant. And after a short pause: "A friend of mine is with that detachment."

"Then you'd better pray for him," said the captain.

Chapter 9

Darkness was already setting in as Marcel and Boris carried the last pieces of luggage up the mountain road from Vieale's car. Before he had driven off Marcel had found the opportunity to have a few words with him alone and he had asked him to say nothing for the moment of their encounter with the men in the truck until it was absolutely certain that Georges would not come back. When Vieale had heard about the incident with Georges he was so flabbergasted that he had not said a word, but Marcel had perceived that Vieale, too, secretly blamed him, and since then he had practically spoken to no one except Boris, who alone kept his feelings to himself. It even seemed to Marcel that since Georges' disappearance the Russian treated him with slightly less reserve than before. However, had he known that this change in Boris's attitude was simply due to the fact that Boris considered him, Marcel, to be a less formidable rival for Anna's attention than Georges, he would not have accepted Boris's more conciliatory tone so willingly.

As they climbed up the road in the first twilight, carrying the heavy luggage on their shoulders—this was now the fifth time that they had made the same journey with the same load—they were both tired and hardly spoke a word. Knopf was waiting for them at the gateway; he had done the journey twice but then had been so exhausted that he could no longer help them.

He accompanied them up the village street and said: "Madame Vieale is cooking up a meal for us. For a change she's giving us spaghetti and tomato sauce and a dish of cold meat."

"Sounds good," said Marcel absentmindedly. His thoughts were elsewhere. He had hoped that Knopf would have had some better news for him and, although he knew the answer in advance, he asked: "Has Georges shown himself again?"

Knopf grew serious. "No."

"And Anna?" asked Boris. "Is she there?"

"She came back twenty minutes ago. I had half decided to go and look for her. Of course, she had lost track of the time, as usual. She's helping Madame Vieale in the kitchen." He turned to Marcel, who was walking beside him with a disappointed expression: "You must not take it to heart so much. There's still a chance that your friend will change his mind."

"I don't know," said Marcel.

Meanwhile they had arrived at their temporary lodging. On arriving in the village earlier in the afternoon Vieale had without hesitation decided on the house next to that occupied by Knopf, Anna and Boris. It was the second from the end of the row on the east side of the village street and had four small rooms—two on the ground floor and two directly above. Some tiles were missing from the roof and the rain had leaked in, but the downstairs rooms were dry and Vieale had said that they would look for a better billet the following day. For the moment they had put all the baggage in the hall and Marcel and Boris added the final pieces to the pile. Then they went out again into the street.

Knopf had sat down on the steps and was watching the sky slowly darken. Madame Vieale's voice, talking to Anna, came through the kitchen window.

"The rain was good," said Knopf to the two men. "It has been unbearably oppressive for several days." He looked at Marcel. "Have you decided where you will sleep?"

"I'll find a place," replied Marcel. "Perhaps I'll lie under our old lean-to."

"It will certainly be cool tonight."

"I have a groundsheet and a blanket."

Boris noticed that while Marcel was talking he kept looking up at the overhanging cliff-face. "Haven't you grown used to it yet?" he asked.

"Once I've been here as long as you have, perhaps I will. Doesn't it worry you?" he asked Knopf.

Knopf smiled. "Forgive me, I am often a little dense," he said. "What are you talking about?"

"I told him that the cliff-face is split from the mountain," Boris answered for Marcel.

"Oh, that." Knopf, too, looked upwards. "I must say that it has never perturbed me. Pierre told us about it. In his opinion it will hold up for a long time yet."

"A pity he didn't come today," said Boris. "He is usually so reliable."

"Let's wait and see if he comes tomorrow," said Knopf.

Marcel, who felt uncomfortable at the mention of Pierre, ran his hand over his chin. "I must have a shave. Perhaps I can do it before we eat. Have you any hot water, by any chance?"

"Go into the kitchen," said Knopf. "Anna will give you some. I always shave out here on the step. You can put the mirror on that window-ledge."

Marcel untied his rucksack and put his shaving gear out on the step. As he was doing this he heard the shots from the tank. His first thought was for Georges and he remained for a few seconds motionless with fright, kneeling beside his rucksack, while Knopf jumped to his feet and walked up to Boris. The Russian stood still in the road and stared into the air with an intent look.

"That sounded like gunfire," said Knopf.

No one answered. Instead Madame Vieale's face appeared at the kitchen window, then the girl's and both looked at Knopf and Boris; the woman said: "Wasn't that shooting?"

"It sounded like it," said Knopf. He turned to Marcel, who was still kneeling on the ground: "You were a soldier. Do you know what that was?"

Marcel got slowly to his feet. "It must have been a tank."

"A tank! Are you sure?"

"Very sure," said Marcel, with the effort of someone making an unpleasant admission.

They all stared at him, then they were distracted by a sound; looking down the street they saw Vieale walking up it. Before he had even reached them he asked: "Did you hear it too?"

"We even heard it in the kitchen," replied his wife. "Monsieur Egli says it was a tank."

"I thought it was," said Vieale. He wiped the sweat from his forehead. "What is one to make of it?"

"Nothing good, at any rate," said Knopf. "Of that I'm sure. I'm afraid that it may have something to do with Pierre."

"Pierre?" Boris shook his head. "Impossible, I should say. Pierre is never out as late as this."

216

Knopf turned to Marcel. "How far away do you estimate that it was?"

"It's hard to say. At any rate, it was on the far side of the pass."

"As far as that?" asked Knopf.

"When I say on the far side," said Marcel, "that doesn't mean to say that it was immediately over the pass. It could as well have been ten or more kilometers to the south."

"But on the road here none the less."

"Not necessarily. You know that the road forks."

"You mean the D206?" interjected Vieale. "It sounded to me too near for that. It may be the Americans already. I can only think that they have clashed with German troops."

"But it would mean," said Knopf, "that troops were on their way here."

He had put into words what they all silently feared; for a while there was not a sound until Boris spoke again: "I don't quite understand it. They must know that the road is impassable."

"It's not marked on any map," said Vieale.

"Then they will notice it when they reach the landslide. As soon as we have eaten I will go down and keep the road under observation."

"I'll go with you," said Marcel. "We can take turns. From where can you watch the road?"

"From the little square in front of the town hall."

"I'll come too, of course," said Vieale.

Boris said: "It won't be necessary. You didn't get any sleep last night."

"I must say I'm beginning to feel it," said Vieale and turned to his wife: "How are you getting on with the meal?"

"It's ready," she said. "I need some light now. Will you fetch the lamp?"

"We have one here," said Knopf. "A paraffin lamp."

"We also brought a paraffin lamp," said Madame Vieale.

The men were just about to go indoors when from the far distance a heavy detonation shook the air and rolled round the mountains like muffled thunder. As it died away the men stared at each other, their faces pale, and Marcel said: "This is beginning to worry me."

"That was no tank," said Vieale. He looked towards the doorway, where Anna and Madame Vieale had appeared.

"What was that?" asked the woman anxiously.

217

"We don't know," answered Vieale. "It sounded like a demolition charge."

Boris ran up the road. He stopped at the end of the houses and looked out over the valley.

"Can you see anything?" Vieale shouted to him.

"Perhaps it ran over a mine," said Marcel; as he spoke his teeth chattered.

"The tank?" asked Vieale.

"It must have been a mine," said Marcel.

For a while they stood uneasily in the road and listened. Nothing more was heard and Knopf said to the others: "I suggest we might as well eat before worrying about it any further."

Vieale agreed. "You are right. Perhaps everything is much more harmless than we think."

They ate the meal in Anna's room. Madame Vieale had placed a dish of sliced cold roast beef on the table. "I hope it's still fresh," she said. "I roasted it two days ago. It doesn't keep long in this hot weather."

"It tastes delicious," Knopf assured her, but none of them had any appetite, and when the dish was empty Madame Vieale got up to go to the kitchen.

Anna forestalled her. "Stay here," she said hastily. "I'll fetch the spaghetti."

"She has hardly eaten a thing," the woman said while Anna was out of the room.

"She never eats much," said Knopf.

He began a conversation with Vieale, but it soon faded out as no one else seemed willing to join in and when Anna came back it was so quiet in the room that she stopped in surprise. "What's the matter with you all?" she asked.

"We couldn't think of anything to say for a moment," replied Knopf.

Anna put the pot of spaghetti on the table. "I've poured the tomato sauce over it," she said. "There's more in the kitchen if that's not enough."

After the meal Vieale offered round his cigarettes. Boris looked out of the window. "Well, it is still quiet. I can't understand it."

Presently, he stubbed out his cigarette and stood up. "I'm going down now," he said to Marcel. "Are you coming?"

Marcel nodded.

"Is it really necessary," said Knopf, "for you to spend the whole night out there?"

218

"Perhaps not so much necessary as reassuring," answered Boris. He took his leave and went out with Marcel.

Knopf sighed. "It's always the same," he said. "Hardly have you persuaded yourself that you're on *terra firma* at last when you notice that you are really only standing on an ice-floe which is melting away all the time."

"Have you been through a lot?" asked Vieale.

"Compared with what others have suffered, no. I should even say that I've been undeservedly lucky. But today that goes for everyone who's still alive."

"Are they all aware of it, I wonder?"

"I'm sure they are, but they will forget it in less time than it takes the grass to grow over those who were unlucky. Every new war is simply the consequence of our own forgetfulness."

"I was at Verdun in 1914," said Vieale reflectively. "Fifty German divisions bled to death round Verdun. Were you ever there?"

"Not at Verdun; I was on the Somme."

"Not a particularly nice place to have been, either," said Vieale. "If you ever go to Verdun take some time off one day and walk along the Route Nationale to Fort Vaux and then on to Fleury and Douaumont. Beyond Fleury there is a cemetery with 16,000 dead. Take a look at the Bois de la Caillette and the Bois Fumin and the shell-holes round Vaux. I have been back three times since the end of World War I, the last time was six years ago. We had no fewer casualties than the Germans, but in France a man like Falkenhayn would have been court-martialed."

"It wasn't Falkenhayn's fault," said Knopf. "He was probably too old to have acted otherwise. In this war it was Paulus. Paulus was still relatively young and merely took orders, whereas Falkenhayn made his decisions more or less independently. In reality there is more in it than the inadequacy of two generals. I don't suppose there are any young people in Germany today who know what Verdun means."

"In France they know," said the woman, who until then had listened without speaking.

Knopf nodded. "For the French Verdun is something like a national shrine, but in the wrong sense, it seems to me. Instead of pointing a warning the military achievement is glorified. But that is not the way to speak for those who paved the road to Verdun with their bones. When we sing the national anthem in a military cemetery it is, of course, a very moving event, but it distorts the

219

true nature of the matter. We should rig up giant loudspeakers and relay recordings of the screams of the wounded and dying and then no one would ever forget that cemetery. Fifty divisions, did you say? Are you sure? I must confess that I have never heard that figure before."

"I read it somewhere," said Vieale. "I think it's correct." He looked at Anna who was sitting in her place and staring vaguely at the evenly burning flame of the paraffin lamp. "I'm afraid we are not entertaining you very well, Mademoiselle."

She appeared not to have heard and did not look up until Knopf cleared his throat.

"Monsieur Vieale," said Knopf, "is afraid that you're bored when we talk about the war."

"No." She shook her head. "No, I'm not bored. I was just wondering in what way soldiers nowadays differ from those who fought in the First World War."

"In their armament," said Vieale. "Today their equipment is better and more modern."

"In what other way?" asked the girl.

"That is a difficult question," said Vieale. "Look at me. I fought in both wars; only for a few days in this one, it's true, but even that was enough."

"I don't think the question is so difficult to answer," said Knopf. "Would you have volunteered in this war too?"

Vieale laughed. "No, Monsieur, certainly not. I remembered the first war only too well. But with young people it's a bit different. Why should they be any more sensible than I was thirty years ago?"

"Somebody should have told them," threw in Anna.

"Some tried to. But when you shout against the wind no one hears you."

"It's the tragedy of inevitability," said Knopf. "If self-destruction is our destiny, the force of reason is powerless against it."

"Is that your philosophy?" asked Vieale.

"I said: if! I don't know. But if it ever came to the point where we had nothing more to live for except ideologies and the motherland, then it wouldn't be too difficult to die."

"Haven't we reached that point already?"

"I don't think so," said Knopf. "Until now it was always a kind of intoxication: they stumbled into death like a drunkard falling under a car. Nobody really went to war to die. They all hoped to escape death and when they realized that it could run faster than they could, they cursed it. We ought not to play anthems over their graves or make solemn speeches in remembrance of them. A people which is proud of its war dead has learned nothing from the war. This is only my personal opinion, but as long as we have no stronger feelings than a bad conscience about our dead when we talk of them, then there will always be other wars. It all began with falsehood and it will one day finish with falsehood: that is what I mean by inevitability. Lies breed death, death breeds lies and so it goes on. By distorting the meaning of our existence we have legitimized mass murder."

"You should have been a politician," said Vieale through his cigarette smoke.

Knopf smiled. "There are enough square pegs in round holes without me."

He looked at Vieale's wife. "You must be tired. As we don't know what surprises tomorrow will bring, I suggest we all go to bed. I expect you will miss your own bed."

"Not tonight," she replied. "I think I could sleep on the bare ground tonight."

"We brought mattresses with us," said Vieale, "so we shall not sleep hard. I originally intended to rent a truck and carry most of the furniture up here, but I didn't want to arouse any suspicion in Eys. Perhaps in about a fortnight we can go down again and return home; for such a short time all that hard work would not have been worthwhile."

"Why do you say that when you don't believe it?" asked his wife.

"I thought that it would please you," said Vieale.

The woman pursed her red lips. "You have not said anything that pleases me for a long time, Monsieur Vieale." She turned to Anna. "I'll help you clear away the dishes."

"Oh, that won't be necessary, Madame," said Anna quickly. "I shall leave it there until the morning. When do you want to get up?"

"We don't know yet," said Vieale. "Provided Boris doesn't bring us any bad news, we shall certainly sleep longer than you."

They got up and Knopf said: "Sleep as long as you can. If the sun shines tomorrow morning everything looks better, even La Peine."

He took the lamp from the table and gave it to Vieale. "We'll go down with you. Do you want to take your chairs too?"

"That can wait until tomorrow," said the woman.

221

They said good night and Knopf and Anna remained alone in the street. They talked for a short while longer until Knopf, suppressing a yawn, turned indoors. "I feel exhausted," he said as they entered the hall together. Anna went into the dark kitchen and lit the lamp.

"Perhaps I should have had a final word with Boris," said Knopf.

"It is too dark now," Anna objected. "You might fall down and break a leg. If Boris sees or hears anything he'll tell us. It has been quiet for two hours. Are you worried?"

"I should be asking you that question," said Knopf and smiled. "You seem to be taking everything very calmly. Aren't you afraid?"

"No." She shook her head. "Not today."

"Why 'not today'?"

Anna avoided his look. "We are not alone now. If we were still alone I would perhaps be afraid."

"I'm glad, too, that they are here," said Knopf. "I like Monsieur Vieale and his wife very much. Are you going to stay up much longer?"

"Not much longer," said Anna.

She stood in the hall with the lamp until Knopf had reached the top of the stairs. Then she quickly went into the kitchen. There were still some embers in the stove. She laid on fresh wood and blew on it. When it was well alight, she put a saucepan on the stove, slipped off her sandals and ran upstairs barefoot. She felt her way to her room, took off her dress and slipped into her three-quarter-length trousers. She put on her pullover and went back to the kitchen.

Four slices of cold roast beef lay on a plate. She cut them into small pieces, put a fork on the plate and waited until the contents of the saucepan were hot. Then she laid the plate on top of it, stuck her sandals under her arm and carefully picked up the hot saucepan. In the hall she blew out the lamp and set off up the street. In the next-door house light still came from a window and she heard the voices of Vieale and his wife. She crept by on tiptoe. When she reached the path she put on her sandals and stood listening. But apart from the painful beating of her heart there was not a sound to be heard and she ran on as fast as she could go in the dark. She could already make out shadowy outlines; then

222

she heard Georges' voice and stood breathless and waited until he emerged between the boulders and came towards her.

"I thought you wouldn't come," he said.

In spite of the darkness she saw that he had shaved and she smiled. "I promised you." She put the saucepan on the ground and shook her hands. "It's hot. I've burnt my fingers."

"You should have wrapped a cloth round it."

"Oh, I managed all right without one. Did you hear that gun-fire?"

"Yes."

"We are all terribly frightened. Do you know what it was?"

"I'm not sure."

"Your friend thinks it was a tank and the big bang was a mine. He and Boris have gone to your lean-to. They are going to stay awake and keep watch. Were you afraid?"

"Very," said Georges.

She laughed. "I don't believe you. You must eat it, or it will get cold. It's spaghetti and tomato sauce. I put it to one side when nobody was looking. It really belongs to Madame Vieale; she invited us to supper. Look! I've brought you something else too."

She bent down and took the plate from the saucepan. "Cold roast beef! Do you like it?"

"You're an angel," said Georges.

"If I were an angel I wouldn't have been able to bring you the roast beef; I had to take it from Madame Vieale."

"If she knew that you had taken it for me she would have given you even more."

"I'm sure she would. She likes you."

"That is an exaggeration," said Georges.

"Oh yes, she does. I asked her."

"What did you ask her? Whether she liked me?"

"Yes."

"You can be embarrassingly frank," said Georges, amused. "What was her reply?"

"That she likes you. Do you like her too?"

"I'm not going to tell you."

"Oh, aren't you!" She looked at him carefully, then shrugged her shoulders. "I don't care; she has a husband, anyway."

Georges laughed. "Of course. Why are we arguing about it?" He looked round. "We'd better get off the path."

"I know a place."

"Is it far?"

"No; just over there among those rocks."

"Then I'll get my things," said Georges.

He had left them lying on the ground a few yards away; he slung the rucksack over his shoulders, picked up his gun and followed the girl between the boulders until they stopped in front of one shaped like a great beetle.

"Up there," she said. "It's my favorite place and from there you can overlook all the other boulders. Hold the saucepan so that I can climb up. I hope it's dry, otherwise we must find somewhere else."

Georges watched her climb first on to a small lump of rock and from there leap over to a big one. For a while she vanished, then her head appeared above the boulder. "It's dry," she said. "Give me the things."

She stretched down her arm and Georges handed her first the saucepan, then his rucksack and finally the gun. When he himself came up and crawled on all fours into the hollow on the uphill side of the boulder, he gave a laugh of astonishment. "It's almost like a bed! How did you find it?"

"By chance," she said. "I once climbed up on another rock and saw it from there."

Georges looked round. As far as he could discern in the darkness the hollow was fan-shaped and its diameter at the top might have been about five feet. It was slightly arched inwards on three sides and sloped diagonally down to its narrowest point. Although the stone was dry he fetched his blanket and groundsheet from his rucksack and gave them to the girl. "Sit on that," he said. "It makes it a bit softer. Who did you pinch those trousers from?"

"I made them myself. Don't you like them?"

"They suit you," said Georges, and took the saucepan between his knees. From where he sat he looked straight over the edge of the hollow and could see the dark cliff hanging like an enormous shadow over the village.

The girl sat with legs crossed and watched him as he first ate the roast beef. When he had emptied the plate he put it down beside him and said: "I'll eat the spaghetti out of the saucepan. If you go on gazing at me like that you'll get a squint."

"Are you embarrassed?" she asked.

"Yes, when you keep staring at my mouth. This spaghetti's delicious."

"I'm glad you like it," she said. "You can eat it all. Listen, I must tell you something."

224

"Yes?" said Georges with his mouth full.

"You won't laugh at me?"

"Of course not."

"Word of honor?"

"Word of honor."

"No, I won't tell you," she said.

"Coward!"

"Coward yourself!"

"Why?"

"Because you haven't given me a kiss yet."

Georges had by now emptied the saucepan. He put it aside, felt in his pocket and pulled out his cigarettes. "Would you like one?" he asked.

She shook her head. "I don't smoke."

"Just as well," said Georges. "I've just noticed that there's only one left. Was that what you wanted to tell me?"

"What?"

"That I hadn't kissed you yet."

"No," said the girl and lay on her back. "It was not."

"I thought a lot about us while you were away."

"So have I," said Anna. "A great deal."

"I shouldn't have done it," said Georges; so far everything was going as he had foreseen it.

Anna sat up quickly. "What shouldn't you have done? Think about us?"

"I'm talking about something else. I'm talking about what we did at the spring."

"Oh!" She was silent for a while and then asked quietly: "Was it something wrong?"

"No."

"Then why shouldn't you have done it?"

Georges turned round so that he could see her face to face. She was sitting near him, and in the darkness he could see the pale oval of her face against the starry sky. "You're making it hard for me," he said.

"You're making it hard for yourself," she said in the same quiet voice.

"Because I'm trying to be honest. I don't want you to be hurt. Anyone who's still as young as you are——"

"You mean naïve?" she interrupted him.

"No, I don't mean that. But the reality is not what you think."

225

"Then tell me what the reality is like," she said cheerfully. "Go on. When I don't understand something I'll ask you."

Georges was silent. For the first time he was aware that he had underestimated her and that the conversation was taking a direction which he had not intended. A few hours ago everything had looked so simple. He had persuaded himself that he had no alternative but to try, with the help of the girl, to get himself out of his self-created blind alley, or at least to gain time until circumstances had altered in his favor. Although he told himself that this was not the only reason why he had kissed the girl, he had subsequently begun to have scruples; the longer he had been obliged to wait for her and the more time he had had to reflect, the worse his behavior towards her had seemed. The actual impulse for his change of attitude had not come until he had made his way back to the boulders and he had been able to think calmly about the three shots of tank gunfire and the mysterious explosion. He had in fact found a satisfactory explanation for them and he ascribed it chiefly to his instinct for predicting events when he had reached the conclusion that the gunfire heralded a new situation which would terminate his dependence on the girl, but from there it was but a short step to the realization that he should never have created that dependence at all. He had intended to be frank with her, and now felt himself on the point of fleeing from one piece of dishonesty by taking refuge in another. But having gone so far he could not turn back.

He noticed that he was still holding the unlighted cigarette between his fingers and he carefully replaced it in his breast pocket so as not to crush it. The girl had lain down again, her long legs crossed and her arms folded behind her head.

The night began to grow strangely brighter. A mysterious light crept along the valley in the midnight silence, spread like a veil over black-rimmed gorges and gullies, crept softly and smoothly between jagged boulders and crept silently along the dark hillsides and made the mountainsides glisten as if they were plated with bronze.

Georges looked at the girl again. "Do you know where I shall be in four weeks' time?" he asked.

She turned her face toward his. "No, I don't know."

"Nor do I," said Georges. "But whatever happens we shall lose sight of each other."

"Yes, of course," said Anna. "And what else?"

226

He had expected something different and shrugged his shoulders. "Nothing else."

"Now I know what you're thinking," she said. "You're afraid I would start thinking about marriage if you were to kiss me. Am I right?"

"You have too much imagination," said Georges harshly.

"Have I?" She leaned over to him. "Then I don't understand why you are dramatizing everything so much."

"Listen," said Georges, growing more and more uncertain of himself, "I can't tie myself to a girl when I'm not sure whether I shan't have to leave her tomorrow or the day after."

"And whether you want to stay with her at all."

"That too," said Georges firmly. "Yes, that too."

"So far I've understood everything," said Anna, and Georges could hear from her voice that she was smiling. "What I don't understand is why you made such a fuss about it all. Or are you afraid of breaking my heart, soldier?"

"Look . . ." said Georges uneasily.

She quickly put her hand over his mouth. "No, don't go on. I just want to know one thing more: I want to know why you kissed me. Just so that I would bring you something to eat?"

"You're quite wrong," said Georges violently. "What do you take me for?"

"I don't know yet. If I felt sure that I knew why you kissed me, I might know."

"People often kiss girls," said Georges.

"You don't. Your friend told me that you don't have much time for girls."

"He's babbling."

"Why did you kiss me?"

"Because," said Georges with irritation, "because I felt like it."

"Then kiss me again," she said and her face was very close to his. "If you feel like it then you must kiss me."

"You don't know . . ." said Georges, but she closed his mouth again and said: "I know everything and you needn't be afraid of breaking my heart. It didn't break when they took away my father and when my mother took so many sleeping pills that she never woke up again. I'm not even . . ."

"Just a moment!" said Georges, sitting up sharply. "Your mother . . ."

"Poisoned herself. You needn't be shocked. Lots of people have

227

done it. I didn't want to tell you and I'd rather not talk about it again. They took away my father in Düsseldorf."

"But they let him go again."

"They did not let him go again."

"But he's here!" said Georges uncomprehendingly.

"That's my uncle. We pretend that he's my father. But what I meant was that I am not quite as naïve as you think. We lived in Lyons for a long time. The people who took us in had a lot of books, including some that I was not supposed to read; once when I was alone in the woods a couple came along and I didn't dare move for fear of being seen. When they had gone I ran home, took those books and read them through again. Do you believe that I am still so innocent and naïve?"

"If you weren't naïve," said Georges thickly, "you wouldn't have told me."

"Shouldn't I have done so?"

Georges took her face in his hands and could say nothing.

"I am stupid," said the girl in a depressed voice. "I wouldn't have told it to anybody else. I liked you from the moment I saw you. I liked Pierre too and Madame Laurat's dog in Lyons. He would only obey me, and Madame Laurat was really jealous, but that was a different sort of liking. I have never wished for anything, because I was afraid that one day someone would come again and take it away from me, but there's nothing wrong in liking something which you know you can't keep. Or is there?"

"Of course not," said Georges with an effort.

"You see?" she said. "And it's also quite normal that two people who like each other often can't stay together, isn't it?"

"Did you get that from books too?"

"Yes. I've read a lot of books where it was like that. I've talked to my uncle about it, too. The same thing once happened to him, you see. He liked my mother, but she only wanted my father and nobody else. Perhaps it's worse for a woman than for a man; but why should it be? My uncle got over it, after all." While talking she had moved away from him and was looking the other way.

"Look at me!" said Georges. He seized her by the chin and forced her to look at him. "You're lying," he said.

"I'm not lying," she said with closed eyes. "Why should I lie?"

"Then look at me," repeated Georges. "I want to see whether you really mean what you've been saying."

228

She said nothing, and when he tried to kiss her she lay back and turned her head away.

Georges bent over her. "You were lying," he said. "Admit that you were lying."

"No," she said, "I won't admit it."

Georges smiled and touched her ear and eyes with his mouth. He was lying half across her; suddenly she wound her hands round his neck and returned his kisses.

"I'd like to sleep beside you," she said. "Let me go to sleep here with you."

"Won't they miss you?"

She shook her head. "Not before tomorrow morning. And by then I'll be back in my room."

"It's a hard bed," said Georges.

"It's not too hard for me. Is it too hard for you?"

"No."

"It is a bit hard, but there are the stars to make up for it."

"A bed under the stars," said Georges, smiling.

"Our bed of stars," said the girl.

"It's cold, too."

"I'm quite hot. Feel my face, how hot it is."

"It's burning."

"Not only my face. My whole body's burning. Is yours?"

"Yes," said Georges.

They were lying closely pressed together. The girl's pullover had rolled up a little way and she had nothing on underneath it. "What are you doing?" she asked.

"Shouldn't I do it?" asked Georges.

"Perhaps I'm too young."

"Yes," said Georges. "You're still very young and I'd better not do it."

"If I were older would you do it?"

"Only if you wanted to."

"If I knew that I would then be quite happy and that I didn't need to be afraid any more and that you wouldn't be disappointed. . . ."

"What are you talking about?"

"Am I ugly?"

"Crazy, at any rate," said Georges breathing heavily.

"No, tell me honestly: am I different from other girls?"

"You're prettier than they are."

"But perhaps there really is something about me which is different. I've always been afraid that there's something about me which would stop a man liking me. They used to laugh at me in school."

"Who laughed at you in school? The girls?"

"Not only the girls."

"They were just stupid children who were put up to it. Didn't your uncle tell you that there is no difference?"

"Yes, but——"

"But what?"

She hesitated, then laid her face against his and said: "If you tell me I'll believe it."

"But I've just told you."

"I want you to tell me after you've seen me."

"You mean——"

"Is that bad?"

Georges swallowed. "It's nonsense," he said after a pause. "Believe me, it's nonsense."

"You don't understand me," she said. "Apart from my uncle I've never been able to talk about it with a man. When my parents were alive I was too young and my uncle still says that I am too young to understand it. He said that there is no difference, but I can't believe that it was only because of the other thing that they hated us so much."

"It's only the other thing," said Georges.

"How do you know?"

"Everybody knows it."

She hesitated. "In school they once shouted something after me."

"What?"

"That I had . . . I can't tell you. It was something horrible."

"Didn't you tell your parents?"

"I was too embarrassed."

Georges shook his head. "I can't quite imagine what it can have been, but it was certainly nonsense."

"I'd rather forget it," she said. "I never really took it seriously, but in spite of that I have never been able to forget it."

"You mustn't think about it any more," said Georges. He pushed his hands under her pullover and said softly: "You crazy little girl."

"Shall I take it off?"

"If it's not too cold for you."

"No, no. Your hands are so warm." She drew the pullover over

230

her head and sat upright for a moment beside him. As he pulled
her down to him he felt her trembling.

"You're freezing," he said.

"No, I'm not," she said. "I'm ashamed and afraid and I know
what I'm doing isn't right, but I've had all evening to think about
it and I wished it would be like this. If you think I'm bad . . ."

"Listen," said Georges pleadingly. "For Christ's sake listen!"

"I don't want to listen, I just want you to hold me tight and tell
me that I'm not different and that a man can want me."

"Any man can want you," said Georges, harshly. "Any man,
d'you hear? And I want you."

"Then show me," she said. "Show me and pull off these trousers so that I can see you want me and that what they shouted after
me isn't true."

She sought his hand in the dark; he felt rough cloth and then
no more cloth. Her head lay on his chest and her body long and
firm against his and her face wet, but she cried silently and he felt
it only because her shoulders quivered. Suddenly she went quite
stiff and bending over her he saw that her eyes were wide open as
if in mortal terror and she asked: "Why don't you say anything?"

"Because I've told you everything already," whispered Georges.
"Don't you understand?"

"Yes," she said. "And it's not true?"

"It's really and truly and absolutely not true."

"Then it's all right," she sighed. "And now I don't care whether
I'm bad or not and you can do it if you want to."

"Shall I really do it?"

"Don't you want to?"

"Yes," said Georges. "Yes, I do, but perhaps you'll be sorry
afterwards."

"Afterwards you will be gone and I don't want to think about
what happens afterwards."

"Good," said Georges. "We won't think about it, but we'll talk
about it again, tomorrow or whenever, and you mustn't believe
that you're bad because you like me. Are you still frightened?"

"A bit, but the other is stronger."

Her sunburned skin felt smooth and warm and Georges put his
mouth on her neck and caressed her. Then he got to his knees and
as he pulled off his jacket, from somewhere a light fell into his
eyes.

He turned his head to look down the valley towards the pass.
Halfway up the distant slope, where the road descended from the

231

pass in a series of tight bends, everything was bathed in light; he could see the brilliant eyes of headlights as they swung round the bends and for a second lit up the opposite side of the valley as they turned. Now he could also hear the dull drone of engines and he held his breath until he felt sure that there were tanks among them. Although he had calculated on this possibility, he felt momentarily stunned; then he looked down at the girl.

Her face was quite white and she had pulled the blanket over herself. "What is it?" she whispered.

Georges dumbly picked up her clothes and put them in her lap. He watched her as she stood up and dropped the blanket. For a few moments she stood in front of him, slim and straight as a wand, and stared towards the pass. Every time that the headlights completed a swing the contours of her body stood out against the starry sky. Then abruptly she began to cry.

This was so surprising to Georges that for a while he sat helpless. As he got to his knees again it seemed that something in him broke in two. Then there was only the girl and his face, cradled in a soft silky bed, cared for and sheltered, her tears dropping on him like soft raindrops. For a few seconds he was driven helplessly onward in a surge of unbridled tenderness, until she began to cry in earnest and he suddenly realized again where he was and why, and as he drew her down to him she laid her head on his shoulder and stammered: "I knew it. I knew all evening that something would happen to stop us and now . . ." She broke off and whimpered like a child; then she stopped and jumped to her feet.

Georges lifted his head. He looked over the edge of the hollow and saw that the convoy had now nearly reached the valley floor and would soon drive through the hollow. Boris and Marcel would see it when it reached the olive grove. They would waken the others and then they would discover that Anna was not there.

He turned round to her. She had put on her trousers and as she picked up her sweater Georges stood up beside her and held her tight. "Let me go!" she said wildly. "Will you let me go!"

Georges shook his head. "Not until you've listened to me for a minute." He took her face in his hands. It was still wet with tears, her mouth in a grimace, and Georges bent down to her and kissed her until, breathless, she let her head fall back.

"There," said Georges. "Now perhaps you will be sensible."

"You don't understand," she said with closed eyes.

"Maybe," said Georges. "But it doesn't alter anything."

232

"I'll never be able to do it again," she said despairingly. "Never, never."

"They all think that."

A quick glance showed Georges that the headlights had disappeared. The trucks must already be in the hollow and he had no more time to lose. "I'd understand it," he said hastily, "if you weren't such a reasonable girl. I tell you that nothing has changed and that it's just the same as if nothing had happened."

"You're just saying that. You don't mean it. I know . . ." She stopped and opened her eyes. "Are you going away?"

"On the contrary," said Georges, "I'm going with you, but you mustn't tell them that we've seen each other."

"But you wanted to go off alone."

"We'll talk about that later. Do you think I'd leave you alone now?"

"Are they Germans?"

"Probably. When they notice that the road's blocked they'll turn round again. We must run, otherwise Boris will come and they'll see that you're not in your room. Hand me down the things."

He quickly pulled on his jacket and vaulted over the edge of the boulder. Moments later they were running towards the path leading to the village. There Georges saw the headlights again. They were climbing steeply uphill and he knew that it could not be long now before Boris and Marcel noticed them.

Breathless, they reached the village street and Georges stopped. "Run inside," he whispered. "Take care they don't hear you."

"I'll take off my sandals," said Anna.

She put the empty saucepan on the ground and thrust the sandals under her arm. Then she walked up to Georges and gazed from below into his face. "What will you do if the Germans come up here?"

"We shall see. If the worst comes to the worst we can always get away over the ridge."

"You could climb over the ridge now," she said. "My uncle is not good at walking. If we have to go over the ridge he'll collapse before he's gone five hundred yards. The doctor has forbidden him to strain himself."

"Then we won't go over the ridge. Don't worry."

She was silent for a few seconds, then asked: "Why are you doing all this?"

233

"For fun."

"Fun?"

"Perhaps that's not the right expression," said Georges. "I like it. It's a man's job."

"Aren't you afraid?"

"Yes, but only when I start thinking about it. Run, before I regret having been so careful about your good reputation."

"That disappeared long ago," said Anna. She stood on tiptoe and kissed him on the mouth. Then she picked up the saucepan and vanished noiselessly indoors.

Georges stood still for another half-minute, then retraced his steps about fifty paces. From here he could look out over the valley and he saw that the convoy was now passing through the olive grove. He was just beginning to wonder why Boris and Marcel had not spotted them when he heard a noise. It sounded like hob-nailed boots on cobbles and then he saw the shape of a man coming up the street in a great hurry.

Georges watched with a grin as he ran into one of the houses. A short while later he reappeared and ran into the next house. This time it was longer before he came out. He stopped in the street, whereupon Knopf and Vieale emerged. They were talking loudly as if in argument and Georges waited until the woman and the girl had joined them, then he slowly strolled towards them.

They were all silent, staring at him. His gun was slung over his shoulder, his hands in his pockets, and when they recognized him Madame Vieale said: "Monsieur Chabrier!"

She made a move as if to run towards him, but her husband was quicker. In three big strides he stood by Georges, put his hand on his shoulder and gazed at him without a word. Then he turned round and said: "He's come back!" And to Georges: "My God, you gave us a fright, Monsieur. Where have you been?"

"I was having a good look at the local terrain," replied Georges, looking over to Marcel who stood there with open mouth and stared at him as if he were an apparition. Anna stayed in the background. She stared at the ground and when Georges looked at her she raised her head and smiled.

Georges nodded to her and turned to Knopf, who had also walked up to him and offered his hand. "I'm glad you're back," he said warmly. "Your friend has been very worried about you."

"So I notice," said Georges.

Vieale gripped him hard by the arm. "There are trucks coming. Monsieur Egli was——"

234

"I know," Georges interrupted. "That's why I'm here. They have tanks with them."

"Tanks?" said Vieale, horrified. "Have you seen them?"

"No, but I've heard them. I suppose they'll turn round as soon as they notice what's wrong with the road. Where's Boris?"

"He ran down the road," said Vieale. "He wants to get a closer look."

Georges nodded and thought for a while. Then he said to Marcel: "How far away were they when you first saw them?"

"In the olive grove," said Marcel.

"Then they still need half an hour. They've probably seen this village; the olive grove is pretty low-lying and the houses stand out against the skyline on a starry night like this. They might like the idea of spending the night here before they drive back. Have you ever been in the fort?" he asked Vieale.

"Once. It's easy to get lost in there. They turned the whole mountaintop into a warren."

"Then there are bound to be plenty of places to hide in the fort?"

"Sure to be, but . . ."

"One moment," said Georges and turned to Knopf: "Can you climb?"

"Hardly," answered Knopf. "Of course, it depends . . ."

"It's only if all else fails," Georges cut him short. "Would you trust yourself to climb over the ridge with us and down the other side?"

"Is it very steep?"

"If you're unlucky you might break some bones."

"No," said Knopf, "I can't. But don't pay any attention to me."

Georges smiled. "Nobly put, but out of place here. Besides it would be as much of a strain for Madame Vieale as for you. I don't think the Germans will come as far as here and if they do I will try and hold them up for a while. I estimate that we have about two hours. By then you must have moved everything, every trace of your having been here, into the fort. Look for a safe hiding place. I'll send Boris up to help you."

"What are you planning to do?" said Vieale.

"For the moment, nothing. Even if all the hard work turns out to have been unnecessary, it won't matter very much." He looked at his luminous watch-face. "It's now one o'clock. By three you must be ready."

"I'll go with you," said Marcel.

Georges looked at him. "You're needed here. Without a rifle you can't help me anyway."

"I'm going with you all the same," said Marcel.

"We'll never manage by ourselves in two hours," interjected Vieale. "We'll have to carry Monsieur Knopf's things up too."

"Marcel will help you," said Georges. And to Marcel: "Do you hear?"

Marcel said nothing. As Georges went down the street he ran after him and said: "Georges!"

Georges stopped. "What do you want now?"

"For God's sake stop talking to me like that," said Marcel, swallowing hard. "I just wanted to tell you something."

"Then hurry up."

"I can't say it as quickly as all that. Where were you?"

"On the moon. What has it to do with you?"

"Don't sound so cross," said Marcel. "I just lost my temper, that's all. It happens to everybody. You've lost your temper often enough."

"Well?"

"Oh, nothing." Marcel blinked and looked upwards. "I'll go and help them now," he said.

He turned round and walked a few paces. Then he stopped again and shouted: "If they have tanks you'd better take care."

"O.K., boy, I will," said Georges and smiled. Marcel smiled too. As he walked back up the street he wiped his eyes.

It was then that Georges caught the sound of a distant hum; he knew that it was made by tanks. It grew louder the farther he went down the road and finally grew to a loud, monotonous drone which sounded like airplanes in the sky.

It temporarily distracted him from his thoughts and he stopped once the better to listen to it. Once sure that the noise was still coming from the other side of the valley, he went on and his thoughts returned to the girl. His feelings for her were stuck in a blind alley, from which there was no way out, since his desire to sleep with her had almost become an *idée fixe* blocking any line of retreat. The concessions to his conscience had even gone as far as confronting the possibility of later marrying her, even though he did it with reservations. But he was honest enough to admit that none of the many girls who had so far come his way had made nearly as strong an impression on him as this one, and as he strode down the moonlit road with the distant drone of tanks in his ears, he thought that he must have fallen seriously in love with her.

And if you were to be worried because she's a Jew, he said to himself, it would mean that you were as pathetic as those who need a race-complex to cover up their own insignificance and inadequacy—to which you are rather prone, if you are honest with yourself. You have always kept your head so high in the clouds that you lost sight of the ground under your feet and you can be grateful to find any girl with the courage to share the rest of your botched life.

He met Boris at the far end of the first tunnel, where the road stopped. The Russian had heard him coming and was standing by the tunnel mouth, his right hand in his pocket, staring unwaveringly at him as he approached. He did not even move when Georges stood beside him, threw down his rucksack and looked out over the valley. From here they commanded a view of its entire length, but the headlights had disappeared. The trucks and tanks were probably already crossing the viaduct and they would come into sight again when they rounded the next bend and reached the demolished section of the road.

Georges sat down on his rucksack, took the cigarette from his breast pocket and lit it. Then he looked up at Boris's face and said: "They'll be here in a quarter of an hour. I told the others you would go back and help them. They are carrying everything movable up to the fort."

"Why should they want to go to the fort?" asked Boris. He had taken his hand from his pocket and was watching the road beyond the landslip.

"It's the best thing to do," said Georges. "The Germans may turn round when they find the road impassable. On the other hand they may decide to go and spend the night in the village."

"How do you know they are Germans?"

"The Resistance have no tanks and the Americans couldn't be here yet. That sound you can hear isn't only made by trucks: they don't make so much noise. If they have infantry with them and decide to climb round the landslip, as we have done, I'll try and hold them up. By then you must have moved everything up into the fort."

"If you hold them up they will know that there are people in La Peine."

"If I don't hold them up they'll be in La Peine in twenty min-

237

utes and they'll find out anyway. We might have tried to get away over the ridge, but for one thing, Vieale would have had to leave all his baggage behind and for another it's highly dangerous at night. If it weren't for Knopf and Madame Vieale the attempt might have been worthwhile, but as things are it's too risky."

"It's equally risky in the fort," said Boris.

"Only if they stay here for a long time, and I consider that out of the question. You've been in the fort and you must know what it's like inside."

"I've only seen a part of it," said Boris. "It's pitch dark in there. Without a light you can very easily get lost."

"So much the better for us."

"We could close the doors behind us," said Boris reflectively.

"Are there any doors?"

"Yes, armored doors. They can be opened and shut from inside."

Georges grinned. "What more could we want?"

"How do you propose to hold them up here if they come over?"

"I'll fire a few rounds into the air. Then they'll turn round or wait for morning to see what they're up against and by that time we shall be sitting tight up in the fort."

Boris turned and stared over the gap in the road. "Why did you come back to us?" he asked after a short pause.

"I heard the shots and thought perhaps I would still be needed."

They strained their eyes gazing in the direction from which the drone of engines was now growing disturbingly louder.

"Now you can hear the rattle of their tracks," said Georges. "In a few minutes they'll be here."

"Shall I stay with you?" asked Boris.

"I don't think you should. They need you up there more urgently than I do."

"I still think we should have tried getting over the ridge. That fort is a rat-trap. Once we're in there it's too late to change one's mind again."

"You know the way over the ridge," said Georges. "The others know it too."

"I'm going to talk to them about it again."

"No one's stopping you," said Georges coolly.

238

Chapter 10

At about the same time that Georges sat waiting for the Germans, Pierre reached the pass. When the bridge had been blown up, he was still making his way up the gorge. There had been two tanks and four trucks and fortunately he had seen their lights in time. Crouching below the steep river bank in the gorge he had let them drive past him and had waited a little longer in case more were following. Then he had sat down on the curb and not moved from the spot until the rifle-fire started and the detonation of the charge roared through the narrow valley like a hurricane. He had felt neither fear nor any other emotion. A quarter of an hour later the German vehicles returned, only this time in reverse gear, and it had been a long time before Pierre had been able to emerge from his hiding-place for the second time. He had run to the bridge; a few of Roger's men had been standing on the far side and he identified himself to them by shouting across the gap. He had given them orders to skirt the gorge via the northern ridge and meet him at the pass.

That had been over three hours ago and he made the most strenuous march of his life in order to reach the pass. He lay down flat on the ground by the roadside, lit a cigarette and stared up at the sky. He knew that everything had been in vain.

Then the tank gunfire started up round La Peine and when it was quiet again Roger and his men arrived. They dropped where they stood; Roger sat down beside Pierre and looked out over the valley towards La Peine.

"Who are they shooting at if there are Germans in La Peine?" he asked.

Pierre did not reply. He had crossed his legs and was chewing the knuckles of his clenched fist.

"I did what I could," said Roger wearily.

"Did you see Gaston?" asked Pierre.

"They threw him down on to the meadow. Jean and René too. All three of them long past doctoring. *Mon Dieu!* I saw you jump out of the truck and run over the bridge and I saw them shooting at you, but I couldn't help you because we would have given away our positions too soon. If I hadn't seen it myself I wouldn't have believed that one man could have so much luck. Everything was going well until you turned up."

"I'm sorry," said Pierre dully. "I was coming to fetch you."

"What for?"

"I'll tell you later. What was the tank doing by the bridge?"

"There were three tanks and four trucks. Jules saw them in time and reported them to us. When they reached the wooden bridge, one tank pulled aside; the others went on. There were troops sitting on the tanks. They looked at the signpost and painted an arrow on the roadway."

"Pointing in which direction?"

"In ours: straight on. They were marking the way for the division. As they were remounting and getting ready to follow the others, you appeared."

"I saw them too late," said Pierre.

"And they saw you. I was still hoping that they wouldn't notice the trick with the signposts, but then they found the ones which you had in the back of the truck—the right ones!"

"Merde!" said Pierre between his teeth.

Roger nodded. *"Merde!* Then they must have radioed to the ones who had crossed the bridge and told them to come back. Anyway they turned round and drove off down the valley. We fired after them and when the others came out of the gorge I blew up the bridge. There was nothing more we could have done. What are you going to do now?"

Pierre stood up. "I'm only interested in one thing: what's going on in La Peine?"

"Do you want to go up there and see?"

"Yes."

"By which way?"

"The shortest," replied Pierre. "We'll go down into the valley, through the wood and climb up the other side. There's a spring up there and a path which leads into the village from behind."

"How many hours will it take?"

"Four, if we're lucky."

Roger looked at his men, who were lying exhausted on the ground and had been listening to the conversation. "Can you still do it?" he asked them.

"Vive la France!" said one of them and the others laughed.

As they gathered together on the road, Pierre told in a few words how Gaston had been shot.

Roger listened in silence. "I thought he was killed when they hit your truck," he then said. "But that makes the business even more mysterious than it is already."

"In a few hours we shall know more," said Pierre grimly. "As soon as we get up there one of us must go over the ridge and fetch the others; they're still waiting where I left them. We need the machine gun."

"If only we were up there already," said Roger. He put himself with Pierre at the head of the men, and as they set off they heard another burst of automatic rifle-fire.

"It's not coming from La Peine," said Pierre, who had stopped for a second, "it must be beyond."

"Sounds like a machine gun," said Roger. Pierre shook his head. "Their machine guns are faster. That one has the same sound as the one which hit Gaston yesterday afternoon. It must be a German machine carbine. They sound like that."

"Right," said Roger. "But I still don't know who's shooting at whom."

"At all events someone fired at them when they were trying to get up there. As we were also fired on, it means that there's someone up there who is as afraid of the Germans as of us."

"But that's impossible," said Roger, baffled.

As he walked along Pierre put his hands in his pockets. "Perhaps it is possible," said Pierre. "Remember the burned uniforms."

"You don't really mean——"

"I don't mean anything," Pierre cut him short. "It's just an idea of mine and in the final reckoning it won't matter who they are up there when I get my hands on them."

"I can believe that," said Roger.

In half an hour they had reached the last hairpin bend in the road leading down from the pass. Then they left the road and struck out directly for the wood. They followed its western edge until they had crossed the valley floor, and then they began to climb the mountain on the far side. As the wood thinned out the

241

going became very hard. Great boulders blocked the way and often the mountain was so steep that the men had to work their way up on all fours. But they were experienced climbers and in spite of the darkness they kept up a good rate of progress. After any particularly taxing stretch Pierre called a short halt.

Within two hours the sky began to lighten and the climb grew easier with the approach of dawn. When Pierre finally stopped to allow the strung-out file of men to close up, Roger joined him and they sat down side by side on a rock and looked down into the valley. As they were on the south face of the mountain and La Peine lay on its western side, they could see nothing of the village. Instead they had an uninterrupted view towards the pass and down the eastward-running side valley. No details were discernible yet, but treetops were slowly emerging more distinctly from the dark, blurred mass of the wood, and as Pierre raised his head he saw the first red streaks in the eastern sky.

"Did you leave the bodies lying there?" he asked.

Roger shook his head. "I sent a man to Jules with orders to pick them up."

"That makes seven now," said Pierre. "We will have their names carved on a stone and set it up in Escarène. A big stone."

"In front of the church perhaps," said Roger. "That would be a good place."

"I thought of that; but would the curé agree?"

"He can hardly refuse when he hears how they were killed. Otherwise nobody would go to church any more."

"We mustn't put any pressure on him," said Pierre. "If he's a good Frenchman he will agree in any case."

He turned to one of his men sitting near by: "Give me your gun. I left mine in the truck."

"What am I to shoot with then?" asked the man.

"You won't be shooting. As soon as we get up there you will climb down the other side and tell Raymond to bring up his men."

"Where is he?"

Pierre described the position and said finally: "You can stay down there and rest."

"He'll meet the Germans who shot at you," put in Roger.

"Of course he can't go by the path," countered Pierre. "There's another way."

"Then I don't understand why you didn't try it yesterday," said Roger.

242

"We had to get Gaston back and it was then too late to make another attempt. The other way is only passable by daylight. I had a better plan. If the Germans hadn't stopped us I was going to send you along this way to La Peine and climb up the other side with my men. Then we would have had them caught in a trap."

"And who would have blown up the bridge?"

"Two men would have been enough for that."

Roger reflected for a while. After a pause he said: "It would have been better still if you had come by this route yesterday morning."

"If!" said Pierre, annoyed. "And what would I have done with the truck? Left it on the road? Besides they would have had us under observation all the way and then been waiting for us at the top. By day this way would have been even more dangerous than the other side. I gave a lot of thought to what I did."

"But you didn't think of the advance detachment of that German division which so successfully ruined our plans."

"Did you think of it?"

"No, I didn't," said Roger, "but I'm . . ." He broke off and stared over to the right, where a white light flared up against the pale sky. As it faded Roger turned in astonishment to Pierre and asked: "Did you see that?"

"It must have been a Very light," said Pierre. "They're signaling to someone."

He jumped up. In the same moment the violent crack of a tank gun thumped across the valley, followed by an almost uninterrupted succession of similar shots. In the narrow space between the sides of the valley it sounded as if two divisions were facing one another and fighting it out. After a while the rifle-fire began. It ended as abruptly as it had begun and then everything was as silent as before.

The men had jumped to their feet and were looking at Pierre; he stood still for a few seconds with his head cocked to one side as if he had cramp in his neck. Then he picked up his gun and set off up the mountain. Roger followed him and the men fell into single file at short intervals. As the mountainside became noticeably steeper at this height, Pierre set a slightly less straight uphill course. Ten minutes later a deep ravine appeared to their left, which seemed to split the mountain from peak to foot. It was over sixty feet wide and Pierre gave a rapid glance at its rubble-strewn

243

floor. Then he nodded with satisfaction and said to Roger: "We're on the right track. In five minutes we'll be there."

Nevertheless a quarter of an hour passed before they reached the path. They staggered on, near to exhaustion, and when the last man was up Pierre approached the man whose gun he had taken and led him to the spot where the path was interrupted by the ravine.

"You must climb up here," he said to him. "The ravine comes to an end a little way below the ridge. When you're at the top, climb down to the valley by the shortest route. Don't break any bones; it's pretty steep on the other side. Tell Raymond to take his time. It will be soon enough if he's here this evening. Only he must be up before darkness, otherwise they'll be stuck until to-morrow morning."

The man looked at the ravine and scratched his chin. "Can I rest a bit first?" he asked.

"As long as you like, but afterwards don't lose any time. Raymond will need at least eight hours to get up. Give me the ammunition in your bag."

"Take the whole bag."

"Right you are," said Pierre. He turned round to Roger and unslung his gun. The men had dropped where they stood; their faces were marked by the hardships of the past night.

The pink light of dawn was now spreading from peak to peak. "We made it just in time," said Pierre to Roger. "Half an hour later and we probably would never have got here."

"What worries me is how we're going to get down again," said Roger.

Pierre shrugged. "On our feet, I hope. It's damned quiet now."

"I don't like it either," said Roger. "They must have pulled back, or else they're in La Peine by now. What do you think?"

"I don't know yet. We must approach the village as carefully as possible. If we find it occupied we'll climb up to the ridge. Once we're up there no one can get us down again." He turned to the men: "Can we go on again now?"

"If we must," said one. "But don't go at such a pace."

"We'll keep to the path now," said Pierre. "Keep wide apart; the fireworks may start at any moment now."

"I shouldn't talk of the devil so much," said Roger, getting up with a groan, "or he'll appear. God, I'm not as young as I was. Thirty years ago I could have done this climb without turning a hair."

"You're in pretty good shape, I would say," said Pierre. "Not many fifty-year-olds could still do it."

He glanced back at the pass, then turned and began climbing the steep path. At each bend he stopped and listened before going on. When he came to the end of the cliff-face on their right where there was a clear view of the ridge he waited for Roger. "How many men have you?" he asked him.

"There are fourteen now," answered Roger. "Why do you ask?"

"I've had another idea. In case we can't go into the village, which is possible, we must block the path. I'll take three men and position myself roughly at the point where the path emerges from the boulders. That will be safer than having us all squatting up on the ridge, because then my group on the path and yours on the ridge can support each other with flanking fire. But see that nobody creeps up behind you; you must have somebody watching the other side too."

"Will three men be enough for you?"

"Even one would be enough to close off the path, but I want to be on the safe side and take three. Tell them to follow me."

"Enjoy yourself," said Roger and looked round for his men. They were rounding the bend at that moment.

Meanwhile Pierre set off down the pathway alone. It led through the scattered boulders, climbed for about a hundred yards and then dropped down to the village. Its numerous bends forced Pierre to move with increasing caution and when he saw that he was nearing the end of the boulders he stopped to allow Roger's three men to catch up. Then they went a little farther down the path, climbed a short way towards the ridge and regained their original direction until the roofs of La Peine appeared between the great rocks. "Stop here," said Pierre softly. "I just want to take a look at the place."

For freedom of movement he took off his gun and heavy ammunition sack, gave them to one of the men and ran off crouching low. Where the boulders came to an end Pierre ran up to a rock large enough to provide cover for two men. He squatted down behind it and cautiously looked over the top.

As he had supposed, he had a direct view of the village street. Having assured himself that nothing was moving in the street, he looked round for a suitable place to put his men. To his left the hillside dropped sharply to the pathway, which ran in a straight line to the upper end of the village street. Looking up the mountainside to the right he could see the ridge and the fort. Behind

245

him was the labyrinth of boulders and the longer he examined his surroundings the more he was satisfied.

He stood and signaled to the men. His carefree movement showed that there was no imminent danger and they quickly came running.

"Looks quite peaceful," said one of them. Named Laroche, he wore a red beret.

"Almost too peaceful," muttered Pierre and turned to the other two: "You can go down to the path. Put yourselves behind a boulder. Don't start shooting until I do."

"What do we shoot at?" asked one and grinned.

Pierre looked down at the village street. "I'll go and take a closer look. You stay here," he said to Laroche. "None of you are to move as long as I am down there."

He waited until the two had reached the path. There they stopped and pointed to a boulder on the uphill side of the path. Pierre nodded and took his gun back from Laroche. "If you see anything," he said to him, "call me or fire a shot. But only if I am in danger."

"Don't worry," said Laroche. "I'm not a beginner."

"Didn't say you were," replied Pierre. He climbed down the valley side to the path. Before he had reached it someone called his name. He looked round.

Laroche had stepped in front of the boulder and was pointing up the mountain. As Pierre turned his head, he saw Roger standing on the ridge and signaling wildly with his arms. His meaning was not clear from his movements and for safety's sake Pierre glanced towards the houses, but could detect nothing suspicious.

He looked up again at Roger, whose thickset form stood out clearly against the sky, and shrugged his shoulders. Then he heard Laroche's voice a second time, this time with an urgent sound. He noticed only now that Laroche was no longer standing in front of the boulder and that Roger also had suddenly vanished from the ridge. For a moment Pierre felt completely alone and noticed that his back was running with sweat; then without further thought he started running uphill.

It was a hundred paces to the boulder and the ground between was covered with rocks and stones. A hundred paces and a steep climb—but Pierre did not notice it. He kept his gaze fixed on the boulder, which threw a long shadow in the morning sun; he had almost reached it when there came a burst of automatic fire.

He fell flat on the stony ground and lay there until he noticed

246

that it was his two men who had fired. Then he stood up and ran all the way to Laroche who was waiting for him behind the boulder.

The firing stopped. Pierre looked towards the village street. At first he could make out nothing, but then he saw a rifle lying in the middle of the street and he knew that it had not been lying there a few minutes earlier. He looked at Laroche, who nodded and said: "You can put a red ring round the date on the calendar today. They came up the road, at least fifty men strong, all wearing steel helmets, with machine guns too. Roger saw them first. I only noticed them when he waved to you."

"Where have they gone?" asked Pierre, gasping for breath.

"Down the street again. They saw you when you started running back. The ones in front were just going to shoot. I could do nothing because you were plumb in my line of fire, but those two down there had their eyes open. You can thank them."

Pierre looked downhill. He could not see the other two, his view being obstructed by rocks. "Did they hit one?" he asked.

Laroche, who had crawled round to the other side of the boulder to watch the street, shrugged his shoulders. "I don't think so. The Germans were fairly well protected by the lay of the ground. The shots must have passed over their heads, but they took them damned seriously," he said with a grin. "I've never seen them run so fast."

"You would have run fast, too, in their place," said Pierre as he stared at the houses. He was well protected and could see everything without having to stick his head far out. The church tower projected over the roof tops slightly to the left of the row of houses on the west side, and as Pierre examined it carefully he seemed to notice something moving in the narrow windows of the belfry.

He pointed this out to Laroche and after watching the belfry windows for some time Laroche said: "Some of them are sitting up there; you can see them clearly."

"Your eyes are better than mine," said Pierre. "It's a pity the distance is so great."

"We could try giving them a burst," suggested Laroche.

Pierre disagreed. "It would be a waste of ammunition. Besides, we would only give away our position."

"It's lucky they have no artillery with them."

"Don't speak too soon. They could soon make things pretty hot for us with a mortar."

"Oh, shut up about mortars, for God's sake!"

Pierre laughed. Two months before they had attacked a German ammunition column, but the last two trucks had had time to turn round and had driven back to the pass. Ten minutes later the sky had rained mortar bombs and Pierre and his men had run for their lives. Since then the subject of mortars had been avoided.

"When the Italians attacked in 1940," he said, "they brought up mortars too. But then we had six feet of concrete over our heads."

"Mortars are a horrible invention," said Laroche with disgust. "They hardly make a crater at all and the splinters shave over the ground like a great scythe."

"Frightened?" asked Pierre.

"What's the use of dying at the end of a war?" said Laroche and spat on the ground.

"Take off your red beret," said Pierre. "It makes too good a target. How's your family?"

"All slightly underfed, thanks."

"No one asked you to bring five children into the world."

"What else has a man to live for?" said Laroche. "I'd like another couple."

"What does your wife think?"

"We agree," said Laroche. "France needs children. Why did the Germans overrun us in 1940? Because they had a population nearly twice as large."

"That wasn't the only reason. There was more to it than that."

"You won't convince me," said Laroche. "The bigger a population a country has, the more divisions it can put into the field. We lacked a hundred divisions in 1940. I'm only a bricklayer, but I can add up."

"Then do some adding up and calculate when the Americans will be here."

"That's a different set of tables," said Laroche with a grin. "I wish they were here already. If they don't come today we shall be in trouble. What would you do in their place?"

"You mean if I were an American?"

"No, I mean the Boche."

"It depends," said Pierre. He opened the ammunition sack belonging to the man he had sent to Raymond. Besides the ammunition it contained an army water-bottle and some bread wrapped in paper. Pierre unscrewed the cap of the bottle and tasted its contents. It was red wine, slightly sourish in taste and still cool from the night air, but its temperature was just right for

248

quenching thirst, and Pierre poured a long draught between his lips, held it for a second in his mouth before swallowing it, then carefully screwed on the cap and pushed it into a shady corner at the foot of the boulder. "If they're clever," he went on, "they'll wait for darkness."

"And then?" asked Laroche.

Pierre carefully studied the terrain in front of him. Most of the ways out of La Peine were either impassable or commanded by the men of the Maquis. "There's not much they can do," he said after a pause. "They may try to escape northwards out of the valley, but that won't do them much good in the end. I'd like to know what's become of the others."

"The people who were up here before?"

"Yes. The shooting that we heard this morning was beyond the village. Why didn't they come back to the village when it stopped?"

"I never could do puzzles," said Laroche.

Pierre took another look at the church, but could see nothing unusual. Then he looked at the house in which Knopf had lived. He could see only its roof, and while he watched it he felt his stomach contract.

As though Laroche had guessed his thoughts, he suddenly asked: "Where did Monsieur Knopf live?"

Pierre told him. "I still hope," he then said, "that they got away in time."

"Where to?" asked Laroche.

This was the same question that Pierre had asked himself countless times since yesterday afternoon and he could still find no answer to it.

The quietness all around was having a soporific effect. It was by now extremely hot and Pierre took off his jacket. He pushed it under the barrel of his gun and made sure that he had a clear field of fire towards the village street. The scattering of small boulders in front of them were fortunately not an effective obstacle. In the street nothing had changed. The houses stood abandoned and neglected beneath the cliff-face. The rusting gutters of the tiled roofs reflected the morning sun with a coppery glitter.

Pierre turned on to his side to escape the sun which beat upon his back. He was just about to check the amount of bread in the sack when there was a loud bang followed immediately by another. In the middle of the village a cloud of black smoke billowed away from the overhanging cliff-face and floated lazily away over the roofs.

249

"Here we go," said Pierre. "That was a tank; indirect fire."

"But where from?" asked Laroche. "They can't hit the cliff if they're on the road."

"It depends on their exact position. If they have gone back to the other side of the valley they could shoot from there."

"Without forward observation?"

"I'm afraid that they have an observation post somewhere. We shall soon see."

A few seconds went by and then a wild burst of firing broke loose. Pierre leaped round and crawled over to Laroche and they both stared up at the ridge, whose jagged outline looked like a cock's comb.

"Roger has caught it now," said Laroche, pale and strained. "That's German machine-gun fire. They've come up behind him."

"It's worse than that," said Pierre between clenched teeth. "The Boches have occupied the fort."

When Boris left him Georges opened his rucksack and filled his pockets with ammunition. Then he released the safety catch of his machine carbine, hung the rucksack over his shoulders again and placed himself against the right-hand wall of the tunnel. He did not have long to wait. Beyond the gap in the road the night was pierced by a sudden light and then a clattering colossus of a tank appeared in the glare from the headlamps of a truck. Georges saw the long gun-barrel, the infantry on the back with rifles at the ready and then came the truck, another tank and behind that two more trucks.

They were going slowly and when they were fifty yards short of the gap a voice began to shout. The leading tank halted as suddenly as if it had struck a wall. In spite of the intervening distance of two hundred yards Georges had a complete view of what was happening. The headlamps of the four trucks gave out so much light that he could even make out the type of tank. He saw the men climb down, to be joined by others running from behind, and then run forward to stare over the edge of the gap torn in the road.

More and more came. They tumbled from the trucks in black clumps and crowded in front of the gap across the whole width of the road until a sharp voice called them back. The leading tank started up and moved close up against the cliff-face on the left side of the road, while the first truck moved forward at a walking pace, passed the tank and stopped a few yards short of the landslip gap.

Although the full light of its headlamps was now shining across at him, Georges did not move. The distance was too great for them to notice him. He presumed that they would just make a close inspection of the situation and then climb back into their vehicles. They would then probably have to reverse down the road as it was too narrow for them to turn round.

A few minutes went by. On the other side they were standing in large groups and arguing, as Georges could tell from their movements. The palms of his hands grew moist. They seemed to be uncertain as to what they should do and Georges gradually lost his patience. He could not understand why they were wasting so much time, but probably the officers could not agree on a plan. If his estimate was correct there must have been well over a hundred men and probably more on the way.

As he watched them a light flashed between the groups of soldiers. It came from a pocket torch and the man holding it walked to the very edge of the abyss and shone the light downwards. Then he turned round and spoke to the others. As far as Georges could discern, the man was an officer. He wore a leather coat, a pistol at his belt and jackboots which shone in the light from the headlamps. He now turned to the spot from which the way led round the landslip débris and began to climb cautiously down.

This was the moment which Georges had been fearfully awaiting. He looked past the truck towards the tank. As long as the truck stood in its line of fire the tank could not shoot and at least two minutes would go by before the truck could be moved aside. Time enough for Georges to get away to safety; there was not the least risk involved.

Georges raised the machine carbine. The officer had stopped, waiting for three soldiers who were slowly following him. Although Georges only intended his shots to frighten them, he hesitated. The thought that they were Germans and that he had belonged to them for three years produced a curious feeling in him; he suddenly felt a smarting in his eyes which did not stop when he quickly wiped them with his coat-sleeve.

Don't be such a fool, he thought. Then he raised the barrel with a violent movement and fired off the whole magazine.

The troops vanished from the road as if the mountain had

251

swallowed them up. Only the officer stood where he was and he was the last person whom Georges saw before the headlights were switched off and there came a savage burst of rifle-fire.

It came much sooner than Georges had expected and he had to run for his life. He slowed down to a walk and breathlessly slung his gun over his shoulder only when he had rounded the bend in the tunnel and the ugly noise of ricochets had stopped. Then from behind came an ear-splitting crack, succeeded by an unbroken series of explosions. It sounded as if the entire mountain was collapsing; when Georges emerged from the tunnel the flashes lighting up the valley and the echoing shots produced the effect of a full-scale battle. The tanks were firing rapid. Georges counted twenty shots before it stopped. The rifle-fire began to slacken and finally ceased. By then Georges had reached the next tunnel.

He dropped breathless to the ground and looked at the road leading from the tunnel; with the mountainside along its right flank and a sharp bend fifty yards away it was an ideal position from which to delay a pursuing enemy.

When he had regained his breath Georges clipped in a fresh magazine. He then took a handful of rounds from his pocket and filled the empty magazine. His hands shook slightly in doing so and he grinned as he noticed it.

You're in a fine state, he said to himself. It's not so easy to fight a private war with them after all. Interesting to know what outfit that is; they didn't learn to shoot like that on the barrack square, for sure. Even so I bet they turn round and give up the idea of a billet in La Peine. No officer would be so crazy as to let his men get shot up just for a few hours sleep in those old hovels—unless, of course, they have a more important reason for going there.

You didn't think of that, did you? he said to himself. You presumed that they only came up this road by mistake and will turn round as soon as they find out that it's impassable. Perhaps it's an independent unit or a reconnaissance detachment. Those tanks could mean that it is and if they didn't come this way by mistake . . . but that's nonsense, he thought. What strategic value has La Peine? None; on the contrary, if the Americans catch up with them they'll be sitting in a trap. You can forget that idea.

He listened attentively. Nothing to be heard. They will have had time to remount their trucks and drive off. Perhaps they don't want to take any risks and will wait until tomorrow. If they don't turn back it will mean that they mean to wait until morning. But

252

why? he at once asked himself. They came so far unopposed and they could equally safely turn back, whereas if they press on they must expect another surprise attack all the time. They would only have to . . . And what about those shots yesterday evening? he thought. And the explosion! And you say they got here without opposition! Or do you imagine they just loosed off those shots for fun? And what did you think when you heard that explosion? Didn't it sound like a detonation charge, as if somebody were blowing up a road-block or . . . or what? A bridge perhaps, was that it? A bridge over the river and then the truck fully loaded with Maquisards. . . .

He sat for a while quite still, until he heard footsteps behind him. The tunnel was about thirty yards long and a figure appeared at its mouth and ran inside. Even before he could fully recognize her, he knew that it was Anna. Then she saw him. She stopped for a second, ran up to him and threw herself on him without a word.

She was quite out of breath. As Georges looked down at her a thick lump formed in his throat and he swallowed a few times, but the lump would not go and he murmured through it: "What are you doing here?"

She gave no answer and pressed herself still closer to him. Georges looked over her head and down the road. There was not a sound to be heard, but he felt certain that they would appear round the bend at any moment.

"You mustn't stay here," he said. "Does your uncle know?"

She shook her head on his chest. "He was in the village," she panted.

"And where were you?"

"I was at the far end of the street. I had been carrying crockery up to the fort and when I was on my way back again I heard it."

"Were you alone?"

"Madame Vieale was with me." She lifted her face and looked at him with tear-stained eyes. "I thought they had . . . you were . . ."

"If they had," said Georges, "you would have run straight into them. Don't do anything like this again. Why didn't Madame Vieale hold you back?"

"I told her that I was going to look for you and that she mustn't give me away."

"You women always gang up on us," said Georges severely, though with difficulty. He looked into the tunnel again. About

253

twenty yards beyond the tunnel the road took another bend; Georges gripped the girl by the hand and led her out of the tunnel and along the road until they were past the bend.

"Stay here," he said to her. "As soon as I fire a shot run up the road as fast as you can go."

"Only if you come too," she said.

"I'll come too, but I can run faster than you and I'll catch up."

He went back to the bend. From here he could see the road as far as the tunnel and through it to the far side. As it was darker in the tunnel than on the road, anyone approaching the tunnel from the other side would stand out clearly. By straining his eyes Georges could even make out the next bend in the road.

When he was certain that there was no movement on the road he picked up his gun, ready to fire from the hip, and stood with his right shoulder leaning against the wall of rock. A glance behind showed him that the girl was standing well covered behind the curve of the road and was looking at him.

"How far have you got with moving the baggage?" he asked.

"When I ran away most of it was already up there," she replied. "There were only a few more of Monsieur Vieale's things to carry up."

"Where have you put everything?"

"There was a long staircase leading downwards and then we went through some doors. I couldn't see much, it was too dark. Boris found the staircase."

"Didn't he tell you that you ought to go over the ridge?"

"No, why?"

He must have changed his mind, thought Georges and said aloud: "Oh, I only asked. You need a good smack on the bottom."

She smiled at him. "Will you do it?"

"Later perhaps," said Georges. As they talked he kept his gaze firmly fixed on the tunnel.

"Why did they shoot?" asked Anna.

"Because I annoyed them."

"It was terrible. I've never heard anything like it."

"And still you ran down here?"

"My legs ran by themselves."

Georges looked at her over his shoulder. "Come here!"

She ran to him and he hugged her with his free hand and said: "You can help me keep watch. But take care that nobody sees you. Are your eyes good?"

"Test me."

254

"Good. How far can you see down the road?"

"Beyond the tunnel."

"No farther?"

"Yes, but then there is a curve."

"Can you see that?"

"Yes."

"Then watch with me to see if anybody comes round the corner."

"I'm sure to see," said Anna. She pressed her head to his shoulder. "Isn't the rucksack too heavy for you?"

"I don't notice it," said Georges. "You're trembling."

"No, I'm not."

"You're trembling," Georges repeated.

"Yes, but I'm not afraid."

"Then you shouldn't be trembling."

"I'm only excited. How many were they?"

"I didn't count them."

"Did you shoot at them?"

"Only into the air."

"And then they shot at you?"

"I ran away at once."

"If anything had happened to you," said Anna, "they would have caught me too. And I wouldn't have cared."

"You must watch out," said Georges.

"I'm doing so," said Anna, looking down the road.

They both saw them almost simultaneously. The shadow of a man and then another appeared at the bend in the road beyond the tunnel and then came a whole file moving slowly towards the tunnel.

Georges pulled his arm away from the girl. "Now show me how fast you can run," he said, "and whatever happens don't stop until you're in the next tunnel. Wait for me there."

"Are you coming? . . ."

"Yes, yes," said Georges nervously. "Get going!" He gave her a gentle push in the back.

The row of shadowy figures had meanwhile drawn nearer to the tunnel. Georges laid the gun-barrel against the sloping rock and aimed at the roof of the tunnel. Then he fired a long burst. Without waiting to observe the effect of his fire he turned round and ran after the girl.

It was about fifty yards to the next bend, followed shortly by another and when Georges had passed them he saw Anna stand-

255

ing in the middle of the road. He seized her hand and ran on with her until they reached the next tunnel; Georges then realized that not a single shot had been fired at him.

"Again you didn't do as I told you," he said, panting for breath. "I told you to run as far as the next tunnel. Do you want your ears washed?"

"I'm sorry," murmured Anna. "In future I'll only do as you say."

"I can never be sure with you. What on earth are you going to tell your uncle when he misses you?"

"I'll tell him that I was with you—what else can I say?"

"That's what I'd like to know. He will be suspicious."

"I'm no longer a child," she said.

"Perhaps he doesn't realize that yet."

"I've already told him."

Georges suddenly said: "I'm fed to the teeth with it."

Anna looked at him in amazement. "What are you talking about?"

"About this whole damned business."

"I thought it was supposed to be fun."

"Do you think it's fun?"

"I never said I thought it was fun—you did."

"I forgot that they weren't Russians," said Georges. "If their officers are any good they'll stop now and wait until it's light."

"You're wishing you hadn't fired at them," said Anna quietly.

Georges shook his head impatiently. "I didn't fire at them. It's only that . . ."

"What?"

"Nothing," said Georges curtly. Then he gripped the girl by the arms and said in a loud voice: "Would you marry me?"

"If you like me," she said, without surprise.

"You must be crazy then," said Georges, and walked on into the tunnel. The girl ran after him. As they emerged from the tunnel and continued their way up the steep road Georges said: "It was just a question, that's all."

"Obviously," said the girl beside him.

"Obviously!" said Georges, irritated. "It's not obvious at all. I might have meant it."

She gave no answer.

"You must know whether you want to marry me or not," said Georges.

"I've told you," she replied calmly.

"But you probably weren't thinking when you did. Have you any idea of who I am?"

She nodded. "Yes. You are Georges Chabrier, the soldier."

Georges laughed in spite of himself. "Quite right; and that's all I am. I wanted to be a Bachelor of Commerce and a big business man; now I shall have to be a street sweeper."

"I'll help you sweep," said Anna.

"I'm quite serious."

"So am I. If you like I will help you sweep streets."

"That sort of talk is easy enough at seventeen," said Georges harshly.

Anna nodded again. "Perhaps. But sweeping streets couldn't possibly be worse than what I've lived through in the past five years. I want nothing but the chance to live one day entirely free from fear."

"Many people want that today. In another five years they will have forgotten it."

"Those who can," said Anna and stopped.

"What's the matter?" asked Georges.

"I heard something."

Georges gave a rapid glance down the road. "You must have been mistaken. They won't be coming before first light."

"Why did you ask me now, of all times, whether I would marry you?"

"It was just a thought that occurred to me," replied Georges. "If you're selling something you want to know what you're going to get for it."

"What are you selling?"

"I think I have sold it already," said Georges and looked again down the dark road.

"I don't understand."

"If I were in your place I wouldn't be able to understand it either," said Georges. "In Zürich I used to know a married woman. I think I would have died for her."

"Were you fond of her?"

" 'Fond' is not the right word: I worshipped her."

"Poor soldier!" said Anna, seriously. "I once read a book . . ."

"For God's sake shut up about your books," Georges cut her short. "She wasn't even worth the zip-fastener on your trousers. Why would you marry me?"

"Keep your eyes on the road."

"I don't give a damn about the road," said Georges in absolute seriousness. "I asked you a question."

"I think it's a stupid question," said Anna.

"I don't care about that either," replied Georges. "I want to hear the answer from you."

"I'm terribly in love with you," she said, smiling.

Georges looked at her for a while and again he had the feeling of having drunk too much. Then he pulled her to him by her long hair and said: "Good God!"

"You are funny," she said confusedly.

"We're both funny," said Georges. "You have no idea how funny we are, otherwise your whole delicious self would be shaking with laughter."

He took her hand and together they walked on. After a few paces Georges noticed the shape of a man standing motionless and staring at them. "Your admirer," said Georges grimly. "He has been watching us."

"What if he has?" said Anna, without letting go his hand.

They had now reached the man and Georges asked: "Are you waiting for us?"

Boris gave him no answer and turned to Anna. "Your father is extremely worried about you."

"My uncle is always worried about me," replied Anna. "Who told you that I was here?"

Her cool tone brought the color to Boris's face. "We guessed it," he said after a pause.

"Don't you mean that you guessed?" inquired Georges.

"What is it to you if I did?" replied Boris.

"Nothing at all now," said Georges and glanced back. "The Germans are coming."

"Thanks to you. If you hadn't shot at them they wouldn't have come on."

"If I hadn't fired on them they'd be up here by now, whether you care to believe it or not. How about the baggage?"

"Finished."

"Then we can move into the fort."

"What good will it do?" asked Boris. "They'll just go on searching for us until they've found us."

Georges shrugged his shoulders. "No one is forcing you to stay here. You were going to talk to the others about it, weren't you?"

"I have done so."

"While I was away?" asked Anna.

Boris looked at her. "Yes."

"What did my uncle say?"

"He couldn't make up his mind. His legs are hurting him."

"He's only saying so: it is certain to be his heart. You know very well that he must not strain himself."

"What does Monsieur Vieale say?" asked Georges.

"He will do what you do. I still believe we should have tried to get away; if we had given ourselves plenty of time and taken it slowly, we would have done the worst of it by the time we had reached the path."

"Or so you imagine," countered Georges. "Just supposing Monsieur Knopf did succeed in climbing down that rockslide, where would you go then? On to the road in the valley? How do you know that the Germans are not already marching up that road?"

"We could go somewhere else," said Boris. "I'm thinking of the wood. If we climb down from the spring we can be down in two hours and can wait there until the Germans have gone. In the wood we have water and whatever else we need."

Georges considered the idea. After a pause he asked: "What's the descent like?"

"Not so steep as on the other side."

"I never thought of that," said Georges slowly. "Of course the wood is a possibility. Have you mentioned it to Monsieur Knopf?"

"Not yet."

Georges let go the girl's hand. His suggestion to go to the fort had been a case of Hobson's choice. If he were honest with himself he had to admit that he had not felt happy about it and had seriously considered whether it would have been better to decide on getting away over the ridge, but the thought of the Maquisards had made him dislike the idea and he had been almost glad that Knopf's weak physical condition gave him an excuse to put aside Boris's objections to the fort. In fact a completely new situation had been created by the arrival of the Germans, and although he had not yet had the chance to give it careful thought, he now almost regarded their presence as a stroke of luck; but he was still not sure to what extent the effects of his impulsive action of the previous afternoon could be neutralized. Nevertheless his situation had already much improved. If he and Marcel were to meet the Maquisards later it would now be much easier to shift on to the Germans any suspicion of responsibility for having shot one of them.

259

Georges approved of Boris's suggestion and he wondered why he had not already thought of it himself. Although he was still convinced that the Germans would not stay long in La Peine, he now had a strong spasm of anxiety whenever he reminded himself that the merest chance could lead to the Germans discovering their hiding-place in the fort. When he had conceived the plan this thought had not occurred to him, but meanwhile the familiar sight of the German uniforms, the violence with which they had reacted to his first shots had all made a deep impression on him; he turned to Boris and said firmly: "I think you're right. If the others agree we shall go to the wood. We should have had to clear the baggage out of here in any case. It's safer in the fort than in those houses."

"We'll take only food and blankets with us," said Boris quickly. "I'll go on ahead and tell them." He set off quickly up the road.

"You should have let my hand go," said Georges as he looked after him.

Anna shook her head. "I held it tight on purpose."

"Can't you stand him?"

"Yes, but he has rather exaggerated ideas about me; I don't want to give him any grounds for persuading himself that I'm in love with him."

"Has he ever said anything of the sort to you?"

"No, but I could feel it. I didn't like it. Shall we go too?"

"Yes, we must . . ." Georges stopped and strained his ears. Softly at first, then louder and louder there came the sound of a dull droning and Georges even thought he could detect a faint vibration of the ground beneath him.

"What's that?" asked Anna. She had laid her hand on his arm and when Georges did not reply she asked: "Are they moving away?"

"It sounds like it," said Georges reflectively. "I'm just wondering though. . . ."

"What is it?"

"It somehow doesn't quite add up," said Georges. "I can't make it out."

With a sigh Anna put her head on his shoulder. "I simply can't understand anything any more. I thought you'd be pleased if they went."

"It's too early in the morning yet." He listened again to the sound of the tanks. It now sounded farther away and when he had satisfied himself that the German unit was in fact withdrawing, he took the girl's hand again and said: "Come on, we must go."

"Tell me what you're thinking."

"Later. Come on!"

They set off at a fast pace, Georges helping the girl to climb over the innumerable rocks scattered over the roadway. Once they stopped and kissed each other. "You frightened me again," she said. "If they go away then all's well."

"Of course it is," said Georges.

Her cool, slim hand lay in his and he held it firmly clasped until they reached the spot where the path led down to the village. Here Vieale was waiting for them.

Georges recognized him by his coat and his broad shoulders and said: "Hello there!"

"Thank God you're here," said Vieale in his loud voice. "Is it true that you think we should go and hide in the wood?"

"Don't you want to?"

"You can hardly see your hand in front of your face. We should have gone there before nightfall."

"Perhaps we needn't go after all," said Georges.

The sound of the tanks was now hardly audible. It sounded like the distant hum of aircraft engines and Georges asked Vieale: "Didn't you hear it?"

"The shooting?" Vieale burst out laughing. "*Mon Dieu,* we thought we'd never see you alive again."

"I'm not talking about the shooting. Listen hard and you'll hear it."

"It must be aircraft, if that's what you mean."

"That's not aircraft," said Georges. "Where are the others?"

"They're waiting just down there," said Vieale. "Your father is very angry with you, Mademoiselle," he said to Anna. "You should not have run away."

"Why not?" asked Georges.

Vieale stared at him in surprise. Then he scratched his head. "It's nothing to do with me."

"Quite so," said Georges calmly. "I suggest that we leave it at that."

He walked on. Vieale and Anna followed him and they met the others in the road by the turning leading to the fort. "You took long enough to get here," said Boris malevolently.

"That is only how it seems to you," said Georges. He turned to Knopf, who was standing next to Vieale's wife and looking at Anna. "I think I owe you an explanation."

"Do you?" Knopf turned to look at him. "I don't know what for.

I'm expecting an explanation from Anna, but that can wait. Boris says that you think it would be better for us to go down to the wood."

"I think we should," said Marcel. He was keeping himself somewhat in the background and looking alternately at Georges and the girl.

"It may not be necessary after all," said Georges. "I'm still not quite sure, but it looks as if the Germans have pulled back."

"Did you see anything?" asked Vieale quickly.

"I didn't actually see them moving away, but what you can hear is not the sound of aircraft: they are tanks. They are driving down the road. As soon as they cross the viaduct we shall see them again."

"Then we can stay here!" said Denise Vieale.

Her husband laughed with relief. "Why didn't you tell us straight away, Monsieur?"

"Because I'm not sure yet," said Georges. He took off his rucksack, laid it on the ground and turned to Anna. "Would you like to sit down?"

"No," she replied.

Georges smiled. "Sit down, you're tired."

She came over and sat down on the rucksack.

"Shall I give you a blanket?" asked Georges.

"No," she said. "I'm not cold."

"You've been running. Take the blanket, or you'll get cold."

She stood up and waited while Georges took the blanket from the rucksack. He put it round her shoulders and said: "That's better, isn't it?"

"Much better," she said.

Georges fleetingly touched her head with the palm of his hand. When he straightened up Knopf was standing in front of him and behind Knopf all the others were looking at him. "I must talk to you," he said to Knopf. He went with him a short way down the road. "I admit that this is hardly the right moment," began Georges, "but I must say what I have to."

"I hope you have thought it over carefully," said Knopf.

"It depends what you're talking about."

"Perhaps not what you have in mind."

Georges stopped. They were now far enough away from the others to be out of earshot. A glance at the sky showed him that it was slowly turning from black to gray and as he looked across the

262

valley towards the viaduct he saw the headlights. "There are only two," he said. "I was afraid so."

"What does it mean?" asked Knopf, who had also seen the beams of light.

"We'll soon see, but until then we have a few minutes."

"You are a strange young man," said Knopf, staring at him appraisingly through his eyeglasses.

"I don't think I am," said Georges. "It may be due to the unusual circumstances that you have this impression. May I speak frankly?"

"Perhaps it can wait until tomorrow," said Knopf.

"One never knows in situations like this. You have at least the right to an explanation. For Anna you are so to speak father and mother in one person."

"When did she tell you all that?" asked Knopf.

"Often five minutes is enough for something for which other people need years. I want to marry your niece."

Knopf took off his glasses, held them in his hand for a while and replaced them. "You must have time to think it over," he said. "To me it seems quite clear that you have not done so."

"So you said just now," said Georges. "I could give you plenty of evidence to show that I have, but we have time for that later."

"It was something else that I called in question a short while ago," replied Knopf quietly. "I said that you and I were probably thinking of different things."

Georges nodded. "Then I suggest that it is a matter which we need not discuss at this moment. I would prefer that, in any case. I should feel that I was being cross-examined and I need a little preparation for that."

"Don't exaggerate the influence that I have on Anna," said Knopf. "I can tell you both my doubts and objections, but that's all. The responsibility is ultimately yours, and here I am very pessimistic."

"That's a hard word," said Georges.

The two trucks were nearing the olive grove. They were widely spaced and Georges saw the tanks in the headlights of the second truck. They were traveling with closed hatches and the rattle of their tracks could be clearly heard. It was now light enough to distinguish the olive trees from the mountain background.

"I hardly know you," said Knopf. "What I think of you will depend entirely on what you are going to do."

263

"Then I'm afraid I shall have to disappoint you. I don't intend to go back home and play the part of the whipping-boy. So many people in Switzerland have already done too well out of our neutrality that I won't give them the pleasure——" He broke off. His attention was again drawn to the column of vehicles. They had drawn level with the olive grove and had stopped, switching off their headlamps as they did so. In the gray dawn light they could hardly be seen against the trees.

"What are they going to do now?" asked Knopf, in a voice of resigned helplessness.

Georges pursed his lips. "In military terminology it's called covering fire. Come on. As soon as they can see us it will get uncomfortable."

They quickly rejoined the others. Vieale's wife had seated herself on the rucksack beside Anna, while the men stood in a group looking across the valley.

"What does it mean?" asked Vieale.

"There were only two," said Marcel. "The others are still up the road."

"Perhaps they all came down but drove without lights," said Boris.

Vieale said: "We would have seen them if they had." He turned to Georges: "I think we should go to the wood after all."

"It's too late for that now," Georges declared. "In five minutes it will be light enough for them to see every movement here."

"In five minutes we can be in the village," said Boris.

"If they see us on the way down they'll drop their shells right on top of us. They're bound to have good binoculars. Do you wish to take the responsibility?"

"We've waited too long," said Boris with irritation. "We were fools to listen to you."

"No one has forced you to stay with the rest of us. I have never had the least intention of being any sort of a leader here."

"And we have never thought of you as such," said Vieale.

Georges looked towards the mouth of the tunnel leading into the fort, then his gaze traveled up the cliff-face to the ramparts and pillboxes at the top. The north face of the cliff seemed to be completely smooth, but as Georges examined it more intently, he noticed a broad crack which started some ten feet above the tunnel and split the cliffside vertically. It ended high up among the fortification works, and when Georges had stared at it for some time he turned to Vieale. "Is that it?"

264

"Haven't you noticed it before?" asked Vieale.

"No, but it looks nice, doesn't it? Let's go inside before it's too late."

He picked up his rucksack and gun and walked a few paces into the tunnel. It was so dark that he could see nothing. A breath of chill, stuffy air met him from the depths of the tunnel.

"The lamp is on the right-hand side if you need it," said Vieale, who had followed him with the others.

Georges put down his things and walked back to the entrance. He could clearly distinguish the two tanks from the trucks. They had placed themselves across the road and their long gun-barrels were trained across the valley.

"I thought I knew something about warfare," said Vieale, "but I don't understand what's going on here. Why are they doing all this?"

"Certainly not for their own amusement," replied Georges. "They've taken it into their heads to go to La Peine and in ten minutes at the latest they will be there."

Vieale sighed. "*Mon Dieu,* I imagined our stay in La Peine slightly differently. It comes from . . ." He stopped and stared down the road, where at that moment a white flare soared up in a parabola over the valley and slowly descended.

"Come on, let's go," said Georges urgently. "I think it's starting."

As if to confirm his words there immediately followed a shattering crash and as they ran into the tunnel a violent cannonade broke out behind them.

They only stopped running after they had gone fifty yards into the tunnel. Vieale had brought the lamp with him and he lit it. By its uneasily flickering light Georges noticed in the walls a whole series of door-like apertures with dark corridors leading from them. The end of the tunnel could not be seen, but the echoes of the gunfire indicated that it led deep into the mountains.

Vieale turned into one of the apertures in the right-hand wall of the tunnel. Knopf was the next to follow him, while Georges and Anna brought up the rear. The girl was still wearing the blanket round her shoulders and she gripped Georges by the hand as they entered the corridor. It was about six feet wide and of roughly the same height. The rough-hewn walls shone with damp and the floor was uneven and slippery. After a few yards the passage took a sharp turn to the left and before Vieale had reached the bend the firing outside had stopped.

265

He stood still and raised the lamp so that he could see Georges. "It has stopped," he said. "Shall we wait?"

"What for?" asked Georges. "It only proves that they will be here very soon."

"I don't understand why on earth they are so eager to come here," grumbled Vieale and turned the corner of the passage. Beyond it a steep flight of steps led downwards. Georges counted forty steps. At the bottom the corridor led on in the same direction and arrived at a heavy steel door which could be opened inwards. Through it they passed into a small room with arched ceiling and walls. It was quite bare; on the opposite side was another door.

Vieale stopped in the middle of the vault and waited until they were all in the little room. "These must have been ammunition chambers," he then said. "We haven't looked to see how many there are. After each chamber there is a thirty-foot corridor."

"Where have you put the baggage?" asked Georges.

"In the third chamber; there seems to be no point in penetrating farther."

Georges examined the door. It hung in a steel frame which was cemented into the rock. On its inner side it had two massive bolts and having shut the door, Georges pushed the bolts into their slots. Then he turned his attention to the second door. Its bolts were on the far side. "They can all only be bolted from this side," said Vieale. "I don't know why they made them like that."

"Perhaps they guessed that we might need them one day," said Georges. "It just makes me think."

They entered the next corridor and Georges again closed the bolts behind them. As Vieale had said, they came to a further vaulted chamber thirty feet long, which likewise had two doors. Georges closed them with the same care with which he had bolted the others and they found themselves standing in the third chamber. It was slightly larger than the other two, about twelve feet wide and thirty feet long. The two doors were placed exactly in the center of each of the long sides, whose walls, in contrast to the other rooms, were straight and only curved where they met the ceiling. Here too there was no trace of plaster or paint: the walls still showed the marks of drill and chisel. Pieces of luggage lay and stood everywhere; even the table and the bench from Anna's room and the trestle table from the kitchen were among them.

Vieale put the lamp on the table. "We must tidy the place up a bit first," he said. "Or do you think that it's not worthwhile?" His last words were directed at Georges, who was still looking round the arched chamber. When Vieale spoke to him he shrugged his shoulders.

"It will be worthwhile in any case. Before we drag everything back to the village we must rest for a few hours."

"It's cold in here," said Vieale's wife, shuddering. She was standing next to her husband, her hands thrust into her coat pockets.

Georges threw down his rucksack. "You can do something about that," he said. "You have mattresses and bedclothes; lie down on them and cover yourselves up."

"Perhaps that is the best idea," said Vieale. He turned to his wife. "Where would you like to lie down, *mon chou?*"

The woman pointed to one of the shorter sides of the room. "There. Four people can sleep along that wall, the rest by the other wall. If we put the table in the middle we shall have more room to move. Will you sleep next to me, Mademoiselle?"

Anna nodded. "If you don't mind, Madame."

"Help me carry over the mattresses," said Madame Vieale to her husband. To Georges she said: "There's room for you beside Monsieur Vieale."

"I have a couple of air mattresses," said Vieale. "One for you and one for Monsieur Egli."

Knopf had sat down on a suitcase. His conversation with Georges had left him with a feeling of dull despair. He glanced frequently at Anna. Since she had come back with Georges she had avoided him and it hurt him that she no longer confided in him. He still did not know what he should say to her, for much as he longed to gain a clear notion of what she was thinking he was equally afraid of alienating her completely by a careless word. Furthermore, he felt disquietingly unwell after the excitements and exertions of the past twenty-four hours. He not only had a permanent roaring in his ears but his legs were almost unbearably painful and in his present condition he would have been quite incapable of climbing down the steep mountainside to the wood, as Boris had suggested.

He absentmindedly watched Vieale and his wife laying the mattresses on the ground, then covering them with bedclothes. Anna was similarly occupied. She had pushed her mattress close to Madame Vieale's bed, while Georges was blowing up Vieale's inflatable mattress on the other side. Although he had no reason for it, Knopf felt uneasy that Georges and Anna had put their beds on the same side, but then he told himself that he was oversensitive and that they all had far greater cares than those which occupied him at that moment.

He stood up in order to put his own bed to rights. Boris had already laid out his mattress for him and had put down straw on the floor. As Knopf approached him he straightened up from his stooping position and said quietly: "You shouldn't tolerate it." In the light of the paraffin lamp his bearded face had an unnatural pallor.

"What are you talking about?" asked Knopf.

Boris glanced over to the other side. "He has turned her head," he said.

"It takes two for that to happen," replied Knopf. "One who does the turning and the other who allows it to be turned."

Boris made an impatient gesture. "You could forbid her."

"Forbid? Try forbidding a bird to fly when it's let out of its cage."

"You know that he's worthless. He's an adventurer."

"Which one of us here is not?"

"Do you really consider him your equal?"

"I'm not in the habit of putting people into categories. Give me time with this matter; one can smother a fire but one can easily burn one's fingers in doing so."

Boris was about to return to the attack when he was interrupted by Marcel who had meanwhile arranged his bedding and had joined Knopf and Boris. "How long are we supposed to be staying here?" he asked.

"Why don't you ask your friend?" was Boris's curt reply. "He brought us here."

"What's the matter?" asked Georges. He had seated himself beside Anna on her mattress and she had just asked him what he and her uncle had said to each other when Boris's loud words caught his attention. When no one answered he stood up. Vieale, who had been arranging the bench and chairs round the table with his wife, also looked up.

"What are you supposed to ask me?" Georges asked Marcel.

"It was nothing important," replied Marcel, throwing a furious glance at Boris. He had purposely avoided putting the question to Georges in order to give him no possible ground for another quarrel. Although he had never seriously considered whether he liked the girl or not, the conversation between Georges and Anna at the entrance to the tunnel had affected him like an ice-cold shower.

268

The image of himself inviting the girl to Zürich and taking her sailing in his boat had become a firm component of his plans for the future and that it should be Georges, of all people, who destroyed this dream aroused his violent resentment. Georges had always overborne him and had always won with ease what Marcel had been obliged to get with the aid of his father's money; he would not have succeeded in suppressing his true feelings at that moment had his awareness of the danger of their position not been stronger than his wounded pride. The cold, oppressive air in the vault, the uncertainty about what might happen in the near future, the nervous strain of the last few days, all combined to put him in a state of fearful expectation, and since none of the others had as much war experience as Georges and himself he felt quite unequal to the situation. Marcel thus found himself willy-nilly in his old state of dependence upon Georges.

Fortunately Knopf now came to his assistance. For reasons of his physical disability Knopf preferred Georges' suggestion of moving into the fort to all others, and he said in place of Marcel: "We were discussing how long we might have to stay here, but I don't think this question need concern us for the moment. The main thing is that we have found a safe place."

"How do we know it's so safe?" asked Boris.

"You bolted the doors behind you, didn't you?" said Knopf, looking at Georges.

"Bolting those doors is useless," said Boris before Georges could answer, "as long as we can't bolt them on the other side. This gallery is bound to have another entrance."

"Have you seen one?" inquired Georges.

"No, but——"

Georges interrupted him. "The fact that the bolt is only fixed to one side seems to indicate that there is nothing to fear from the other side. Marcel and I will just go and take a look and see where the passage goes from here. There must be a place where the fresh air is coming in, otherwise the air in here would be much fouler than it is. We'll wait until evening and then go and investigate."

"And if the Germans stay here for a long time?" asked Boris.

"I don't believe they will."

"Why not?"

"Because I can't see any sense in it. Unless I'm very much mistaken they will have gone again in a few hours at the very most. As soon as they realize that this is only an access road to the fort they'll probably climb over the ridge."

"Why over the ridge?" asked Vieale, puzzled.

"Because they have no other way to go, but it's only a guess of mine."

"A pretty wild one, too," said Boris sarcastically. The others also looked disbelieving.

Georges did not care. He went to the corner where he had put his rucksack and took out his pocket torch.

"Where are you going?" asked Anna. She was sitting on her bed talking to Madame Vieale.

"I'll be back in a moment," replied Georges.

"I'm coming with you," she said and started to get up. Georges pushed her back on to the mattress. "This time you're staying here," he said so softly that only she and Madame Vieale could hear him. "Don't try and run after me again."

"Please. I won't be in your way," she pleaded.

The other woman put in: "Monsieur Chabrier is right, you know, Anna."

"He can do what he likes," said Anna, "and I shall do what I like. After all, we're not married."

"Not yet," said Georges. "But I have told your uncle."

"What?" she quickly asked.

"That I want to marry you."

"You haven't!"

"I have."

Anna sat there with her mouth hanging open, then blushed scarlet and turned to Madame Vieale. "He said it to me an hour ago. One shouldn't take it seriously."

"You don't seem to take me seriously at all," said Georges angrily. "I at any rate am completely serious about it, do you understand?"

"Don't shout so," she said. "We're not even engaged yet."

"Holy Mother of God!" said Madame Vieale in amazement at the sudden tension that had sprung up between Georges and Anna. "Whatever's going on between you two?"

"What's all this?" asked Vieale, who had caught the tail-end of her remarks and came quickly over to them.

Georges bit his lip. Then he picked up his gun and said to Marcel: "Come on!"

As they passed through the second door Georges switched on his pocket lamp. The scene was as before: first a short corridor, then a vaulted chamber, another corridor, and as they entered the

270

next chamber Georges stopped and said: "Do you notice something?"

"Fresh air," answered Marcel. "Where does it come from?"

Georges turned his torch on to the ceiling until the ray of the lamp picked out a circular hole. It was about two feet in diameter and led obliquely upwards. "An airshaft," he said with satisfaction. "If we could climb up it we should come out somewhere into the open."

"Inside the fort?"

"Yes. What a task, building those fortifications."

"No greater than excavating these tunnels and galleries in the rock."

They went on and came to yet another chamber. Then there was a violent thud and they felt the ground shake beneath them. Simultaneously they heard a dull pattering as if heavy stones were dropping, then a long grinding noise which sounded so uncanny in the dark, subterranean vault that the sweat started from Georges' forehead.

They stopped and listened until it was quiet again. Marcel's fingers had clutched Georges' jacket and he asked in a whisper: "God almighty, what was that?"

Georges did not answer. After waiting a half-minute he walked out of the chamber into the corridor beyond. It was longer than the others and took a slight bend to the right; suddenly the way was almost blocked by a heavy rock and when Georges shone the feeble beam of the torch upwards he noticed a large hole in the roof over his head and alongside it a broad crack which extended parallel with the corridor into the darkness ahead. It was wide enough to hold a clenched fist.

Georges stepped over the rock and went cautiously on. He had only gone a few paces when he found the passage blocked to the roof with rubble. Although he had guessed at something similar, the sight sent a chill up his spine. He swung round and ran back to the chamber where Marcel had not moved from where he stood.

"Seen anything?" asked Marcel excitedly.

"We must turn back," said Georges.

"If only we had never come to this damned fort," said Marcel.

When they rejoined the others Georges saw from their anxious expressions that they had been as frightened as Marcel and he had been. Knopf, Vieale and Boris had sat down at the table while Anna and Madame Vieale were still sitting on their mattresses.

271

"What have you found out?" asked Knopf.

"The passage is blocked," said Georges.

"Where?"

"Not far from here; maybe fifty yards farther on."

"That could happen to us in here," said Boris. "We must get out."

"Where to?" asked Georges.

"Give me your torch. I'm going to have a look and see what's happening outside. Perhaps they've gone already."

Georges put his hand in his pocket and put the torch on the table. "There you are," he said.

"I'll leave the doors open behind me," said Boris.

When he had gone it was quiet for a while until Vieale broke the silence: "Wouldn't it have been better, Monsieur, if you had gone with him?"

"He didn't ask me to go, so why should I suggest it?" said Georges.

"He hasn't so much experience as you," put in Knopf.

Georges looked at Marcel, who was still standing near the door. "Why don't you sit down?"

"I'd rather stand," answered Marcel.

"And I'd rather you sat down," said Georges. "You make me nervous."

He waited until Marcel had sat down on the bench, then turned to Knopf. "Any of us here is free to do as they wish; I can't stop Boris from going out."

"He could put us all in danger," said Knopf. "Shouldn't we at least shut the door?"

"Then we can't hear anything. If they see him they'll shoot at him. Perhaps I should have tried to hold him back, but you know as well as I do that it would have been useless. Like all Russians, he's pig-headed."

"He doesn't like you," said Anna.

Georges gave a thin smile. "Quite so."

"And if they catch him?" asked Marcel.

Before Georges could reply the flame of the paraffin lamp suddenly began to flutter and then the same thing occurred as had happened a few minutes before. The ground shook as if from a distant explosion, followed by a nerve-shattering noise of grinding like the splintering of rotten wood; the silence which came afterwards seemed to be charged with electricity.

Georges looked at Anna. She was staring up at the arching roof

272

and the skin of her face was stretched so tightly that the lines of her cheekbones showed through.

"This is getting unbearable," said Vieale in a whisper. He had put his hands on the table in front of him and nervously clenched his fists. Knopf sat stiffly in his place and did not move when Marcel leaped to his feet, ran to the door, stopped and shouted in a voice hoarse with fear: "We must do something; the mountain is caving in."

"It's still standing so far," said Georges, pointing to the lamp. "The lamp felt it before we did. The ground shook before we heard the crash. They are bombarding the fort."

"The Germans?" asked Vieale anxiously.

"Who else is there with artillery?" answered Georges. "Just a few more shells and——"

He stopped. Boris appeared in the doorway, his face gray. "They're in the fort," he said and locked the door behind him. "I've heard their voices."

"You needn't have gone outside just to discover that," said Georges. "I could have told you that they were up here."

"Did you know that there's a battle going on?" asked Boris. Georges looked up sharply. "A battle! Where?"

"I don't know," said Boris and dropped on to the bench beside Vieale. Anna, Marcel and Madame Vieale also drew closer and they all looked at Boris, who had turned to Georges. "You can hear machine guns," he went on. "From the passage I couldn't make out where the firing was coming from, but it sounded as if it was in the fort."

"Then it is merely covering fire," said Georges. "Perhaps they think that the people who shot at them have taken refuge in the fort."

"I didn't have that impression," said Boris. "Go out yourself and listen to it. There are several weapons firing at once. The fire is being returned from somewhere; you can clearly distinguish the sound of one from the other."

"How far out did you go?" asked Vieale.

"I wanted to go into the tunnel, but before I came to the end of the passage I heard voices. They were Germans. They must have been standing quite close and shouting something to each other, but the noise of firing was so loud that I couldn't hear what they were saying."

"It's impossible!" said Georges impatiently. "If there were anybody else here we would surely have seen or heard something."

273

"They may have only just come," replied Boris and looked at Knopf. "I'm thinking of one certain person."

"So am I," said Knopf in a worried voice. "I hope we are mistaken."

Georges exchanged a rapid glance with Vieale and asked: "Who is that person?"

"Pierre," answered Knopf. "Perhaps he tried to come up here today and ran into the German troops."

The same thought had occurred to Georges. If this had in fact happened, he had no further need to worry about Maquisards and his first feeling was of relief. But then he remembered that Pierre had not been alone. Perhaps the Resistance had collected reinforcements in the night and were barring the way to the Germans across the ridge.

As he listened with half an ear to the conversation between the others he reasoned to himself that the Maquis must have been aware of the arrival of the Germans, since only that would explain their summoning up reinforcements in such strength, and the longer he considered it the more uneasy he became. Then he felt a hand on his shoulder. Looking round he saw Anna standing behind him.

"Is the mountain going to break up?" she asked quietly.

"I can't imagine that it will," replied Georges.

"You don't really believe what you say," she said. "I can tell from your face."

Georges was spared from replying by Vieale, who turned to him and said: "What do you think?"

"I wasn't listening," said Georges. "What were you talking about?"

"Your friend says we can't stay here."

"Then I suppose he also said where we should go to."

"It was your idea to come in here, not mine," said Marcel with irritation.

"Nobody seemed to have a better one."

"I told you what would have been better," interjected Boris.

"Somewhat too late," said Georges.

Boris said sharply: "It wouldn't have been too late if you hadn't dawdled. You made us lose a lot of precious time."

"As far as I'm concerned," said Georges quietly, "I wish you had lost no time at all and taken the next boat to Timbuctoo. Better still, I wish you had stayed where you came from."

"Messieurs!" said Vieale imploringly.

274

Georges waved him aside. "All right, all right. It's my own fault that I'm sitting here and I don't need a scapegoat; the same goes for most of the rest of you. If ever anybody somewhere else in the world feels oppressed I shall send them a food parcel with an expression of my profound sympathy. In thirty years the Russians will have all Europe and then all these little problems will be solved." He stood up and collected his gun from the corner. "Where's my torch?" he asked Boris. Boris produced it from his pocket and put it on the table.

"I'm just going out to listen for myself," said Georges. "If the Germans really are going to spend some time here there is nothing we can do about it. We have enough food to eat and enough time for waiting."

He walked over to the door and pushed back the bolt. Then a thought came to him. He looked at Knopf. "I didn't mean you."

"I didn't think you did," said Knopf. "But you have forgotten one thing."

"I'm sorry," said Georges, looking at him inquiringly.

"We have no water," said Knopf. "The bucket is empty."

His words produced a silence of several seconds. Georges was leaning against the door, and when he spoke again his voice sounded husky. "When did that occur to you?"

"When you said that we had enough to eat."

"Who carried up the empty bucket?"

All eyes turned on Boris, who hung his head.

"That really was worth a moment's thought, wasn't it?" Georges said to him. He stood for a while by the door and then pushed back the bolt. "In this case we can't risk being discovered. We must try to get water this evening. Until then we must not stir from here."

"We still have two bottles of wine," said Vieale.

Georges replaced his gun in the corner. "I always get thirsty after drinking wine. I suggest we lie down and sleep."

"Sleep!" Marcel gave a nervous laugh. "How do you think we can sleep? This mountain is going to collapse round us at any moment."

"You won't know much about it if it does," said Georges. "First it will fall on to the village and then about another thousand feet into the valley. By then you will be past caring."

Vieale attempted a grin. "Cold comfort."

"What else is there?" asked Georges.

Chapter 11

It was early evening when Georges was awakened by a noise. Before going to sleep they had put out the lamp and the chamber was in pitch darkness. Georges lay with eyes open and listened. As he was not sure whether he had merely dreamed it he closed his eyes again, but then he heard Vieale's voice beside him.

"Are you awake, Monsieur?"

Georges sat up. "Yes. Did you hear something?"

"It was the same noise that we heard this morning," replied Vieale softly.

"I heard it too," said his wife. "What's the time?"

Georges looked at his luminous watch. "Seven o'clock."

"That means we have slept for nearly nine hours," said Vieale slightly more loudly.

"You'll wake up the others," whispered Madame Vieale.

"I think they're already awake," said Georges, fumbling in the dark for his torch. When he had found it he shone it past the table towards the three men. They were awake and all three sat up as if at a word of command.

"I've been awake for a long time," said Knopf. "Did you hear it too?"

"We were awakened by it," answered Georges.

"That was the third time in the past hour," said Knopf. "Each time it was louder."

"Was there an explosion first?"

"No, it began by itself."

Georges threw off his blanket. "In an hour it will be dark out-

side," he said. "We might as well start getting up." He shone the
torch past Vieale to Anna. There was just room enough on the
narrow side of the chamber for four people to lie. The Vieales had
covered themselves with an eiderdown and they had laid it sideways to cover Anna as well. Georges could only see her face.

"Slept well?" he asked.

She shook her head. "No. I'm not used to sleeping in my
clothes."

"Nor am I," said Denise Vieale. She crawled from under the
eiderdown and looked at her dress in horror. "I can throw it away
now. It was my best and I put it on specially to avoid it being
crushed in the suitcase."

"You could easily have taken it off, *mon chou*," said her husband.

Georges went to the table and lit the paraffin lamp. His mouth
felt dry and he stood for a while in uncertainty until Vieale came
over to him, sat down on the bench and looked up into his face.
"What are you thinking about, Monsieur?"

"I'm wondering whether I'm hungry or not."

"We could eat something. We have some tinned sausages."

"I've no appetite for food," muttered Marcel.

Georges stared at him. "Are you sick?"

"I could hardly shut an eye all the time. That noise gets on my
nerves."

"We can all hear it. It's probably always there. When a mountain is shifting there is bound to be noise."

"I don't like it," said Vieale and lit a cigarette. "I'd like to know
what's happening."

"We'll know in an hour's time," said Georges. His glance fell
on Madame Vieale. She was talking to Anna, who had also got
up and was putting on her sandals.

"I don't know either," said Anna aloud.

"What don't you know?" inquired Georges.

Anna blushed slightly and said to the woman: "You ask him,
Madame."

"I was wondering what the weather was like outside," said
Madame Vieale. "Where can we go to when we have to?"

"Must you?" asked Vieale.

"You don't have to ask that in a coarse way," said his wife.

Georges suppressed a laugh. "No harm in talking about it, I
suppose," he said. "Take my torch and go into the last chamber."

"How does one know that it's the last one?"

"You can count them; there are three altogether."

"I hope I don't miscount," she said, taking the torch from Georges. "I must look ghastly. I haven't combed my hair or washed myself for two days."

"You look fine to me," said Georges.

"If I were you I would pay my compliments somewhere else," she said and disappeared through the door.

Vieale grinned. "What we have to put up with from these women, Monsieur!"

"It's my own fault," said Georges. Anna had turned her back on him and was busy with her bed. Her shoulders were shaking as though with suppressed laughter.

Knopf, Boris and Marcel had listened in silence to the brief conversation. When Madame Vieale went out Marcel got up from his bed and came to the table. As he had found no opportunity to shave the previous day his beard had grown still thicker. His face looked haggard, with dark rings under his eyes. "Do you think we shall get out?" he asked.

Georges shrugged his shoulders. "I hope so. If we don't we shall just have to spend another night here."

"It's like a tomb," said Marcel. "I feel as if I hadn't seen the sun for a month."

"So do I," said Vieale. "Even so we must eat. Have you lost your appetite?" he said to Knopf, who had taken off his glasses and was polishing the lenses.

Knopf continued rubbing them for a while. Having slept for a few hours he now felt better. He replied: "I have no great appetite, but I could eat something."

"Then let's wait for Madame Vieale. I don't know where she packed the tinned sausages."

"I'm beginning to get thirsty," said Marcel and licked his dry lips with his tongue.

"We'll drink a bottle of wine with them," said Vieale.

While he took the bottle from the luggage, Knopf stood up and walked over to Anna. She wore an expression of cool reserve, and as Knopf sat down by her she moved slightly to one side.

The men at the table chatted aloud until Vieale's wife returned. "I didn't know where you had packed the tin of sausages," Vieale said to her. "Will you fetch them for us, *mon chou?*"

"What else do we need?" she asked.

"Bread and glasses; I already have the wine."

278

Anna watched as the woman busied herself with the luggage. "Can I help you?"

"I can easily find it myself," said Madame Vieale. "We shall need your glasses, though. Mine will not be enough."

"They're in the little wooden chest," said Anna.

Knopf sat frowning beside her. Although he had come over to talk to her, he was unable to find the appropriate words. It seemed to him that an invisible wall stood between them and her persistent silence increased his discomfort. "I'm worried about Pierre," he said at last. "I hope nothing has happened to him."

"I've been thinking about him too," said Anna. She had clasped her hands round her knees and was watching the men at the table.

It occurred to Knopf that no one was paying any attention to Anna and him. Even Georges was managing to avoid looking at them. Boris was still sitting on his straw bed, but the men sitting round the table blocked Knopf's view of him.

"Perhaps we should have stayed in Escarène," said Knopf after a pause. "We might have spared ourselves all this."

"It was Pierre's idea," said Anna.

"If we had told him that we preferred to stay in Escarène he would have agreed."

"I don't regret it."

"That we came to La Peine?"

"I shall never regret it," said Anna.

"Never is a long time," said Knopf. "You're only seventeen."

"You once said yourself that my years count double."

"In endurance, but not in experience."

"If you don't mind," said Anna, "let's talk about it some other time. We may die here."

"You mustn't say things like that," murmured Knopf uncomfortably.

"Why not? We have always talked about such things," she replied calmly. "Since Georges has been here I have ceased to care whether we die or not. You have had sixty-six years of time, while I will perhaps have only seventeen. I thought you would understand."

"Have I said that I don't understand you?"

"You haven't said so, but I feel it all the same."

"I'm only thinking of you," said Knopf.

"You think so, but I could never love you again if you tried to change anything now."

279

Knopf was silent and watched Georges, who was talking to Vieale, Marcel and Madame Vieale. She had laid glasses and plates on the table. "What do you know about him?" asked Knopf after a further pause.

"You never know more of a person than your own belief in him."

"He might change his mind one day."

Anna looked at Georges and smiled. He was sitting beside Marcel on the bench. Vieale and his wife were sitting on the folding chairs. "He might indeed," said Anna. "If he stops loving me one day, why should he stay with me?"

"You're out of your mind, child," said Knopf, shaking his head.

Still smiling she laid her hand in his. "He said that to me too. I'll give him time to think it over thoroughly and then if he still wants to marry me, he can. One is never so sure of the other person as to exclude the chance of losing them one day, but that's no reason why one shouldn't at least have a try."

"I seem to have heard that before."

"Of course you have. I got it from one of your own books."

"That was twenty-five years ago," said Knopf. He slowly stood up. "Are you so very fond of him?"

"Yes. If we ever get out of here he will come with us or I will go with him and I will take good care that he doesn't change his mind."

Knopf looked down at her for a few seconds and as he did so he made a strange discovery.

"Why are you looking at me like that?" asked Anna.

"I have been asleep too long," replied Knopf.

He quickly bent down to her and kissed her on the forehead, then turned round. As he walked past the table the other men watched him in silence, but he did not notice them. He sat down on his mattress and stared absentmindedly in front of him.

Vieale exchanged a meaningful look with his wife and leaned over to Georges. "Shall we wait any longer before eating?"

"It makes no difference to me," said Georges, looking at Anna. She held her head down and Georges felt a surge of anxiety. For a moment he had a strong desire to get up and ask her what she had been talking about with her uncle, but it would have been too conspicuous and he did not want to give Knopf any further cause for disliking him.

Madame Vieale had already prepared the meal. Slices of bread lay on the plates and Vieale had opened the tin of sausages and poured wine into the glasses. As long as Knopf had been talking to Anna neither Vieale nor his wife had mentioned the subject of food and even Marcel, who noticed that Georges wanted the two to be undisturbed, had mastered his impatience. But now he saw no further reason to wait and said to Georges: "Couldn't we start now?"

"I thought you had no appetite," said Georges.

"I had none just now," said Marcel, "but since we're all sitting here . . ."

"Boris has fallen asleep again," said Vieale, after a glance at the Russian, who was lying on his back with his eyes closed.

"He's only pretending," muttered Georges. "Five minutes ago he was wide awake."

A slight sound turned his attention to Anna. She got up and came to the table. "Is there room for me?" she asked.

Georges moved up closer to Marcel. "There's always room for you. Sit down beside me. Did you have a good talk?"

She smiled and laid her head on his shoulder for a moment. "Yes."

"Then all's well," said Georges with relief. "Let's eat. Ask your uncle whether he minds if we start."

"What do you mean—uncle?" asked Marcel in astonishment. He was the only one who still did not know about it. Madame Vieale had learned of it that morning from Anna when Georges and Marcel had gone out, and later had told her husband.

"I'll explain later," said Georges to Marcel. "Don't pull such a stupid face!"

Anna stood up. "Where's the torch?"

"What do you want it for?" asked Georges.

"For the last chamber, you inquisitive soldier."

"I left it over there on the suitcase," said Madame Vieale.

Anna fetched the torch and Georges showed her how it worked. Then she went over to Knopf and said: "We're going to eat. Are you coming to the table?"

"I'll wait until you're back," said Knopf, who had heard the last part of the conversation.

As Anna turned she glanced at Boris. He had put his right arm under his head and she noticed that his eyes were open and he was looking at her. "Don't you want to eat anything?" she said to him.

"I'm not hungry," replied Boris. He watched her as she went to the door.

"I thought you were asleep," said Knopf, who was sitting next to him. "Won't you really have something to eat?"

Boris shook his head. He had only slept for two hours. His disillusionment was now complete and only weary resignation remained of all the emotions which had tortured him since realizing that Anna was lost to him. He could not even hate Georges any more.

Knopf had noticed nothing of all this. The rush of events had in any case left him no time to think about Boris. Each of them had been absorbed in himself and as Boris had always been of a reserved nature Knopf had not noticed his depressed behavior. He had, of course, been aware of the tension between Boris and Georges, but he had attributed it to mere personal dislike; the possibility that Boris, too, might be in love with Anna would have struck him as so unlikely as to be not worth consideration.

The conversation with Anna had set his mind whirling, and he was still so preoccupied by it that he had no time to wonder at the Russian's sudden loss of appetite. Only when Boris began to talk again and asked him how his legs were did he tear himself away from his thoughts. "I think I am stiff after all that exercise," he said.

"You should have spared yourself," said Boris. "We could have managed it quite well without you." He dropped his voice. "Did you talk to Anna just now?"

"Yes."

"What does she say?"

"She wants to get married."

Boris nodded bitterly. "He knows exactly what he wants. I hope that you know too."

"What do you mean?"

"Perhaps I'll tell him myself," answered Boris. "I will find a suitable opportunity to do so."

"Don't you like him?"

"No."

Knopf crossed his legs and looked over at Georges, who was talking with Vieale and his wife. They were speaking so quietly that Knopf could only hear snatches of their conversation and after watching Georges for a few seconds he turned again to Boris. "He feels the same about you."

"Yes, because he has noticed that I've seen through him."

"Neither of us knows much about him," said Knopf guardedly.

282

"At the moment we are thrown together in each other's company. I must beg you not to start another quarrel with him."

"You've reconciled yourself to the situation pretty rapidly," said Boris after a while.

Knopf made a weary gesture. "Not really, although I've become reconciled to something else in the last five minutes; at least I'm trying to."

"Will you tell me what it is?"

"Until now I've treated Anna like a child," said Knopf.

"You were right."

"Perhaps you would think differently if you were ten years younger. When I was seventeen I felt myself old enough to take on the whole world." He stood up. "Come to the table. You must eat something."

"I really have no appetite," said Boris.

"Then for once eat something without being hungry. Who knows when we'll get our next meal?"

When they reached the table, Anna again had taken her seat on the bench next to Georges.

"There's not much room, I'm afraid," said Vieale.

"It doesn't matter," said his wife. "I've laid all the places now and divided the bread. One person must sit on the suitcase."

Hardly a word was spoken while they ate. The liver sausage was rather fatty but tasted good with red wine and when they had finished Vieale handed round cigarettes.

A glance at his watch told Georges that it was now dark outside and he decided to wait another ten minutes. He noticed that the palms of his hands were damp. He wiped them on his jacket and drained his glass.

"Would you care for a drop more?" asked Vieale.

Georges picked up his wineglass and then put it back on the table. "We must go carefully with the wine," he said. "I don't know whether I shall be able to bring you any water."

"Where will you find water?" asked Marcel. "You surely won't go to the spring?"

"Where else?"

"That's impossible," said Anna forcefully. "You can't go to the spring."

Georges said nothing and blew his cigarette smoke at the lamp-chimney, where it was driven upwards by the heat.

"That would be foolish," said Knopf. "As long as we have wine there is no need to risk your life."

283

"By tomorrow afternoon at the latest the wine will be finished."

"Then will be the time to go; perhaps the Germans will have gone by then."

"Perhaps," said Georges. "But it's equally possible they will still be here the day after tomorrow and I'd rather try to get through to the spring this evening than tomorrow morning. Monsieur Vieale has an alcohol-stove. If we have water we can make some coffee. We must get something warm into our stomachs."

"I can go for another three days yet without anything warm," said Anna.

Vieale agreed with her. "You should think it over, Monsieur. Don't go out there for our sakes."

"I'm not going for your sakes," replied Georges. "I want a cup of coffee." He threw down his cigarette and ground it out under his boot. "You can come with me for some of the way," he said to Marcel.

"Don't do it," begged Anna, her face white.

Georges took the torch from the table. "If it gets unpleasant I'll turn back. Once in Russia we had no water for three days. By tomorrow evening not one of us here will be able to think of anything but their craving for a drop of water and we don't want things to get to that stage."

He went with Marcel to the door and unbolted it. "Shall I come as far as the spring?" asked Marcel uncomfortably.

"Only as far as the staircase," replied Georges. He felt Anna staring at his back and strode into the corridor, where he switched on the torch.

"I would have waited until tomorrow if I were you," whispered Marcel.

"Now don't you start that," said Georges and opened the door.

The nearer they came to the steps the more cautious he became, and when they reached the last door he stopped for a while and listened. "Can you hear anything?" he asked softly.

"Not a sound," whispered Marcel.

"Stay here," said Georges. "As soon as you hear someone coming down the steps, bolt the door. If it's me I'll knock on it three times. I'll take the torch with me. Hold it for a moment." He gave the lamp to Marcel, changed his empty magazine and refilled it.

"And another thing," said Georges when he was ready. "In case they're chasing me I'll shout. Then you mustn't shut the door until I'm in the chamber with you."

"And if they're close behind you?"

"If they're too close behind me I won't be able to shout because I'll already be dead."

He carefully pushed back the first bolt and as he gripped the second Marcel put his hand on his back and said: "Georges! I'm going back to Zürich in spite of everything."

"In spite of what?"

"In spite of everything. If we get out of this business in one piece I'm going to Zürich. I've sworn to do it."

"I won't stop you."

"Won't you come too?"

"No."

Disappointed, Marcel took his hand away. "Is it because of the girl?"

"No; on principle," said Georges, and opened the second bolt. Then he put his foot against the door and said: "Give me the lamp." He shoved it into his pocket and opened the door a few millimeters, always ready to counter a sudden pressure with his foot. Now the gap was wide enough for him to put his head through and for a while he stared into the pitch-dark passage beyond. Although he strained his ears he could no longer hear noises of battle, and when he was sure that no immediate danger threatened he turned to Marcel. "You know what to do. If I'm away for too long get Vieale or Boris to change places with you."

"How long do you think . . . ?"

"It depends whether the way to the spring is free or not. Half an hour there, half an hour back and half an hour while the bucket fills up; let's say two hours. If I'm not here by then you needn't wait any longer."

"Don't talk nonsense," murmured Marcel. "Where should we be without you?"

"The Germans won't stay here forever. This valley is not a cage; it has a hundred ways out."

"One would be enough."

Georges grinned in the dark. "It won't do you any harm to spend two or three days in this pile. It'll be a little foretaste of what's to come. The prisons in Switzerland are not much more comfortable."

"At least you know you'll get out of jail alive."

"They say prisoners have died of measles before now," said Georges and stepped out into the passage.

He felt his way through the gloom to the steps and slowly climbed up. At the bend in the corridor he stopped again and

285

listened. If they were shooting outside he would have heard it from here, but all was quiet and he went on his way until he reached the spot where the passage debouched into the tunnel.

The bucket hindered him. He put his left arm through the handle and slung it over his shoulder. Before entering the tunnel he made sure that he had released the safety catch of his carbine. The stillness was so absolute that he began to sweat with anxiety. He felt his shirt clinging damply to his armpits and pressed his forehead against the cold wall as he fought against his impulse to turn back.

He knew that never for a moment had he seriously considered reaching the spring. He had only taken the bucket in case of a lucky chance. However, as he felt himself increasingly responsible for their unpleasant situation, the empty bucket had been a welcome excuse to give way to his extreme unease and to go and see for himself how things looked outside without betraying his growing doubts about the safety of their hiding-place. Boris's objections to the fort and Marcel's increasing anxiety caused by the uncanny noises within the mountain had struck a sharp blow at his original confidence. Furthermore he was being more and more plagued by the suspicion that the Germans really intended to stay for some time in La Peine; this would make the drinking-water problem as acute as he had pretended it to be.

As he passed from the passage into the tunnel he did so like a man crossing a minefield. His eyes were now so accustomed to the darkness that he easily found the tunnel's exit. It looked like a semicircular spot in the darkness, through which he could see a tiny patch of star-dotted night sky.

Georges' fear that sentries might be posted at the tunnel mouth was groundless. Although he walked most of the way on tiptoe, he reached the open air unhindered and here too his excessive care proved to have been unnecessary. Nothing suspicious was to be heard in the village below and Georges stood indecisively for a while, unable to formulate a plan of action.

After sixteen hours spent in the cold chambers of the rock, the warm fresh air did him good. He felt the pleasant breeze on his face and took several deep breaths, while his brain worked feverishly. Although he might well have been satisfied with the results of his scouting trip so far he could not get rid of the uneasy feeling in his stomach. Something prevented him from believing that the Germans had withdrawn, although for the moment it seemed that not a soul was to be found near or far. He wondered whether to

286

go back and fetch Marcel, but then decided to go down first of all to the village and look round. If fighting really had taken place it would have left traces in the village, although he was half convinced that Boris had been mistaken.

He set off along the road, trying to step as quietly as possible. The crescent moon was still low in the sky and the light from the stars was feeble. In an hour's time it would grow lighter, but he preferred the darkness.

He had now reached the path and began walking slowly down. In spite of the care with which he put down each foot, he started a pebble rolling and halted, holding his breath, until its clatter finally stopped. In the night the noise must have been audible for miles and Georges resisted with difficulty the twitching in his legs which tried to make him turn back. But having come so far and finding semi-certainty even more unbearable than ignorance he forced himself to go on.

Before reaching the little square with the cypress tree, whose outline now emerged vaguely from the darkness, he stopped and watched the gateway of the town hall for a minute and more. Then he stepped into the square, taking an indirect route in order to approach the gateway from the side. Pressed close to the outer façade of the town hall he slowly felt his way nearer; at the fountain-trough he stopped and listened. In the surrounding quietness the thumping of his heart sounded as if a little rubber hammer was beating a tattoo on his ear-drums. The dampness under his armpits had spread over his whole back; his face too was wet and he wiped his forehead with his sleeve. Then he slowly edged towards the gateway and stared in: he saw from his first glance that it was empty.

His relief, which felt like a sudden slackening of bonds round his body, was so great that it produced a sensation of emptiness and he stood motionless for a while, until he noticed that he was still holding his gun at the ready. He lowered it and walked through the gateway to the village street. Here under the overhanging cliff it was darker than outside the village.

Georges now moved with less caution. He no longer made any effort to conceal the sound of his steps; even if he had walked on tiptoe the double row of houses would have magnified and echoed even the creaking of his boots.

Walking up the street, he slung the carbine over his shoulder. He was now almost certain that there were no more Germans in La Peine, and when they appeared in front of him they were so

287

near that he could clearly recognize their uniforms. They were standing in the small square in front of the church and there were more of them than he could count at one glance.

He checked himself so violently that his stomach heaved. Horror enveloped him like a narrow-meshed net and robbed him of the power of movement for a fraction of a second, while his thoughts reeled through his mind like a flock of wounded birds. Then he turned and ran across the street into the doorway of the nearest house.

He did it without thinking. His legs reacted before his brain had time to give an order and if it had started to function a moment sooner he would have been lost, because he would have started running down the street, his reason rejecting the notion of running into a house which possessed no second exit. But that did not occur to him until he was in the house and rifle-fire started to shatter the plaster on the walls of the narrow hall—the same rifle-fire which would have caught him with deadly certainty after the first ten yards if he had been running down the exposed street.

He raced up the stairs and heard the bucket clatter down as it fell from his shoulder; as he reached the landing his hands struck a wall and there was a hole in it through which he felt fresh air on his face. In a flash he remembered the gap between the row of houses and the rockface and the windows giving on to it which Marcel had pointed out to him. As the first soldiers came running into the house he quickly slung his carbine over his back, swung himself through the rectangular casement into the open and dropped six feet to the ground.

He landed on stones and fell so awkwardly that he struck and cut his elbow. The pain went through his body like an electric shock, and for a moment he lay twisted on the ground while fireworks exploded in front of his eyes, then he got groaning to his feet and ran blindly on, his hand pressed to his elbow. He crashed into boulders, stumbled against sharp-edged rocks and tripped over treacherous potholes; behind him he could hear voices and he knew that they were now climbing out of the window and that others would be running down the street to cut him off. He had no chance of reaching the end of the village before them. In the pitch darkness it was like somebody running amok against a multitude of obstacles, all of which conspired against him, and once again he ran headlong into a boulder. He stopped and looked back.

He had run about fifty yards from the spot where he had climbed through the window; it had been impossible to go farther

288

in that short time, but the pursuing soldiers had to contend with the same difficulties. He could heard their suppressed cursing, the trampling of their hob-nailed boots over the stones and then a light suddenly shone from one of the windows.

The light from the torch was not strong enough to put him in danger yet, but it could only be a matter of seconds before the man with the torch followed the others. Georges might perhaps have tried to make a dash for the end of the village, but it would have had little sense; even if he had been able to maintain his lead and there were no Germans waiting for him at the far end, he would have presented them with a perfect target as he clambered up the steep pathway to the fort.

All these thoughts flashed almost simultaneously through his mind, and from the moment when he stopped to the moment when, by the light of his pursuer's torch, he spotted a breast-high window frame in the dark wall, less than two seconds had gone by. Without the light he would have run past it; he first had to clamber over the boulder, then he reached the window, threw his gun into the room beyond and pulled himself up with both hands. The pain in his elbow brought tears to his eyes and in jumping down he tripped over the carbine and fell flat; in doing so he again hit his injured elbow and if the Germans had come in at that moment he would have been past caring. He forgot the pain and raised his head only when he heard them running past and realized that one of them might shine the torch through the window.

In front of him there was a rectangular hole in the surrounding darkness. He looked at it more carefully and realized that it was a doorway. It led into the street and the room in which he lay was the hall. Perhaps this house had only one story; he remembered that there were some single-story houses in the village street.

It was now quiet behind and there was no sound to be heard from the door. Judging by the footsteps only a few soldiers had followed him through the window. As he was not sure whether any more were standing in the street, he crawled to the door on his knees. He felt as though his whole body was covered with bruises and the pain in his elbow was making itself felt again. The uncertainty over what awaited him quickly damped the brief mood of relief caused by his escape.

His progress grew slower the nearer he drew to the door. It seemed to be getting somewhat lighter outside. He could make out the cobbles in the street and the opposite row of houses. When he thought how bright the night had been when he had watched the road from the tunnel yesterday, his plan seemed hopeless and he told himself that he must either get out of the village within the next ten minutes or await the dark hour before dawn—though by then it would be too late.

He stood up and put his head out of the doorway. Although it was no longer so dark he could only see a short stretch of the street. The house through which he had come stood roughly in the middle of the village. Confused voices could be heard from the direction of the church, and as Georges took a few steps down the street he heard talking somewhere near the town hall. He turned back into the house and leaned out of the rear window. Here there was silence. In the meantime the soldiers must have reached the little square and it was unlikely that any of them were still lurking behind the houses. He quickly made up his mind, climbed out of the window again and gingerly felt his way between the scattered rocks. The ground beneath him sloped away sharply. It had the same gradient as the village street which ran parallel to it and there was a ten-foot gap between the houses and the rock-face.

He progressed about twenty paces, then heard voices murmuring in front of him. Where the houses and the cliff came to an end a gray patch was visible in the darkness and across it several dim shapes were moving. Georges could only recognize them by their outlines and he was in no danger of being seen by them as long as he remained where he was. For safety's sake he looked around for any near-by windows; there was an opening in the wall of the very next house and as he went on he counted his steps. Then he realized that the sound of voices had ceased.

Suspiciously he stopped and listened. He thought he could vaguely hear the sound of retreating footsteps, but he was not sure and continued on his way with increased caution. He finished the last few yards on all fours, until he could see the square with its cypress tree. In the last quarter of an hour it had grown so light that he could make out some detail. The square was empty, but a new sound from his right made him look in that direction. It sounded as if several men were climbing up the steep path towards the road and Georges listened until the noise died away.

The puzzling behavior of the Germans made him uneasy and he tried to think what their aim might be. Possibly the whole thing was nothing but a trap to lure him from his bolt-hole, but they could have achieved the same object by simpler means.

For a while he lay flat on the ground. If the soldiers who had gone up the path belonged to the same group that had chased him, there was one possible explanation of their action: they must have supposed that he had already reached the square and had made off in the direction of the fort. However, this seemed hard to reconcile with the fact that another group had been running down the street; one group or the other would surely have stayed behind in the village.

The longer he considered it the more unsafe he began to feel. In the past half-hour he had at no time felt so helpless and undecided as now, when everything could depend on a single quick decision. Once again he looked up the mountainside to his right. There in the darkness lay the road and the entrance to the fort, and he debated whether to avoid the path altogether and climb up the north face of the cliff, but the mountain was very steep and smooth at this point and anyone who slipped on it would smash more than his elbow. As things stood he would have chosen the path without hesitation, if only he could get an inkling of where the Germans were whose footsteps he could still just hear. He was nagged by the thought that they had by now reached the road and were effectively barring his way back to the fort. For the moment he was safe where he was, and if he were to wait for another half-hour it would perhaps be light enough for him to see as far as the road.

He turned on to his side and rested his injured arm on his hip. When he cautiously felt the elbow he noticed that his coat was soaked in blood. Fortunately he had taken a clean handkerchief from his rucksack that morning and he pushed it up the sleeve so that it covered the wound. Then he examined his immediate surroundings. He was lying between two large rocks, with room enough to move. The ground in front of him was strewn with stones and sloped gently downwards. The wall on his left probably belonged to the town hall. If he were to crawl forward another six feet he could look round the corner of the building towards the gateway, but that would have meant leaving the cover of the cliff-face.

It suddenly seemed to him pointless to be lying on the ground instead of shooting his way through to the fort. As soon as it became light enough for him to see the road, it would also be light enough for the Germans to see him from their position above him. He got to his feet and looked up the steep mountainside. It was about thirty yards to the path and from there another thirty yards up to the road. Sixty yards, he thought, they'll shoot you like a sitting duck. He began walking.

291

When he reached the path still no shot had been fired; with every step it became clearer that there was nobody on the road and this was finally confirmed when he reached the top of the path. It seemed so incredible that he felt no relief and he walked stiffly along the road, all the time expecting to see the muzzle-flashes of rifles firing in front of him; but nothing happened, and by the time he was ten paces inside the tunnel he began to believe in miracles.

It was about thirty paces to the point where the passage branched off. He had counted them that morning, but either because he now took longer paces or because he had made a mistake in counting, the passage which he now entered emerged into another chamber after a few yards. Georges first noticed it from the different acoustics and when he tried to touch the walls his hands could find only emptiness. He took the torch from his pocket. Its glass had been broken by his fall, but the bulb still burned. Its feeble light revealed a hall-like vault which ran parallel to the tunnel and whose length could not be estimated. He went back to the tunnel and felt his way along the left-hand wall in the direction of the exit. Almost at the same moment that he found the passage he heard the murmur of voices. At first he thought it was an illusion, but after listening for a while there was no longer any doubt: the Germans were somewhere in the fort.

Although this answered the question of the whereabouts of the soldiers who had climbed up the path before him and partially explained their puzzling behavior, Georges would have preferred the answer to have been a different one, since their occupation of the fort confirmed a suspicion that had been growing in his mind since he had seen them standing around on the little square in front of the church. The voices came from deep in the tunnel and he realized that he need no longer fear being discovered. He slung his gun over his shoulder, switched on the torch and turned into the passage. As he went down the stairway he found himself wondering how long a man could hold out without water.

Marcel heard him coming down. He had passed an uncomfortable hour. The vigil in total darkness, the innumerable noises imagined by his overstimulated senses would have been bearable had not the uncanny creaking sound been twice repeated during his wait. His nerves would not have lasted another ten minutes, and when he finally heard footsteps he slammed the door so violently that it echoed like a cannon-shot through the vaulted chamber. He held his breath and waited until the agreed signal was

given, then pushed back the bolt and saw Georges standing before him in the light of the torch.

"Have you gone mad?" asked Georges.

"I couldn't help it," Marcel murmured. "The door slipped out
of my hands."

"One day something will slip out of your head," said Georges.
Steps were heard in the darkness and when he shone his torch
on the door opposite he saw Anna come through it. "Shut all the
doors behind you," he said to Marcel. He gave him the torch and
walked over to the girl. As he looked into her face he felt his legs
trembling in sudden reaction from the nervous tension. He leaned
down to her and she put her arms round his neck. For a few seconds they clung to each other, until Marcel came up to them.

"Do you mind if we go on?" he said sulkily.

Anna tore herself away from Georges and ran through the door.
"You are and always will be a fool!" Georges snapped at Marcel
and ran after her. She was waiting for him in the next chamber
and he almost knocked her over.

"I was half dead with fright," she whispered. "Did you reach
the spring?"

"No. Did you hear me coming?"

"Monsieur Vieale heard you. He was standing by the door. I
think that's him."

Georges turned round; as all the doors stood open, light was
visible from the third chamber and the Frenchman's broad-shouldered outline now appeared in the doorway. "If you're looking for
us, we're here," said Georges.

"Monsieur Chabrier!" cried Vieale with relief. "Thank God!
How was it?"

"Difficult. I couldn't get any water."

"Then the Germans are still here?"

"Yes."

Marcel came in and bolted the door. Seeing Vieale he asked:
"Did you hear it again?"

"If you mean that noise, yes. But this time it wasn't so bad."

"It was quite bad enough for my liking," muttered Marcel. "I
tell you, the whole place is collapsing, mark my words." To
Georges he said: "What's going on outside? Can we go out?"

"You can go out if you like. Didn't you hear anything else?"

"What else should I have heard?"

"Rifle-fire."

"Not a sound. Was there more shooting?"

Georges smiled. "A bit."

When they came into the chamber Madame Vieale, Knopf and Boris were seated round the table.

"Here he is again!" said Vieale, with rather forced cheerfulness. "I think he——" He stopped. He had noticed Georges' elbow, where the pale material of his jacket was stained dark red.

"Are you wounded?"

"Only a graze," replied Georges and leaned his carbine against the wall. "It looks worse than it is."

"Where?" asked Anna quickly. Then she saw the red stain and went pale.

"It's all right," said Georges.

"Don't play the hero," said Madame Vieale and stood up. "That could give you blood-poisoning if you don't take care. Take off your jacket."

Anna helped him as he did so. Her face stiffened with fright as Madame Vieale turned Georges' arm round and examined the wound. "Can you move it?" she asked.

"I think so, but I'd much rather not try."

"It's gone right through to the bone."

"The stones round here are harder than my elbow. Don't twist it so much, or it will drop off."

Knopf looked at it anxiously. "That wound must be cleaned. Were you not able to fetch any water?"

"I lost the bucket," said Georges.

"You fool!" said Boris. He alone had remained seated and held a cigarette between his fingers.

Georges turned to look at him. "I'll give you a new one some time."

"Don't mind him," said the woman. "He's had a bad day. We have another bucket in case you need one. Can you bear it if I put something on it?"

"It depends what it is," said Georges.

Madame Vieale went to her suitcase and returned with some cotton wool, a piece of lint and a small bottle. "Iodine?" asked Georges.

"I always take it with me when we travel," said Madame Vieale. She moistened the lint with iodine and quickly pressed it to Georges' elbow. "Does it hurt?"

Georges grinned as tears started to his eyes. "You told me just now not to play the hero." Anna, too, was nearly crying and turned her head away when Georges looked at her.

"It's all right; I saw," said Georges.

"What did you see?" asked Madame Vieale, busy with his arm. She had removed the lint and was putting cotton wool on the wound.

"You're doing it magnificently," said Georges, still looking at Anna. "I must have lost my handkerchief. Or is it still in the sleeve?" he said to Anna, who was holding his jacket.

She felt inside the sleeve. "It's not here."

"Then I have lost it. I may still have a field dressing in my rucksack."

"We'll use a towel," said Madame Vieale. "It will support the arm better."

"I'll get one," said Vieale and went to the suitcase.

Marcel, who could no longer suppress his curiosity, asked: "Where did you lose the bucket?"

"In the village," said Georges. "There were some Germans standing in front of the church. I saw them as they saw me. They ran after me for a bit and it was then that I dropped the bucket."

"Did anyone see you go into the fort?" asked Knopf.

Georges did not reply until Madame Vieale had finished bandaging him. He made sure that the tightly-bound towel was not stopping the circulation in his arm and said: "*Merci,* Madame." Then he said to Knopf: "No, I was not seen coming in, but the Germans are in the fort too. I heard them talking."

"That's bad," said Vieale, and sat down heavily in a chair. His angular face had turned gray. "It almost looks as if they were preparing to stay here for quite a long time."

"We must get out of this hole as quickly as possible," said Marcel urgently.

"You can try if you like," said Georges. "You won't get far."

"You managed to get out."

"Yes, and I was forced to come back again."

"We could go down the road."

"Their trucks are parked along the road and they are sure to be guarded."

"God damn and blast it!" said Marcel, staring at the ceiling.

Georges went to his corner and lay down on the inflatable mattress. He was in great pain and had a violent thirst, but he did not want to be the first to start complaining of it.

"We might as well go to bed and sleep," said Madame Vieale, coolly. "I don't know why we are standing around."

"I don't feel like sleep," said Marcel. He had stuck his hands in

295

his trouser pockets and sat down at the table with Boris and Vieale. "If we don't get out of here," he went on, "we're done for."

"We were done for when we came here," said Boris. His cigarette had gone out and he was rolling the stub from one side of his mouth to the other.

"We can always comfort ourselves with the thought that it was not your idea," retorted Georges.

Anna sat down beside him on the mattress. She was still carrying his jacket and asked: "Do you want to put it on again?"

"I'd like to put it under my head as a pillow."

"You mustn't move your arm; I'll do it."

She folded the jacket, and as she bent over Georges she brushed his face with her cheek. "Is that all right?"

Georges smiled. "Very good, thank you."

"Does it still hurt?"

"Not much."

"I have some tablets."

"Keep them, you might have toothache one day."

"After a week in this place none of us will be having any more toothaches," growled Marcel.

"Did they shoot at you?"

"Not exactly," said Georges evasively.

Knopf sat down at the table between Vieale and Boris. "Let us wait until tomorrow; perhaps they will only spend one night here. I blame myself for the situation; but for me you could have escaped to the wood."

Madame Vieale countered energetically: "You mustn't say that, Monsieur. I would never have been able to climb down the mountainside at night. We're not all as nimble on our feet as Monsieur Boris. And I don't think we would have been as comfortable in the wood as we are here."

"We would have had water," said Boris.

"We still have another whole bottle of wine," said the woman, irritated. "If you're thirsty you can drink my share; I'll go without." She went over to Georges and Anna and sat down on her bed.

Boris was blushing deeply. He took the cigarette stub from his mouth and said to Vieale: "You know I didn't mean it like that, Monsieur."

"I don't care how you meant it," said Madame Vieale. "What we might have had in the wood is of no use to us whatever as long as we're in the fort. Am I right?" she said to Georges.

"Definitely," replied Georges in an admiring tone.

He was not so pessimistic as Marcel. Although there was plenty of evidence in support of Vieale's fear that the Germans were preparing for a lengthy stay in La Peine, something in him refused to believe it. It not only ran counter to his previous assumptions, but also made the behavior of the Germans still more incomprehensible. It would have been an easy matter for them to have caught him if they had been seriously intent on doing so. The fact that they had only sent a handful of men after him and that even they had given up the chase after a few minutes pointed to only two conclusions: either they were being incredibly careless—which in their situation they could ill afford to be—or they had no further time to spend chasing him. The second alternative seemed to him the most likely, although as it was still only a guess he decided to keep it to himself for the moment.

"I shall try again tomorrow evening," he went on. "Then if they are still here we can consider what we should do. We may even find water somewhere in the fort. If it was supplied from the underground lake there must be a pipe somewhere."

"I've never seen one," said Vieale, "and even if there were one it is certain to have been shut off."

"Have you inspected the whole fort?"

"One would need a whole day to do that. Last time we were here I went a bit further into the tunnel. I had no torch and had to turn back."

"Where do the passages go that lead off the other side of the tunnel?"

"Boris can tell you that," put in Knopf. "He has been up here twice. I think they lead to the gun emplacements."

"They didn't need any water in the gun turrets," said Marcel. "If the lake was on a lower level than the fort they must have pumped the water up. Where will you find a pump?"

Georges smiled. "Write to your father to send us one. There must be a letter-box somewhere in La Peine."

"Oh, for God's sake shut up," said Marcel, and threw himself offended on to his bed.

Madame Vieale sighed. "*Mon Dieu!* Each one of you is touchier than the other."

"They don't mean it," said Vieale. He was anxious to conciliate them and turned to the Russian: "No one could foresee that the Germans would stay here."

"It was a possibility that should have been taken into account."

"Did anyone prevent you from thinking of it?" asked Georges.

"You seem to have left something else out of account—that the Germans would lose the war."

"Did it occur to you?"

"It was part of the risk—as it also was for you. You are complaining to the wrong person. Anyway, I have never quite understood why you deserted your own side. Didn't you owe something to your country? After all, you studied at the university at the state's expense."

"Georges!" cried Anna, and laid her hand on his arm.

He sat upright. "I simply want to know what sort of a person he is. Since I've been here he has never missed a chance to provoke me; but two can play at that game."

"I have already had occasion to notice that you're not stupid," said Boris coldly.

"Really?" Georges stared into his expressionless face. "Then you have successfully kept this opinion to yourself. What caused you to notice it?"

"You know that."

"I'm sorry to seem so stupid, but I really don't know."

"You can't go back to Switzerland, can you?"

"Well, so what? Anyway, that's not true: I could, but I don't want to."

"But you want to go to Germany?"

"Somebody seems to have told you so."

"Your friend has told me," said Boris. "You were lucky in meeting Monsieur Knopf, weren't you? Without him you would have had little chance of going to Germany. And if he happens to have an impressionable young niece, to whom you know he is devoted, you are even luckier."

"Hmm. You know how to draw blood," said Georges. He turned to Anna. "Do you understand what he's saying?"

"It's not very difficult," she replied. "I had no idea that he could be so hateful."

Boris winced as if someone had slapped him.

"You asked for that," said Georges with a grin. "Usually you only get ideas like that when you've been thinking along the same lines yourself. But I wouldn't like to impute that to you."

"But he insinuated it about you," said Anna. She turned to Knopf, who was sitting at the table with bowed head; he seemed lost in thought. "Why don't you say anything?" she asked. "Boris has been speaking about you."

"Yes, I heard him," replied Knopf absentmindedly. "I haven't

298

yet asked Monsieur Chabrier whether he wants to go to Germany with us."

"You have talked to me about it."

"We shall discuss it again, but not here and now."

"I should like you very much to do so now," said Anna resolutely. "I have nothing to hide from anyone. You invited Boris to go to Germany with us; why shouldn't Georges come with us?"

"I advised him not to."

"You didn't!"

"Yes, I did."

Anna turned anxiously to Georges. "You never told me about this."

"I hoped your uncle would change his mind."

"I have no reason to change my mind," said Knopf. "I think it is also better for Anna if you straighten out your past before you start thinking about the future. As a Swiss citizen you have not the slightest prospect of applying for asylum in Germany. You will be arrested and deported to Switzerland."

"I can't believe that," interjected Madame Vieale. "After all, Monsieur Chabrier fought for Germany."

Knopf took off his spectacles and put them on the table before him. "For which Germany? When the war is over it will not be the same Germany." He turned again to Georges. "In any case you would not be dealing with Germans but with the occupation forces. Did you think of that?"

"You seem to be doing my thinking for me," said Georges. "But Germany is a big place."

"I'm sure that when this war ends it will no longer be very big."

"Big enough for Boris," said Anna. "Why not big enough for Georges too?"

"For a real emigré even Switzerland is big enough," answered Knopf. "But it will be hard to pass off a man from Zürich as a political refugee; it's a paradox."

"Why shouldn't one emigrate to escape from stupidity, indifference and complacency?"

"And where can you go where you will not find these things?"

Georges looked at Boris, whose face was still white with red flecks on his cheeks. "Not everyone has the good fortune to be a genuine emigré," said Georges after a pause.

Knopf replaced his glasses. "I don't think you can call it good fortune. Ask Boris whether he prefers being here or in Gorky."

"I don't know why he's here. He ought to be grateful to the Communists, after all."

"What for?"

"For letting him be a teacher. In Russia that's an honor. There's no room in high school for people who are politically unreliable."

"A hypothesis," said Knopf, dismissing the idea. "Even Communists are not thought-readers. That is why all dictatorships eventually collapse."

"Not in Russia."

"Another hypothesis."

"It is true," Boris broke in. "I haven't told you, but I was in the Party."

A moment's stillness followed his words. Knopf drew his hand over his forehead as if to wipe away something. "Now I don't know where I stand with you, Boris."

Marcel gave a malicious laugh. "What did I tell you, Georges!"

"It fits into my theory," answered Georges, but he said it without satisfaction and with a trace of admiration in his voice.

"Your theory has a gap in it," replied Boris coldly. "Do you know what Russia was like before the revolution?"

"I know what it's like today and that's enough for me."

"You don't even know that. To understand the Russian revolution you must know what came before it. The Communists gave the people a new faith."

"Yes; faith in materialism," scoffed Georges.

"No. Faith in ourselves," Boris retorted. "Faith in a more decent life. At first I was as enthusiastic as the rest, I closed my eyes for ten years because I told myself that the revolution had its own laws and later when my own family fell victim I still regarded it as a personal sacrifice which the revolution demanded of me."

He paused, then went on: "Perhaps I should still feel the same today if I had not chosen to study languages. It was pure chance, a particular talent of mine. What others took years to learn was child's play to me, and by the time I was conscripted I was fluent in six languages. I was made an interpreter in a propaganda unit. We drove along the front line with loudspeakers trying to persuade German troops to desert, until one day I seized my chance and deserted myself.

"I often used to talk to foreigners, particularly with one, an "American newspaper correspondent. We became friends; in 1934 he was expelled for writing too much about the great purges in the Party. He taught me what democracy was, I learned to make comparisons and when I realized that the Party was violating its original principles and still using methods which were only justifiable during or just after a revolution, I drew my own conclusions. I then waited for my chance and when the Germans marched I thought it had come."

"That explains everything," said Knopf.

Boris smiled bitterly. "For me, perhaps it does; but not for the rest of Russia. The man who grows up in a cage has no idea what a life of freedom means. Instead of languages I should have studied astronomy; at least the universe doesn't change."

"Neither does God," said Knopf. "In 1914 we could still say: God is with us. I remember wondering why he should be on our side. Did we pray more than the others, were we better than they?" He looked at Vieale and smiled. "Better than you, Monsieur? But at least our generation still believed in Him. Nowadays they believe in new ideas. But even though they may want to build paradise on earth because the way to heaven is too steep, they cannot do without God." He stood up. "Excuse me. I have a headache again."

They watched in silence as he went, slightly stooping, to his bed. Vieale was first to move. He had listened to the argument with only half an ear. Since Georges had returned without water he had been overcome with anxiety. He was not a timorous man and he would have come to terms with their situation had he not been worried about his wife and he blamed himself more and more for not leaving her with Philippe. He looked at Georges and Anna who were sitting close beside one another. Georges was biting his underlip and did not even look up when Vieale got up and walked over to him.

"Don't feel angry," said Vieale. "You can't make people better than they are; not even us French." With his big hand he tenderly stroked his wife's head and sat down beside her. "We might as well go to sleep again and save paraffin."

"Ours is finished," said Anna.

"I brought a full can," said Vieale. "It won't last long, either, if we have to burn the lamp night and day."

"We have a torch, it's on the table," said Georges. Boris stood up and went to his bed. Knopf seemed to be already asleep. He had got under the bedclothes and turned his face to the wall.

"Then I must go back to my bed," said Anna to Georges. "Otherwise Madame Vieale will be angry with me."

"Perhaps she won't," said Georges.

Madame Vieale pretended not to hear them. "Put out the lamp," she said to Vieale. "I want to undress, or this frock will be ruined."

As Vieale went to the table, Anna quickly leaned over to Georges and touched his face with her mouth. "Later," she breathed.

Georges nodded. He watched her go back to her place, then the light went out and he heard Madame Vieale's soft voice beside him: "Monsieur!"

"Do you mean me?"

"Yes. Don't trip over my legs."

"I'll take care," promised Georges with a smile. "*Merci*, Madame."

He heard Vieale feeling his way back from the table and unlaced his boots. Before undressing further he waited until Vieale and his wife were lying down. Then he slipped out of his clothes, draped a blanket round himself and felt his way barefoot through the darkness until he touched the opposite wall. As he bent down to Anna, Madame Vieale began to talk quietly to her husband and for a moment Georges felt the girl's hands. Then he was lying beside her; she had drawn her knees up to her chest and pulled up the blankets as far as her neck.

Someone was snoring on the other side; it was impossible to say who it was. The sound brought the conversation between Vieale and his wife to an end and after a while it sounded as if they had fallen asleep. "Go back," whispered the girl. "I'll come to you."

"Why?"

"I'll tell you later."

Georges kissed her. "If you're not there in ten minutes I'll come and fetch you."

"I promise to come," she whispered.

He went back to his place. Beside him Vieale had also begun to snore and while Georges waited for the girl he could feel his heart beating. After ten minutes she came, but it seemed to him that he had been waiting for hours. She crawled under the blanket with him and pressed her knee to his chest.

"Why didn't you undress?" whispered Georges.

"I didn't know whether you wanted me to," she answered softly. "Have you any clothes on?"

"No."

"Nothing at all?"

"No."

302

"Show me!" Her hands glided over his shoulders and chest. Her fingers felt hot. Georges held them tight and whispered: "Take your things off."

Then she was lying beside him again and the smell of her hair was the same as the evening before. Everything about her was light and fresh as sunrise as she drew closer and touched him— the pressure of her legs and her firm little breasts, her hips as they nestled up to him and the clumsy tenderness of her hands. For a few seconds he had the sensation that he had felt three days earlier when he had stood up to his neck in the icy crystal-clear water of the mountain stream and his heart had stopped for a moment; then he felt a sudden flush, he pressed his whole body to hers and she wound her arms round him and lay quite still.

"Why didn't you want me to come to you?" asked Georges.

"We can't do it next to Madame Vieale," she whispered.

Amused by this piece of feminine logic he said: "It doesn't matter who is next to us."

She shook her head. "It does matter. Besides, they're hardly asleep yet."

"So they'll know in any case."

"Once they're sound asleep they won't know. I don't want anyone except us to know." She laughed softly. "How they snore!"

"Is that your uncle over there?"

"I've never heard him snore before. It must be Marcel."

"He often snores, but what about Vieale!"

"Like a bear," whispered the girl and her shoulders shook with suppressed laughter. Then she put her mouth to his ear and whispered: "Do you want to do it?"

"Not here."

"Why not?"

"They would hear."

"Can't one do it quietly?"

"Not the first time. It wouldn't be right if we did it now."

"Waiting is so hard. Do you want children?"

"I think so."

"Lots?"

"As many as you like."

"I'd like lots of children," she whispered. "But I'm afraid the same thing might happen to them as happened to me."

"That will never happen again."

"Think so?"

"Yes."

"I don't know. I somehow think it's too deeply engrained in people. They always need someone to despise and as long as we Jews are here they will look down on us."

"No one will look down on you in Switzerland," murmured Georges. It slipped out unconsciously and he bit his lip.

"But I thought you didn't want to go back," said Anna after a pause. "I'd gladly go to Switzerland with you. In Germany I'd always be afraid for you. Could we stay in France?"

"They'd hand me over."

"Perhaps Pierre can do something for us."

"You can forget——" Georges broke off. The men's snoring had stopped almost simultaneously and it was so quiet that he could hear Madame Vieale's gentle breathing. He pressed Anna's hand to her lips and for a while they lay motionless together until Vieale began to snore again.

"I must think it all over again," Georges then whispered. "You know that they'll put me in jail in Switzerland; we couldn't get married."

"Couldn't we marry in Germany?"

Georges hesitated. The idea had never occurred to him, but he suddenly realized that it would be impossible. A man alone could always go underground anywhere, but with a girl by his side it would be much worse, especially when he had to take care to avoid doing anything which might give Anna or Knopf the idea that Boris had not been entirely wrong in his suspicions of Georges' motives.

Cunning bastard, he thought. What he said is far worse than if he'd tied a millstone round my leg.

"I must think about it again," he answered her. "There'll be time enough when we get out of here. You'd better go back to your own bed now."

"Five more minutes," she whispered. "Just let me lie by you for another five minutes."

An hour later she was still lying beside him and he noticed that she had fallen asleep. She had drawn one knee up to her chest again and her head was resting on his shoulder. He couldn't bring himself to disturb her, although he knew that he was being careless. He was kept awake by the fear that the noise in the mountain might be heard again and waken the others. It had been quiet since his return and he supposed that the noise had been set off by shellfire and that meanwhile the mountain had settled down, but he could equally be wrong, and the thought that Knopf and

304

Boris might discover him and the girl in bed together had become like a thorn which bored into the very center of his weary brain.

He lay staring into the darkness, while he felt the girl's body at his side. He silenced his growing scruples by telling himself that they were both old enough to know exactly what they were doing. He found that he had ceased to have any feelings about Marcel. You can't look after both Anna and Marcel at the same time, he told himself.

His elbow was starting to hurt again. He turned over cautiously to avoid waking the girl and rested his injured arm in a more comfortable position. He was growing gradually more tired. The thorn in his brain was being blunted by drowsiness and he thought that he should at least put his clothes on again. Once he tried to do so, but the contact of his bare shoulder with the cold air in the chamber was so unpleasant that he at once crept back under the warm blanket and lay down very close to the girl.

I will wake up in time, he thought. I will wake up as soon as somebody stirs; she only has to pick up her clothes and she'll be back in her bed in a moment. Before he fell asleep he saw himself and Anna in his mind's eye walking down a broad, beautiful, well-kept avenue and the water beyond was the Lake of Zürich.

When he awoke he immediately had the impression of having slept for a long time, and his first waking sensation was of unease. He looked at his luminous watch-face. It was half past five; outside it must already be daylight. Although he could not discover what caused his qualms, they increased with every second and as he stared into the darkness he suddenly felt that something threatening had happened.

He leaned over to the girl and placed his hand over her mouth. As she tried to sit up he held her tight and waited until she was wide awake. Then he said softly: "Take your clothes and go back to your bed."

"Has something happened?" she whispered.

"I don't know yet. Go on!"

She obeyed in silence and Georges let another minute pass before he looked for his clothes. He dressed himself lying down. The towel hindered him and he hastily untied it and felt his elbow. The blood-soaked cotton wool had hardened into a crust and whenever he moved the arm the pain jarred him to his finger-tips. Finally he laced up his boots, then stood up and felt his way to the

305

table. The previous evening he had put the torch on the side of the table nearest to his bed and carefully noted its position in order to be able to find it again in the darkness, but he now discovered that it was no longer there. He found it at the other end of the table and it could only have been used by one of the men who slept on the other side. As Georges switched it on his first glance fell on the right-hand door. It was half open.

He turned round and looked over at Boris's bed; it was empty and then Georges noticed something else: Knopf was awake. He had clasped his hands behind his head and was gazing steadily at him. The expression on his face gave Georges a shock.

For seconds they stared at each other and Georges thought: he knows everything, he has been awake and watching all night. The thought made him sweat and for a while he could say and do nothing. Then he slowly went over to Knopf and asked awkwardly: "Where is Boris?"

"Boris!" Only now did Knopf seem to realize that the Russian was not lying beside him. He quickly sat up. "Where has he gone?"

"That's what I should like to know," said Georges. He picked up his gun and went out.

The other doors were also open and when he reached the steps he thought he could hear voices from above. He stopped and listened. He could still hear them, but they were far away and he could not understand what they were saying. He had already almost decided to venture up the stairway when he heard footsteps behind him. Before turning round he knew that it was Anna, and then she was clinging to him.

"You must stay here," she murmured. "If you go up this time you will never come back."

Georges caressed her head, trying to calm her. "I'm not going," he said. "Boris has left all the doors open behind him. I'm afraid they may have caught him."

"The Germans?"

"Yes. Quiet a moment, you can hear them talking."

They both listened and it seemed to Georges that the voices had grown louder. Then he stiffened with amazement. As he started incredulously up the stairway, he heard the girl's voice beside him. "Those are no Germans," she whispered. "They must be French."

"It's not possible," said Georges flatly.

"But it is, just listen! Perhaps it's Pierre!"

"Pierre?"

"It must be Pierre," she said aloud. "I recognize him by his voice." She pulled herself away from him. Before he could hold her back she ran up the steps and Georges leaned back against the wall and thought: are you pleased with your work, Cain?

Chapter 12

Raymond and his men arrived in the early evening. Roger had left behind a man as a guide and he led them to the boulders, where Raymond crawled forward to join Roger and Pierre in their position under cover. Since the Germans had set up their machine guns in the turrets of the fort, the Maquisards among the boulders could only move by crawling about on their stomachs.

"Glad to see you," said Pierre to Raymond. "Where have you left your men?"

"They are waiting down there on the path," replied Raymond. "It looks bad here, doesn't it?"

"Could be worse," said Pierre. "They tried to register their tank guns on us, but they were unlucky: the houses were in the way. They can only hit the fort or the ridge."

"Are none of our men on the ridge?"

"We've all come down, thank God," said Roger. "I was up there with eleven men when the Boches occupied the fort."

"*Merde!*" said Raymond, and spat at the rock behind which they lay. Then he grinned and said: "They marched right past us."

"The Boches?"

"Must have been a whole division. When Leroy came from you to fetch us they had been streaming by for six hours and no sign of the end of the column. They had a lot of artillery. Heavy stuff, I can tell you."

"Were you all still in the wood?"

"That would have been too dangerous. When the first units appeared we went a little way up the mountainside. I immediately thought that all your plans must have gone wrong."

Pierre was about to expostulate when a burst of machine-gun fire rattled out from one of the gun turrets and bullets grazed the tops of the boulders. The bullets smashed against the rocks with an ugly sound and for a few seconds the air was full of the hiss and whine of ricochets. The firing ceased as suddenly as it had begun.

Pierre calmly lit a cigarette. "They do that every ten minutes," he said to Raymond, who had ducked his head still further. "You can set your watch by it, they're so punctual."

"They have too much ammunition," said Roger. "They just bang away for fun."

"I don't think they are quite so cheerful," Pierre countered. "They know that they have very little chance of getting out of the village again."

"Nor we of getting in," murmured Roger.

Pierre drew on his cigarette. "We have time, more time than they have. They will attack tonight. If they knew how many we are they would give up the idea." He gave Raymond the wine-bottle. "Have a drink, there's still a drop left. It's been a tough day."

"Tomorrow won't be much better," muttered Roger. Raymond gave the bottle back to Pierre and thanked him with a nod. "Why do you think they will attack?" he asked.

"Because they must. They have maps and can easily work out that there's a shorter route to the D206 than over this ridge here. Did you see the aircraft?"

"Yes. They were American."

"Where did they drop their bombs?"

"It must have been somewhere near the frontier, but we couldn't see anything."

"Good. That means that the Americans are pressing the Germans hard," said Pierre with satisfaction. "Meanwhile they will have found out that the division is on the D206. I wouldn't like to be a Boche when they reach the Col du Tende tomorrow morning. They won't get over it without taking the devil of a beating."

Raymond pushed his head very slightly over the top of the rock and looked down the village street. "Nothing to be seen, I suppose?"

"They're not as stupid as that."

"Lucky they haven't any mortars," said Raymond. "With a mortar they would have smoked us out of here long ago."

309

"Then thank God the whole division didn't come up this way," said Roger. "Imagine how it would have been if they had been able to bring all the divisonal artillery to bear on us. Personally I'm glad it has worked out this way. I was unhappy about the plan from the start."

Pierre shrugged his shoulders. "Because you have no imagination. I have seldom given so much thought to a job as this one."

"Oh, it was a good plan," Roger agreed.

"Of course it was good," said Pierre. "But there was one single fault in it and now I want to find out who is responsible for that fault." He looked at Raymond. "If my memory is correct you have brought twenty-nine men with you. Am I right?"

"Twenty-eight," replied Raymond. "Leroy stayed down below to keep the Germans under observation."

"Yes, I told him he could rest. I want you to go to your men now and tell them to disperse themselves among the rocks. As soon as it's dark you must bring them forward. . . ." He was again interrupted by the chattering of the German machine gun and he waited until it had stopped. Then he stubbed out his cigarette on a rock, wiping away the black stain that it made.

"The machine gun must take up a position on the path," he then went on. "Take care that it has an uninterrupted field of fire on to the houses. Do you see that boulder over there?"

"The round one?" asked Raymond.

"The one which looks like a ball. Laroche is somewhere behind it. Get in contact with him; he knows the positions of our men. When it's dark Roger will take them up to the ridge again. You will stay here with the remainder and take charge of this flank, but don't put more men behind a boulder than it will cover; we are not going to lose any men in this operation."

Roger sighed. "I wish we could have convinced their wives of that."

"Leroy ought to do that," said Pierre. "He wanted to be a priest once. As usual, though, it will be my job to tell the wives."

"Rather you than me," sighed Roger.

"The women of France," said Raymond with pathos, "know what they owe to the Republic."

Roger grimaced as if he had a mouthful of vinegar. "He ought to be War Minister," he said to Pierre.

Pierre grinned. "If the women of France had their own way there would be the death penalty for making or bearing arms."

310

"No patriot talks like that," muttered Raymond into his dark beard.

"I leave patriotism to you," replied Pierre. "Since the Communists have lately started playing the patriot I prefer to be a simple Maquisard. Get on with your job before I get angry!"

"One more thing," said Raymond. "How long do you think we shall have to stay here?"

"Until the Americans come. Roger has left two men at the bridge and they will guide the Americans to the pass. When that will be I have no more idea than you. There'll be no sleeping to-night."

"We didn't come here to sleep," grumbled Raymond as he crawled away.

Roger watched him go until he disappeared behind the next boulder. "Now you've annoyed him," he said.

Pierre put the bottle to his mouth and emptied it, then wiped his lips with the back of his hand. "I just want him to realize that I know where he and I stand. Since the Russians have been pushing back the Boches he has suddenly discovered a great sympathy with the Communists. A Frenchman can either be a Communist or a patriot."

"Try telling that to the Communists," murmured Roger. "Louis is firmly convinced that he's the greatest patriot of all time. He'll die laughing when he hears that the whole German division got away from us."

"That shows you that he's no patriot," said Pierre.

He rolled over on to his other side and saw that evening was approaching. The sun's rim had reached the western mountain peaks and for a few minutes the village seemed to be bathed in a red cloud; then the redness vanished from the roofs and only the top of the church tower continued to glow for a while in the pink light, which gradually faded and was finally extinguished.

"They're no longer in the church tower," said Pierre.

"They can observe us better from the fort," said Roger. He was sitting propped up against the boulder and polishing the metal parts of his machine-pistol with a handkerchief. Then he held it up and inspected it critically. "The machine gun hasn't fired for a quarter of an hour," he said casually.

"Well?" said Pierre. He had also noticed it, but thought no more of it. He had now been lying for fourteen hours behind the boulder, time enough to make a complete mental review of the situa-

311

tion. When he considered with what hopes they had begun the operation and compared it with what they had achieved and the price they had paid for it, he felt tempted to take his men back to Escarène and let the Germans go. It was as if he were a hunter who had set off, at the cost of tremendous effort and sacrifice, to hunt an elephant and who had come home with a rabbit. He was only kept going by the urge to find out exactly what had been going on in La Peine and to learn what had happened to Knopf, Anna and Boris; even if they were past helping he could at least discover what their fate had been and who had shot Gaston.

It was already dark when the machine gun in the turret began hammering again and shaving the boulders with bullets. Almost simultaneously a second gun started to fire, but those shots came from below, and as Pierre peered round the left-hand side of his boulder he was able to fix its position.

"They've set it up on the road," he said to Roger. "A bad place. We could shoot it up from here."

"Shall we?" asked Roger.

"Why? As long as it stays there it can do us no harm."

"Let's hope we hear them coming. We shan't be able to see much in the next two hours; it will bet a bit lighter around midnight."

'We'll hear them all right," said Pierre. "They would have to take their boots off if they wanted to move without making a noise and even then we should hear them when they kicked a stone. Send your men up to the ridge and don't forget to come down again before it gets so light that they can see you from the fort."

"This time I'll go a bit farther to the right," said Roger. "There are some big rocks there which we can use as cover against machine-gun fire."

"I'll leave you here for the moment," said Pierre and stood up. "I just want to check the position where Raymond has put the machine gun. Collect the empty bottles from your men. I'll send a few of my boys to the spring to fetch water."

He took the shortest way down the mountainside. Men were lying behind almost every boulder that he passed. He called five of them to him and told them to collect bottles and go to the spring. To the others he said: "Keep your eyes open. If they come they'll come in the next two hours or tomorrow morning before daybreak."

The machine gun had been sited beside a boulder about five yards above the path. Pierre saw at a glance that the position was

312

well chosen and he exchanged a few words with its crew. There were four men. They had made a pile of stones and set the machine gun behind it.

"We can't hit the machine gun down on the road," said one of the four. "It's too low for us."

"There's no need for you to try," said Pierre. "Let them loose off as much as they like. You mustn't fire until they start coming out of the village."

"A pity that division got away from us," said another. "We ought not to have allowed that to happen."

"As you've got such a big mouth why didn't you stop them from getting away?" asked Pierre coldly.

"I'm not on the general staff," retorted the man. "You're the one who gives the orders."

Pierre opened his mouth to reply just as there came a sudden and violent burst of rifle-fire. They threw themselves flat on the ground and stared over to the village. The firing only lasted for a few seconds and then stopped, but voices and loud shouts could be clearly heard and then seemed to be retreating into the distance.

"*Parbleu!*" said one of the machine-gun crew. "Now the Boches are shooting at each other. What do you say to that?"

"They're up to something," said another. "Their machine gun hasn't fired for twenty minutes."

They looked at Pierre, who had gotten to his feet again and was staring towards the village. The outlines of the houses were only dimly discernible against the starry sky and as he watched the village he suddenly felt certain that the two men and the girl were still alive and were hiding somewhere in the village.

He gave the machine-gun crew a few more brief instructions, then set off again up the path and followed it for a short way between the boulders until he was far enough away from the fort to be able to climb up to the ridge in safety. He found Roger and his men hard at work. They were hauling great rocks into a pile to form a breastwork to protect them against machine-gun fire from the fort. Their position lay at about a hundred and fifty paces from the fort and on the same level, as the southern end of the ridge rose steeply. As Pierre approached them they stopped their work and surrounded him.

"What was that firing?" Roger at once inquired.

Pierre told them. "It gets more and more mysterious," said Roger. "We no longer know who's shooting at who. Can you explain it?"

313

"No more than you. Perhaps it's something to do with those deserters."

"They've stopped firing now," said Roger, gazing at the fort. "I hope they've run out of ammunition."

"They must have more," said Pierre.

Roger turned to the men. "Carry on and let's get it finished. In an hour it will be so light that they can see us from the fort."

To Pierre he said: "What's the matter with you?"

"What do you mean?"

"Come on, I know you. What's worrying you?"

"Something has been troubling me for the past twenty-four hours. When this business is over you can find yourself a new boss."

"Are they refusing to carry on with you?"

"They need a scapegoat because that German division got away from us. In a war you can do ninety-nine things right and one wrong, but afterwards the only thing that people remember will be your one mistake."

"We had bad luck," said Roger. "What you say about doing things right and wrong has nothing to do with it. If anybody says anything stupid I'll stop up his mouth for him. Are you going to stay here?"

"No. I'll hear them coming sooner down below."

"If they come."

Pierre returned to his position behind the boulder where he found Laroche. He said: "I've been looking for you everywhere. The water has arrived. Here's your bottle."

"Merci," said Pierre, and poured a stream of ice-cold water between his lips.

"Nothing's happening," said Laroche, looking down at the village. "I wish they would come."

The night passed and the Germans never came. Their machine gun in the fort, after a three-hour silence, began firing again at midnight and fired a burst over the boulders at regular intervals, while the second machine gun remained silent. As the sky began to lighten before dawn Roger and his men came down from the ridge.

"The war seems to have stopped," he said and sat down beside Pierre. Their faces looked gray and overstrained and were covered with long stubble.

It was now light enough to see the houses and Pierre said: "It's already too late for them."

"I can't help myself," said Roger, "but when this affair is over I shall say a paternoster. What's the matter?"

Pierre seemed not to have heard him. He was staring in bewilderment towards the village street, where in the gray light of dawn the shape of a man had appeared and was approaching them; the figure reached the last house in the row, stopped for a few seconds, looked around and then came slowly forward. "Now I believe in ghosts," murmured Pierre. "Pinch me, will you?"

Roger, who had also seen the man but did not recognize him, did not know what to make of it. He asked: "Do you know him?"

"It's Boris," said Pierre in a strangled voice. Then he stood up and ran down the mountainside, followed immediately by Roger.

They paid no heed to the fact that they could be seen by the Germans in the fort, nor to the shouts of their men behind the boulders. The machine gun from the turret only opened fire when they were already in dead ground from its field of fire and were approaching Boris. He had stopped on hearing the shots and looked up to see the two men bounding towards him down the rock-strewn valleyside. As he recognized Pierre his tense attitude relaxed.

The firing had stopped and the only sound to be heard in the sudden stillness was the panting breath of the two men, who had now reached the Russian and stared at him as if he were a supernatural apparition.

"Is it really him?" asked Roger.

Pierre was still out of breath and speechless. He looked past Boris and down the village street. It lay as empty and peaceful in the dawn light as if German soldiers had never been in La Peine; then he seized Boris by the arm and asked hoarsely: "Where is Monsieur Knopf?"

"In the fort," Boris replied. "They are in one of the store chambers. We hid ourselves there from the Germans."

"Has anything happened to you?"

"No, they didn't find us."

Pierre let go his arm with a sigh of relief. He was so relieved that for a while the news supplanted every other thought in his mind. He left further questioning to Roger, who now asked: "Where are the Germans?"

"I don't know," answered Boris, following Roger's glance down the row of houses. "As I came out of the fort I heard the machine-gun fire. At first I wanted to turn back, but I kept on and came down into the village."

"When was that?"

"About half an hour ago. There are no more of them in the village; I haven't seen a single person here."

Roger turned to Pierre: "I can't understand it. Can you? They've been shooting at us all night."

"Yes, but from the fort," said Pierre. "I'm afraid they've fooled us."

"How?"

"Fetch the men," said Pierre. "Tell them to keep under cover as they go; the path is out of sight from the fort."

As Roger set off, Pierre turned to Boris. "Tell me briefly what happened when the Germans came and what you did."

"There's not much to tell," said Boris. "But you don't yet know that since the day before yesterday we have not been alone here."

Pierre jerked up his head. "Did somebody come?"

"Three men and a woman."

"Are they French?"

Boris waited a moment before answering. He had had to get up once in the night and had used the pocket torch. He had seen that the girl's bed was empty and, shining the light towards the Swiss, he had seen them. He had almost been sick and once back in bed he had been unable to sleep again. The sight of Anna lying beside Georges, the blanket pulled aside to reveal her naked shoulder, had eaten into his brain like acid. Having already decided, after his quarrel with Georges, to go outside by himself and spy out the situation, the incident served to confirm him in another decision and he regarded his meeting with Pierre as a lucky coincidence which increased his determination to carry out his plan.

"You may know one of them," he said. "His name is Vieale and before he came here he was mayor of Eys."

"Vieale!" Pierre whistled. "Do I know him! What's he doing here?"

"He came with his wife. He has enemies in Eys who are accusing him of being a collaborator."

"And they're right; he was hand in glove with the Boches."

"If he were," Boris countered, "I wouldn't be here. He helped me to get away."

"You're joking!" said Pierre, perplexed.

"I'm not joking," said Boris and described briefly how he had come to Eys and had been taken in by Vieale. "Without him I

316

wouldn't have known where to go," he said finally. "He sent me on to La Peine."

"An astonishing story," said Pierre after a moment of reflection. "Who are the two others?"

"Two Swiss. They fought in the German army against the Russians. When their division was transferred to France a few days ago they deserted."

"Deser——" Pierre stopped. He turned round and looked towards the boulders. It had grown still lighter in the last quarter of an hour; Roger and the other men were just emerging from cover. Raymond and Laroche were with him. They approached at a fast walk and Raymond shouted from a distance: "Have they really got away from us?"

"Don't shout so much," said Pierre. "Take a few men and run up to the fort as fast as you can. No one must be allowed to get out." He turned to Roger and Laroche. "I have some news for you two."

As Raymond ran down the village street with eight men, Pierre said to Boris: "Tell them again who is with Monsieur Knopf."

Boris repeated what he had said, and when he mentioned the two Swiss, Roger exchanged a meaningful look with Pierre and asked: "When did those two come?"

"They came first on Monday," answered Boris. "Early on Tuesday morning they went away again."

"Why?" asked Pierre.

"I advised them to," said Boris. "But the next day they came back with Monsieur Vieale."

"And otherwise there were no Germans here? Except, of course, the troops who came yesterday?"

Boris shook his head uncomprehendingly. "No. Why do you ask?"

"I'll tell you later. Have the Swiss got guns with them?"

"Yes."

"Automatic rifles?"

Boris was still puzzled by his great interest in the two Swiss. He said: "I think they are machine carbines, but I don't see——"

"I must get up there," Pierre cut him short. "Come with me!"

Boris stood in his way. "Just a moment. Will you take Monsieur Knopf back to Escarène?"

"When we're finished here," replied Pierre. "You'll come too, won't you?"

"No."

317

Pierre smiled in surprise. "Why not?"

"I shall stay here," said Boris. "The war isn't over yet."

"You can just as well wait for it to end in Escarène," said Pierre. He set off towards the village, and as the other men followed him Boris felt obliged to do the same.

The sky in the east was beginning to redden as they reached the lower end of the village and began to climb the steep path towards the road where Raymond and his men were waiting for them. Between them, hands held on their heads and faces gray with fear, stood two German soldiers.

Raymond came forward carrying a German machine gun. "Here is your garrison," he said grimly. "The Boches cleared off last night."

Pierre showed no surprise. He had guessed it, but now that he had met Boris and believed he had found out who had shot Gaston, the confirmation of his guess produced no reaction in him. He was surprised, however, that the Germans had left behind only two men. They were young, tall and dark, and standing there they seemed sulky rather than afraid. Nothing but their ash-gray features betrayed their feelings.

"Where did you find them?" Pierre asked.

Raymond put down the machine gun. "They came out by themselves. We had positioned ourselves on both sides of the tunnel mouth. We had hardly been there five minutes when they came creeping out. They were going to follow the others."

"Where?"

"They say they don't know."

"Then how could they follow them?"

"I asked them that," said one of Raymond's men. He had been a prisoner-of-war in Germany for two years and had learned the language. "They say their officer only gave them a general direction to take."

"Which direction?"

"Northwards."

"We must go after them!" said Raymond urgently. "They have a six-hour start."

Pierre looked up the valley where the endless sea of mountain peaks stretched northwards.

"They won't go far," he said. "If they're lucky they'll run into the Americans, otherwise . . ." He grinned and turned to Roger. "If you were them, which way would you have gone?"

318

"I would have gone the way Leroy went," answered Roger. "Through the gorge and over the ridge."

"You can only do that if you know the gorge."

"Then I would have gone by the same way that we came: over the pass and along the western ridge as far as the wooden bridge."

"And then down the D206?"

"Yes."

"Which is probably by now in American hands."

Roger scratched his chin and looked at the two Germans. "All the same," he said, "I certainly wouldn't have gone north. They'll either get lost or break their necks."

"Well, then," said Pierre to Raymond, "do you want to break your neck too?"

"I'd rather do that than be made to look a fool," muttered Raymond. "The Americans will kill themselves laughing."

"Allow them that small pleasure," said Pierre. "They'll have little enough to laugh about until they're in Germany." He took another look at the prisoners. They were still holding their hands on their heads and staring at the ground.

"What shall we do with them?" asked Roger. "Shall we hand them over to the Americans?"

"Why bother?" shouted one of the men. "Let's knock them off now!"

"Let them jump over the mountainside," shouted another.

Pierre turned to the man who had interrogated them. "Why didn't they leave earlier?"

"Their orders were to stay here until daybreak."

"Perhaps there are still some more in there somewhere. If the Boches left a rearguard it must have consisted of more than two men. Ask them again!"

While the man questioned the prisoners, Pierre looked round for Boris. He saw him standing at the back of the group of men and elbowed his way through to him. "Where is the chamber?" he asked him.

Boris described its location, then looked towards the prisoners. "Are you going to shoot them?"

"Why not?"

"If I were you I would let them go. They were only doing their duty. Think of Monsieur Knopf."

"He won't see them," answered Pierre and walked back to the prisoners. "What do they say?" he asked the man who spoke German.

"They still maintain that they were the only ones to stay behind. The officer asked for volunteers and they were the only ones who came forward. They are brothers, by the way."

"Brothers, are they?" Pierre turned to Raymond.

Raymond shrugged his shoulders. "Brothers or not, they are Boches."

"We can't do it here," said Pierre. "We must think of Monsieur Knopf and the girl. Roger!"

Roger stepped up to him. "Take two men and do it farther down the road. Push them over the edge so that nobody sees their bodies."

"I'd rather Raymond did it," muttered Roger.

"And I'd rather you did it," said Pierre.

"Are you afraid I couldn't do it?" asked Raymond sharply.

"On the contrary," said Pierre. "You would do it only too well. After all, you're a butcher!"

The men laughed. They made way for Roger to lead the prisoners off. Their faces were now a paler shade of gray and one of them had beads of sweat on his forehead.

Roger beckoned two men to him and set off with them behind the prisoners. When they had gone about twenty paces Pierre ran after them and took Roger aside. "When you get to the next tunnel let them go," he ordered.

"*Bon*," said Roger and went on with a grin.

Pierre stood for a moment and watched them go. He had not done it out of pity and he knew that it was simply a whim of his. Raymond would be furious, but the meeting with Boris had put him in a magnanimous mood and he felt that he should show a little gratitude to fate for having saved Knopf and the girl.

When he rejoined the men Raymond said to him: "What did you want with Roger?"

"I'll tell you later." Then he said to Boris: "Show us the way."

"We shall need a torch," said Boris. "It's pitch dark in there."

"But you got out without a torch!"

"It was extremely difficult."

"We have good eyes," said Pierre. He turned to Raymond. "You and Laroche can come with us. The others—stay here and wait."

They went into the tunnel and found the entrance to the passage without difficulty. "Here it is," said Boris. "It leads straight ahead for about five yards, then turns left and goes down some steps."

"Aren't you coming with us?" asked Pierre.

Boris shook his head. He had been debating with himself whether he shouldn't at least say goodbye to Knopf and the others, but he was afraid that they would not let him go, and if Knopf were to ask him for his reasons he would have to lie to them for the truth would have made everything worse. He had made up his mind and when he thought of the future he did so with the indifference of someone who has come to terms with his lot. Everything was as it had been before he had met Knopf and Anna, no better and no worse, and the loss of one illusion no longer meant anything to him. He would stay in La Peine for as long as necessary and in case of extremity he always had his pistol. He was determined not to be caught alive, and if it should prove that there was no place in the world for a man like him to live without fear of being extradited, he would make an end of it. Twice in the past he had staked everything on a single chance and now he had nothing more to stake, but he found that he no longer cared.

"I'll wait here until you come back," he said. "You only have to follow the passage. It may be that they are all asleep."

Pierre, who had turned to go down the passage, stopped again. "Don't they know that you went out?"

"I didn't tell them."

"They'll get a surprise!" said Raymond.

"Especially two of them," said Pierre and went into the passage. Raymond and Laroche followed him.

"It's damned dark," muttered Raymond.

"I have a cigarette lighter," said Laroche. He felt in his pocket and said to Pierre who was leading, "Where are you?"

"Here," answered Pierre. "Where's your lighter?"

"It won't work, damn it."

"Throw it away; we'll find the way without it."

He waited for the other two to catch up with him. Almost at the same moment he heard a voice call his name; as he reached the steps and looked down he noticed a light at the bottom, just bright enough for him to recognize the girl, who was coming racing towards him three steps at a time, and then she was hugging him, sobbing and laughing at the same time.

Laroche had at last made his lighter work. As it flared up, Anna unclasped her arms from Pierre and turned to look at Raymond and Laroche who grinned with embarrassment and wiped their hands on their trousers before shaking hands with the girl. She was on the borderline between laughter and tears and immediately

321

turned back to Pierre. "I don't want to cry," she said. "Perhaps I'd better swear to make me stop, but I don't know how to swear in French."

"You can learn that from Raymond," said Pierre and laughed. It helped him to cover up his emotion, and he said to Raymond: "How much do you charge for lessons?"

Raymond grimaced. "I'll do it for nothing if you tell me why you ran after Roger."

"I ordered him to let the Boches go."

The two men blinked at him in amazement. Laroche was holding the still burning lighter in his hand. As Raymond took a step towards Pierre he caused a draft which extinguished the lighter.

"Look out!" said Laroche.

Raymond felt his way towards Pierre and stopped in front of him. "We'll talk about this later," he said, hoarse with anger. "I took those prisoners; you had no right to let them go."

"Keep your distance," said Pierre coolly. "You spit when you talk. As long as I'm in charge I shall decide what happens to prisoners, and it if suits me to let them go there is nothing you can do about it."

"You should at least have told us," grumbled Laroche. He flicked his lighter again and it lit up Pierre's face.

"What are you fighting about?" asked Anna uneasily.

Pierre grinned. "He wanted to slaughter two skinny little piglets. I took them away from him and now he's furious, but I shall give him a couple of fat sows in exchange. Come on."

Going down the steps Anna looked around for Georges. She had expected him to follow her and although she was slightly surprised when there was no sign of him down below, she gave the matter no special thought. Seeing Pierre again had so excited her that she had even forgotten to ask about Boris and she only remembered him when she rejoined the others in the chamber.

They were already expected. The paraffin lamp was burning and the men were standing in the doorway, with the exception of Georges, who was sitting at the table next to Madame Vieale. They were already awake when Georges had come back. He had listened to the meeting between Anna and Pierre, then had returned, put his gun in the corner and sat down at the table. He was so preoccupied that he had not replied until Vieale questioned him a second time about the new arrivals.

As Anna and the three men came into the chamber Georges

322

felt perspiration break out on his forehead. He saw the smallest of the three approach Knopf and greet him. The other two remained in the doorway for a moment and eyed the inmates suspiciously. With their unshaven faces, their berets and short-barreled automatic weapons they presented a terrifying aspect which was in no way modified by the warmth with which they greeted Knopf. After the first few words Georges realized which of them was Pierre and he watched him with special attention. With his big scar across his right cheek and low hairline on his forehead he looked like a picture-book Maquis chieftain. As Georges looked at him he had the impression of having seen him before. He wondered whether he could have been one of the two men who had run into his fire two days ago. Although for a fraction of a second he had seen their faces as clearly as though through field-glasses, he could not be sure. In their berets they all looked alike.

He was temporarily distracted by Anna who had been glancing his way and now came over to him. "Why are you making such a face?" she asked quietly. "Aren't you pleased?"

"Yes, yes I am," replied Georges vaguely.

He watched Knopf talking to the three men. Their entrance had thawed the icy crust which had overlain his features since Georges had returned, but Georges knew that it was only to be short-lived and that he could count on a nasty scene with Knopf before much longer. "Where is Boris?" he heard him ask.

Pierre nodded towards the door. "He stayed outside. We wouldn't have found you so quickly but for him. The Germans pulled out last night. Unfortunately we only realized this when it was too late, otherwise we would have helped them on their way." He turned to Vieale. "Monsieur Vieale from Eys! Do you remember me?"

"I can't say that I do," said Vieale defensively.

"But I remember you. It was more than a year ago. You were paying a visit to the mayor of Escarène, Monsieur Michaud. He introduced you to all the members of his council; I was one of them."

Vieale forced a smile. "It's quite a long time ago, Monsieur . . ."

"Fournier," said Pierre. "I didn't think that you would recollect my name. A man like you with such good connections with the Prefect must have had more important matters to think about. Are you spending your holidays here?"

"I rather think you know why I am here," said Vieale brusquely.

323

"Boris told me. When I heard that you were here I recalled our last conversation. Do you remember what we talked about?"

"I think we talked about many things."

"Yes, we did, but one thing in particular that you said stayed in my mind. You declared that the Resistance could have no influence on the outcome of the war. I imagine that you have altered your view now."

"I have had no cause to do so. The war was decided in Russia. In France it might last a week or two longer without the Resistance, but it has contributed nothing to the final result."

Pierre turned to Raymond and Laroche, who had been listening to the conversation with growing interest. "Listen to this! You can learn something here."

"I don't know why you listen to that drivel," said Raymond with annoyance. "Anyone who has worked with the Boches should keep his trap shut."

At this moment Knopf spoke up. He had hoped that they would avoid this subject until he had discussed it alone with Pierre, but now he could no longer be silent. "I must disagree with you," he said quietly. "I am convinced that what is being said in Eys about Monsieur Vieale is nothing but an excuse for resentment and jealousy with the usual motives."

"That I can't judge," said Pierre. "If Monsieur Vieale has made himself disliked in Eys that is his own affair. But this concerns something else which happens to affect me too."

Vieale shrugged his shoulders. "You asked me for my opinion, Monsieur. We're not living in Russia. A Frenchman has the right to express his opinion, just as he has the right to fight in the Resistance if he wants to."

"But you don't think it's right?"

"Is it a crime to think so? I have never prevented anyone from joining the Resistance."

"You do of course concede that we have shortened the war by a fortnight. That will have saved the lives of many Frenchmen."

"That is only one side of the reckoning," said Vieale. In his good brown suit he looked, standing beside Pierre, like a factory-owner talking to a workman. "If you look at it in that way you must also take the casualties of the Resistance into account. Not to mention what we have lost through German reprisals against the Resistance. I have been through two wars and I can tell you, Monsieur, I am sick of it all. If you are not yet sick of it, that's

324

your business. The war was decided at Stalingrad and I am as happy about the outcome as you are."

"So you say. But for me the outcome has not been decided until the last German has left France. Even if your reckoning was right something would still be missing. Do you know what I mean?"

Before Vieale could answer, Knopf interrupted. "I have discussed all this at length with Monsieur Vieale and I believe that his only crime consists in being humane. If you condemn him for that you must condemn me too. No one should be forced into anything which conflicts with his convictions. I don't know whether my opinion in this matter means anything to you."

"It means a great deal to me," said Pierre.

"Then help Monsieur Vieale; I ask you that expressly. The war has piled so many injustices upon us that we must at least try and prevent any more from being done if it lies in our power. If you are on his side, Pierre, no one in Eys will dare to lift a hand against him."

Pierre stared at the ground for a few seconds. Then he quickly looked up. "You know that I wouldn't refuse you anything, Monsieur. But first there is something which we must clear up. Let's sit down for a moment; it may take a few minutes. You too," he said to Vieale. "One can talk better sitting down."

The two men sat down at the table and Marcel, who had been standing next to Vieale, took a seat beside them. Raymond and Laroche were leaning against the wall near the door. When Pierre looked at them and gestured towards the table, they shook their heads.

"We'd rather stand," said Laroche. His dark, leathery face with the deep furrows across the forehead had a disagreeable and suspicious look. Raymond, too, wore a grim expression. They distrusted Pierre's behavior and were only prevented from venting their feelings by the presence of Knopf.

Raymond had lit a cigarette and was looking round the vaulted chamber. In doing so he glanced towards the corner where Georges had stood his machine carbine. He walked over and inspected it, then picked it up and asked aloud: "Whose is this thing?"

"It belongs to me," answered Georges.

"A lovely weapon," said Raymond and stuck his cigarette in a corner of his mouth in order to leave his hands free. Then he sniffed the muzzle and asked: "Have you fired it much?"

"No."

325

"But you have fired it, haven't you?"

"That's why I was given it."

Raymond gave him a rapid glance. "I thought as much." He gave the weapon to Pierre, who had stepped up to him and was also examining it.

"When was the last time you fired it?" asked Pierre, without looking at Georges.

"Yesterday."

"At whom?"

"He fired into the air," said Anna. She was sitting on the bench between Georges and Madame Vieale and smiling at Pierre.

Pierre turned to face her. "Into the air?"

"Yes, when the Germans came. He held them up until we had carried our belongings into the fort, otherwise we should have had to leave everything behind."

"Where was that?"

"At the gap in the road," said Georges. "Then later on once farther up the road. Each time I let them come in sight and then fired in the air. After the second time they stopped and waited until daybreak."

"Did they shoot back?" asked Pierre, as he stared at the gun.

"Yes."

"With tanks too?"

"Yes."

"Then that was the firing that we heard," said Laroche. "I never thought that the answer would be so simple."

"Nor did I," said Pierre. He turned to Vieale. "Where did you get to know these two?"

"In Eys. Monsieur Chabrier and Monsieur Egli . . ."

"Who is Monsieur Chabrier?" Pierre interrupted.

"I am," said Georges. He waited for Pierre to look at him, but he did not and instead continued to stare at the ceiling and said: "Are you Swiss?"

"Yes."

"Where were you born?"

The men at the table were beginning to grow uneasy. Vieale and Knopf glanced at Pierre and Georges. Only Marcel looked straight ahead, his face the color of cheese.

"In Lausanne," replied Georges. "Why do you want to know?"

Pierre did not answer the question. "Go on," he said to Vieale. He walked over to the table, put his right foot up on the bench, rested his gun-butt on the ground and folded his arms over his knee.

Vieale hesitated. "Perhaps Monsieur Chabrier can——"

"I want to hear it from you," said Pierre.

He said it in a voice which conveyed to Vieale that he would be wiser to do as he was told. "They were billeted on me. I understood that they wanted to desert."

"Why did they want to desert?"

"They joined the Germans to fight against Russia. Then when they were posted to France . . ."

"They deserted."

"Yes."

"A nice story," said Pierre. "Did you send them to La Peine?"

"I thought they would be safe in La Peine. We agreed to meet here."

"And where did you meet them?"

"On the road."

"By the bridge?"

"Yes. Boris had told them——"

"It was a misunderstanding," put in Knopf. "Boris was afraid of complications. I only heard their full story later."

"That doesn't matter for the moment," said Pierre. "Did you come by car, Monsieur Vieale?"

"Without a car we couldn't have brought all our baggage. I put it away in a quarry by the viaduct."

"That was on Wednesday?"

"Yes."

"At about what time?"

"I didn't look at my watch."

"It must have been at about one o'clock," said Knopf. "They arrived when the storm began."

"That fits in," said Pierre. "When did you leave Eys?"

Vieale reflected. "Tuesday afternoon. It was already dark when we met Monsieur Chabrier and Monsieur Egli. I knew that the road to La Peine was very bad and we decided to stop and drive on next morning."

"Then you spent the night by the bridge?"

"Yes."

"And burned their uniforms?"

Vieale started. "How do you know?"

"We found the remains of them in the ashes," said Pierre. "If

327

you want to burn . . ." He broke off and looked curiously at the ceiling. Softly at first and then growing in volume the grinding and creaking of the mountain was heard again. The sound lasted for about half a minute, while simultaneously the floor shook and the empty wineglasses on the table began to tinkle. When the noise stopped Pierre looked at Raymond and Laroche, whose faces had turned pale. "What's that?" he asked.

"Time we were going," said Raymond hoarsely. "It began just like that when the mountainside broke off and the road was cut. A few days later the whole lot was down below in a heap."

Pierre turned to Knopf. "Have you heard it before?"

"At least seven times since we've been here," replied Knopf.

"But it has been very quiet since yesterday evening," said Vieale.

Knopf shook his head. "It happened last night also; not so violently, but it woke me up. Didn't you know about it?"

His question was directed at Pierre, but the answer was cut short by the sudden appearance in the doorway of Roger.

He was out of breath. Without noticing the others, he at once strode up to Pierre. "What was that?"

"The mountainside," said Pierre. "It's moving."

"Then it won't last another week," said Roger.

Laroche anxiously examined the ceiling. "Let's hope it doesn't fall on our heads."

"Shame to spoil your red beret," muttered Roger. "I was standing on the steps when it started. It gave me a shock, I can tell you." He saw Anna and Knopf and at once went to shake their hands. "Pierre said he would kill somebody if anything had happened to you. We're all glad he hasn't had to do it."

"So am I," said Knopf.

Anna turned to Pierre. "Is that true?"

"I was prepared to," said Pierre.

"I almost forgot," said Roger to Knopf. "I had to give you a message from your friend."

"From Boris?"

"Yes, I had a little job to do. When I came back he had already gone. The men said that he had gone back to the village and asked you not to follow him and not to wait for him. Did you quarrel with him?"

Knopf shook his head in amazement. "I don't understand it. Didn't he say where he was going?"

"No. I thought you would know."

"He intends to stay in La Peine," said Pierre. "He told me when we met him."

"I wouldn't do that if I were him," said Roger. "La Peine can't last much longer."

"He knows that," murmured Anna.

"Then he must be warned again," said Pierre. "He can't stay here."

"It's too late for that," said Knopf quietly. "I'm afraid he wants to stay there."

They all looked at him, but he said no more.

Raymond cleared his throat. "I suggest we waste no more time. It's too dangerous here."

"We'll be ready soon," said Pierre. He walked round the table and stood behind Vieale. "I want to finish this matter."

"What matter?" asked Roger. As Pierre did not answer he walked over to Raymond and Laroche and whispered to them.

"So you spent the night by the bridge," said Pierre to Vieale. "When did you leave the next morning?"

Vieale looked uncertainly towards Georges, but he was staring at the table as if the conversation had nothing to do with him. "I can't remember exactly," said Vieale evasively.

"Well, it can be worked out," said Pierre. "We reached the bridge towards seven; you had gone by then."

"That's possible. We started early."

"About six o'clock in fact. How long do you need with your car from the bridge to La Peine?"

Vieale said nothing.

"Let's say an hour and a half," said Pierre after a short pause. "You should have been in La Peine by eight o'clock at the latest, instead of which you didn't arrive until about one o'clock. Did you have a puncture?"

The three Maquisards by the wall had stopped whispering and were looking at Vieale. Madame Vieale turned and said firmly to Georges: "Why don't you tell him, Monsieur? You can see that there's no more sense in it."

"No one has asked me," replied Georges.

"Then tell him. We intended no harm. I don't think Monsieur Fournier will chop off our heads for that."

"It would be a shame to lose such a pretty head," said Pierre gallantly. "I don't mind if you want to tell me."

The woman firmly returned his look. "It was stupid, Monsieur, but we didn't know that on Wednesday. Monsieur Chabrier told

329

us that we shouldn't go to La Peine because Monsieur Knopf and Boris didn't want us to and because on Wednesday a car from the Resistance was going there. But we had been preparing for this for weeks and we couldn't go back to Eys. From what Monsieur Chabrier had heard from Boris we supposed——"

"You can go ahead and tell him that it was my idea," put in Georges.

"That no longer matters. We all agreed and we all went together. We had the chance of getting out—and we didn't."

"But it went very well!" said Vieale, with a short laugh. "Monsieur Chabrier achieved what he wanted."

"What *we* wanted," his wife corrected him.

"And what did you want?" asked Pierre.

"We wanted you to turn round," said Vieale. "We wanted to give you the impression that La Peine was occupied by German troops."

"Yes—and . . . ?"

"And?" Vieale shrugged uncomfortably. "You know what happened because you were there. Monsieur Chabrier and Monsieur Egli put on their uniforms . . ."

"I thought they had burned them!"

"They burned their proper uniforms. But they still had their camouflage overalls and they wore those."

Pierre nodded. "Now I see it. They positioned themselves with weapons in the hollow."

"Yes, but we expressly agreed that there would be no shooting . . ."

Vieale was interrupted by Raymond. Like Roger and Laroche he had been listening to the story with mounting astonishment. When he realized the implications of what he heard he gave a curse and broke out: "You fool! Do you realize what you were doing?"

Vieale blushed. "We know now that it was wrong. But that's no reason for you to be abusive. You reached La Peine two days later, that's all."

"That's all! roared Raymond. He turned to Pierre. "Did you hear that? That's all, he says!"

Pierre waved him aside impatiently. "Don't shout so; we're not deaf." To Vieale he said: "You got us into a fine mess. Did you at least tell this to Monsieur Knopf?"

"We meant to, but the arrival of the Germans prevented us."

330

"You should have told me sooner," murmured Knopf. He seemed very disturbed by what he had heard.

Madame Vieale leaned over to him. "We are sorry, Monsieur. We didn't know you. We assumed that you would betray us."

"None of it was anything to do with them," put in Georges. He had been silent so far because Pierre had ignored him, but he felt that the time had come to enter the lists and he said firmly: "I would have carried it out even if Monsieur and Madame Vieale hadn't agreed."

Pierre looked at him for the first time. "What would you have done if we had simply driven on?"

"Tried to stop you," said Georges.

"How?"

"That's difficult to say after the event. I would probably have fired at the tires of your truck."

"Besides you we saw two others. They came down the road from the olive grove."

"That was us," said Madame Vieale. "We were getting impatient. Monsieur Chabrier told us to drive into the olive grove and wait for him there."

Knopf spoke again. Having recovered from his surprise he now regarded the incident from a viewpoint of much greater understanding; he said: "It was a chain of unfortunate events. We are all lucky that we came out of it so well."

"Very lucky," growled Raymond. "You have no idea how lucky, Monsieur."

"What do you mean?" said Knopf, offended by his tone.

Pierre put his hand on Knopf's shoulder. "We came up on Wednesday to fetch you away from here. I'll tell you about that later. For the moment I'm very interested in hearing the rest of this story. What did you do when you reached the end of the road?"

His last words were directed at Vieale who shrugged impatiently. "We sat down in the tunnel on the other side of the gap and waited until the rain stopped. When the storm was over Monsieur Knopf, Boris and Anna came to meet us."

"They came to you?"

"Boris had seen the car coming," put in Knopf. "We wanted to make sure who it was, but we were caught on the way by the storm."

"And then?"

The tenacity with which Pierre pursued the story obliged Knopf to smile. "Then we had a talk—which was, I think, a most useful one. When the rain stopped we carried up the baggage."

"How long did that take?"

"Until evening."

For a moment Pierre seemed unsure of himself. He scratched his cheek with his finger and reflected.

"I don't see where all this is leading," said Vieale nervously. "Surely it would be simpler if you told us in so many words what you want to find out."

"I agree," said Knopf. "Is it to do with the Germans?"

Pierre gave him a puzzled look. "I don't think so. It would of course be the simplest explanation, but on Wednesday afternoon there were no Boches here yet."

"Except Anna and myself," said Knopf with a smile.

"When I say Boches," replied Pierre hastily, "of course I mean soldiers."

"You don't have to apologize. Have you any reason to suppose that there were any Germans in the neighborhood on Wednesday afternoon?"

"Reason enough, but it is not possible. When did you first see them?"

"I only saw their trucks and tanks. We heard the shots and explosion that evening. Do you know where they occurred?"

"Do we know!" Roger grinned bitterly. "Pierre can tell you better than we can."

"That can wait," said Pierre. "Were you still awake when the German column arrived?"

"We were asleep," said Knopf. "Monsieur Egli woke us up. We were worried by the sound of firing and Boris decided to stay up all night to keep watch. He and Monsieur Egli went to the little square at the end of the village. They saw the column from there."

"Lucky for you!" said Laroche.

Knopf nodded. "Yes. Otherwise they would have caught us sleeping."

"Monsieur Chabrier also woke us up," said Madame Vieale. "He saw the trucks too."

"Wasn't he asleep?" asked Pierre.

"No; he was away."

"With Boris?"

She turned to Marcel. "You can better tell him that, Monsieur."

"I'd prefer you to tell me," Pierre said to her.

"They had quarreled," she said. "Monsieur Chabrier was

332

angry and said he was going to leave us. But he came back during the night."

"When did he go away?"

"Quite late."

"Before four o'clock?"

"Oh, much later," said Knopf. "It must have been at least six o'clock."

This answer disappointed Pierre. He looked at Anna, who was listening with close attention but without taking any part in the discussion herself. "What did they quarrel about?" he asked Knopf.

"I didn't bother to inquire."

Pierre stared hard at Marcel's pale face. "Well—what was it about?"

"It was a personal matter," said Marcel uncertainly.

"You won't tell me?"

"No."

"Do you know what it was?" Pierre asked Vieale.

"I have no idea," said Vieale unwillingly. "I didn't see Monsieur Chabrier the whole afternoon. He went ahead of us. He wanted to see for himself what was going on in La Peine."

"When was that?"

"Perhaps about half an hour after we had reached the tunnel; it was still raining."

"Had Monsieur Knopf joined you by then?"

"No," said Vieale.

"We met Monsieur Chabrier," put in Knopf. "He came up the road while we were waiting in one of the other tunnels, where the storm had caught us. He told us that Monsieur and Madame Vieale were waiting farther down the road and that he intended to go on to La Peine. I asked him to send Anna to me with my raincoat."

"And Monsieur Chabrier went to La Peine?"

"Yes."

"What did he do there?"

Knopf shrugged his shoulders in silence.

"That is interesting," said Pierre with satisfaction and looked at Vieale. "You arrived at one o'clock and half an hour later Monsieur Chabrier left you. To walk from the tunnel to La Peine takes thirty minutes. Did he stay long with you?" he asked Knopf.

"Five minutes at the most."

"And with Anna?"

333

The girl said nothing. She gave an impression of vacancy and did not speak even when Knopf said to her: "Pierre is asking you something."

"What's the matter with her?" Pierre inquired.

Knopf gazed at her for a few moments. Then he said quietly: "Monsieur Chabrier can't have spent long with her. She brought me my coat a short while after he left."

"And then you didn't see Monsieur Chabrier again until late that night?"

"Yes. When we returned he had already left. I learned this from Monsieur Egli."

"Where did you meet Monsieur Chabrier?" Pierre turned to Marcel.

"In the village."

"What was he doing there?"

Marcel looked helplessly over at Georges. It was a decisive question and if he told the truth he would incriminate Georges heavily. He cursed his own dullness which prevented him from finding a plausible explanation in a hurry and he waited for Georges to take the opportunity of answering in his stead. But Georges sat with bowed head and said nothing, and when Marcel looked at him he saw that his features were bathed in a thin film of sweat. He heard Pierre's impatient voice repeating his question and he then heard his own voice answering: "He was asleep."

It was the stupidest thing he could have said, but he only realized it when he saw Anna wince. "Why are you lying?" she asked sharply. "You told me that you met Georges on the path!"

"On which path?" asked Pierre.

"On the path to the spring."

"That's enough for me," said Pierre with satisfaction. "I assume Monsieur Chabrier knew that there is another way of reaching La Peine."

"Of course he knew," said Vieale guilelessly. "When he and Monsieur Egli went there the first time they went over the ridge. They lost their way by night and took the D206. But I don't see why . . ."

"You'll see in a moment," Pierre interrupted. He was now absolutely sure of the facts and said to Knopf: "Gaston is dead."

Knopf swung round and stared at Pierre. "Gaston! But he was going to come up with you on Wednesday."

"He did come," said Pierre. "He was sitting beside me in the cab when we drove down from the pass and we saw these two standing in the road. We then tried to get up here by the other route and in doing so we were shot at. It was a German automatic rifle. Gaston got three bullets in the chest."

"But it's not possible," murmured Knopf. "There were no German troops here at that time."

Pierre nodded. "That's the point. It can only have been one person. Here he sits: Monsieur Chabrier!"

There was deathly silence as they all stared at Georges. With a chalk-white face Vieale leaned over to him. "Say it isn't true, Monsieur."

"He cannot," said Pierre coldly. "Gaston was shot at half-past four. No one saw Monsieur Chabrier between two and six o'clock. The shots came from this weapon." He struck the muzzle of the machine carbine with his fist. "Do you still wish to deny it?" he said to Georges.

Georges lifted his head. He saw Vieale's sallow face looking at him, Knopf's eyes filled with anger and revulsion, and he saw Marcel shrug his shoulders in resignation and despair. But none of these affected him, nor the horrified look of Madame Vieale who stared at him in bewilderment. He might have even raised a grin at the laborious way in which Pierre had proceeded, had Anna not been there. Before the interrogation had started he had imagined her sitting, as she sat now, staring vacantly into a corner of the chamber. That she might react in this way had been his only fear; but now that it had happened he felt nothing.

He looked into Pierre's eyes. "Have I denied anything?"

"You admit it?"

"Everything points to it."

"Yes, everything," said Pierre. "You have taken a long time to notice it."

"I didn't want to spoil your fun."

Pierre frowned. "It was as little fun for me as for you. One thing I'd like to know: why did you shoot?"

"I can't explain."

"As you wish." Pierre beckoned to Raymond. "You can take him outside."

"What about you?" asked Raymond.

"I'm handing him over to you. Hurry up!"

Raymond turned to Georges. "Come on."

As Georges stood up, Madame Vieale said to Pierre: "What are you going to do?"

"I'm going to drive to Eys with you," he replied. "If necessary

335

I'll even post two men outside your front door so that you can sleep in peace. Isn't that enough for you?"

"For me, perhaps, Monsieur. But ask Mademoiselle Anna whether she's happy about it."

"Anna?" Pierre turned to look at the girl. "What has Anna to do with it?"

"Can we go?" asked Raymond impatiently. He was standing by Georges while Laroche and Roger were waiting at the door.

"Yes. At once," said Pierre. He gave another look at the girl. Her face seemed petrified and he let a few seconds pass. Then he went up to her and asked: "What is it?"

She gave no reply and seemed not to have heard. Madame Vieale had clasped her hands in front of her with anxiety.

"You must be mistaken," Pierre said to her. "Anna knew Gaston well. I know that she was very fond of him."

"At a moment like this a woman can only be fond of one person," said the woman to Anna.

"But which?" asked Pierre. He waited for half a minute more, then took Georges' pocket torch from the table and gave it to Raymond.

"Whose is this?" asked Raymond.

"It's a German army torch," said Pierre. "You can keep it."

Raymond switched it on and gave Georges a slight push from behind. "*Allez!*"

From the doorway Georges heard Marcel's voice call his name. It sounded as if his mouth was stuffed with rags.

Then he set off down the dark passage with the three men. Raymond led the way, the torch in one hand, his gun in the other. They climbed up the steps and when they emerged from the tunnel into the open air, Georges shut his eyes for a moment against the harsh sunlight. But he soon opened them again and saw the men. They were squatting by the roadside and there were many more of them than Georges had supposed. One looked up and said something. The man beside him looked up at the same time and then all the others took notice. They jumped to their feet and formed a wall diagonally across the road.

Georges heard the three men whispering behind his back. Then he was gripped by the arm and someone said: "Stay where you are." It was Raymond. He and Roger walked forward to the others and began talking to them, while Laroche stayed with Georges.

Laroche pulled a squashed blue cigarette pack from his pocket and offered it to Georges. "Take one."

"I won't smoke now," said Georges.

Laroche shrugged and lit one for himself. The smoke went up Georges' nostrils and he thought: I should have had one. I even think I should have enjoyed it, but it's so horribly banal.

He looked up at the blue sky and the mountains on the far side of the valley and he told himself that it was an impressive background for his end. At any rate it was more impressive than in Russia, he thought, and if you come to think of it you've had plenty of luck in spite of everything. You've survived the whole war without so much as breaking a bone and the prospect of death should be no surprise to you. The only thing wrong is the beautiful blue sky, he thought. I always hoped it would be raining when the moment came. Death matters less when it's raining and one is less liable to feel regrets for what one might be missing.

His elbow was hurting him. He felt it with his finger tips and moved it until the pain brought tears to his eyes. There's another side of it too, he said to himself. Before you start thinking about the girl and what life might have been like with her, kindly remember the abscess you had on a back tooth six months ago which drove you so nearly mad for a week that you would gladly have put a bullet through your brain. You only need a rotten tooth-stump in your mouth and no dentist in reach and you're prepared to give up all the pleasures of life in exchange for a moment's peace and you can bet there would have been worse cases than one miserable tooth. Still, there's more to life than toothache and I do wish it would rain.

He looked at the group of men, who were standing in a huddle about twenty yards away, and he couldn't hear what they were talking about, but he knew all the same. The man beside him was puffing happily at his cigarette and staring across the valley, which lay calm and peaceful in the morning sunlight. As Georges looked down it he calculated his chances of escape. From where he stood the mountainside had a sheer drop of about a hundred feet. There was little hope.

His glance lingered for a while on the floor of the valley with its thick undergrowth and large boulders and he tried to imagine what he would do if he were down there now and free of the Maquisards. The tanks had disappeared and the road lay empty in the sun. This afternoon or this evening Vieale would drive back down the road to Eys and Marcel would be sitting between him and his wife. Anna too would be with them and Georges mentally

337

followed their route over the pass, through the gorge and into the valley.

I hope they have all the luck in the world, he thought. Especially Marcel. If he's clever he'll find his way to the nearest consulate, and if he doesn't, try to reach the frontier first. He'll never do it without me. Perhaps Vieale or Knopf will look after him. He can't just be left alone; he's as helpless as a child. And Anna will get over it. She's been through so much already that she should survive this too. I'd rather not know what she thinks of me now, but whatever she thinks, if it helps her to get over this affair then I don't mind.

A noise made him look towards the men. They were moving. The group divided itself into two long rows forming an open triangle with the apex towards the fort. Then Georges saw the two men who had been in the chamber standing at the tip of the triangle and one of them raised his arm.

Laroche threw away his cigarette. "Get moving," he said to Georges. Early as it was, it was already very hot and Georges felt the sweat running down his body. His face, too, dripped with perspiration. He wiped it off with his sleeve, watched by more than forty pairs of eyes.

He stood in the center of the triangle, the open road before him. It was about two hundred yards to the next bend; he found himself, for no particular reason, gauging the distance. As he had walked towards the group he had wondered why they had formed a triangle; if they had formed two ranks with a space between it would have been obvious that they intended to make him run the gauntlet. He disliked nothing more than uncertainty, but even this feeling soon ceased to trouble him.

Raymond came up to him. "You're lucky," he said loudly for all to hear. "It won't take you as long as it took Gaston. He was four hours in dying; for you it will be only a second." He stopped and grinned. "We're even giving you a chance. You can run fifty yards before we shoot. Fifty yards down the road. Before that none of us will fire a shot."

"How many will fire?" asked Georges, still looking down the road.

"All of them," said Raymond with a sweep of his arm.

Georges nodded. He now saw the significance of the triangle and he thought: you won't know much about it. You always wanted it to be quick and painless and if forty men shoot simultaneously at least ten will be sure to hit you with their first round.

338

It's better than being caught by a shell, a shell can be awful, much worse than this.

"That's no chance," he heard himself say.

"At least you know that you're being shot at," Raymond replied. "Gaston didn't know, and everybody here was a friend of Gaston."

He left Georges and joined the others at the tip of the triangle. They were all holding their automatic rifles and Georges stared back at forty dark-skinned, motionless faces. He was half a head taller than most of them and could see over them towards the fort. At the moment when Anna came running out of the tunnel he heard Raymond's voice saying: "Run!"

Georges looked at his bearded face and back to Anna. As their backs were turned to her none of the men had seen her and Georges waited until she had covered half the distance. Then he turned round and ran down the road. He ran as fast as he could and after about fifty paces he stopped and looked back.

The men had dropped their weapons and were all staring at one point. Georges heard a piercing scream and then another and recognizing Anna's voice his heart missed a few beats. The right-hand row of men began to sway, then bulged out at one point and was torn apart. In the gap appeared the girl with Raymond behind her, holding her firmly with his great butcher's hands. She fought like a wildcat, punched his face and lashed out at him with her feet; unable to shake him off in this way she fell to the ground, rolled over, jumped free and raced down the road.

Not one of the men followed her. Even Raymond stood where he was and merely stared after her in complete amazement. She ran straight for Georges, trying to shield him with her body and Georges, realizing her intention, let her come within ten paces, then ran on ahead of her and only stopped again when they had rounded the first bend.

Both were gasping for breath. Georges looked at the girl's agonized face. She stood before him, her mouth wide open, her hands pressed to her chest and her long black hair in disorder over her shoulders. As Georges took a step towards her she shook her head and said breathlessly: "We mustn't stay here; Pierre's coming. Here!" She pressed two small keys into his hand. "These are the keys of Vieale's car. He gave them to me. We must keep running, or else Pierre will catch us."

She started to run on, and as Georges did not follow her at once she screamed: "Come on!"

It was unbearably hot. Georges pulled off his jacket as he ran.

He was still unable to think clearly: everything had happened so quickly that his consciousness had not yet reacted. Then as the girl began to slacken her pace and to stumble with exhaustion his consciousness began to function again and he held Anna by the arm and said breathlessly: "You must go back!"

She looked past him up the road. "I won't go back. I'm coming with you."

"You can't," said Georges. "It's impossible."

"Why?"

"Because . . ." Georges stopped. He took her face between his hands and she said: "You're crying!"

"I'm not crying," said Georges. "Can you imagine someone like me crying?"

"No, I couldn't," she said. "Why did you kill him?"

"I didn't want to."

"Swear it to me!"

"Yes."

"I don't think I can ever forget it," she said. "He was always so cheerful and it's as bad as if you had killed Pierre. I'm afraid of you."

Georges was silent.

"Why don't you say anything?" she asked. "You said nothing, either, when Pierre was questioning you. I was so hoping that you'd say something, if only that you were sorry. But you didn't even say that. Doesn't it mean anything to you to kill somebody, just like that, who has never done anything to you?"

"Anna——"

"Does it mean nothing to you?"

"If you think like that about me——"

She interrupted him again. "I know too little. If I marry you I don't suppose I shall have an easy life."

"You have four years to think it over," said Georges.

She looked quickly up at him. "Four years?"

"Yes."

"You mean . . ."

"Perhaps it's better after all. I'd rather you had time to change your mind, than let you in for a dog's life."

"Is that the only reason?"

"In four years' time perhaps I can express it more exactly. It's a long story. But for you I should be dead now."

"I would never have let them," she said. "When they led you out I wanted to run after you. Pierre held me back. Then I thought

340

you might need Monsieur Vieale's car, but I had to get the keys without Pierre noticing it. He was talking to my uncle about Boris and when I had the keys I ran out. You won't get over the bridge; it has been blown up."

"I'll go over the mountains. Did Pierre run after you?"

"He started to, but somebody must have stopped him. I think it was Monsieur Vieale. As he gave me the keys he stood up and placed himself behind Pierre."

He chanced to look up the road just as a man came running round the corner. Anna saw him almost at the same moment. She dug her fingers into Georges' arm and whispered: "Pierre!"

"He's by himself and unarmed," said Georges. "He's come to fetch you."

"You mustn't stay here," she said urgently. "Run, I'll try to hold him up."

Georges looked again at Pierre, who had just noticed them. He slowed down to a walk, stopped for a moment and then slowly approached them. He wore no jacket and his black and white striped shirt had a long tear on the right shoulder. It had probably happened when Vieale tried to stop him and Georges remembered what big hands Vieale had.

One day I'll go and see him, he thought and said aloud: "He doesn't want me, otherwise he would have come armed and in more of a hurry. He can do nothing to me without his gun."

"As long as there are no more of them behind him," said Anna. "Wait here; I'll talk to him."

She began to run up the road; Pierre stopped and let her come. His expressionless face was wet with sweat. He mopped his forehead with a handkerchief and stuffed it under his torn shirt below his right armpit.

"Your uncle sent me," he then said. "He begs you to come back with me." His voice sounded harsh and impersonal and it hurt her to hear him use that tone with her.

She looked past him and asked: "Did you come alone?"

"Yes."

"I'll be back in a moment," she said and returned to Georges. "You were right; he's come to fetch me, but I don't know whether I should go with him."

"I think it would be better for both of us if you did."

She nodded and stared at the ground. Then she looked up at him. "What will you do?"

341

"I shall go to Monaco. There's sure to be a Swiss consulate there. I'll report to the consul."

"And then?"

"And then!" Georges looked up again at the houses of La Peine. "Then they will take me to Zürich and give me my four years. If I behave well they may let me go sooner."

"You will behave well," said Anna. "I don't want to wait four years for you. It's a terribly long time."

"Too long, perhaps," said Georges, looking at the old houses. "In four years you'll be twenty-one and you will have met a hundred other men."

"Or two hundred," said Anna. "Are you afraid of losing me?"

"Very much."

She smiled. "You can't lose something like me. You have to chase me away to get rid of me. Where can I write to you?"

"I don't yet know in which hotel I shall be staying," answered Georges. He took a notebook from his pocket, thumbed through it and tore out a page. "That's my father's address. I'll tell him about you."

"Don't tell him anything bad about me or he'll throw me out if I go and see him." She read the address, then carefully folded the piece of paper and held it in her hand.

"You can take that back too," said Georges and gave her Vieale's car keys. "You tell him that I shall see him again without fail."

"Perhaps we could do that together," said Anna. "You can still change your mind. You only have to say one word and I'll go with you wherever you like. I don't want them to put you behind bars just for my sake."

Georges looked up and saw Pierre watching them. "No. I've put off the evil day quite long enough—too long, probably. Let's hope we're doing the right thing for once. You must go now."

"I don't want to go," she said as the tears ran down her cheeks. She wiped them away impatiently and smiled again. "Give me a kiss!"

Georges bent down to her and he saw her face dimly through a haze and her mouth tasted salty. "I could die for you," he said. "For you and for nothing else in the world."

"I'd rather you lived for me," she murmured and pulled herself away from him. "Pierre's watching us. *Au revoir,* soldier. Go before we regret it. My uncle has done so much for me."

Georges turned round and walked quickly away down the road.

About seventy yards farther gaped the dark mouth of a tunnel and he had covered three quarters of the way to it before Pierre came up to Anna.

He looked at her from the side and started to blink. She touched his arm with her hand and said: "Hold on to me very tight, Pierre. If you don't I'll run after him."

"I didn't realize," murmured Pierre and laid his arm round her shoulders. "As far as I was concerned he could have stayed here, but the men . . ."

"No, no," said Anna. "This was the right thing. Even he said so."

Georges had reached the tunnel. He stopped for a moment and looked back. Then the tunnel swallowed him up and Anna pressed her face to Pierre's chest and he clumsily stroked her hair with his coarse hands. After a while she raised her head and looked into his eyes. "It's not easy to be a human being in this world, Pierre. Do you know that?"

"Yes," said Pierre. "By God, it's not easy."

"Then let's go now," said Anna. They set off up the road. Pierre was relieved to see that she was no longer crying.

When they reached the fort the men were standing about in small groups and watching them as they approached. Knopf, too, was among them. He had taken off his glasses and in the harsh sunlight his face looked almost transparent. Beside him Anna saw Vieale, his wife and Marcel, who, when he saw her, came running towards her.

"Where is Georges?" he stammered.

"He's going to Monaco," replied Anna, but she had to look away from him as her eyes were filling with tears again.

Marcel looked at her uncomprehendingly. "What does he want in Monaco?"

"He's looking for the consulate. He wants to go back to Switzerland."

"To . . ." Marcel stopped. He stood petrified for several seconds and then set off down the road with huge strides.

Anna looked after him and smiled. As if from a great distance she heard Vieale's voice: "He's forgotten the rucksacks!"